WESTWIND

Also by Ian Rankin

The Inspector Malcolm Fox Series

The Complaints

The Impossible Dead

The Detective Inspector Rebus Series

Knots & Crosses

Hide & Seek

Tooth & Nail
(*previously published as* Wolfman)

A Good Hanging and Other Stories

Strip Jack

The Black Book

Mortal Causes

Let It Bleed

Black & Blue

The Hanging Garden

Death Is Not the End
(*a novella*)

Dead Souls

Set in Darkness

The Falls

Resurrection Men

A Question of Blood

Fleshmarket Alley

The Naming of the Dead

Exit Music

Standing in Another Man's Grave

Saints of the Shadow Bible

The Beat Goes On: The Complete Rebus Stories (*a story collection*)

Even Dogs in the Wild

Rather Be the Devil

In a House of Lies

A Song for the Dark Times

Other Novels

Witch Hunt

Blood Hunt

Bleeding Hearts

Watchman

Doors Open

Dark Entries (*graphic novel*)

IAN RANKIN

WESTWIND

BACK BAY BOOKS
Little, Brown and Company
New York Boston London

Back Bay Books / Little, Brown and Company
Hachette Book Group
1290 Avenue of the Americas, New York, NY 10104
littlebrown.com

Originally published in Great Britain in 1990 by Barrie & Jenkins Ltd.
First published in hardcover in the United States by
Little, Brown and Company, January 2020
First Back Bay trade paperback edition, January 2021

Back Bay Books is an imprint of Little, Brown and Company,
a division of Hachette Book Group, Inc.
The Back Bay Books name and logo are trademarks of Hachette Book Group, Inc.

The publisher is not responsible for websites (or their content)
that are not owned by the publisher.

The Hachette Speakers Bureau provides a wide range of authors for speaking events. To find out more, go to hachettespeakersbureau.com or call (866) 376-6591.

ISBN 978-0-316-49792-3 (hc) / 978-0-316-49793-0 (pb)

Cataloging-in-publication data is available at the Library of Congress

Printing 1, 2020

LSC-C

Printed in the United States of America

For my sisters,
Maureen and Linda

WESTWIND

West wind, wanton wind, wilful wind, womanish wind, false wind from over the water.

—George Bernard Shaw, *St Joan*

INTRODUCTION BY THE AUTHOR

Westwind was originally published on Thursday March 1 1990. My diary entry for that day announces the fact thus: 'Yes, *Westwind* was published to ONE review (in the *Guardian* and very small). Jesus. A flop from the word go.'

As you can see, I was not in what is these days referred to as 'a good place' in the early months of 1990, as my diary of the time regularly records. Here's Wednesday February 28: 'I was wondering today, when will *Westwind* be published? I knew it was scheduled for March and books are always published on a Thursday. But it *can't* be tomorrow surely – Barrie & Jenkins (my publisher at the time) would have been in touch re possible sources of publicity. Surely my author's copies should have arrived? But on returning home a gift bottle of whisky greeted me. Must be tomorrow then – with so little ceremony!'

It's easy to be sanguine as I look back at my younger self, but I was demonstrably starting to lose belief in my abilities, doubting my future as a publishable writer. I was also slogging my guts out, working a day job in London and trying to find space to write in what free time remained to me. My first Rebus novel, *Knots & Crosses*, had been published without fanfare in 1987. On May 12 of that year I record in my trusty diary that 'I should be doing the satellite novel (*Westwind* in other words). I'm doing nothing.' Well, not *nothing* exactly because at the same time I was also polishing the spy thriller which would appear the following year as *Watchman*. I was living in Tottenham and working as an assistant at the National Folktale Centre, based at what was then Middlesex Polytechnic.

Unusually for London, this meant I could walk to work. It also gave me access to a computer, while at home I still hammered away on a noisy electric typewriter. Not that the computer, with its large floppy disks, was much use to me – I didn't know anyone else (my publisher included) who used one. My first Amstrad word processor was still a ways off, while the fax machine in my workplace remained as mysterious to me as the Sphinx.

I'm not sure what gave me the idea that a techno-thriller would be my next project.

Knots & Crosses had been a fairly traditional whodunit. *Watchman* was a spy novel influenced by Graham Greene's *The Human Factor*. *Westwind*, on the other hand, would start with a space shuttle plummeting to earth and a malfunctioning satellite. It seems to me now that I was feeling my way towards what kind of writer I wanted to be. High on the list was: successful enough to give up the day job. I'd tried the crime novel and the spy novel and now I was going to attempt to write the sort of high-tech thriller that sold by the pallet-load in airports and railway stations. So it was that I visited my local library on Tottenham High Road and asked the librarian for anything they could give me to do with space shuttles and how satellites work. Many of the resulting books proved too technical for me – my degree was in English literature rather than mathematics and physics – but a few proved useful. (I'll admit now that one of them was a children's book.) Then there was the trusty Rand McNally *Road Atlas of the USA*, since part of the book was going to be set there (international sales ahoy!) and I'd yet to visit that country outside of novels, movies and TV shows.

As you can see, I was young, hungry, naïve – and driven.

Turning to my diaries again to help me with this introduction, I was surprised at the long gestation of *Westwind*. The first mention I can find is May 1987, and by June I was happily at work on it. At this time it was called *Coffin Burial*, and my one issue was that my typewriter needed repairing. In July 1987 I was chipping away at it while also editing *Watchman*. By August, I was having doubts, but in September, I was finding some of the writing 'v exciting' and 'heart-pounding'. By December, the first draft of the book was finished and the title had been changed to *Westwind*. (I'm not sure where *Coffin Burial* came from – I did think it was a poem, but I can't find it on the internet. My memory was, it might have been John Masefield, but again I can't find it in a list of his works – though I did come across a poem of his called 'The West Wind'. Coincidence?)

My agent read the book over the festive period and got back to me in January 1988. He was not enthusiastic and wanted major revisions before submitting it to a publisher. Okay, so by March I'd tweaked the book, but then everything seemed to go quiet. There was TV interest in *Knots & Crosses* and I was also working on a script for a potential film of my first novel *The Flood*. I was also getting ready for publication of *Watchman* and applying for jobs with a bit more pay than I was getting at Middlesex Poly. By May, I was at work on a new Rebus novel (which would eventually see the light of day as *Hide and Seek*) and by the summer I'd secured work as a journalist on a monthly magazine called *Hi-Fi Review*. *Watchman* was out and receiving some good reviews (if decidedly sluggish sales) and *Westwind* was languishing. By September, my agent was apologising that he still had no takers for the revised book. I was almost too busy to notice. My new job came with a ninety-minute each-way commute, during which I was devouring novels which I'd started reviewing for the newspaper *Scotland on Sunday*. I'd also been approached to pitch script ideas to ITV's *The Bill*, and I was working away between times on the Rebus book . . .

Then, praise be, my agent phoned with news. My old editor from Bodley Head (who had taken both *Knots & Crosses* and *Watchman*) had switched publishers and was now at Barrie & Jenkins. He wanted to revitalise their meagre fiction list. In short, he wanted *Westwind*. By January 1989 I was discussing further edits to the book and by March I'd signed a contract. Nineteen eighty-nine saw me continuing to write *Hide and Seek* (at this point titled *Dead Beat*) while revising *Westwind*, and still working as a hi-fi reviewer. *Westwind* was eventually finished by July. I had a new editor by then, however, and she disliked some of the book's tone, finding it too humorous for a thriller. She wanted a tougher book and I did my best to comply, meaning a further edit. Which brings us to March 1 1990 and publication.

Not that anyone noticed. There was one hardcover printing, one paperback, and one in large format for readers with limited sight. It didn't sell to the USA and no foreign-language publisher wanted it. What's more, the book had taken so long to get into print, and been through so many permutations and revisions, that I could muster very little enthusiasm for it myself. Every time my agent or editor had asked me to rework it, I had acquiesced, until it felt like it wasn't really my book at all – certainly not the one I'd set out to write.

So I decided that it would rest in a dark corner of my consciousness, never to see the light of day again.

Until Twitter changed my mind.

There had been the odd occasion where a fan at a signing would tell me they'd read it and liked it. Those fans had either got lucky in charity shops or else had shelled out a lot of money to a book dealer. Yes, the book had its fans, but I wasn't among them until someone on Twitter persuaded me to give the book another look. 'It's better than you think it is, Ian.' It had been so long since I'd read it that it felt like reading another writer's work. This proved to be a good thing – I could be objective as I raced through the pages. Yes, it had a few faults and some of the sentence construction was overwrought. It also felt a little bit dated, but on the other hand it also seemed prescient. I had set it in an alternative 1990 where American troops are being pulled out of Europe. International tensions are high. The US is retrenching and the military is worried about the future direction Europe will take. Satellites circle Earth, being used potentially to spy on everyone and everything. No one knows who to trust, or what's about to happen.

Yes, I saw plenty of parallels with the current geopolitical situation, but I also enjoyed reading it. The characters came to life, the plot was pacy, the villains were scary and the heroes believable. And oh the nostalgia! Central locking for cars was obviously a fairly new thing (not *remote* central locking, mind), since I mentioned it more than once. Then there were the Filofaxes, floppy disks and cassette tapes. People smoked on aeroplanes, Tower Records had arrived at Piccadilly Circus, and Germany was still divided into East and West.

I'd forgotten that the listening base where Martin Hepton works was sited at Binbrook, Lincolnshire – a location I'd chosen because my sister Maureen (married to an RAF technician) had lived there for several years and I'd stayed with her as a teenager over the course of one or two long, hot school-holiday summers, back in the days when I was convinced I was going to be either a rock star or a poet. This is partly why I have the notion that 'Coffin Burial' must have been a poem. But during the course of writing the book, I started disliking that title. My British spy satellite was called *Zephyr*, and a zephyr is a light breeze or 'the west wind'. Bearing in mind that (influenced by Alan Moore's comic *Watchmen*) I was calling my spy novel *Watchman*, maybe I had the idea that my novels could all start with the letter 'w'. The third Rebus novel, after all, would be titled *Wolfman* (before an astute editor in the US asked me to alter it to *Tooth and Nail* so as not to deter non-horror book buyers). The George Bernard Shaw quote at the start of the book was probably another piece of serendipity – the 'false wind from over the water' might refer to either the US or Russia. It certainly hints that those you think of as your friends may actually have hidden intentions and ulterior motives.

I've given the original printed text a polish, hopefully ridding it of those flawed sentences and scenes. A few words have been added here and there, while others have been removed or altered, but it is essentially the same book that it always was, just thirty years older and a little wiser . . .

Ian Rankin, 2019

Part I

Today may mark the end of a great alliance as hundreds of US forces personnel await the transport planes which will take them home, away from the country they have for so long helped defend. Many were tearful last night as they said their farewells to the friends made in this country. They are sorry to go, and we are sorry to see them go. But Britain is a part of Europe now, and it was a democratic decision to part from our erstwhile allies. Let us hope to God it will not prove a foolhardy decision to boot. Already, there are whispered doubts about the efficacy of European defences, and as an island we should be doubly worried about our reduced defensive capability, robbed as we now are of much of our protective power. The mortar may have been removed from the bricks, and who knows when the wolf from the East may come, demanding entry?

Editorial in *London Herald*, 15 July 1990

1

He watched the planet earth on his monitor. It was quite a sight. Around him, others were doing the same thing, though not perhaps with an equal sense of astonishment. Some had grown blasé over the years: when you'd seen one earth, you'd seen them all. But not Martin Hepton. He still felt awe, reverence, emotion, whatever. If he had called it a spiritual feeling, the others might have laughed, so he kept his thoughts to himself. And watched.

They all watched, recording their separate data on the computer, keeping an eye on earth from the heavens while their feet never left the ground. Hepton felt giddy sometimes, thinking to himself: this is the only earth there is, and we're all stuck with it, every last one of us. At such moments, the thought of war seemed impossible.

The ground station at Binbrook was small by most standards, but quite large enough for its purpose, and it was sited in the midst of the greenest countryside Hepton had ever seen. He had been born here in Lincolnshire, but had grown up in 1960s London; 'swinging' London. It had swung right past him. With his head stuck in this or that textbook he had never quite noticed the bright clothes, the casual attitudes, the whole hippy shake. Too often, when his head wasn't in a book, it had been raised to the sky, naming a litany of stars and constellations. And it had led to this, as though by some predetermined scheme. He had reached for the skies and had touched them. Thanks to *Zephyr*.

Zephyr was the reason behind all this activity, all these monitors and busy voices. *Zephyr* was a British satellite. *The* British satellite. It wasn't the only one they had, but it was the best. The best by a long shot. It could be used for just about anything: weather-watching, communications, surveillance. It could drop from its orbit to within a hundred kilometres of earth, take a pristine picture, then boost back into the higher orbit again before relaying the information back to the ground station. It was a clever little sod all right, and here were its nursemaids, keeping a close eye on it while it kept a close eye on the British Isles. Nobody seemed quite sure why Britain was *Zephyr*'s present target. Word had gone around that the brass – meaning the military and the MoD – wanted to survey this sceptred land, which was fine by Hepton. He would never tire of staring at the various screens, seeing what his satellite saw, making sure that everything was recorded, filed, double-checked. And then viewed by the generals and the men in the pinstripe suits.

He had his own ideas about the present surveillance. The United States was pulling its troops out of Europe. It all looked amicable and agreed, but rumours had started in the press, rumours to the effect that there had been a good amount of shove on the part of the mainland European countries, and that the American generals weren't entirely happy about leaving. The rumours had led to some demonstrations by right-wing parties, asking that the 'USA stay! USA stay!', and an organisation of that name had quickly been formed. More demos were now taking place, and vigils outside the embassies of Britain's partners in Europe. Not exactly powder-keg stuff, but Hepton could imagine that the government wanted to keep things nailed down. And who better than *Zephyr* to follow a convoy of protesters or keep tabs on rallies in different parts of the country?

All at the touch of a button.

'Coffee, Martin?' A cup appeared beside his console. Hepton slipped his headphones down around his neck.

'Thanks, Nick.'

Nick Christopher nodded towards the screen. 'Anything good on the telly?' he asked.

'Just a lot of old repeats,' answered Hepton.

'Isn't that just typical of summer? Honestly, though, I'll go mad if we don't get some new schedules soon.'

'Maybe we're due for a little excitement.'

'What do you mean?' asked Christopher.

'Well,' said Hepton, cradling the plastic beaker, 'I've heard that the brass are around today. Maybe Fagin will put on a simulation for them, show them we're on our toes.'

'Anything for a shot of adrenaline.'

Hepton stared at Nick Christopher. Rumour had it that at one time he'd shot more than just adrenaline. But that was the base for you: when nothing was happening, the rumours seemed to start. Christopher was reaching into his back pocket. He brought out a folded, dog-eared newspaper, its crossword nearly completed. Hepton was already shaking his head.

'You know I'm never any good at those,' he said. Nick Christopher was a crossword addict. He'd buy anything from a kiddies' puzzle book to *The Times* to feed his habit, and over by his desk he had weighty tomes dedicated to his pursuit: dictionaries, collections of synonyms and antonyms and anagrams. He often asked Hepton's help, if only to show how close he had come to solving the day's most difficult puzzle. Now he shrugged his shoulders.

'Well, see you at break time,' he said, heading back towards his own console.

'Biccies are on me,' Hepton said.

There was a sudden wrenching of the air as an alarm began to sound, and Christopher turned back to smile at him, as if to congratulate him on his hunch. Hepton put down his coffee untouched and checked the screen. It was filled with flickering white dots, static. The other screens nearby were showing the same electronic snow.

'Lost visual contact,' someone felt it necessary to say.

'We've lost *all* contact,' called out another voice.

It looked as though Fagin had set them up after all. There was immediate activity, chairs swivelling as consoles were compared, buttons clacked and calls made over the intercom system. Despite themselves, they all relished the occasional emergency, contrived or not. It was a chance to show how prepared they were, how efficient, how quickly they could react and repair.

'Switching to backup system.'

'Coding in channel two.'

'I'm getting a very sluggish response.'

'So stop talking to snails.'

An arm snaked past Hepton's shoulder and punched numbers out on his keyboard, trying to elicit a response from their own. Nothing. It was as if some television station had packed up for the night. All contact had been lost. How the hell had Fagin rigged this?

Hepton lifted his coffee to his lips, gulped at it, then squirmed. Nick Christopher must have dropped a bag of sugar into it.

'Sweet Jesus,' he muttered, the fingers of one hand still busy on his keyboard.

'Coded through.'

'No response here.'

'I'm getting nothing at all.'

A voice came over the speaker system, replacing the electronic alarm.

'This is not a test. Repeat, this is not a test.'

They paused to look at each other, reading a fresh panic in eyes reflecting their own. *Not a test!* It had to be a test. Otherwise they'd just lost a thousand million pounds' worth of tin and plastic. Lost it for how long? Hepton checked his watch. The system had been inoperative for over two minutes. That meant it really was serious. Another minute or so could spell disaster.

Fagin, the operations manager, had appeared from nowhere and was sprinting from console to console as though taking part in some kind of party game. Two of the brass were in evidence too, looking as though they'd just stepped out of a meeting. They carried files under their arms and stood by the far door, knowing nothing of the system or how to be of help. That was typical. The people who held the purse strings and gave the orders knew nothing about anything. That was why the budgeting on *Zephyr* was so tight. Hepton glanced at the pair again. Grey, puzzled faces, trying to look interested and concerned, unsure what to be concerned about.

Suddenly Fagin was at his shoulder.

'Anything, Martin?'

'Nothing, sir.'

'What happened?' Fagin trusted Hepton, and knew him to be fastidious.

Hepton shrugged his shoulders, feeling more impotent than he could say. 'It just started snowing,' he said, gesturing towards the screen. 'That's all.'

Fagin nodded and was gone, his reputation for competence on the edge of being wiped out. Like sticking a magnet on a floppy disk: it was *that* easy to lose it all in a moment.

Then:

'Wait a minute!' It was Nick Christopher's voice.

'Yes,' someone else called from further off. 'I'm getting something now. We've regained radio contact.' There was a pause. 'No, lost it again.'

The brass exchanged glances at this news, and both checked their watches. Hepton couldn't believe what he was seeing. They seemed to be worrying about the time. All the while, a billion pounds' worth of high-tech was whizzing about blindly, or crashing towards earth, and they were worrying about the time.

'Are you sure you had it?' yelled Fagin.

'Yes, sir.'

'Well then, get it back!'

'Trying.'

Despite the adrenaline gnawing at him, Hepton felt a sudden inner calm. All would be well. It was just a matter of trusting to fate and pushing the right buttons. Who was he kidding? *Zephyr* was lost for good.

Someone was standing behind him. He glanced back and saw Paul Vincent watching intently over his shoulder. Vincent was the youngest of the controllers, and the least confident.

'Come to see how the professional does it, Paul?' Hepton said, grinning nervously at the screen. He saw Vincent's reflection smile wanly back. Then he began pushing buttons again, trying every combination possible. He had used up all the rational choices. Now he was trying the irrational, asking the computer to do the impossible.

Paul Vincent's face was suddenly at his ear, though the young man's eyes still appeared to be studying the monitor.

'Listen, Martin, there's something I want to show you.'

'What?'

Vincent's gaze remained fixed to the screen. His voice was low, just audible over the noise all around.

'I can't be sure,' he said, 'not a hundred per cent, at any rate. But I think there's something happening up there. Either that or I've been doing something wrong. I had it on my screen a little while back.'

'What do you mean, "something happening"?'

'I'm not sure yet. Foreign data.'

'Have you reported it?'

'Of course.'

Perhaps that was why the brass were on the scene, and why they had looked momentarily scared.

'Are we talking about interference?' Hepton's voice was low too.

'I don't know. I could make a wild guess, but I'm not sure it would help. I'd like you to confirm the data.'

'When did it start?'

'About half an hour ago.'

'Coincidence?'

There was a sudden whoop, then cheers and some applause.

'We've got her back!'

Hepton's eyes went to his screen. They had indeed got her back. He was staring at a fuzzy but identifiable picture of Britain, taken from all that unbelievable distance. The image was out of focus, but they could soon put that right. What mattered was that *Zephyr* was working again.

'Panic over,' he said, turning now to face Paul Vincent. 'So what about this foreign data?'

'I've saved the readout on disk. Come and see.'

Paul spoke without blinking, and still softly, though the clamour around had grown. He was young but, Hepton knew, not an idiot. A first in astrophysics from Edinburgh, then research in Australia. No idiot, but not a hands-on expert either. It was his job – his sole responsibility and specialism – to monitor the space around *Zephyr*, seeking space trash, debris, meteorites, waves of interference. He'd never made a mistake when it had counted. Never.

'Okay, Paul,' Hepton said. 'Give me a couple of minutes to put things right and I'll come take a look.'

'Thanks.' Vincent looked relieved, like a man who needs reassuring that those pink elephants he can see really are there. Maybe they were, at that. He left Hepton's side and returned to his distant console. Then again, maybe the kid was losing his touch. There had been a bout of sulking a week ago to do with some girlfriend or other. Hazard of the job. Shift work, odd hours, occasional days on end cooped up in the base. Sleeping four to a room in two sets of bunk beds. Hepton wasn't sure he could take much more of it himself, despite the pleasures of earth-watching. Who ever thought to ask him if *he* were lonely? Nobody. He thought of Jilly, and wondered what she was doing while he sat here. He didn't want to think what she was doing.

The brass were looking pleased about something. Well, they'd got *Zephyr* back, hadn't they? One said something to the other, and Hepton, watching the man's lips move, caught the words 'three minutes forty'. The other nodded and smiled again. So they were discussing the length of time the satellite had been lost to its ground base. Three minutes and forty seconds. Longer than ever before. Almost too long.

Things were calming down all around. Fagin had gone to speak with the brass. They were in a huddle now, their eyes glinting. Hepton couldn't see their lips any more. Well, it was none of his concern.

He busied himself with putting his console right. He had pushed a few too many of the wrong buttons in the wrong sequences. Adjustments were needed. And then he would visit Paul Vincent on the other side of the room.

'More coffee?' It was Nick Christopher.

'You put sugar in the first.'

'An honest mistake. I'll fetch you another.'

'Don't bother. What do you think went wrong back there?'

'Put it down to a hiccup. Everything malfunctions from time to time. Between the two of us, I think *Zephyr* was cobbled together like its namesake, the old car. We'll be lucky if it stays the course.'

'It was out for three minutes forty seconds.'

'What?'

'The brass were timing it.'

'Then maybe it was an exercise.'

'I don't think Paul Vincent would agree.'

'Martin, you're talking in riddles.'

'Sorry.'

'Now what about that coffee?'

'No sugar this time?'

'Promise, no sugar.'

'Okay then.'

The brass had disappeared, and Fagin with them. Waving them off, probably. Hepton wondered what the weather was like outside. He could check by using the computer, but wouldn't it be so much nicer just to walk outside and take a look? Sunny, showery, cool, breezy. Inside, the air conditioning kept things temperate, and the lighting was designed specially so as to be bright without giving glare. Same went for the screens. You could stare at them all day without getting a headache, which didn't stop him succumbing to the occasional migraine. He pushed back into his chair. It, too, had been designed for maximum comfort and minimum stress. He stuck a thumb either side of his spine and pressed, feeling vertebrae click into place.

'No sugar,' said Nick Christopher, handing him the beaker.

'Thanks.'

'Only another twenty minutes till break.'

'Thank God.'

'So what were you saying about Paul?'

'Oh, just that he's got some data he wants me to check.'

'Data?' Christopher sipped his own coffee. 'What sort of data?'

'I don't know till I've looked. Probably nothing important. You know what Paul's like.'

Christopher smiled. 'He's like a kid with a train set.'

'Exactly,' said Hepton.

But by the time he wandered across to Paul Vincent's console, Vincent himself had vanished. Hepton looked at the computer screen. It was blank. He tried coding in, but it remained blank.

'Temporary fault,' said Fagin from behind him. 'Was there something you wanted?'

'Just checking.'

'Checking what?'

'Oh, you know . . .'

'Well you won't get much joy. Part of the disk's been wiped.'

'You mean the hard disk?'

'Yes.'

'Because of the malfunction?'

'Or more likely Vincent's panicking.' Fagin had it in for Paul Vincent, everybody knew that. It was whispered that Paul reminded him too much of his own son, who had left home at seventeen and never returned.

'Where is Vincent, by the way?'

Fagin shrugged. 'I don't know. The little boys' room perhaps.'

'What happened back there?'

Fagin seemed to think about this. 'I'm just glad we got her back,' he said at last. 'We'll find out eventually.'

'It wasn't a test then, to impress our friends?'

'Friends?'

'Those two generals.'

'Not at all. What makes you say that?'

'Oh, they just seemed to be timing our response, that's all. And they looked fairly happy with the outcome.'

'Nobody likes to lose a satellite, Martin.'

'Of course not, sir. If you'll excuse me, it's almost my break. I think I'll try to find Paul.'

'Fine.' Fagin was picking up the internal telephone, pushing buttons. The panic was over; things had to go on.

Three minutes and forty seconds. Usually a malfunction could be located and corrected within sixty seconds. There were backup systems, a computer locked into every function of the satellite, ready to pinpoint the failure and repair it. After sixty seconds, you could assume that the computers had failed to find the fault, and you began to worry. So you went to manual, checking everything yourself. At the two-minute mark, you panicked.

Three minutes and forty seconds. The brass had seemed satisfied. Fagin seemed satisfied. Paul Vincent had reported his findings, but nobody seemed to want to know. *What the hell was going on?*

Hepton went to the toilets, then checked the canteen, the recreation area and the TV room: nothing. The table tennis players hadn't seen Paul Vincent, the guys watching a porn film hadn't seen Paul Vincent, nobody had seen Paul Vincent. He had disappeared. Hepton sat down in the TV room to think. The porn film was in German, not that a degree in languages was necessary to understand the plot. The film was being beamed via satellite, probably from a mainland European station. One bored weekend they'd spent several hours using the base's sophisticated communications technology to home in on a couple of television satellites. Now they could pick up just about any station they liked and decode any scrambled signal. The picture today wasn't the sharpest, but the cameraman was in close enough so that this didn't really matter . . .

Zephyr. What did Paul Vincent know about *Zephyr*?

Hepton caught up with Nick Christopher in the canteen, where he was scooping up chips and beans with a fork and holding open a book with his free hand.

'What are you reading?' Hepton asked.

Christopher showed him the cover, 'Albert Camus, *The Fall*. I found it in the library.'

'What's it like?'

'I don't know. Nothing's happened yet. What's wrong?'

Hepton realised that he was sitting with head in hands, elbows propped on the table.

'I can't find Paul,' he said.

'Perhaps he doesn't want to be found,' said Christopher, scooping up another mouthful of beans.

'Maybe you're right at that,' said Hepton, stealing a limp lukewarm chip from the plate.

The afternoon drifted back into ordinariness. After the break, it was back to the consoles. The system, though, was failing to yield the source of the malfunction. Fagin walked from monitor to monitor, for all the world like a factory-line foreman. He stopped at Hepton's desk.

'It seems Paul Vincent has been taken ill,' he said, scribbling something on his clipboard.

'Ill? Can I go see him?'

'He's not in the rest room. They've had to take him to hospital.'

'Christ, that was a bit sudden.'

'The doctor thinks it might be simple exhaustion.'

Exhaustion. Paul was not only the youngest of the crew, he was the fittest too. Twice a day he jogged around the perimeter fence, a haul of two and a half miles. He was the only one of them who used the multigym. He had the stamina of an athlete. Hepton sat at the console, his mind whirling. The nearest hospital was twenty miles away. He had to go there.

Fagin had walked away now and was examining another monitor. Hepton looked across to where Paul Vincent's monitor sat untended, the chair pushed in beneath the desk with the finality of a coffin lid being nailed down. He shivered. There was something very odd about this whole thing. A curious mind had brought him into the world of astronomy and astronautics, and that same mind was now needling him to look a little further into things. And yes, he would.

2

He tasted smoke in his nostrils and felt blood gouge its way along the creases in his spacesuit. The vibration in the shuttle intensified still further, becoming more than a roller coaster. A roller coaster had once terrified him as a child, and he had determined never to be afraid of anything again in his whole life, a decision that was ending here and now with the most complete terror he had ever felt.

Through the glass he caught a quick glimpse of the ground crew; already the fire engines were racing forwards, but too late. Sparks flew from the seared undercarriage, and a final all-encompassing ball of flame sent him veering towards pale darkness.

But then suddenly Adams was at his side, his head bloodied, and Adams' hands slid around his throat, growing tight, and all the time he was shouting:

'You sonofabitch! You sonofabitch! I won't forget! Not ever! The burial's what matters! Coffin's got to be buried!'

It was all so unnecessary, Dreyfuss thought. We're dying anyway; why don't you let me die in peace? The tarmac below was churning like the sea, as unsteady as a fairground ride. Adams' hands were still there. Blood pounded in Dreyfuss' ears, tortured metal, the whine of the uncontrollable engines. How could it have happened? Total malfunction. Absolute and total, just as they were starting the descent. *How could it have happened?* It was typical of his life that he should die with a question unanswered in his mind.

And then, finally, he blacked out.

The emergency team were ready. They'd been ready since the first warning that something was wrong on the space shuttle *Argos*. Now they started to jet, engulfing white foam over the stricken craft, snuffing out flames until the whole thing looked like a children's toy in a bubble bath. The crew had come from the ground station to watch. There had been six men on board: five Americans and one Briton. Most of them were praying that the Americans, at least, would still be alive. They didn't really give much thought to the only Briton, Major Michael Dreyfuss. These days, it was strictly a case of looking after number one.

The few small fires were quickly put out. Thankfully, the *Argos* had little fuel left in its tanks to burn. Nevertheless, the surface metal of the shuttle was too hot to touch, even with asbestos gloves. But they managed at last to wrench open the doors. Inside, they could smell smoke, singed rubber and something less pleasant still. They expected to find corpses, but the last thing anyone expected to find was five of them, one of which had its hands embedded in the neck of the single crew member left alive . . .

3

General Ben Esterhazy sat in the back of his chauffeur-driven limo and wondered why there was no bourbon left in the drinks cabinet. He hoped there'd be some at the airbase. Not that there was much left of the base. They were dismantling and moving, shipping the boys back to the States. Lousy damned country anyway. He'd spent a few years in Germany just after the war. People starving. A mother really would lie down and open her legs for a tin of beef and some powdered whatever.

The country didn't seem to have changed that much. But now Europe had forgotten all about World War Two, had gotten eyes bigger than its belly. All the talk now was of Europe, a Europe that saw no place for the US forces lined up in a thin defensive wall against the East.

'Well, fuck them.'

'Sorry, General?' Esterhazy's aide, Lieutenant Jerry Bosio, sitting in front beside the driver, had turned his head to catch the words.

'Never mind,' growled Esterhazy. He picked up a bottle of Glenfiddich whisky and poured himself an inch. Esterhazy had a jutting, aggressive face ending in a nose like that of Punch. He'd put on weight since they'd given him a desk job, but not much weight. His tits didn't sag the way some middle-aged men's did, and he could wrestle marines half his age.

'Where the hell's the soda?' he muttered. The streets of Bonn were in a mid-evening hiatus. Nobody seemed much bothered about the official car or its cargo – there had been so many such cars in Bonn of late – and this suited Esterhazy fine. The last thing he needed was either cheers or jeers. If they cheered, were they cheering because they were glad to see the back of the American forces? Or because they were glad of those forces and wanted them to stay? God alone knew. Ben Esterhazy didn't. The talks had dragged today. The interpreters seemed to be in some kind of stupor, and the delegates likewise. It was winding down, the pull-out already being implemented. All they were really talking about now was the dotting of a few i's. That had never been Esterhazy's way.

But now his part in the comedy was over, and tonight he was flying back to the States. He relaxed, sipped his drink, rested his head on the seat-back. He was going home. The work was done. He'd put in an appearance for the sake of appearances, he'd signed this and that piece of paper. Now he could go back to the men in Washington and tell them it was done. Not that they really cared. If Europe wanted to go it alone, let them. That was democracy's attitude. But if there were to be a war, the men in suits would be the first to take cover, and the first to order the troops straight back into the kill zone.

'Well, fuck them.'

'Sir?'

'Never mind.'

'Sir . . .'

Esterhazy realised that the aide's hand had reached into an attaché case and come out with an envelope, towards which he was trying to attract the general's attention.

'What the hell is it?' said Esterhazy, snatching at the paper.

'Message came through for you, sir,' said Bosio. 'Sorry, I forgot to give it to you earlier.'

'Idiot.' Esterhazy tore open the envelope and unfolded the note inside.

SORRY YOU COULDN'T MAKE IT TO THE BURIAL.

For the first time that day, General Ben Esterhazy smiled.

4

Martin Hepton put down the telephone. At the third attempt, he had found out something concrete about Paul Vincent. He had found out that Paul was no longer in the hospital. He had been sent on to a rest home for a period of 'recovery', as the hospital doctor had termed it. Exhaustion, that was all it was. That was all.

Hepton walked along the corridor, paused outside the gym, then pushed open the door. It was a well-equipped gym. Healthy bodies meant healthy minds. Not that anyone ever used the gym. No one except Paul Vincent. Hepton went to the multi-gym, the so-called 'torture machine', and hoisted himself up on the arm-lift bar. He brought his chin up to touch the bar, then relaxed his arms until his toes touched the floor.

'That's one,' said the voice behind him. It was Nick Christopher, smiling, letting the gym door swing shut behind him.

Hepton smiled and pulled himself off the floor again, straining this time, coming down heavily.

'Two,' counted Christopher.

'Enough for today,' said Hepton, feeling the blood pound in his chest.

'Is this man out of condition? I ask myself.'

'Okay, let's see you do some.'

'Stand aside, shrimp.' Christopher pulled a crossword book out of his back trouser-pocket and handed it to Hepton, then gripped the bar and heaved himself aloft. He managed fifteen pulls, then rested, breathing hard.

'I'm impressed,' said Hepton.

'If there's one thing regular sex does for you,' explained

Christopher, taking the book back, 'it gives you a strong pair of arms.' They both laughed.

'I wouldn't know sex if it hit me in the face,' Hepton said.

'That's your problem then,' Christopher said. 'You can't tell the difference between sex and a slap in the face.' He paused. 'How are things with Jilly?'

'What things? I haven't heard from her since she went to London.'

'Have you tried calling her?'

'Only every day.'

'So do you get the feeling it's all over?'

'Just a little.'

'Sorry to hear that, Martin.'

Hepton shrugged. He gripped the bar again and managed two more hoists.

'What about Paul?' Nick Christopher asked.

'What about him?'

'Have you managed to find out anything?'

'Apparently he's gone off to some rest home.'

'Jesus, it must be bad then. I thought those places were for the dying and the dead.'

Hepton tried a third hoist, failed, and dropped to the ground. 'Better book me a room in one then,' he said. 'After you've bought me a drink.'

They sat down in the cafeteria, drinking cans of cola and eating crisps.

'Is this supposed to be brain food?' Christopher asked. Then: 'What do you think of that shuttle, the *Argos*, crashing like that?'

'I think our man was lucky to get out in one piece.'

It was front-page news, of course. Tomorrow it would be relegated, but for today, Major Mike Dreyfuss was famous, which was, Hepton supposed, what the bastard had always wanted. Hepton had two very good reasons for being jealous of Mike Dreyfuss. For one thing, the man had actually touched the skies, while all he, Hepton, could do was watch them.

For another, Dreyfuss and Jilly went back a long way. They had never been lovers, perhaps – though he had her word alone on that – but they had been friends, very close friends, and while she had allowed Hepton into her bed and her body, her mind had stayed closed to him. Yet she had spoken of Dreyfuss with such tenderness . . .

'Well,' Nick Christopher was saying, 'I can't see him having an easy time of it. I mean, there he is in America, the sole survivor of a disaster in which all the Americans on board perished, and here we are kicking the Yanks out of Europe, making us not very popular over there.'

'I see what you mean,' said Hepton. It was all he could do to stop himself from smiling. He stuffed his mouth with crisps instead. Yes, front-page news Dreyfuss might be, but for all the wrong reasons.

5

The light was diffuse and coloured the burnished gold of . . . The description ended there. His mind wasn't up to it. He decided to open one eye, just a little, and saw an underwater blur of greys and blues and whites, bathed in the same golden light. He blinked, opened both eyes and saw that he was lying in a hospital bed. A private room. Lavender paint on the walls, machines standing beside the bed, a drip feeding his left arm. Through the slats of the blinds streamed the day's raw sunshine. Golden light.

He was alive then.

A nurse sat dozing in the heat, a paperback novel on her lap. Where was this? Why was he so sore? His mouth was raw. Then he remembered – the shuttle had crash-landed. Couldn't get the undercarriage down. Couldn't get anything to work. Total shutdown of the onboard computer. Now how the hell could that have happened?

And what about Heinemann, O'Grady, Marshall, Wilson, Adams? Were they alive or dead? The fate of Hes Adams especially interested him. He let out a little whistle of air, as much as he could manage without feeling pain. It was enough. The nurse stirred, opened her eyes and smiled at him. Then closed them again as she stretched. A good big early-morning yawn, and then another smile, as though they were waking up in bed together; lovers.

'Good afternoon, Mr Dreyfuss. How do you feel?'

Dreyfuss. That was his name. It was as good a name as any. He tried answering her question, but his throat was dry and sore. He swallowed painfully, and she seemed to understand. Rose from her chair and poured some water from a jug into a glass. There were flowers on his bedside cabinet. Not many of them, a couple of small bunches.

The water was tepid. He had trouble swallowing.

'Thanks,' he rasped. 'Needed that.' Speaking was like rubbing something raw against sandpaper.

'You've been asleep a long time.'

'How long?'

'Several days, I think. I've only been on shift a couple of hours.'

'Where am I?'

'Sacramento General.'

It sounded like the title of a bad western. He supposed it was a hospital in Sacramento. He'd never been to Sacramento before. One of his reasons for wanting the shuttle mission was so he could see a little more of the States. He'd only been three times previously, and then never for long. As a child, growing up in the rapidly disappearing slums of east Edinburgh, he had dreamed of all this, of spacemen and of America, playing out the dream with toy spaceships that he would send hurtling to their doom.

'The others . . .' he began, but already the nurse had pushed at a buzzer above his bed. God, her body looked good, wrapped in the flimsiest layer of white cotton. He could almost taste . . . What was it he could taste in his mouth, right there behind the caked dryness and the lees of water?

It was smoke, blood, fear. And hands tearing at him. Why were hands tearing at him?

'Good afternoon, Major Dreyfuss.'

A man in a white coat, stethoscope swinging reassuringly around his neck, had pushed open the door. Behind him came two others, one in a general's uniform, the other looking like a worrier from the State Department. They stood slightly to left and right of the doctor, like tumours growing out of his sides. Good, thought Dreyfuss: his powers of description were coming back.

'Hello,' he said, but the doctor was studying his chart, and then studying the nurse. He smiled at her.

'I don't think I've seen you before, have I?'

She smiled back. 'No, Doctor. The name's Carraway.'

'Well, Nurse Carraway, has the patient been behaving?'

'Yes, Doctor.' Now she was looking towards Dreyfuss, and there was that smile again. The doctor turned towards him too.

'How do you feel?'

'One hundred per cent, Doctor. When can I get up?'

The doctor laughed. 'Not for a while yet, I'm afraid.'

'What's the rush?' snapped the general. It was a serious question.

Dreyfuss closed his eyes.

'I've had a relapse, Doc,' he said. 'I'm allergic to goons.'

'Why, you sonofabitch—' started the general, only to be stopped by the civilian's upraised hand.

Dreyfuss opened his eyes and stared at the slats of the blind, trying to recall where he had seen that colour before, that golden colour, and heard those words before, too.

A ball of flame. Fuel igniting. And the voice of Hes Adams in his ear: *you sonofabitch*.

'Leave him be, Ben,' the civilian was saying. 'He's traumatised, probably doesn't know what he's saying.'

'He knows all right.'

'Come on,' the civilian insisted, leading the general towards the door. 'I'll buy you a drink and you can bore me with the story of Bonn.'

The doctor watched them go and seemed to relax a little. He approached the bed.

'Nice chaps,' Dreyfuss commented. The doctor seemed not to understand, then smiled.

'You mean General Esterhazy and Mr Stewart.'

'If that's who they were.'

'That's who they were.' The doctor watched Dreyfuss sip more water. 'Throat sore?'

'A little,' said Dreyfuss. 'Listen, I meant what I said back there. When can I get up?'

'Just hang on in there.' A pencil-fine beam of light shone into Dreyfuss' left eye, then his right. 'What do you remember about the accident, Major?'

'What accident?' Dreyfuss smiled at the doctor's look of alarm. 'Only joking,' he said. 'I remember a ball of flame; it really did look like a ball, too. I felt like I could have given it a kick. I didn't, though. It kicked me instead. Then I suppose I must have passed out.'

'And where were you when this happened?'

'On the shuttle, of course. The shuttle was called *Argos*, and we were coming in to land, and there were six of us.'

'And what had the shuttle been doing?'

Dreyfuss made a show of trying to think.

'Major?'

'I . . . don't seem to remember that,' he lied, though why his instincts told him to conceal his returning memory was a mystery.

'Well, don't worry about it.' Dreyfuss caught Nurse Carraway staring at him fixedly. But when his eyes met hers, she slapped a smile onto her face again. 'Do you remember the names of the other crew members?' the doctor was asking.

'Let's see.' Dreyfuss tried to look as though he was thinking hard. He wondered why Nurse Carraway was so intent on his answer. 'Heinemann,' he said at last, 'Adams, Marshall, O'Grady, Wilson.'

'Good, Major Dreyfuss. Now think back.' The doctor began to check his pulse. Dreyfuss had the idea that this was less even than a routine check; that it was a cover under which the doctor could ask his questions. Without knowing exactly why, he had the feeling that there was a good reason why he shouldn't tell him everything he knew. 'What,' the doctor was saying, 'is the next thing back that you remember *before* the fire?'

This was perfect: they expected – *wanted* – him to have amnesia.

'Major?'

'Well . . .' Dreyfuss started, licking his lips. He stared at the lavender walls, at a concerned Nurse Carraway, at anything that might appear to be jogging his memory. 'I remember taking off, the whole thing with ground control, with Cam Devereux – he was my contact on the ground. Everything was going according to schedule. But . . . I'm not sure why we were up there in the first place. No, wait, we were launching a satellite, right?'

The doctor smiled.

'That's right, Major. Launching one of our communications satellites. Don't worry.' He patted Dreyfuss' shoulder. 'It'll come back to you in time. This sort of thing is quite usual in cases of trauma. And you took a few nasty bumps when you landed.'

'Nothing serious, though?'

'No, nothing serious. You just need to rest. Does your head hurt?'

No, his head didn't hurt. He put his right hand to his forehead and felt a plaster there.

'Yes,' he said, 'a bit of a headache.'

'We'll get you something for that. I'll be back to see you shortly. Meantime, if there's anything you need, just ask Nurse . . .?' The doctor had forgotten her name.

'Carraway,' she said. She smiled at Dreyfuss again, her hair the colour of honey. And he smiled back. By which time the doctor had left the room and the door was swinging shut. A voice was raised somewhere in the corridor. The goon, thought Dreyfuss, the one called General Ben Esterhazy.

'Can I see a newspaper?' he asked Nurse Carraway. She was

sitting down with her book again, legs crossed. Were those silk stockings she was wearing? Since when were silk stockings regulation issue for nurses?

'I'll have to check on that, Mr Dreyfuss.'

'Didn't you hear? It's *Major*.'

'Of course it is. I'm sorry.'

'That's okay.'

She had risen to her feet, but instead of leaving to fetch a paper, she approached the bed.

'Can I just ask one thing?' she said.

He smiled. 'How can I stop you?'

'I was just wondering . . .' Her fingers stretched towards him, stopping just short of his throat. 'I was wondering how you got those bruises on your neck.'

Hes Adams' fingers trying to wrench the life from him, when they were both already dead.

'What bruises?' he said, his eyes clear and honest.

She smiled, but uncertainly. Then walked to the door and opened it, turning back to look at him before leaving. Dreyfuss checked that there were no cameras trained on him from the corners of the room, no holes drilled in the wall. Seeing none, he allowed himself the luxury of a smile.

6

Parfit stared at the security room's various screens as they relayed the passing parade outside the embassy. Most days now there was a demonstration of some kind. It might be the French embassy or the German embassy. But mostly, as today, it was the British embassy. Today's crowd was small. Thank the unseasonal Washington drizzle for that perhaps. They were yelling something, but the cameras hadn't been wired for sound, not outside the perimeter wall at any rate. It didn't matter. He knew the gist of their chants. You don't want us, we don't want you – that sort of thing. And he took their point. Whether he agreed with it or not was irrelevant.

There had been some ugliness in other parts of the country. It was tempting to say the less civilised parts. A section of the USA would forever stay frontier country, and God help any unwary English tourist straying too far from the safety of their metropolitan hotel. So far this week, Parfit had had reports of two firebomb attacks on British businesses in Boston and New York, several broken windows, threats, casual violence, and sixteen muggings, one of which had taken place in a picnic area of Yosemite National Park.

Then there were those who were merely annoyed: the British businessmen who were losing contracts, the British immigrants who were being harassed at work. And all of it filtered back via the great brown fan to the Washington embassy, where some of it landed squarely on Parfit's too-small desk.

'Looks peaceable enough, Mr Parfit,' said Tom Banks, one of the security team whose job it was to watch the screens, seeking breaches in the line of defence.

'The rain will cool their tempers, Tom,' said Parfit. 'See you later.'

'Bye, Mr Parfit.'

He was headed for Johnnie Gilchrist's office, the inner sanctum. Towards Gilchrist's door, the carpet pile seemed to grow discernibly deeper. It was said that this was because so few people dared disturb Gilchrist in his lair. Like many myths, there was a core of truth to it. But Parfit knocked anyway, his distinctive three short raps and one long.

'Come in, Parfit.' Seated behind his desk, half-moon glasses resting precariously on his aquiline nose, Gilchrist could look tame enough, more the retiring scholar than the shrewd – and vicious – career diplomat. He and Parfit had sharpened claws on one another in the past, but at least each understood the other's territory. Gilchrist's job was to get things done, no matter what. Parfit's job was damage limitation. There could never be one without the other.

'Sit down.'

Parfit sat, crossing his legs. The chair was as uncomfortable as it needed to be. It was not designed for long-stay visitors.

'Another demo outside.' It was a statement of fact.

Gilchrist removed his glasses and rubbed at the red indentations either side of his nose.

'It seems quiet enough today,' Parfit commented.

'Thank Christ for that at least then.' Gilchrist slipped the glasses on again, pushing them down firmly onto the bridge of his nose. 'Now, what about Dreyfuss?'

'What about him?'

'Come on, Parfit. What's your game?'

'I don't know what you're talking about.'

Gilchrist waved the comment aside. 'You should be there in Sacramento. *Somebody* should be there at least. Has he regained consciousness yet?'

'We think so.'

'*Think*?'

'It's not easy getting straight answers just at the moment. You should know that, or haven't you noticed that our dealings with the cousins have become rather frosty? We keep in contact with the hospital authorities, who pass us on to somebody else, and that somebody else tries to sell us a call-back-tomorrow or an I'll-check-and-call-you-back.'

'All the more reason why somebody from the embassy should be there.'

'I'm going.'

'Yes, but when?'

'Maybe tomorrow.'

Gilchrist stared hard at Parfit, who didn't flinch. 'Is that a maybe-maybe or a maybe-definitely?'

'It's a maybe-probably.'

Gilchrist smiled in defeat, then took off his glasses again to rub at his nose. He had been doing this ever since Parfit had known him, and it irritated him more than he could say.

'So,' Parfit began, 'is there anything I should know about the state of play on the pull-out?'

'No. NATO's making its usual balls-up of the whole thing. Nobody seems able to agree with anybody else. Fallings-out left and right. If only we had the right bloody government in power . . .'

'But we don't.'

'Quite. So instead it's complete chaos, and what are the Soviets doing? Have you noticed?'

'I wasn't aware they were doing anything.'

'Exactly. They're just sitting back enjoying the bloody show. Oh, and speaking of bears, Ben Esterhazy's back from Bonn. Not the happiest of soldiers, by all accounts. There's talk that he'll be heading for Sacramento.'

'Oh?'

'Well, most of that shuttle crew were his men after all.' Gilchrist sighed. 'We really could have done without this on top of everything else.' He pulled a newspaper from the drawer of his desk and began to read aloud. '"The Jonah Factor. Major Michael Dreyfuss, the Briton they did not want on the tragic shuttle mission, was still seriously ill in Sacramento General Hospital today. Ground observers report that the shuttle's undercarriage appeared not to operate during its descent towards Edwards Air Force Base."' He looked up at Parfit. 'Et cetera,' he said, 'until this at the end: "Whatever happened, one thing is clear. The people of the United States will long remember the dealings of the past few weeks with the British government, the British people, and one British subject in particular."' He threw the paper back into the drawer. 'They're talking about Dreyfuss, and yet you're letting him lie there—'

'I have a good reason.' Parfit snapped his mouth shut, but too late. He had already said it. Gilchrist smiled again, nodding.

'I thought there must be a reason. So come on, what is it?'

Parfit sighed. 'Not here.'

'Very well then, let's stretch our legs as far as the secure room. I'm all ears, I'm sure.'

7

At last, Hepton had two clear days free from the base, and could take a drive into the country. Ripening fields, the sun beating down as it had no right to do in the course of an English summer. An occasional splash of garish yellow where rape – vegetable cash to the farmers – had been sown. But mostly the fields were green, or were delivering up golden buds of wheat and barley. A beautiful country. He so seldom noticed it, but it was the truth. He had become blind through living his life underground, but like a mole, he had burrowed his way to the surface and was now scenting the air anew. He checked in the Renault's rear-view mirror. The Ford Sierra was still with him, a hundred yards back but quite noticeable, there being so little traffic on these winding roads.

Twenty minutes ago, he had slowed behind a tractor, though overtaking would have been easy, and had watched the car behind him edge forward until the face of the driver – female – was clear in his mirror. The face of a businesswoman, but she didn't appear to be in any rush. So that when he had waved her past, she had flashed her lights once in acknowledgement, but shaken her head too. And stayed behind him.

She was still behind him, sometimes gaining, sometimes losing. He thought of pulling in to a café, to see whether she would follow him. After all, this might be innocence itself, a chance encounter that might lead . . . well, anywhere. Except that he had to press on. Paul Vincent was in the Alfred de Lyon Hospital, and the Alfred de Lyon Hospital was an inconvenient forty or so miles away yet. So he drove on.

He thought of *Zephyr*, of the miracles satellites could perform. He stuck an arm out of his window and waved towards the sky, wondering if he could be seen. There was no doubt that *Zephyr* could see him if it wanted to. It could give close-ups of his car, of his number plate. But *Zephyr* wasn't trained on him. It was trained on a series of air force bases, where the US personnel were preparing for their flights back home. Or at least that was what it had been watching yesterday evening, on Hepton's last shift.

Something niggled, though, something he had noticed and mentioned in passing to Nick Christopher. It was to do with Buchan Air Force Base in the north of Scotland, just outside the town of Peterhead. Buchan had been an RAF radar station, but then the American forces had moved in for a time. Hepton had watched it before. He liked the quality of light in northern Scotland. That was what niggled: the sun was setting early in Buchan.

'Cloud cover,' Christopher had explained. 'I've seen the weather reports. Overcast skies.'

'Yes,' Hepton had said, 'but they're not overcast.'

And Christopher had shrugged his shoulders, then placed a hand on Hepton's own.

'Maybe when you go to visit Paul, you and he should swap places. What do you say?'

Then they had both laughed and gone to watch the night's television.

Was something wrong with the weather, then? Or had the *Zephyr* malfunction caused some tinting of the lens, some aberration to appear on the glass? What the hell. He'd think about it some other time. For today, he had forty-eight hours' worth of off-base permission, and he intended to use the time well. He switched on the radio and found a station broadcasting a phone-in about the Geneva arms talks. The Soviets were offering yet more deals. Jesus, what were they going to do with all those redundant guns and tanks and missiles? Better yet, what would they do with all that redundant manpower?

On another station, two critics discussed the latest high-grossing American film, *Gun Law*. They'd had a bootleg tape of that on the base last week. Usual vigilante stuff, all about how the USA should pull up the drawbridge and let everyone outside the moat rot. Laughable really, yet some of the men on the base had started acting tough the very next morning, and come in wearing black T-shirts and white jeans, the way the hero did.

'Strange times,' Hepton said out loud, flicking to another

channel. Mahler. Radio 3, he supposed; some lunchtime concert. He didn't know which Mahler it was, but he knew it was Mahler. Jilly had listened to Mahler before, during and after each session of love-making. Which had seemed weird to him at first. In fact, it had seemed weird *all* the time. She would push his prone body away from her so that she could go and change the cassette tape and then would come to him again and give him a hug, just to show that she liked him a little bit too.

But not enough to stop her taking the newspaper job in London, not enough to stop her zipping a bag and throwing it into the back of her MG, giving him a brief embrace while her eyes glazed over with thoughts of leader columns and front-page scoops. A peck on the cheek, and then into the driving seat where she belonged, no seat belt necessary, though he had warned her before.

'Phone me!' he had called, but she never had. And now it was over. He had toyed with the idea of using *Zephyr* to track her down, to peek through some bedroom window as she pushed away another prone body and went to change the tape.

It was a nice dream.

After the Mahler, there was the one o'clock news, including a small item on Major Mike Dreyfuss and the American reaction to the shuttle disaster. Predictable stuff. He had watched the TV pictures. Orange flame, the nose of the craft crumpling, turning in on itself, more explosions. It was a funny thing about Dreyfuss, though. He was in his late thirties, a few years older than Hepton, not exactly his physical prime. Hepton had read about the other candidates who'd been in the running for the UK's only place on the mission. They'd been young, strong. So why Dreyfuss? Not that it was any big deal. Not the big deal it was when the first Briton in space had gone up on that Soviet mission, or when the second one had gone up soon afterwards, courtesy of the Americans. No, to be Britain's third man in space: well, there was something pathetic about that, wasn't there? He allowed himself a guilty smile.

The Alfred de Lyon Hospital was, for the most part, a rest home, and had been chosen not because it was so far away from the base but, in Fagin's words, 'because Paul is suffering from some kind of nervous exhaustion, and they specialise in that'. Now that Hepton re-ran that statement in his head, he saw an ominous ambiguity to it. He checked in his mirror but couldn't see the Sierra. He signalled and came to a halt by the side of the road, where he waited for three minutes. But there was still no sign of the car. Somehow, he felt disappointed. Maybe he should double back. The woman might be in trouble, her car might have gone off the road . . .

Or, more likely, she had taken a turning and was heading towards her destination.

Maybe Nick was right, Hepton said to himself. Maybe I do need to book myself into this place. He started the car again, and within quarter of an hour was turning the Renault through an imposing main gateway and up a country house driveway of gravel so clean it might have been polished that very morning. Therapy for the patients, perhaps?

As he rounded a bend, a rabbit leapt into his path and he nearly hit it. He braked hard and watched it flee across an expanse of manicured lawn and into some shrubbery. Skin tingling, he opened the car door and stepped out. He could hear a car approaching the gateway. When he turned, he saw the same Ford Sierra driving past. He listened as its engine faded into the distance. Smiling, he got back into the Renault and drove up to the imposing entrance of the Alfred de Lyon Hospital itself.

'I must have made a mistake then, it's as simple as that.'

They were sitting in the morning room, a modern extension to the main building fitted with patio doors and filled with pot plants. It was like a hothouse, and Hepton, who had already taken off his jacket, now dragged his tie loose from his neck. Paul Vincent, dressed in slippers, thick dressing gown and sunglasses, didn't exactly look ill. He looked rested and a little tanned. In fact, he looked a good deal healthier than Hepton felt.

'Still,' Vincent continued, 'it's good to see you, Martin. Thanks for coming. So tell me, what's happening back at the base?'

Hepton shook his head. He hadn't driven all this way for gossip. 'What makes you so sure you made a mistake?'

'Well,' Vincent opened his arms in supplication, 'like you say, nothing's been done about it. And Fagin doesn't seem to think anything's amiss.'

'Fagin can make mistakes.'

'Not while I've been working for him he hasn't.'

'So how come we lost *Zephyr* for over three minutes?'

'You can't blame that on him.'

'Why not? He's in charge, isn't he?'

'Martin, what's wrong?' Vincent seemed genuinely concerned.

Hepton rubbed sweat from his forehead. It was a good question. What *was* wrong? Why was he so keen to see mysteries where there might be none? Paul Vincent didn't seem anxious. Nick Christopher didn't seem anxious. Fagin didn't seem anxious. So why was he bothering?

'I don't know, Paul. It's just . . .' He sighed. 'I really don't know.'

Vincent smiled. 'It really was nice of you to come. I haven't seen anybody since I came in here.'

'What happened to you? I mean, back at the base?'

He shrugged. 'I'm not exactly sure. One minute I was fine, the next I was in hospital.'

'And what did the hospital say?'

'You know what they're like. The patient always gets to know the least.'

'Who was your doctor?' Hepton had asked the question in a rush. It seemed almost to catch Vincent out; he stared at Hepton before replying.

'McGill, I think. Yes, a Dr McGill.'

Hepton sat back in the chair and looked around. A few elderly men were seated in wicker chairs. Two were playing a game of chess so delicately they looked to be moving in slow motion. The heat was prickling Hepton's neck and back. He rubbed a finger beneath his shirt collar and glanced towards the doorway, where two muscular male orderlies stood, their jaws fixed. Like soldiers on parade, he thought, rather than nurses caring for the sick.

'So what's it like here?' he asked.

'The food's good,' said Vincent. 'Mind you, the sex isn't up to much.'

They laughed, but Hepton was beginning to catch something behind his friend's eyes, something trapped behind that dead, unfocused look.

'Are they giving you any drugs, Paul?'

'No more than I usually take.' Vincent laughed again, but Hepton managed only a smile, listening to that laughter, to its nervy hollow centre.

'Know what I think, Paul?' he said. Then he leaned towards his friend and lowered his voice. 'I think you're in trouble. I think you're frightened. I think this is all bullshit.' He nodded in the general direction of everything around them. 'And I think you need a friend like me. Maybe I'm wrong.' He rose to his feet. 'Give me a call if you feel like talking.'

'Martin!'

But Hepton knew that the only way to end the scene effectively was for him to walk and keep on walking. So he did. He wasn't going to learn anything here, not unless he could scare Paul enough to make him say something.

He was practically at the car when he heard footsteps hurrying across the gravel behind him.

'Martin, wait!' Paul Vincent caught up with him, looking paler now after the exertion. 'Martin.' He paused for breath. 'At least stay for afternoon tea.'

It wasn't the answer Hepton wanted. He opened the driver's-side door. Vincent's hand came down onto his own level.

'Look,' he said. He glanced around him. 'I'm going to say this just the once, but that should be enough. You always were a good listener, weren't you?'

'I still am, Paul.'

'Well, listen now. Stay out of it. Take a holiday. Suggest it to Fagin. He'll approve it. Go off somewhere warm.' He laughed at this, the sweat gleaming on his face. 'I mean somewhere exotic, somewhere quiet.'

'That's friendly advice, is it?'

Vincent shrugged. Hepton could see the two orderlies in their white uniforms watching them from the main building. Could he bundle Paul into the car and make a getaway? Not against the fitter and younger man's will. He climbed into the Renault and closed the door.

'Tell me,' he said through the open window. 'Really, just between us, what did you think you'd discovered?'

Vincent sighed. His voice when he spoke was no more than a whisper. 'There was something up there, Martin. Something big.' He glanced over his shoulder towards the orderlies. 'But that doesn't seem to be the point.'

'How do you mean?'

'The point seems to be that no one *cares*. One name, Martin.'

'Yes?'

'A man called Villiers. He came to see me, to ask a few questions. He didn't give his name, but I asked at the desk afterwards and they told me. I didn't like him much. Steer around him if you meet him.'

'What questions did he ask?'

'Oh, I don't know, routine stuff. What happened at the base? What happened with my computer? That sort of thing.' Vincent paused. 'The disk got wiped, didn't it? The hard disk?' Hepton nodded, and Vincent sighed. 'They're being pretty thorough.'

'You're saying the disk wasn't wiped accidentally?'

'I'm not sure, but I never was a great believer in coincidence.'

'No, me neither. But then someone in the control room must have wiped it.'

'I suppose so, yes. I got the impression Villiers wanted everything kept as quiet as possible.'

Which, Hepton thought, seems to mean keeping you out of the way.

'Thanks, Paul,' he said.

'Remember what I said about taking a holiday.'

'Goodbye, Paul. Look after yourself.'

'You too, Martin. And I mean that. You too.'

Driving off, Hepton checked in his rear-view mirror and saw the two orderlies approach Vincent. Vincent had the look of a lonely man, of a man unfairly imprisoned. Hepton felt his hands harden around the steering wheel. He pressed down a little on the accelerator and enjoyed the momentary feeling of complete control.

8

The Palladio Bookshop was sited not far from Holborn Underground station, and every weekday morning the shop's proprietor, Mr Vitalis, would take the Piccadilly Line Tube from his home in Arnos Grove. He always walked up the escalators rather than standing, but this was due not so much to impatience or any need to be getting on as it was a keen desire to keep himself fit. After all, Mr Vitalis was nearing fifty, though he looked older. Some said his background, to judge from his voice, was east European, and that he had come to England at the outbreak of World War Two. Others, examining his olive skin, proclaimed him Greek, while a few guessed at Italian and fewer still north African. In a sense, they were all correct, since Mr Vitalis liked to think of himself, in the truest sense of the phrase, as a man of the world.

The Palladio was fairly quiet in the mornings, busying at lunch-time with customers from the offices and shops, browsing as they munched on a sandwich or sipped from a carton or can. In the afternoon, a few of the regulars usually dropped in either to buy or to sell. Mr Vitalis had a good reputation with the city's book reviewers, who would offer him the latest titles, once they had been finished with, for one third of the cover price. These books Mr Vitalis sold on to libraries and, it must be said, other bookshops. And in this way he made his money.

He kept few friends, but those he did keep, when entertained for the first time at his home, could not help but comment on its size, and on the superb works of art he had collected over the years. He would smile, and then move the conversation along to literary gossip or some commentary on current affairs. For Mr Vitalis loved conversation.

Today, however, the few regulars who called at the Palladio for an afternoon's tea and chatter found the usual pavement stall locked up inside the shop, and the shop itself deserted, with a neatly written note sellotaped to the inside of the glass door: *Apologies, friends, but Palladio closes early today. Business as usual tomorrow.*

They'd never heard the like: Mr Vitalis shutting up shop early? Perhaps there was a woman behind it. After all, he *was* a man of the world. They were sure there would be *some* story in it, and surer still that Mr Vitalis would be telling the story tomorrow afternoon over tea.

Not many would have looked for Mr Vitalis in the back of a black cab, for he was known to abhor the things, always choosing to travel by Tube or bus or foot.

'I'm a social animal at heart, you see,' he would explain.

And while he was considered something of an aesthete, his tastes could not be said to be expensive in most areas, so some might have been more surprised still to see the taxi drop him outside a Park Lane hotel called the Achilles, where, having paid the driver, he talked animatedly for several minutes with the uniformed doorman. He then entered the hotel lobby, while the doorman stared evenly at the traffic roaring past the entrance.

Mr Vitalis looked as though such hotels were part of his everyday existence, walking up to the reception desk with a polite smile on his face and his eyes as dark as the shiniest black olives.

'Good afternoon,' he said. 'I'm expecting a friend. I wonder, has he arrived yet? His name is Mr Devereux, an American.'

The clerk checked the register, then remembered.

'Oh yes, sir,' he said. 'No, Mr Devereux hasn't arrived yet. We have some mail waiting for him. That's why I recall the name.'

Mr Vitalis looked surprised.

'But I am right, am I not? I mean, he *is* due today?'

The clerk flipped over a page of the register. 'No, sir,' he said. 'We have Mr Devereux's name in for tomorrow.'

'Ah.' Mr Vitalis nodded. 'I must have a crossed line then. Well, tomorrow it is. Thank you.'

And with that he turned and walked back through the lobby, pushing his way out of the main door, which he held open courteously for an elderly lady and the fruits of her shopping trip. On the hotel steps, he paused again to exchange some words with the doorman. Not many words this time, but they seemed to leave their impression, for the doorman's cheeks were crimson with shame as Mr Vitalis walked towards the taxi rank, where he opened the door of a waiting cab, heaved himself in and slammed it shut behind him.

9

Hepton had been thinking about it all the way back to the base. So much so that when he glanced in the rear-view mirror and saw no sign of any car following him, he merely shrugged and kept on driving.

They were surprised to see him at the gate.

'Thought you'd got a couple of days' leave,' one guard said.

'Can't keep away,' Hepton replied, starting the car forward as the barrier rose to let him into the compound.

He parked, then went straight to Fagin's office, a small white-washed room next to the female toilets on the second level. There was always a faint aroma of urine and disinfectant in the room, which nobody mentioned and everyone put down to its location. But Fagin seemed happy there; some might have said disturbingly so.

Fagin, too, was surprised to see him, but admitted as much only by the raising of his thin eyebrows when Hepton walked in through the door.

'Sit down, Martin, please.' Hepton sat. 'Have you seen Paul?'

'Yes.'

'And how is he?'

Hepton looked around the room before answering. There were photographs of satellites, spaceships and aircraft covering the walls, and three pinboards filled with postcards and other memorabilia. Then he looked towards Fagin.

'He's fine,' he said.

'Good,' said Fagin, returning the look. 'So what can I do for you?'

That was the question, thought Hepton: what *could* Fagin do for him? What was it Paul Vincent had said . . .?

'Actually,' he began, 'it's about Paul. He looks so fit, he reminded me it's a while since I've had a break. I mean a proper break. I was wondering if I could be spared for a week or two.'

Fagin seemed to consider this. 'Well . . .'

'I know I'm not due any additional leave right now,' Hepton continued. He was waiting for a shake of the head. Fagin hated to see people go off on holiday. Work was what he lived for, and he didn't see why others shouldn't be the same. So Hepton waited. He knew he wasn't owed any holiday time, and Fagin knew it, too. Besides which, there was a strict routine to be obeyed, which meant giving four weeks' notice of intended vacations.

Fagin's face wrinkled.

'I'm not sure we *can* spare you just at the moment, Martin. I take it you'd want your leave to start immediately?'

'If possible, yes.'

Fagin was shaking his head, but slowly. 'I'm not sure,' he said again.

'Nick Christopher could stand in for me,' Hepton said, thinking fast. 'He knows the set-up on my console as well as I know it myself. And Curtees could take over from him.'

'I'll have to think about it, Martin. I'll try to give you an answer one way or the other as soon as I can, but no promises.'

'Well, thanks anyway.' Hepton made to rise, but paused. 'Oh, one more thing, sir.'

'Yes, Martin?'

'Have you discovered what went wrong with *Zephyr*?'

'Not yet. I'm just thankful we didn't lose her altogether.'

'Yes, so you keep saying.' Hepton rose from the chair. 'It couldn't have anything to do with whatever else was up there, could it?'

Fagin smiled quizzically. 'How do you mean, Martin?'

Hepton shook his head. 'No, maybe not. I just thought that whatever it was that was up there interfering with *Zephyr*'s airspace might have caused the satellite to malfunction temporarily.'

'There wasn't anything else up there.' Fagin seemed bemused. 'What made you think there was?'

'Oh, just Paul's data. Have you checked it yet?'

'I told you, the disk—'

'Oh yes, the disk malfunctioned too, didn't it?' Hepton shook his head. 'Well, these things happen, don't they, sir?' he commented archly.

'Yes, they do, Martin,' said Fagin coolly, watching as Hepton walked to the door and made his exit.

Hepton descended the metal stairs to the ground-floor level and walked along the corridor towards where two telephone booths were situated. As usual, one of these had a notice taped to it saying *OUT OF ORDER*, to which some wag had prefixed the single word *BANG*. But the other telephone was working. Hepton dialled directory enquiries. His call was answered immediately.

'Hello,' he began. 'I'd like the number of a hospital in Grimsby. It may be the only hospital, I'm not sure.'

A few moments later, he had several numbers in the back of his diary. He drew lines beneath them all with his pen, thanked the operator and rang off. Then, finding more change in his pocket, he dialled the first number.

'Hello,' he repeated, when the call was finally answered. 'Could you put me through to Dr McGill, please?'

It took the receptionist a little time. 'I'm sorry,' she said at last, 'there's no Dr McGill working here.'

'Thank you,' Hepton said, ringing off. He felt actual relief: it would be something of an anticlimax if Vincent's Dr McGill were to exist outside of the young man's imagination. He called the other two numbers with the same negative result.

So there was no Dr McGill. Had Paul Vincent ever even been taken to hospital in the first place? Or had he been at the Alfred de Lyon all the time? It was a question Hepton couldn't yet answer. He took his pen and wrote the name *VILLIERS* in his diary. Another figment of Vincent's imagination? A second visit to the nursing home was becoming absolutely necessary.

Two hours later, Hepton was playing pool with Nick Christopher when the internal note arrived. He read it out aloud.

'"Leave can begin at once. Send us a postcard. Henry."'

Christopher came to see. 'Jesus,' he said, 'he really signed himself Henry. Fagin *never* uses his Christian name. Never.'

Hepton wafted the note in Christopher's face. 'Now will you believe that something's going on?' he said.

He had spent the past half-hour trying to make sense of his suspicions to Nick Christopher, but it seemed that the more he talked, the flimsier everything became. But now this. The granting of an immediate holiday, courtesy of Fagin.

Courtesy of Henry.

Christopher returned to the table and played a shot, but it went wide of the pocket and he sighed, putting down his cue.

'Okay,' he said. 'Run through it again for me, starting at the beginning.' And this time he was concentrating as Hepton told his story.

10

Hepton went to his dorm, pulled a suitcase out from beneath one of the bunks and started packing. Nine months ago, he'd taken out a year's rental on a small flat in the market town of Louth, plumb in the middle of the town's market area and not far from Binbrook. He'd reckoned it would make a little love nest for Jilly and him, whenever they could find a couple of days or more free to spend together. But then she'd taken the London job, forsaking her own local paper, where she had been something of a star. There had been a murder, made to look like suicide, and Jilly had investigated. She hadn't exactly been able to prove anything substantial, but she had goaded the police into taking another look, and from there they had pronounced the suicide a murder. From where it was a short step to declaring the murderer (the dead woman's son) found and guilty (twelve years).

Jilly's story had found its way into the national press, and then the *London Herald* had jumped in with the offer of a job. Of course she'd been right to take it. It was the perfect career move at the right time. So the flat had gone unused and unloved, but Hepton had kept it on, using it for the occasional tryst, more or less unsatisfactorily.

He didn't pack much, just enough to make people think he really was going to take a holiday. Then he waved farewell to Nick Christopher, who waved back, and made for his car.

At the security barrier, the guard came out of his hut.

'Off again, are you?'

'That's right, Bert,' said Hepton, smiling.

'I don't know, some people . . .' Bert went back to his post.

Hepton waved at him, too, as he drove underneath the rising barrier and took a right turn onto the main road. Louth was less than twenty minutes away.

There had been a market that day, but the only signs in the town centre were scraps of vegetables in the gutter outside the entrance to Hepton's flat. He lifted his suitcase out of the car and unlocked the main door. There were three flats in the house: one on the ground floor, one on the first floor and another in the attic. His was the first-floor flat, and he took the winding stairwell with accustomed awkwardness, manoeuvring the suitcase around the twists of the climb.

There was no mail waiting for him on the matting that covered his hall floor. The neighbour downstairs, Mrs Kennedy-Hall, had a key to the flat and sent the mail – bills always – on to him at the base. He unlocked the door. The flat smelt musty. He hadn't been here in over a fortnight, and then only to play the gigolo in a failed seduction.

The place looked tidier than he remembered it. They had drunk a lot of wine that night, and rather a lot of neat gin (there being no tonic water to hand). None of it had helped. He couldn't remember clearing up afterwards, though. Perhaps Mrs Kennedy-Hall . . . But no, it would be more her style to hire someone to tidy.

Then he heard the sounds, at first placing them in the street below. The sounds of running water, of things being moved, breakable things. There was someone in his kitchen . . .

He ran towards the source of the noise and stood in the kitchen doorway, dumbstruck. At the sink stood a tall, attractive woman, perhaps a year or two younger than him. She had rolled up the sleeves of her white blouse and was up to her elbows in soapy water. Clean dishes stood on the draining board, the worktops shone, the whole place was sparkling. The woman turned, saw him and smiled.

'Hello,' she said. 'You must be Martin.'

'That's right,' Hepton said at last. 'And who the hell are you?'

'Harriet,' she answered, letting the water out of the sink. 'My friends usually just call me Harry.' She dried her hands on a dish towel, then held out the left one towards him. There were no rings on her water-reddened fingers. 'How do you do?'

Hepton shook her hand awkwardly, right-handed himself, and she noticed his hesitation.

'Oh dear,' she said, 'I'm always doing that – shaking with the wrong hand, I mean. Sorry.'

'Not at all,' said Hepton. The shock of finding a stranger in his flat, a breaking-and-entering charlady, was ebbing. Questions filled the space. 'But who are you?' he asked. 'How did you get in?'

'Care for some tea?' Harry had turned her back on him and begun to fuss with the kettle.

Hepton stared down at her legs, supple, slim legs wrapped in thin black stockings. She wore a blue pinstripe skirt to just below the knee. It was half of a suit, the jacket of which he now saw was hanging over one of the chairs beneath the freshly wiped foldaway table.

'There's today's milk in your fridge,' she was saying, 'and some Assam tea in the cupboard. The place was quite barren. I hope you don't mind. I went to that little shop on the corner.' She turned to smile at him, and despite himself, he smiled back.

'I think you should know—' he started.

'Oh,' she interrupted, sniffing the interior of the teapot speculatively, 'but there's very little I *don't* know, Martin. Very little indeed. That's why I've been sent along here. Do you take milk?'

'Who sent you here?'

She smiled again, with her unblemished English rose of a face, then waved an expansive arm around the kitchen.

'All neat and tidy,' she said. 'That's how I like things. I can't remember, did you say you took milk?'

'Yes,' he said, beginning to feel distinctly uneasy. It was difficult to find an order for all the questions welling up within him. 'How did you get in?'

'Didn't I say?' She began pouring water from the kettle into the teapot. 'Your door was open.'

'Open?'

'Wide open. No breaking and entering necessary. Well, no breaking at any rate. So I suppose the worst I can be accused of is cleaning with intent.' She had placed everything on a tray, which she now double-checked. Satisfied, she lifted it. 'Shall we go through to the living room?'

There was little Hepton could do but follow her, knowing that he needed answers but knowing also that she seemed determined to give them in her own way and in her own time. Well, he had lots of time, didn't he? He was on holiday. All he needed was patience.

They sat down and she poured, handing him a cup.

God, he hadn't used this tea set in living memory, preferring a chipped red mug. It had come with the flat, the tea set. But then so had the mug.

'I thought it was odd,' Harry continued, 'your door being open like that, so I called in to report it. I'll pay for the call, of course.'

'Called in to whom?'

'To my employers,' she said, 'who are, ultimately, *your* employers. It'll be useful to keep that in mind.'

'Why?'

She chose to ignore this, lowering her fine eyelashes as she sipped from her cup. Hepton drank too, playing her at her own game. The tea was strong and aromatic. Harry put down her cup and crossed her legs.

'You saw your friend this morning. Paul Vincent. And now your little holiday begins.'

'That's right.' Then it hit him. 'And you,' he said, 'drive a black Ford Sierra.'

She smiled, but did not reply.

'You were following me?' he said.

'Why were you so anxious about Mr Vincent?'

Hepton shrugged. 'It's no secret. Paul was taken ill. He's a friend of mine, as you yourself said. So, naturally, I was worried.'

'But there's more to it than that, isn't there?' Her voice had taken on a hard, professional edge. He stood up.

'Look,' he said, 'I'm sorry, but I've got no proof that you are who you say you are – not that you've said very much.' He walked to the window and stared down into the street. An old man was stooping to pick up a discarded piece of fruit from the side of the road.

'Very good, Martin. I was beginning to wonder if you'd ever get round to asking. I thought you'd forgotten procedures. Take this.' She produced a slip of paper from her skirt pocket and rose from her chair to hand it to him.

From close up, he could smell the subtle soap she used. She wasn't wearing perfume, though; either that or his nose wasn't attuned to it. He stared at the numbers on the paper.

'It's a telephone number,' she said. 'Ex-directory; you won't have come across it before. If you dial it, you will find yourself speaking to your superior, Mr Fagin. It's a direct line. He'll give you clearance to speak to me, and he'll promise also to give that permission in writing. Don't worry, nothing you might say to me will get back to him.'

'You don't have any identification on you?'

'Nothing formal,' said Harry. 'It's against the rules. I can let you have a library ticket or my credit card, but that's about it.'

Hepton smiled but was already picking up the telephone. The receiver at the other end was answered after the very first ring.

'I suppose that's you, Martin. I was told to expect a call. Listen, I want you to tell them *everything*, do you understand? It may be more important than you think. Don't let it spoil your holiday, though; just get it all off your chest and then you can enjoy yourself.'

As Hepton listened to Fagin's unmistakable voice, saying little himself, he watched Harry picking invisible hairs off the arms of her chair. His head was spinning. *What is all this about?* A little while ago, Fagin hadn't seemed interested in anything he or Paul Vincent might have to say. Yet now he was ordering Martin to tell all. He wrenched his thoughts back to the here and now in time to catch Fagin's final statement:

'If you keep anything from them, you could get into serious trouble, and they'll *know* if you're hiding something. That's their job. I must go now. Goodbye.'

As though she had heard everything, Harry raised her head at this, staring towards him with a righteous look on her face. Hepton put down the telephone and sank into his chair, feeling not at all comfortable in his own home. He pinched the bridge of his nose, then straightened up.

'So what do you want to know?' he said.

'What I really want, Martin,' Harry began, 'is not so much to be told as to do the telling. As I said before, there probably isn't much you could tell me that I don't know already. You should be aware, however, that this is a matter of national security. It sounds like a cliché these days, but I'm in absolute earnest. It is in everyone's interest for you to forget whatever Paul Vincent told you.'

'Told me about what?'

Her look was that of a disappointed schoolmistress, some favoured pupil having let her down. Hepton stared at her evenly.

'Told you,' she said, 'that he had noticed something on his monitor.'

'Then there *was* something up there?'

'Certainly there was . . . interference. We're looking into it.'

'But who's "we"?'

'You could say that I do PR work for the armed forces.'

'Public relations?' Hepton sounded doubtful. Harry shrugged. 'But I don't understand,' he persisted. 'What have the army got to do with it?' Then he remembered. *Zephyr* was watching for civil unrest during the US pull-out. The army must be on standby, of course.

'As a matter of interest, Martin, what do *you* think happened?'

'Me?' Hepton seemed genuinely surprised. 'Why should anyone be interested in what *I* think?' He remembered his final sighting of Paul Vincent, looking scared and beaten. For some reason, the memory stirred him to anger. 'I'll tell you what I think,' he said. 'I think you know *less* than you're saying, not more.' He was out of his seat now, standing over her. 'I think you should get out and leave me alone. That's what I think. And if I want to tell anybody about all of this, then I'll damned well tell them.'

She stood too, her eyes on a level with his. Her face had tightened, and there were spots of red on either cheek. Her voice when she spoke was as cold and lifeless as a deep freeze.

'Of course you must do whatever you see fit. I'll get my jacket.' He followed her to the kitchen and watched her put the jacket on. She surveyed the newly cleaned work surfaces. 'Neat and tidy,' she said, 'that's how I like things, Martin.'

'Is that a threat?'

She smiled at this, but not pleasantly, and moved past him into the hall, opening the front door. She paused on the threshold, reached into her jacket pocket and brought out a laminated business card. Well, it looked like a business card, but in fact all there was on it was a printed telephone number. 'You can contact me at that number,' she said.

Hepton stared at the card. 'What did you mean when you said we work for the same bosses?'

She chose not to reply, but reached again into her pocket and held out a ten-pence piece towards him. 'For the call,' she said. He accepted the money. She was leaving now, but she turned one last time. 'You know Major Dreyfuss, don't you?'

'How do you know that?'

'It's my job,' she said.

He watched her descend the stairwell, then listened as she walked along the passage to the main door. He closed his front door and walked briskly to the living room window, but there was no sign of her in the street outside, no sound of her shoes moving away. His head was spinning. His flat, his private life, everything had been suddenly whisked away from him, reshuffled and brought back altered beyond repair. The old man was still examining stray scraps left by the market stalls. Dispossessed, but no more so than Hepton was himself. As Hepton watched, the man arched his back, straightening it, and in that moment looked up at the window. Hepton flinched, shrank back into the room. Was he being watched? Who was watching him? He realised that he wasn't just confused. He was afraid. Terribly afraid, and yet without knowing quite why.

Harry used a small infrared device to disconnect her car alarm as she walked towards the black Sierra, then unlocked the boot and took from it a large attaché case, which she carried with her to the driver's-side door. Sliding into the seat, she quickly opened the case and studied the telephone equipment inside. She should check in, but she still wasn't sure how much of a threat Hepton was. He seemed at the same time quite innocent and quite devious. Of course, as she knew from experience, even the innocent could be dangerous. She had to be sure. She closed the case again, unlocked the glove compartment and removed from it a small black plastic module. Switching it on, she was rewarded with a high-pitched bleep and a strong green light at the centre of a series of radiating LEDs. It wasn't the world's most sophisticated tracking device, but it would do. She placed the tracker on the passenger seat and sat back, hands on the steering wheel, eyes staring straight ahead, waiting . . .

Part II

A United States National Security Agency plan to expand considerably the eavesdropping facilities of its spy base at Menwith Hill, North Yorkshire, is likely to be given the go-ahead by Harrogate district planning committee . . . The Conservative-controlled council was recommending approval . . . 'They do a good job there, not only for the protection of America but for every man and woman in the free world.'

Independent, 21 September 1987

11

Days were passing. Dreyfuss felt sure of that, though he slept mostly. Probably because of the drugs they were giving him: the ones he could see, the ones they asked him politely to swallow; and perhaps the ones he couldn't see, concealed in his drinking water, his meals.

But after his latest bout of unconsciousness, he awoke not to the restorative sight of Nurse Carraway, but to two stern figures, the same men as before, the ones the doctor had named as General Esterhazy and Mr Stewart.

The general was examining the cards attached to the few flowers that had been sent to the invalid.

'Who's Jilly, for Christ's sake?' he asked the other man, unaware as yet that Dreyfuss' eyes were opening.

'Just some woman he knows. They used to date in school apparently.'

God, they know so much about me . . .

'He was married, though?'

'Divorced now. The ex-wife lives somewhere in Australia.'

'I notice *she* didn't send any flowers,' the general commented, taking pleasure in the fact.

Dreyfuss noted that Stewart seemed subdued, while the general himself was as abrasive in his speech as a grinding tool. Now Stewart had noticed that Dreyfuss' eyes were opened to slits.

'General,' he warned, and both men came to the bed. Dreyfuss could smell salt and something sweeter, an aftershave perhaps. 'My name's Frank Stewart,' said the civilian. 'I'm from the State Department.'

He's CIA, Dreyfuss thought. Either that or NSA.

'And this is—'

'Jesus Christ, Frank,' snapped the general, 'I can make my own introductions, can't I?' He turned his eyes to Dreyfuss. The pupils were inky, like staring down the barrel of a pistol. 'The name's General Ben Esterhazy.'

Esterhazy, one of the biggest of the cheeses. He had been on a mission to Europe and hadn't been able to meet with the *Argos* crew to offer them good luck. Instead, an aide had come to give them the general's best wishes.

'Pleased to meet you,' said Dreyfuss in a voice weak from sleep. In fact, he didn't feel at all bad, but he didn't want the hospital thinking he could be moved. He felt safe here, safe from choking hands. And he still had to find out a few things. 'They're all dead, aren't they?' he asked.

'Every goddamned one of them,' Esterhazy said bitterly, while Stewart threw him a look that said he shouldn't have told Dreyfuss that. Dreyfuss had the feeling there was no love lost between these two men, or between their respective organisations.

Stewart dragged the nurse's chair closer to the bed and sat down. He was a heavyset man in his early fifties. Dreyfuss thought his hair had probably been grey for quite a few years. In build, however, he was Joe Frazier to Esterhazy's Ali. The general was tall, and as broad as Americans liked their heroes to be. Esterhazy had been publicly and vociferously opposed to the European pull-out, and had received a polite but stinging slap on the wrist from the White House as a result.

Which hadn't stopped them sending him to Europe to negotiate the terms of the pull-out itself.

'So,' Frank Stewart was saying, 'how are you doing?'

Stewart had slipped out of his jacket, which he was now hanging over the back of the chair. Dreyfuss noticed the gold armbands on his shirtsleeves. He had never seen anyone wear bands before, outside of old movies. Maybe a snooker player or two, but only of the old school. Perhaps they were there to cut off the supply of blood to Stewart's fists, so he wouldn't sling a punch at General Esterhazy. Stewart's eyes were as murky as prunes swimming in semolina, and the cracks on his face weren't there from laughing. He reached into his pocket for a crisp white handkerchief with which to mop his forehead. Dreyfuss knew who he was now: he was Spencer Tracy playing the tired, put-upon father in some film.

'I'm doing okay,' Dreyfuss answered, pouring himself a little water. He saw for the first time that the drip by his bed had been taken away. There was a fresh sticking plaster on his arm where the syringe had been removed.

'Better than some,' spat Esterhazy.

'Ben, for Christ's sake—'

'Well, what do you want from me?' Esterhazy exploded. 'Tears and flowers?' He slapped at the bunch of flowers nearest him and sent some petals spinning floorwards. 'Five good men died up there.'

'Do we know what happened yet?' asked Dreyfuss.

'*We* don't, no,' said Esterhazy. His eyes drilled into Dreyfuss'. 'Do you?'

Dreyfuss took his time, sipping the water, thinking over his reply. But Stewart was ready with another question.

'The doc says you've got a case of partial amnesia. Is that right?'

'Yes.'

'So what *do* you remember?'

Dreyfuss rested his head against the pillow. 'I was chosen as the British member of the *Argos* mission. We were launching a communications satellite. Everything went fine . . .' He stared at the ceiling, seeing the control panel again, the computer screen, the readouts, which had stopped making sense. Heinemann had been watching the screen, too, but hadn't said anything. He didn't seem to think there was anything wrong.

But there was.

And at first Dreyfuss hadn't said anything, in case the answer was simple and they all sneered at him again, thinking him underqualified to be on the flight, thinking him stupid. But then he had mentioned it to Hes Adams . . .

'Yes?' Stewart prompted.

'Everything went fine, like I said. But when we were coming in to land, the onboard system failed.'

'Christ, we *know* that!' shouted Esterhazy. 'Tell us something we don't know.'

'Ben, please.' Stewart's voice was pleading. He smiled at Dreyfuss.

Techniques for the survival of interrogation, number one: trust no one, and especially not anyone who appears to be your friend. That was what they had taught him. He would have to be careful of this man Stewart.

He had a question to ask for himself.

'How far is Sacramento from Edwards Air Force Base?'

'Maybe three hundred miles,' Stewart said.

'Why was I brought here then? Why not a hospital closer to Edwards?'

Stewart turned to Esterhazy. 'Yes,' he said, 'why was that, Ben?'

'I told you, Frank, we were trying to throw off the press. They've been round this thing like vultures. We were also trying to avoid any ugly scenes, public demonstrations, folks wanting him strung up.' Esterhazy was relishing this. 'So instead of taking him to Bakersfield or LA, which would have been obvious choices, we landed him at McClellan and brought him here. And what do we get by way of thanks? Squat!'

Stewart ignored this, his attention still on Dreyfuss. 'Those bruises on your throat aren't love bites, are they, Major?'

'I suppose we all panicked when the shuttle was coming down.' Dreyfuss had had time to prepare this story. 'We all got a bit crazy.'

'Bullshit,' hissed Esterhazy. 'They were the best. They wouldn't panic. They'd take it like men. I *know* they would.'

'If you say so,' Dreyfuss said.

'Sonofabitch,' Esterhazy growled.

There was that word again. *Sonofabitch! The burial's what matters. Coffin's got to be buried!* But what coffin? Whose? Had Hes Adams meant the shuttle itself?

Esterhazy was coming towards the bed. He looked massive, and not a little dangerous. 'What the hell is it with you, Dreyfuss? Just what is it you're trying to hide? I *know* you know something. Damn you, I want to know what it is.' He turned to Stewart. 'Get out, Frank. Give me ten minutes with this bastard.'

'Ben, don't be stupid. You're a general, not some damned sergeant in the marines. And this isn't Vietnam. This is the United States. That's not the way we work.'

Esterhazy's voice had become almost neutral. 'Yes it is, Frank,' he said. 'You should know that. Now either you get out of here, or I'll have a couple of my men drag you out.'

'Ben . . .' Stewart's face was purple with blood. Nobody had talked to him like this for quite some time, which, Dreyfuss supposed, meant he was fairly high up in his organisation. But he held his rage and got slowly to his feet. 'You're making a mistake,' he said. Esterhazy was smiling now.

'Hell, Frank, what do you think I'm going to do? Wire electrodes to his nuts? Your gang might have stooped to that once upon a time. But all we're going to do is talk. Just a one-to-one. Because the major is holding back on me, and I don't like that.'

Stewart was at the door now, hesitant, but ready to leave.

Techniques for the survival of interrogation, number two: when a team of two is involved, everything they do is calculated, everything is a trick. Don't be fooled.

'Tell me something,' Esterhazy was saying, his breath close to Dreyfuss' ear, 'how come nobody from your own embassy has even bothered to come see you? Huh? Answer me that.'

Esterhazy's hands were leaning on the edge of the bed, and Stewart was turning the handle, opening the door, making to leave.

But there was someone outside the door, and as Stewart opened it, they walked in, as though they had been standing there for some time listening, awaiting the moment to make the most effective entrance.

'Good day to you, gentlemen,' the intruder said by way of introduction. 'The name's Parfit, British embassy.'

What was he, some kind of child? To be ignored like that, to be left here in his room while the three of them went off for a meeting. Parfit, British embassy. Just like that.

'Well, Jesus, it's about time one of you guys turned up,' Esterhazy had sneered. 'If this' – jerking his head in Dreyfuss' direction – 'if this had been one of ours in your country, we'd have been at his bedside before the goddamned shuttle had stopped smoking! We look after our own, and I'll tell you—'

'I'm sure you will, General.' Parfit's voice was as clean as a polished window. 'Is there a room where we can sit down and discuss things?'

'There's the administrator's office,' offered Frank Stewart.

'Excellent,' said Parfit. He came to the bed and touched Dreyfuss' shoulder. 'I'm glad to see you looking so well, Major. We'll talk soon.'

And then they'd walked out of the room and left him. Dreyfuss fumed for a couple of minutes, his heart racing, angrier than he'd been since the crash. Then he pulled at the bedcover and swung his legs off the mattress and onto the floor. The floor itself was warm to the touch, yet the room was cool. He stood up, feeling his legs wobble from inaction. He locked them at the knees and drew himself to his full height. A few hesitant steps took him to the washbasin, where he splashed cold water onto his face. He looked in the mirror, and saw a pale face, a gaunt face, the hair cloying and in need of shampoo. The skin was singed from the shuttle blaze, and cream had been smeared onto his cheeks and forehead. And yes, those bruises on his neck were prominent. He looked a mess.

He dried himself with a towel, feeling sweat trickling down his back from the effort thus far. Then he shuffled over to where the flowers sat. There were two cards: one from Jilly, and one from Cam Devereux.

Cam! He held a snapshot in his head of Cam's beaming face, that air-hostess-style voice: 'Hi, I'm Cameron Devereux. Call me Cam, everyone does. I'll be your contact down here while you're up there.' The day they'd gone to visit the *Argos* ground station, meeting with the men who would be their eyes and ears on earth while they were circling in space. The controllers, with their crew cuts and striped shirts, seated in front of screens that could show anything from the height and trajectory of the shuttle to the pressurisation of the cabin and the heartbeats of the men inside it.

Cam, too, had a striped shirt and a crew cut. He also had a smile. God, that assured smile, a fortune in dental work. Even the mechanics in this country smiled like movie stars. But he had a weak handshake, and would melt like wax if a hand grabbed at his smooth lapel or threatened to tweak his WASP nose. However, there was every chance that he would know something about what had gone wrong, or at least would have his suspicions.

I shouldn't have been up there in the first place, Dreyfuss said to himself now. He had been chosen over younger men and better men, men more computer-literate, men fitter, more intelligent. He had told the selection panel at his third and final interview: 'I'm just an airman who wants to be an astronaut.' Hoping that candour would stand up where his credentials had faltered. It had: the Americans wanted him. Everyone had wondered why . . .

'Major!' It was Nurse Carraway, entering the room on her silent rubber heels. 'What are you doing?'

'Just taking a look at my flowers.'

'I didn't think you were strong enough to walk.'

'Willpower, that's all.' He shuffled back to his bed and sat down on its edge, where General Esterhazy's heavy knuckles had recently rested.

'Well, anyway, it's time for your medication.' She was holding a tiny paper cup filled with liquid in one hand, and a yet smaller cup containing a mixture of tablets in the other. Dreyfuss accepted both. He put the liquid down on his bedside cabinet and picked one of the tablets out at random, holding it between forefinger and thumb. It was oval-shaped and purple in colour.

'What's this?' he asked. He felt bolder now that Parfit had arrived.

'What do you mean? It's just medication.'

'No, come on, you're a nurse. What *kind* of medication? What's its purpose? What's its medical name?'

She seemed flustered. Dreyfuss had not seen her flustered before.

'Well?' he goaded.

She smiled. 'Major Dreyfuss, if you don't want to take the tablets, that is your concern. But I should warn you that I'll have to report—'

Dreyfuss laughed, shaking his head. 'Get out of here,' he said. 'Go on, shove off.' His grin was purposeful. 'You're not a nurse. A nurse on the wards would know what the drugs were called, nicknames, medical names, Christian names. A real nurse would know that. But you, Nurse Carraway, you don't know anything. As General Esterhazy might put it, you don't know squat! Incidentally,' he was on his feet again, shuffling forwards, 'which one of them do you work for, Stewart or Esterhazy?'

'Major Dreyfuss,' she spluttered, 'I . . . I don't know what you're talking about.'

'What's more,' he went on, enjoying this, 'the doctor who came to see me that first time had never seen you before. Plus,' he said, staring at her legs, 'I can't see too many nurses wearing silk hosiery, can you?'

She was staring at her legs too now, as though unable to believe their treachery.

'Go on,' he said tiredly, 'go and make your report.' And with this he fell back onto the bed and lay there shading his face with his arms. There was a pause of several seconds before he heard her shoes squeak. She had turned round and was going to the door, which opened silently. Dreyfuss felt tired and tricked and used. His head was thumping, and he wondered if any of the tablets in the cup would ease it.

'Bravo.'

It was Parfit's voice. Dreyfuss took his arms from his face and jerked his head up. Parfit was standing in the doorway, holding the door open with the tip of a polished black leather brogue. He came into the room, letting the door close softly. His shoes made a solid clacking noise on the flooring as he approached the bed.

'Do you always eavesdrop on people's conversations?' asked Dreyfuss.

'Goes with the territory, I'm afraid. So how are you?'

'Fine.'

'Yes, for the moment perhaps. But everyone around you seems ever so slightly agitated. I shouldn't think your safety here could be guaranteed for much longer. What do you say?'

'You mean I can leave?'

'Well of course you can leave. Nobody's been forcing you to stay.'

Dreyfuss groaned.

'Unless, of course,' Parfit said, 'they got you to sign any papers.'

'What kind of papers?'

'Papers committing yourself to their care?'

'I haven't signed anything.'

'You're sure?'

'Positive.'

'Very well then. I'll just make a few arrangements, and then we'll have you out of here.'

'Have you told them I'm leaving?'

'Who?' Parfit seemed amused. 'Esterhazy and Stewart? Good Lord, it's not up to them, is it? It's up to the doctors and the hospital administrator. I foresee no problem.'

'They won't be very happy.'

If anything, Parfit's smile broadened. 'No,' he said, 'no, they won't, will they?'

He was about to leave, but Dreyfuss stopped him.

'One question, Parfit,' he said.

'Yes?'

'What took you so long to get here?'

'We'll talk about that elsewhere,' Parfit said, looking around the room. His meaning was clear: walls really do have ears. Dreyfuss nodded. Parfit again turned to leave.

'Parfit?'

'Yes, Major Dreyfuss?'

Dreyfuss was smiling too. 'It's nice to see you again,' he said.

12

Cam Devereux arrived at London's Heathrow Airport desperately tired and in need of the vacation this was supposed to be. His cotton sports shirt was sticking to him, and his scalp tingled as he ran his hands over his thinning hair. He was so tired. But how could he rest? His mind felt inflamed. How could he stop himself replaying events, seeing that stranger arrive at the ground base control room? Seeing the stranger given an office of his own and a console, ignoring the curious looks of the other controllers? Seeing *Argos* itself gliding erratically towards earth, flailing across the runway . . .?

Yes, he needed a vacation. They'd told him that. He needed a complete break; everybody did, everybody connected with *Argos*. They had *ordered* him to take a break. So he had chosen to come to London, despite their protests about leaving Europe well alone. London was a city he could happily get lost in, and wander through all day from district to district. He liked almost everything about it, including the things the Londoners themselves seemed to loathe, such as the subway system. So, having waited for his baggage, he headed downwards, beneath the ground, far away from the sunlight and the sky, and bought a ticket to Green Park station, from where it would be only a short walk to his hotel. The other people who got into his compartment of the Tube train were travellers like himself, hauling too much baggage behind them. He himself was travelling light by comparison. You could always buy what you hadn't brought, especially with the thick wallet of travellers' cheques they had given him.

'Look on it as a bonus,' they had said. A bonus for what? he was tempted to ask. But he had never questioned anything in his life . . .

until now. Now, his head was full of unanswered questions and fears. He again examined his fellow passengers, and saw that they looked every bit as nervous as he felt. First-timers in London, he supposed, and wary of every step.

Maybe at last he could stop looking over his shoulder. Maybe he could stop worrying about what he had seen, what they seemed to *know* he had seen. And had paid him to forget about, paid him by way of a holiday, a swanky hotel, a plastic wallet full of paper money. Maybe they'd leave him alone. And maybe when he stopped worrying, he'd stop thinking about it too.

Maybe, but he doubted it.

Still, he had to make it look like a holiday. He would visit a few of the sights, do a little shopping. All the time waiting for his new controller to make contact. He had asked for one, and they had agreed to his request, though reluctantly. But he had negotiated from a position of strength. He had information after all, didn't he? He had something to tell. If only he knew what it was . . .

13

The morning was bright, despite Martin Hepton's mood. He awakened to his clock radio, just in time to catch a studio debate between someone from the Pentagon and the Minister for Defence turning into a full-scale shouting match. The radio presenter sounded genuinely alarmed as accusations were hurled across the table. Lack of co-operation, distinct misunderstanding of the mood of the European Community, defenders not terrorists, never asked to be here in the first place. Et cetera.

Hepton smiled to himself as he listened. If intelligence and communications were good enough, he reasoned, there would be no arms race: everyone would *know* what everyone else had. That was why he felt no jab of conscience at his job, even when attacked at parties by people who could not understand why he did what he did. Not that he did very much. There would be the occasional full-scale surveillance operation, covering the movements of a suspected spy or some military attaché. Someone in a car might just notice that another car was following, but they couldn't suspect that they were being watched from space. Mostly these jobs were for the security services. Now and again they were for the military. There had been illicit peeks at what this or that US listening post was up to; the one at Menwith Hill, for example. Against the rules, of course. Snooping on the enemy was all well and good, but spying on your allies . . .

Maybe that was why NATO was in such a shambles. European countries were squabbling with each other. America was pulling its defences out and retrenching back in its homeland. A ring of steel was going up around the USA: not just missiles and tanks and manpower, but economic steel and the steel of mistrust. The USA could be self-sufficient if it wished, and that was the way things were headed. Companies were finding it harder to export their goods to the States. Diplomacy had about it the air of the refrigerator. What had gone wrong? Just over a year ago, Hepton had been delighted with the way the world was going. The EuroGreens were keeping things sane as far as the environment went, the left wing of the European Parliament was pushing through some worthwhile legislation. The mood was distinctly upbeat. Even Britain was becoming more . . . well, European.

So what had happened? Hepton had blinked and the edifice had started to crumble: squabbles, economic downturns, the troubles in Pakistan and Turkey . . . And now the pull-out. He fumbled for the radio's off-switch and made for the shower. Standing beneath the spray, he thought of the dream he'd had in the night. Mike Dreyfuss had been in it. So had Jilly. They'd been seeking each other, finding each other, but then losing each other again.

When he came out of the shower, he heard the telephone ringing. He ran, naked, to the living room and picked up the receiver.

'Hello?'

'Martin? Is that you? Thank Christ I've found you. I tried at the base but they said you were on leave.'

It was Paul Vincent, sounding edgy. No, more than that, sounding frightened.

'Where are you?'

'I'm still at the nursing home. I've been trying to reach you.'

'What's wrong, Paul?'

'They've got guards watching me, Martin. I mean, they watch me *all* the time. I can't stand it. They said I could leave soon, but I think they're planning something, God knows what. Please, come and get me, Martin. I want out of here.'

'Okay, Paul, just hang on. I'm coming. It'll take an hour, maybe a bit longer. Just keep calm. Okay?'

'Okay. But hurry, please.'

'Paul, I know there isn't any Dr McGill. They never did take you to hospital, did they? And you didn't become ill. Isn't that right?'

Vincent sighed loudly. 'Yes. They said they were security. I was on my break. They asked me to go with them. They brought me straight here. I drank some tea and the next thing I knew I'd crashed out for a solid day.'

'Drugs?'

'They wouldn't admit it, but I get the feeling they'd been questioning me during that time. The bastards won't admit *anything*.'

'You mean the staff?'

'Not all of them. No, these were other people. People brought in by Villiers.'

'With Fagin's knowledge?'

'I don't know.'

'Okay, Paul. Hang in there. I'm on my way.'

'Thanks, Martin.'

Hepton pulled on a pair of denims and a T-shirt, hardly aware of what he was doing. He slipped on his shoes, grabbed his jacket, then took a last quick look around and left the flat, pausing to check that the lock had connected and to turn the key in the mortise. He didn't believe Harry's story of finding the door ajar. He had spent over an hour checking for bugging devices that she might have left behind. He hadn't found any, but that didn't mean anything. There were many other possible points of entry into a closed environment or a telephone line: no one knew better than he what technology was capable of.

Shit, if they were listening in on his telephone, they would already know about Paul. He had to hurry.

Outside, he glanced around as he unlocked the door to his Renault. He crouched beside each wheel arch and peered beneath the vehicle, running a hand around the body in search of a tracking device. Nothing. No black Sierra parked in sight. No tramps picking fruit off the ground. He got into the car, fired it up and sped down the cobblestoned street. He started to think about Paul Vincent, and the line of thought led him back to *Zephyr.* How often did Fagin entertain bigwigs? Three, maybe four times in a year? A large coincidence then that he should have one such party in tow on the day *Zephyr* chose to blow a fuse. Hepton smiled grimly at this, remembering how he had once used the phrase 'blow a fuse' when talking with Jilly about the satellite.

'You mean those things actually have fuses?' she had said, and he'd had to explain that he was using layman's language. She had bristled at this, and insisted that he explain things to her in more technical terms. So for over an hour he'd spoken of SIGINTs and COMINTs and geostationary orbits, while she had listened intently, asking occasional questions. At the end of his explanation, she had smiled.

'You really are a clever little sod, aren't you?' she had said, and he'd nodded. What else could he do?

Clever, Martin, but perhaps not clever enough. He was used to being given orders, used to doing what he was told, to being nothing more than an operative. He seemed a long way from that now. Those uniformed high-ups were still in his mind. Three minutes and forty seconds, and they'd looked pleased. What was it about *Zephyr*? What was it that was so classified even the control personnel couldn't be told of it? For he was sure now that the malfunction had been a test of sorts, that it had been being put through its paces, with the brass there to watch, and that it had passed the test.

But what *was* the bloody test?

If anyone was following him, they were good. He didn't catch sight of a single suspicious car or person on the drive to the Alfred de Lyon Hospital. Everyone was doing his or her bit to seem genuine, from the lady driver who nearly hit him at a junction to the man whose dog ran into the road, causing him to brake hard.

So far so good. Paul Vincent had sounded on the verge of a breakdown. Hepton didn't feel too good himself. His body seemed extraordinarily tired and sluggish, his brain befuddled. He was hoping that Vincent knew more than he had been saying to date. It seemed the only way to unlock the hoard of answers to this whole thing.

He made good time on the drive, steered the car through the gates of the Alfred de Lyon and sped up the gravel drive. He didn't bother with the small car park, leaving his Renault outside the main doors to the building. In the reception hall, he went straight to the admissions desk, where the white-coated lady on duty smiled, recognising him from the previous day.

'I've come to see Mr Vincent,' he said.

'This must be his lucky day,' she said. 'Two visitors—'

'Two?' Hepton interrupted.

'Yes, a young lady arrived half an hour ago to see him.'

'A young lady? Short fair hair?'

The woman nodded thoughtfully. 'Yes, that sounds like her.'

'Is she still here?' snapped Hepton. He was growing afraid now. What if he had missed them? What if Harry had already whisked Paul Vincent away somewhere . . . somewhere Hepton couldn't find him?

'Well, I haven't seen her leave. I'll try Mr Vincent's room.' She picked up the telephone, pressed two digits and waited while the extension rang. Then she frowned. 'There's no answer. Perhaps they've gone to the sun lounge.' An attendant was coming from that direction. 'Oh, Roddy,' she called. 'Have you seen Mr Vincent?'

'I thought he was in his room,' the attendant called back. Hepton felt the hairs bristle on the back of his neck.

'Where's his room?' he said.

'The end of the corridor on the first floor, but you can't just—'

He couldn't just, but he already was: he ran to the sweeping staircase, took it two steps at a time, stumbling at the top, and ran along the first-floor corridor. He pushed open the last door he came to and looked in. It was a large, airy room, the walls cream-coloured and the bed a double. Some of Paul's things were lying about, but not untidily. There was an en suite bathroom, and Hepton paused at this door before turning the handle, expecting the worst.

'Paul?' he called. Then he pushed the door and let it sweep open on its silent hinges. But the bathroom was empty. He felt momentary relief, though he couldn't say exactly what he had thought he would find. Then his neck prickled again. Paul wouldn't have left knowing that Hepton was on his way. He would have stayed close to his room. He wouldn't have let Harry take him away without a struggle. Not unless he'd been drugged . . .

The woman from the front desk was standing at the bedroom door, with the attendant peering over her shoulder.

'He's not here,' she said.

'So where is he?' Hepton's voice was loud, and the woman recoiled a little.

'The stool from beside the bed's not there either,' she said. 'Maybe he's taken it into the garden . . .'

'I'll go and look,' said the attendant, skipping away, glad perhaps of a little bit of action. Hepton was back in the corridor again. He examined the other doors. Three, like Vincent's, were unmarked. Other bedrooms, he supposed. And one was marked *Stores*.

'Where else might they have gone to talk?' Hepton asked the woman.

'Well, there's the television room, of course, but it's not ideal for conversation. Some of our patients are slightly deaf, and they like the volume turned up. Then there's the morning room and the library.'

'Library?'

'Downstairs. It's usually empty. But I'm sure I would have seen them go in there. They'd have had to go through reception to get to it.'

'Would you check anyway?' The woman seemed doubtful. Hepton tried a smile. 'Please?' he said. 'It's very urgent that I talk to Mr Vincent.'

She hesitated. 'Very well then,' she said, and turned and walked back along the corridor.

Hepton stared into Vincent's room. Where the hell could they be? Wait, though: a building like this would need a fire escape, wouldn't it? He walked back along the corridor and continued past the staircase. Just around the next corner was a door marked *EMERGENCY STAIRS*. He smiled and pushed it open.

He was standing at the top of an enclosed stairwell, its steps winding and made of concrete. There was a window looking out onto the hospital's rear car park. He glanced at the dozen or so cars and saw the black Sierra parked there. He smiled again. Then he heard a sound from below him. Heels scuffing on stairs.

'Harry?' he called. He started to descend, then stopped. There was no sound now from below. 'Harry?' he repeated. He listened and heard the sound again. Footsteps, not descending now but climbing. Coming towards him. He was about to approach them, but something about the sound stopped him, something distinctly ominous. The steps were slow and even, and he could hear only one pair of feet. No Paul, then. Only a woman's heels. Silently he retreated a few steps until he was back beside the door and staring down the twelve or so steps to where the staircase turned a corner. There was a shadow on the wall below him. Then a figure appeared on the lower landing.

Harry.

And she was holding a gun.

Her face was devoid of emotion as she saw him and angled the gun up towards his head. Hepton dived towards the door and yanked it open. He threw himself through it and into the corridor, looking to left and right. He heard Harry's feet quickening on the stairs behind him and ran back along the corridor. The receptionist was standing at the top of the main staircase.

'There you are,' she said. 'I've looked, but there's no sign—'

'Get back downstairs!' yelled Hepton, startling her. Then he was past her, running towards Paul Vincent's room. He realised that he should have pushed past her and down the stairs, well away from Harry and her gun. But there were people downstairs, lots of them. He couldn't endanger all those lives. Very noble, Martin, he thought. But now what could he do? He stared at the door marked *Stores*. Beneath this sign was a smaller one indicating that a fire extinguisher was located within. Well, any weapon was better than none.

He saw as he approached that the door was ever so slightly ajar.

Behind him, he could hear the receptionist. She hadn't gone downstairs; instead, she had followed him along the corridor. Any second now, Harry would round the corner and be upon them. Hepton pulled open the cupboard door.

His eyes met a pair of legs. They were hanging a couple of feet above the ground, and on the floor lay an overturned stool. Hepton's eyes started to move upwards, his teeth gritted in growing horror. The body's arms hung limply; the head lolled at a tight angle. A thin metal tube, almost certainly carrying electrical wires for the building's lighting, ran the breadth of the large cupboard's ceiling, and this was what the green garden twine had been tied to.

The green garden twine that was cutting into Paul Vincent's neck.

His face was purple, eyes and tongue bulging obscenely. Somewhere behind Hepton the receptionist shrieked. He leapt forward and wrapped his arms around Vincent's legs, lifting them a little higher, then reached up with a finger to pull the twine out from where it had cut into the neck.

'Get me scissors!' he hissed. 'Or a knife – anything that'll cut this.'

The woman had a small pair of nail scissors in her pocket and handed these to him. After that initial shriek, she had quickly calmed. Hepton supposed she had seen this sort of thing before, working here. He cut the twine and eased Paul Vincent's body down, bringing it out into the hall and laying it on the carpeted floor.

'I didn't know,' the woman was saying. 'I never realised the poor man might—'

'He wouldn't!' Hepton snapped back at her. 'He wouldn't do this.'

He looked past the receptionist, along to the end of the corridor, and saw Harry standing there. Their eyes met, then she turned swiftly and was gone, back towards the emergency stairs.

'Wait!' he shouted.

The receptionist saw him staring and glanced back along the corridor too, but saw nothing. No doubt she thought him emotional and in shock.

Hepton stared at Paul Vincent, then at where Harry had been standing. He made his decision and bent over his friend, pushing Paul's swollen tongue out of the way and sticking two fingers into the young man's mouth, searching down towards the throat, checking if there was a clear flow for air. Then he pinched Paul's nose and gave mouth-to-mouth resuscitation.

'Come on, Paul,' he said. He pushed down with both hands on Vincent's chest, once, twice, three times. Pause. Once, twice, three times again. He checked for a pulse. There wasn't one – but then there was! Faint, but there.

'Is he . . .?'

Hepton turned to the woman. 'Go get a doctor,' he hissed.

'Yes, of course.' She hurried away.

Hepton kept trying the mishmash of life-saving techniques, remembering bits of each of them from the training sessions he had attended more than a year ago. He pushed down hard again on Vincent's chest with the heels of his hands. There was a palpable groan from the inert body. He crawled back to Vincent's head, his mouth close to the deep-red ear.

'Paul? Paul, it's Martin. Come on, Paul. You're going to be fine. Paul?'

The opaque eyes seemed to clear, the mouth trying to form words. But the voice box was shattered, the windpipe raw. Hepton brought his own ear close to Vincent's mouth. There were white threads of saliva at the edges, hanging from swollen lips. The word was hoarse, barely recognisable as speech. But Hepton heard it, where others might have thought it mere babble.

'Arrus . . . Arrus . . . Arrosss . . .'

And then the breath seemed to rattle within, the eyes became filmy, and Hepton could only crouch there, staring at his friend. The doctor was rushing along the corridor now, and would do what he could. It was already too late, Hepton knew. His own ministrations had served only to extend the waning life by a moment. But in that precious moment, Paul Vincent had given him something. A word.

Argos.

He left the body, rising slowly to his feet. Then he remembered Harry, and turned on his heel. He ran along the corridor, swung round the corner, pushed open the door to the stairs. He didn't mind now, didn't care if he ran straight into her and her gun. All he held in his mind was burning rage. But a glance through the window showed him that the black Sierra had gone. He leaned his forehead against the glass and closed his eyes.

'Paul,' he whispered. Then he began to cry.

14

They sat him on a sagging chesterfield sofa in the musty library, declared the room off-limits to the inquisitive patients and gave him sweet tea to drink. Meanwhile, Paul Vincent's body was being laid out on the bed in his room, his possessions gathered together, his family informed. A tragic suicide: that was what it would become. But Hepton, sipping his tea, knew this was not the truth. A policeman came to see him, a detective in plain clothes. Hepton told him about Harry.

'Yes,' the detective said. 'Mrs Collins on reception said Mr Vincent had had a visitor.'

'She killed him.'

The detective raised one eyebrow. He had already been informed that Hepton was in shock.

'She killed him,' Hepton repeated. 'She had a gun. I saw her.'

'But Mr Vincent wasn't killed with a gun,' the detective said slowly, as though explaining something difficult to a child. 'He hanged himself.'

'No, she did it. She hung him up there.'

The detective decided to ignore all this. He referred to his notebook. 'The name we have for the visitor is a Miss Victoria Simmons.'

Hepton shook his head. 'Her name's Harry.'

'Harry?' The detective sounded doubtful.

'Short for Harriet.'

'And her second name?'

Hepton shrugged. 'I don't know. She's something to do with the military. That's what she told me, anyway. You can ask my boss, Mr Henry Fagin. I'll give you his number . . .'

'Yes, well, meantime just you rest, Mr Hepton. You've had a bit of a shock.'

'I'm fine. But I'm telling you . . .' He looked up at the policeman. A simple-looking face, disguising a simple-working mind. He shook his head. 'Never mind,' he said. 'Never mind.'

The duty doctor gave him a couple of tablets, but Hepton refused them. He didn't need calming down, or cheering up. He didn't require the proffered lift home. He was quite capable of driving himself.

Paul had given him a name: *Argos*. Perhaps the truth had been too obvious, too glaring, too outrageous. But now that he thought it over, it was quite true that the United States space shuttle *Argos* had been in space at the time *Zephyr* had malfunctioned. But *Argos* wasn't supposed to be anywhere near *Zephyr*'s orbit. It had been a thousand or more miles away, launching another satellite. With Dreyfuss on board, now its only survivor. A coincidence? Paul had given him that one word because he had suspected *Argos* of interfering with *Zephyr* in some way. One person would know for sure.

Dreyfuss.

But how the hell could Hepton get to him? There had to be some way. The Foreign Office, perhaps. Their people in the United States would have access to him, surely? That might mean a trip to London . . .

London.

Of course! Jilly would have been keeping in touch with him. Hepton just *knew* she would. Partly from friendship – mostly from friendship, even – but partly because she had a nose for a story, and Dreyfuss was news. That was that then: he'd pack a bag and head for London. But first there were more questions to be asked of him, more tea to be served up and drunk. Why garden twine? Why suicide? Why by hanging? Why in a cupboard? He kept his answers to himself. Garden twine was strong. It wasn't suicide, but murder. Hanging to make it *look* like suicide. A cupboard to prevent the body being found too quickly.

Because Harry had known Hepton was on his way, and there hadn't been much time. Not enough time for an overdose, and not enough time for an abduction. No one, of course, had seen anything. No one had heard anything No chair falling. No choking or kicking. It was a neat operation. Neat and tidy. Hepton couldn't get Harry's face out of his mind.

Eventually they had to let him go. He gave his address in Louth, got into his car and drove off at a steady pace, picking up speed only when he was out of the nursing home's gates, picking up more and more speed until he caught himself doing seventy. Too fast on these roads. Braking, slowing. He didn't want there to be any other accidents.

Parking outside the flat, though, locking the car door, he felt a fresh wave of foreboding wash over him. Harry had killed Paul to stop him saying anything about *Zephyr* and, more especially, about *Argos*. Hepton thought of Harry again: *I like things neat and tidy.* With Paul gone, he knew he himself had become a target. Perhaps the only target left.

He stood at the bottom of the stairwell for a long time, listening. Then he climbed quietly to the first floor. He slowly pushed open his letter box and listened for sounds in the flat. There were none. Then he unlocked the mortise and the Yale lock and opened the door. There was a piece of paper lying on the floor of the hallway. He unfolded it and read: *Need to speak with you. Please come to the Coach and Four, 7.30. Nick.*

Hepton looked at his watch. It was 7.25. He'd have to hurry; the Coach and Four was a good seven or eight minutes' walk away. He'd never been to it before, there being two other pubs nearer the flat. He wondered why Nick wanted to meet him. Perhaps he had discovered something. Well, Hepton had things to tell him too, didn't he? Things about *Zephyr* and *Argos*. Things about Paul Vincent. Things about his death.

It hit him then, standing in the hall with the note in his hand. A huge tremor ran through him, and the strength left his body. He leaned against the wall for support and thought he was going to be sick. Was this what delayed shock felt like? He stumbled into the bathroom and ran cold water into the basin, splashing his face and neck. He wasn't going to be sick; the feeling was passing. He had to be strong, for his own sake. And he wouldn't be late for his appointment.

There was only one real route to the Coach and Four. It took him up a narrow, cottage-lined street, a street he'd always admired. But the people who lived there these days weren't farmhands or labourers or even small merchants. They were estate agents and accountants, most of them working in London during the week, coming here only at weekends. And as this wasn't yet the weekend, the street was deserted. At the end of what might seem to some a cul-de-sac, he turned right into a narrower lane yet, which would bring him out across from the pub. It too was quiet; one side being workshops and garaging, the other the backs of some houses, high fencing protecting the privacy of the gardens. A few brave motorists used this lane as a shortcut, though its surface was rutted and booby-trapped with potholes. He could hear a car now, slowing in the street behind him, turning into the lane. But there was plenty of room for it to pass him.

He turned to look at the car and saw the nose of the black Sierra as it started to speed towards him. Harry, clearly visible behind the windscreen, seemed to be enjoying the look of terror on his face. She gunned the vehicle forwards just as Hepton turned and ran.

He was no judge of distance but reckoned that he couldn't make the end of the lane before the car caught him. He quickly sought an open door to one of the workshops, some garage that hadn't been locked up. But it was useless. The Sierra was only a few yards from him when he made up his mind. He braced himself against the metal door of one of the garages, then pushed off from it and sprinted across the line of the oncoming vehicle. Harry accelerated harder yet, but Hepton had judged it right, and he leapt at the high wall of one of the gardens, his fingers seeking the top edge of the brickwork. They found it, and he pulled himself upwards as the Sierra curved towards him, its front wing searing against the wall. He swung his legs upwards so that the roof of the car just missed them, and hung there, teeth gritted, thinking suddenly and absurdly of the multigym's chinning bar.

The Sierra screeched to a stop at the end of the lane, just as Hepton was about to drop back to the ground. Then its wheels spun and it started to reverse hard towards him. Christ, he couldn't hang on much longer, and he hadn't the strength to pull himself over the wall. But then the car stopped, idled for a moment.

'What's going on?'

Hepton turned his head and saw that a man had appeared from a gate in one of the garden fences. He was in his shirtsleeves and carried a folded newspaper, obviously having just been disturbed from an evening's reading in his garden. Hepton dropped to the ground and watched the Sierra start forwards slowly, turning out of the lane and speeding away.

Of course: there couldn't be any witnesses, could there? It had to look like an accident. Hepton saw it all clearly. The note from Nick was a fake. *She* had chosen the pub because she'd known he had to walk along this lane to get to it. And in the lane there would be no escape, and no one to see the car hit him. But it wouldn't have been hit-and-run. That might have looked too suspicious. No, she would have stopped and played the innocent. She would say he had jumped in front of the car, perhaps, and everyone would come to believe her, because it would be shown that Hepton was distraught, unstable after watching his friend die earlier in the day.

Just another suicide.

'I said, what's going on?'

Hepton snapped out of his reverie, went to the man and shook his hand.

'Thank you,' he said, then began to jog back the way he had come, leaving the man standing there uncomprehending.

He arrived at his car without further incident. They wouldn't want his death to look suspicious, so he didn't bother to check for bombs under the chassis or snipers on the rooftops. He just got in and drove, trembling throughout his body, heading south towards Boston and further on to Peterborough, and beyond that London.

He stopped once for petrol and asked the attendant where he might find a telephone. There was a payphone on the wall outside the gents'. A man was coming out of the toilets, his face wet. Hepton had noticed a car parked beside the pumps. The man smiled.

'Never any bloody paper in these places,' he said, explaining the wet face. Hepton nodded. 'Needed a bit of a splash, though,' the man went on. 'Driving to Leeds tonight. Bloody long way, but the roads are quieter at night than through the day. I'm a rep, you see. You get to know these tricks.'

Hepton smiled again, but offered no reply. The last thing he needed was a lengthy conversation with a professional traveller. The man seemed to take the hint and moved past him, towards the station shop. Hepton turned his attention back to the telephone. He lifted the receiver, slipped a ten-pence piece into the slot and dialled the number of the base.

'Hello,' he said. 'I'd like to speak to Nick Christopher if he's around.'

It took a minute or so, then Nick's voice came over loud and clear.

'Nick here.'

'Nick? It's Martin.'

'Hello, Martin. What can I do for you?'

'I just wanted to check something. You didn't leave a note at my flat, did you?'

'A note?'

No, of course he hadn't. Because he was in Binbrook, not Louth. Because the note had been written by Harry. Which meant she knew Nick Christopher was Hepton's best friend . . .

'Nick,' Hepton said. 'There hasn't been someone there asking questions about me, has there? A woman in her late twenties, short blonde hair, attractive?'

'No, can't say there . . . Hang on, yes, there was somebody here like that. Saw her go into Fagin's office. Tasty piece.'

That was it then. All she'd had to do was ask Fagin who Hepton's closest friend on the base was. Then she'd used his name to lure Hepton into the trap. Not the cleverest of traps, but then it had probably been devised in haste, now that she saw him for the threat he really was.

He rang off and found another ten-pence piece, then took from his pocket the card Harry had given him. He had begun to feel a kind of strange elation at having cheated death. In fact, he felt more alive than he had done in months, perhaps even years. He dialled the number, ready to taunt whoever answered, but heard only a continuous whine from the receiver. He tried again, with the same result. Disconnected.

Had they cleared out then? Or changed the number when they had decided Hepton must die? There didn't seem any other explanation as to why Harry would have given him the card. Unless . . . He studied it more closely. Thick card, inflexible, covered in a plastic coating. Quite a robust thing, really, given that all it contained was a telephone number, and a discontinued one at that. He asked the attendant if he possessed such a thing as a knife. The man looked dubious, but they went to the shop, where he found a Swiss Army knife. The rep was whistling cheerily, selecting a dozen or so chocolate bars before moving on to the sparse display of music cassettes. Hepton chose the thinnest blade on the knife and began to cut along the edge of the card, the attendant watching, unsure what to expect. The rep came over too, his selections made.

The plastic was tough, but once he was through it, Hepton noticed that the card itself was very thin, more like paper. He began to peel it off, revealing a thin piece of metal studded with solder.

'What is it?' asked the rep, intrigued now.

'It's a PCB,' Hepton answered, quite calmly.

'A what?' asked the attendant.

'A printed circuit board. Smallest one I think I've seen.'

There could be no doubting that it was a transmitter of sorts. Crude, as something this size needed to be, but probably effective. Hepton smiled, shaking his head. No need to check your car's wheel arches these days for an unwieldy magnetised box; something the size of a business card would do the job every bit as well.

'Can I pay for these?' the rep asked the attendant and, show over, the attendant nodded, taking back his knife and going behind the counter. Hepton stood beside the rep, waiting his turn to pay for petrol.

'I'd like a receipt too, please,' the rep said to the attendant as Hepton held the transmitter between forefinger and thumb and gently, surreptitiously, slipped it into the man's jacket pocket. He held his breath, then stepped away. But the rep hadn't noticed anything, and with any luck he would continue all the way to Leeds still in blissful ignorance.

'Have a good trip,' Hepton called to him as the man went out to his car. Then, having paid for the tankful of petrol, he went out to his own vehicle, started it and headed off in the opposite direction, whistling.

As he drove, he remembered something and reached into his pocket, bringing out the note Harry had left for him, the one that had led him by the nose towards his intended death. He rolled down the window and threw it out. Was there anything else she had given him? No, nothing, not unless she had planted something on him without his knowledge. He would have to check his clothing.

Wait a minute, though . . . she *had* given him something else: a ten-pence piece to pay for the call she said she had made yesterday evening. He angled a hand into his trouser pocket and brought out all his loose change, scattering it on the passenger seat. Then he picked out the three ten-pence pieces that lay there and threw them out of the window too. He hoped someone would pick them up. If one of them contained a backup transmitter, Harry might have another long, hard and fruitless journey ahead of her.

Something else was niggling him. Several things really. For one, Fagin had ordered him to talk to Harry, to tell her everything he knew. So was Fagin in on it too? Or was he merely obeying orders? And who the hell was Villiers? What was it Harry had said? Something about 'my employers, who are, ultimately, your employers': but who – ultimately – was Hepton's employer? The Home Secretary? The head of the MoD? Someone in London, he'd bet on that. But it might take a journalist's nose to discover the final answer. A good journalist. Someone he could trust.

Supposing, that were, Jilly would even want to speak to him again.

15

In fact, the smooth-dressed, smooth-spoken Parfit did not return, and Dreyfuss, who had been keening like a young whelp, grew first agitated and then worried and then frustrated. Parfit had said he was coming back to take him away from Sacramento General, away from the vicious General Esterhazy and the cunning Frank Stewart, away from nurses who weren't real nurses and drugs that did more than merely put a man to sleep. So where the hell was he? What was he doing?

The evening stretched into night, and the night saw Dreyfuss sleepless, pounding the floor of his room on aching feet. A night-duty nurse looked in on him, but he growled at her and she quickly fled. A male attendant, black, uncertain, asked him if he wanted anything.

'Nothing,' he snarled, and paced the cage again.

When breakfast arrived, he found himself waking on top of the bed, still wearing slippers and a dressing gown, his forehead damp with sweat.

'Hot in here,' said the nurse, a teenager who certainly looked more like a nurse than Carraway had.

'Yes, it is,' Dreyfuss answered, sitting up with his back against the mound of pillows. She placed the tray on a trolley and wheeled the trolley over until it was positioned in front of him.

'Ham and eggs,' she said, removing the cover from the plate. Dreyfuss nodded hungrily and started to tuck in. Three or four chews later, he remembered about Parfit, and the hunger left him. He sipped at the coffee, still chewing the food in his mouth, desperate to swallow it but somehow unable to. Eventually he spat it back into his paper serviette.

The nurse returned after twenty minutes and took the tray away. She didn't say anything about the untouched food.

'How are we this morning?' the doctor asked brightly, pushing open the door.

'We're fine,' said Dreyfuss glumly. 'When can we get up?'

'I did hear,' the doctor said mock-conspiratorially, checking Dreyfuss' pulse at the same time, 'that we *had* been getting up. Pacing the floor at all hours of the night.' He stared at Dreyfuss with soulful eyes. 'Hmm?'

'I'd like to leave today.'

'Fine.' The doctor had stopped checking the pulse. He now peered into Dreyfuss' eyes. 'Where will you go?'

'I don't know; a bit of sightseeing, maybe. Book into a hotel, see a few shows . . .'

'In Sacramento?' The doctor laughed. 'No, I think you'd be better staying just here, Major Dreyfuss.'

And that was what he did. Though he willed himself to move, to just open the door, walk down the corridor and leave by the hospital's front door, he had no idea what he might be stepping out into. A demonstration, perhaps; an angry mob; some lone gunman looking to make the news?

He sat tight, his gut quivering whenever someone walked noisily past the door of his room. But Parfit didn't come. Someone else came instead.

Frank Stewart.

'Can I speak to you for a minute?'

'Can I stop you?' Dreyfuss' voice had bite, but he waved for Stewart to sit down. Secretly he was glad of some company.

'How do you feel?'

How *did* he feel? He felt strange, staring into Spencer Tracy's eyes like this.

'I know what you're thinking,' Stewart continued.

Dreyfuss doubted it. 'Go on,' he prompted.

'You're thinking that somehow you're to blame for what happened to *Argos*. Forget it; you couldn't have done anything.'

'I couldn't?'

'Well, could you?'

Dreyfuss thought about this. What was Stewart trying to get him to say? 'I don't know,' he said at last.

Stewart seemed pleased with this reply and drew his chair closer to the bed.

'I know there's something wrong,' he said, his voice almost a whisper. 'I know there's something cooking.'

'Are you CIA or NSA?'

Stewart seemed surprised by the question. 'I'm State Department,' he said.

'Right,' Dreyfuss said, sounding as unconvinced as he felt.

'Okay, okay. I'm on secondment to the NSA.'

Dreyfuss nodded. 'And what,' he said, 'makes you so sure something's "cooking", as you put it?'

'Just a feeling. When you reach my age, you get a nose for these sorts of things.'

Now if that wasn't a line from a Spencer Tracy film, what was? 'What sorts of things?' Dreyfuss asked, enjoying throwing Stewart's statements back at him as questions. This way, he gave himself a little room for manoeuvre.

Stewart's voice grew quieter yet. 'When General Esterhazy was in Europe, another of our staff generals, William Colt, very high up at the Pentagon, sent him a message. It said, and I quote, "Sorry you couldn't make it to the burial." That message was sent at almost exactly the time your shuttle was crashing.'

The burial! Hes Adams' face swam into view amidst the smoke and sparks and heat.

Stewart could see his words having an effect. 'What is it?' he hissed. 'That means something to you, doesn't it? Has it jogged your memory, Major? Not that I believe for one moment that you really *have* got partial amnesia. I've got to hand it to you, though. You've got the doctors fooled.'

'Nurse Carraway wasn't a real nurse.'

Stewart nodded. 'So I understand. Ben Esterhazy had her planted here. I didn't know anything about it.' His voice fell again. 'It's him you've got to be careful of, not me.' Dreyfuss stared at him stonily. Stewart shrugged his shoulders. Then he changed tack. 'I hear tell,' he said, 'that when you landed, the ground crew had to prise Major Adams' fingers from off your throat. Adams was one of Esterhazy's men too. He was his golden boy at one time, but then he screwed up on a mission. Got himself compromised. Then suddenly he ends up on *Argos*. That made me a little curious. What was going on up there?'

Dreyfuss was thinking. Yes, it was true: Esterhazy and Adams had the same words at their disposal – "coffin's got to be buried"; "sorry you couldn't make it to the burial" – and it meant something to both of them, something worth dying for, worth killing for. He *had* to tell someone. His brain was feverish. He felt he would burst if he didn't speak. Where was Parfit? Parfit should be here, not this American secret serviceman. The confessor was wrong, but still the need to confess was strong. Too strong.

He cleared his throat as a prelude. 'We were up there to launch a communications satellite,' he said. 'That's what *I* thought. But it was like some joke was being played on me, like I wasn't being let in on something. They were grinning . . . I think the rest of the crew knew. Hes Adams definitely knew what was going on. We launched the satellite okay. Then I saw some figures on the screen, co-ordinates I thought at the time. And a series of numbers. There was one sequence that kept repeating itself. I tried to memorise it, but it was way too long. I remember how it started, though: Ze/446. I wondered about that, but nobody seemed too bothered. Then I asked Hes – Major Adams – about it, and he laughed.' Stewart's face was so intent at this point that Dreyfuss felt nothing would tear the older man's eyes off him. 'I knew then that something was wrong. And I felt that I wasn't intended to get off the shuttle alive, because I'd been stupid enough to tell what I'd seen to the one man aboard who knew what it all meant. Then later,' he continued, swallowing, 'when we were dying and everything went haywire, Adams started choking me. He was mad, screaming at me, "Coffin's got to be buried!"'

Stewart looked startled at this, then sat back in his chair, as though he were thinking hard. He folded his arms and seemed to require no more from Dreyfuss for the moment. Dreyfuss was thinking too, thinking how hungry he suddenly felt.

'Now hold on,' Stewart said at last. 'Let me see if I've got this straight . . .'

'Got what straight, Mr Stewart?' asked Parfit, stepping into the room.

Stewart looked embarrassed, but recovered quickly. 'Just asking the major here some questions about the flight.'

Parfit looked towards Dreyfuss. 'And does the major want to be questioned?' he asked.

'The major wants to be told he can get out of here,' Dreyfuss said, remembering now that he was angry with Parfit, who had left him here for so long.

Parfit made a sweeping gesture with his arm. 'Your carriage awaits,' he said.

Stewart was rising to his feet. 'Wait a minute. Major Dreyfuss can't just walk out of here. He's under medical care.'

'Nonsense,' Parfit replied. He went back to the doorway, leaned out into the corridor and picked up a large paper carrier bag. 'I hope these fit,' he said, bringing the bag to the bed.

Dreyfuss was already on his feet. He opened the bag and brought out trousers, underwear, a cotton shirt, socks and a pair of canvas shoes.

Stewart watched him dress, but his words when he spoke were directed at Parfit.

'You know this is crazy, don't you? Esterhazy will blow all his fuses when he finds out.' But he sounded as though this was not a wholly unpleasant thought.

'I'm hoping he does just that,' Parfit returned.

Dreyfuss knew there was some undercurrent to this exchange, something they were managing to say to one another without his understanding. He slipped on the shoes. The clothes were a near-perfect fit.

'Ready?' said Parfit.

'Ready,' answered Dreyfuss.

'I'm glad we managed to have some time together, Major,' Stewart was saying. Dreyfuss smiled but did not reply. Parfit had already turned in the doorway, and held the door open as Dreyfuss took his first steps out of the room, into the bright, disinfected corridor.

Parfit kept a couple of steps ahead of him as they walked. Dreyfuss felt elated at first, light-headed, but then started sweating. He had paced his room, but that had called for little real exertion. Now, after sixty or so strides, his hair was prickling and his back began to feel damp. The corridor was quiet: no staff, and all the doors except his own looked to be locked tight. They came to a set of swing doors and opened them. Now they were in a larger, noisier, busier corridor, one of the hospital's main arteries. Dreyfuss looked back at the doors they had just come through and saw that a large *NO ADMITTANCE* sign and a radiation symbol warned the unwary against entering his own silent corridor.

He had been expecting to see an armed guard at least. What had been stopping journalists from trying to visit him? Not just that sign, surely. Then he noticed an orderly sitting on a chair by the door, pretending to be on his break and browsing through a newspaper. His eyes were toughened glass as they fixed on Dreyfuss and

Parfit, and Dreyfuss knew he was a guard of some kind, but an unobtrusive one.

'Does he know who we are?' he said to Parfit as they walked on.

Parfit glanced back towards the orderly. 'Well, he knows who *I* am. I've had to get past him to see you, yesterday and today. But he's here to stop people getting in, not coming out.'

'What took you so long to come back?'

But Parfit was flurrying on again, and it took all of Dreyfuss' energy and concentration to keep up with his pace. The question lapsed.

'How much did you tell Stewart?' Parfit asked.

'Quite a bit.'

'Mmm. That's all right then.'

'What do you mean?' But Parfit wasn't about to answer this question either.

Everybody was too busy being sick or being a comforter of the sick to pay them much attention, but at the main door, Dreyfuss hesitated. Something would happen. They'd be stopped. He'd be dragged back to his room and questioned again. They wouldn't get away with it. As Parfit approached the glass doors, they opened on a motorised hush, and then both men were outside.

Outside, it was warm, but with a strong breeze. And there was cloud cover. A storm was coming. Dreyfuss began to shiver as the sweat on his body cooled. A large sedan pulled up to the kerb, and Parfit opened the back door, ushering him inside. The driver was a thickset man with the face of a well-used hammer. He stared at Dreyfuss in the rear-view mirror. Parfit closed the door after him and they drove off.

'This is Ronald,' Parfit said to Dreyfuss.

Ronald nodded, unsmiling, then concentrated on his driving.

'Where are we going?' asked Dreyfuss.

'Washington. There's a private jet waiting for us at the airport.'

'A private jet? Is that standard Foreign Office issue?'

Parfit smiled. 'It's not ours, I just borrowed it from someone who happened to owe me a large favour.'

Dreyfuss nodded.

'So,' Parfit was saying, 'I think you'd better start at the beginning, hadn't you?'

'I nearly died up there.' Dreyfuss turned towards him. 'Why didn't you warn me?'

'But if you'll remember, I did warn you. That's why we're sitting here today.'

Yes, Dreyfuss remembered all right. The telephone call telling him he'd been picked for the *Argos* flight, and then the arrival at his home of a man in a pinstripe suit, introducing himself as 'Parfit, Foreign Office'. He had come, so he said, to give Dreyfuss a pre-briefing briefing. In fact, he had come with a warning.

The first thing he had done was go through Dreyfuss' curriculum vitae, but in much more detail than the interview panel had done. He had cited Dreyfuss' age as a point against him. Other minus points included lack of experience and slight problems of stamina. Dreyfuss, who had been elated at the news of his selection, began to feel distinctly uncomfortable at this.

'Yes, but they still chose me,' he had said.

'Exactly, Major Dreyfuss,' Parfit had replied. 'Exactly.'

So there had to be a good reason, and Parfit was intrigued to know what it was. Dreyfuss had been bottom of the British list of candidates – no disrespect intended – and they couldn't figure out how he could come top of the American list. But there *would* be a reason, and it was judged worth warning Dreyfuss to be on his guard, and to give him a few tips, a few lessons in the art of survival in a hostile environment.

'You were right about that,' Dreyfuss said now. He had just been telling Parfit what he had told Stewart, but in a little more detail this time. 'I didn't get into a space shuttle, I got into a coffin.'

'So you think the shuttle itself is the coffin that had to be buried?'

'Don't you?'

Parfit rested his head against the seat-back, thinking things through. 'No,' he answered at last. 'No, I don't, not entirely.'

'So what *do* you think was being buried?'

'I don't know. Perhaps we should just ask General Esterhazy. He seems to be involved after all, doesn't he?'

'But you don't think Frank Stewart is?'

'If he were, he wouldn't have been asking you questions the way he did. He wasn't questioning you to find out how much *you* knew. He was doing it because *he* doesn't know much of anything himself.'

'It's a military thing then?'

'Perhaps. Whatever it is, someone's going to a lot of trouble over it, which would seem to indicate that it is fairly special and not very small in scale.'

'Such as?'

'I could only posit a few guesses.'

'Posit away.'

Parfit sighed. 'Anything between an assassination and a war.' He paused. 'They're not mutually exclusive.'

'A *war*?'

'Why not? Look at the way things are going.'

'Christ . . . a war.' Dreyfuss felt weak again. 'But wait, if it's such a big thing, why did they keep me alive?'

'Well, that's easy enough. Five men had already died, and yet you had been pulled alive and in surprisingly good health from the wreckage. The TV cameras and newspapers caught all that. So your sudden death in hospital would have looked a mite suspicious.'

'We were all supposed to die, though, weren't we? All the crew?'

'It looks that way. A kamikaze mission to launch a communications satellite. An unlikely scenario, you'll admit.'

'But it wasn't just a comms satellite, was it?'

Parfit turned towards Dreyfuss and smiled, seeming pleased that he had worked this out. 'The question is,' he said, 'what was it?'

'I know one way we might find out.'

Parfit seemed interested now.

'How?'

'My controller on the ground, Cam Devereux. He might know.'

Parfit nodded. 'It's an idea. But even supposing he knows anything, why would he tell us?'

Dreyfuss seemed not to understand the question.

'I mean,' Parfit said, 'why should he be friendly towards us? Can we assume he's not in on it – whatever "it" is?'

'Well,' said Dreyfuss, 'can you think of anyone else who might have the answers?'

Parfit considered this. 'Off the top of my head, no.'

'Besides which,' Dreyfuss continued, 'I got on well with Cam. He sent flowers to the hospital. We struck up what you might call a special relationship.'

Parfit raised an eyebrow. 'Any particular reason why?'

'We had something in common,' said Dreyfuss. 'As kids, we were both scared to death of roller coasters.'

Parfit stared at him. Dreyfuss smiled back.

'Well,' Parfit said, 'I suppose we've nothing to lose by talking to Mr Devereux. Best wait until we're safely back in the embassy compound, though. We'll try and contact him from there. All we need to do now is find someone who would know what that readout meant. Ze/446 – you've really no idea?'

'No, but if Cam Devereux can't help, I might know someone who can.'

Now Parfit looked genuinely impressed.

'A friend of a good friend of mine,' he continued. 'He works with satellites in the UK.'

'And what is his name?'

'His name's Hepton,' said Dreyfuss. 'Martin Hepton.'

16

Hepton took his car to the long-term car park at Heathrow and slept the night there. He awoke cramped and stiff, locked the car and wandered off towards the terminal building in search of breakfast. He hadn't been to Heathrow in what seemed like years. The place was huge, a city almost in itself. Eventually he found what he was looking for, and drank two cups of coffee before buying an over-priced croissant, then another, then a third, chewing each one slowly as he considered his options. His first plan still seemed the best: get in touch with Dreyfuss.

It was early, but the cafeteria section was busy with business executives and security men. Hepton felt scruffy and a little too obvious. He went to the toilets and washed, tidying his hair as best he could. At the sky shop, he bought a comb and a toothbrush. He also bought two newspapers, neither of which carried any mention of Paul Vincent's death. Not that he had expected them to.

He found a cashpoint machine, and was about to empty it of his day's maximum allowance when he hesitated. Would they have access to his bank account? By 'they', he meant Villiers and Harry. If so, they could track him as far as Heathrow just by tapping into the present transaction. On the other hand, he had to have money, and if he took it out now at least they wouldn't be able to pinpoint him to London itself. He might even be about to get on a plane, mightn't he? Running scared and flying for cover. So he pushed the card home, tapped in his identity number and withdrew ten crisp ten-pound notes.

He had decided to leave the car here. For one thing, they had his licence plate number and the car's description, so he didn't want to drive it around London. Besides, he had the feeling that in London a car might actually slow him down. It wasn't a series of roads out there; it was a jungle. Which was all to the good. He wanted to lose himself there, and hope the big-game hunter in the black Sierra went home without a kill.

He took the uncrowded Tube train towards town. It filled up as it hit west London, then became claustrophobic as it neared the centre. South Kensington came as merciful release. But all he was doing here was changing platforms to the District and Circle Line, and the train that eventually arrived was again crowded. How could people live like this? He thought of green fields, of Louth. Of hangings and cars trying to crush him . . . Safety in numbers: that was what a city provided.

So he stopped hating the packed carriage, and rubbed shoulders with an extraordinarily pretty young woman until Westminster, where, despite the temptation to keep travelling, he finally alighted. Tourists were already busying themselves with the day's chores, cameras and video cameras trained on the Houses of Parliament and Big Ben. Hepton headed up Whitehall and realised suddenly that he didn't know which of the large, anonymous buildings he needed. Understated signs beside the impressive doors were the only indication as to their identity. A man was striding purposefully towards him, black briefcase in hand. Hepton recognised the style of the briefcase: soft leather, more a school bag than a business case. There was a small crown above the nameplate. He had seen visitors from the MoD carrying such bags when they came to the base. He stopped the man.

'I wonder if you can help me,' he said. 'I'm looking for the Foreign Office.'

The man said nothing; merely indicated with his head before walking on. Hepton stared at the building towards which he had nodded, then started towards its arched main door.

ALL PASSES MUST BE SHOWN declared the sign just inside the doors. Below it, another notice advised that security alert was condition Amber. Security alert was normally at Black. Hepton knew this from his own dealings with the MoD, though Binbrook had its own, different grading system. Above Black came Black Special, which meant there was cause for caution, and after Black Special came Amber. Amber was what government departments had gone to after the Libyan bombing. Amber was serious, only marginally less serious than Red. Hepton had never seen a Red alert, and, knowing what it meant, hoped he never would.

The uniformed guard was eyeing him suspiciously.

'Can I help you, sir?'

'I hope so,' Hepton said. 'I'd like to speak with someone about a friend of mine. This friend is in the United States, and it's vital that I contact him. Is there anyone here who might help?'

'Why not just phone your friend, sir?'

It was a fair question. Remembering Paul Vincent and Harry, however, Hepton knew that speed was of the essence. He hadn't time to muck around, to engage in little games of 'let's pretend'. He needed to get past this first obstacle quickly, and he knew of only one sure way to do it.

'Well,' he said, 'it's not quite that simple. You see, he's Major Michael Dreyfuss, the man from the shuttle crash.'

Eventually he was given a visitor's pass to fill in, which he did, using the name Martin Harris. Then he was shown to an office along a sweeping, red-carpeted corridor. There were many doors, bearing room numbers and sometimes the name of an individual or a section. The room Hepton eventually entered, however, had neither. A young man sat behind a desk. He stood as Hepton entered, leaned across the table to shake his hand and gestured for him to take a seat.

'Would you like some coffee, Mr Harris?' There was a percolator standing on a table beside the small window.

'Please,' said Hepton.

As the man poured, Hepton studied the room. It had bookshelves, but no books, and the desk looked to be unused. Though it boasted some papers and a box of biro pens, there was a layer of dust covering its surface, evidence that this room wasn't often occupied. He wondered if he had walked into some kind of trap.

'Milk?'

'Please, no sugar.'

He was handed a cup and saucer. The young man sat down again, sipped, then looked up.

'So then, Mr Harris, what can we do for you?'

'Well, I'm a friend of Major Michael Dreyfuss . . .'

'Yes, so you said.'

'And I really would like to get in touch with him.'

'Any particular reason why?'

'To wish him a speedy recovery, of course.'

The man nodded. 'It's taken you a while to get round to that, hasn't it?'

Hepton reminded himself that he had no time to play games. 'Look,' he said firmly, 'there's just something I need to speak with him about. Something personal, but very important.'

'Oh?' The civil servant had picked up one of the new biros and was examining it. It struck Hepton that he didn't know who this man was.

'I'm sorry,' he said, 'I didn't catch your name.'

'Sanders,' the civil servant said. 'And you said yours was Harris.'

'That's right.'

'Well, Mr Harris, it's just that we have to be careful. A lot of people would like to speak to Major Dreyfuss. I'm sure you understand. Reporters from the less scrupulous newspapers, and other people. So, if there's some way we can establish your identity . . .?'

Hepton cursed silently. Sanders was shrewder than he had anticipated. He shook his head. Sanders appeared to have been expecting this.

'Or,' he said, 'if you can prove your relationship with Major Dreyfuss . . .?'

Hepton thought this over. 'We have a mutual friend,' he said at last. 'Miss Jill Watson. She's a reporter on the *Herald*.'

The civil servant looked up from his pen. 'And she sent you here?'

Hepton saw the implication and shook his head. 'No, no, of course not. She doesn't even know I'm in London, for Christ's sake.'

'No need to lose your temper, Mr Harris.' Sanders was writing Jilly's name on a sheet of paper. 'But you've no proof of identity on you?'

Oh, what the hell, thought Hepton. If they're going to check on Jilly, they'll get my name eventually.

'My name's Hepton, not Harris,' he said.

Sanders seemed satisfied. 'But you signed the visitor's pass Harris. That could get you into trouble, you know. Why the deception?'

'Look, I just want to get in touch with Major Dreyfuss. If you could help me contact him . . .'

Sanders rose to his feet. 'Wait here a moment, would you, please?' He walked smartly to the door. 'Help yourself to more coffee,' he said, making an exit.

Hepton stayed seated, but couldn't relax. This had seemed such a good idea at the time. There was bound to be someone from the FO in contact with Dreyfuss. It had seemed so simple . . . But now he had given them so much, and they had given him nothing. He got up and went to the window, pushing aside the net curtain to look out. All he saw was other windows in another building. They too had net curtains, making it impossible to see into the rooms.

He crossed to Sanders' desk and examined it. The papers, as expected, were just blank sheets. The drawers of the desk were locked. Over at the bookcase, he wiped a finger along one surface and it came away carrying a bud of dust, which he blew into the air. There was another door, a cupboard perhaps, but it too was locked. He went to the percolator and refilled his cup, drinking slowly. What was happening? Where had Sanders gone? Would Harry walk in through the door? Had he delivered himself to her on a plate?

When the door did finally open, Sanders himself stood there, looking composed.

'If you'd like to follow me, Mr Hepton,' he commanded, and they set off together back along the silent corridor and up an imposing staircase. There weren't so many rooms on this second level. A large and busy reception area was the hub of the activity as people walked briskly in and out of the various offices. Telephones rang, and a few visitors sat on modern upholstered chairs, flicking through magazines.

Sanders approached the reception desk and said something to the prim woman seated there. She filled in another pass, which was torn from its pad and handed to Sanders, who in turn gave it to Hepton.

'Sign it, please,' he ordered, and Hepton accepted the proffered pen. 'Best stick to calling yourself Harris,' Sanders advised. 'That way it doesn't get complicated when you've handed back both passes and somebody tries to collate the day's visitors in and out.'

'Right.' Hepton signed himself as Martin Harris and followed Sanders towards one of the doors. This led into a smaller reception, where a young black secretary tapped away at a computer.

'Morning, Sarah,' said Sanders, passing her and pausing at yet another door. Sarah smiled at Hepton, and he smiled back. He was thinking now that everything was going to be all right.

Sanders had knocked at the door. There was a command from within, and he opened it, ushering Hepton into the room before him.

It was a decent-sized office, its furniture a mixture of the antique and the up-to-date. Books lined one wall, while another contained paintings and prints. The fourth and last was taken up for the most part by a large window, again net-curtained. At the window stood a middle-aged man, an important-looking man. The cut of his clothes was expensive, and where his cheeks had been shaved there was a bright ruddiness that bespoke health and wealth. Hepton had the feeling that he had seen this man before somewhere, on television perhaps.

'Ah, Mr Hepton. Do come in, please. I'm George Villiers.'

Villiers! Hepton's heart shrank to the size of a peach stone. But he kept his face neutral, betraying no emotion, and finally shook the proffered hand. It struck him that Villiers wouldn't – couldn't – know that Hepton knew about him. He had to stay calm, not give anything away. He breathed deeply to stop himself from hyperventilating. His heart was racing, but he kept his posture stiff.

Villiers motioned for him to sit, and Hepton did so. Then Villiers seated himself and drew his chair in towards the table. Something about his actions – a clipped, rehearsed quality, a feeling that each movement of the body possessed its own cause and effect – told Hepton that he was ex-military. And not all that ex either.

Villiers lifted a sheet of paper from his desk. It was a typed sheet, not the one Sanders had taken with him from that first room. 'Can you tell us why you wish to contact Major Dreyfuss?'

'No,' said Hepton briskly. 'If you could just pass a message on to him that I'm trying to reach him, perhaps—'

'You're on holiday at the moment, aren't you?'

'Yes, but how could you—'

'These things aren't difficult. All right, Mr Hepton. We'll see what we can do. Where will you be staying while you're here?'

'I haven't decided yet.'

'With Miss Watson, perhaps?'

'No, I don't think so.'

'Oh?' Villiers stared past Hepton's shoulder, towards where Sanders stood. 'I was under the impression the two of you were friends?'

'We are. That is, we were.' Hepton's thoughts were quicksilver now. This was a man he'd been told to avoid, told by Paul Vincent, who was now dead. He couldn't afford to let Villiers know anything, and already the man knew too much . . . 'We broke up. We haven't seen one another in months.' Hepton sounded bitter, and made his face look the same. They had to be made to think that he wouldn't be contacting Jilly.

'Ah.' Villiers went back to studying the typed sheet of paper. Hepton noticed that there was a buff-coloured file on the desk, down the edge of which was written a name: *Dreyfuss, Major M.* The paper had undoubtedly come from the file. Villiers seemed to know who Hepton was, and didn't seem overcurious about Jilly. Therefore he already knew as much as he needed to know. Had he gleaned the information from the typed sheet? Hepton doubted it. No, there was another reason why Villiers knew about him.

Villiers looked up suddenly and caught Hepton staring at him. He smiled, as if to say: I know what you're thinking. Then he read through the sheet again, and Hepton relaxed. Villiers *couldn't* know he knew.

'So how will we contact you, Mr Hepton, should we get through to Major Dreyfuss?'

'As soon as I know where I'm going to be, I'll let you know.'

'Yes.' Villiers sounded sceptical. 'That would probably be best.' He seemed preoccupied.

'Is there anything wrong?'

'Wrong?' Villiers looked up.

'I mean, wrong with Major Dreyfuss. Any reason why I shouldn't be allowed to speak to him.'

Villiers smiled. 'Oh no, nothing like that. Nothing like that at all. But procedures, you know . . .'

'Red tape?'

'Exactly. A bore, but it's what we're paid for.' He smiled again, and Sanders laughed quietly.

'Is there someone from our embassy with Major Dreyfuss?'

Villiers' smile vanished. 'Why do you ask?'

'Well, I would have thought it usual to have someone there beside him. To make sure everything's all right.'

'There's someone with him,' Villiers said in a cool voice. 'Don't worry on that score, Mr Hepton. Now, if you'll excuse me . . .'

'Of course.' Hepton stood up.

Villiers reached out a dry, cold hand for Hepton to shake.

'Just tell us when you get settled in somewhere, and then when we get through to Major Dreyfuss, well, we'll take it from there. All right?'

Not really. Hepton felt that he had failed badly. But at least the mood in this office had alerted him to the fact that something was going on out in the States. Perhaps Dreyfuss was in danger from the rednecks who had nicknamed him 'Jonah' after the crash. Perhaps, though, there was another kind of danger altogether. On the other hand, he had walked into the lion's den, and here he was walking out again. He decided to classify this fact a minor victory.

'Thank you,' he said, following Sanders out of the door.

As soon as Hepton had gone, Villiers took a fountain pen from his pocket and scribbled down a brief summary of the meeting. Then he amended the information about Hepton and Miss Watson on the typed sheet of paper, initialled the summary and slipped it into the Dreyfuss file. From the top drawer of his desk, he took out another folder. This one was unlabelled, and into it he slipped the single typed sheet to which he had been referring throughout the meeting. This was the file on Martin Hepton.

He locked his drawer and picked up one of the two telephones on his desk, punching in three digits.

'Sanders is seeing someone to the front door,' he said in a monotone. 'Have them followed. But keep it low-key. A one-man job, if you can.' He listened for a moment. 'No, no forms to fill in on this one. I want it kept strictly off the books.' He listened again, his cheekbones showing red with suppressed anger. 'Yes, I know,' he hissed. 'I'll assume full responsibility, just bloody well do it!' Then he slammed down the receiver and stared at it, thinking hard. Hepton wanted to speak to Major Dreyfuss. If he did so in Villiers' presence, then Villiers would find out all he needed about what both men knew. So why keep two old acquaintances apart? He picked up the other receiver.

'Sarah?' he said. 'Put through a call to Washington, will you? I want to speak to Johnnie Gilchrist.'

17

The city was swarming, and there was no shade to be found. Hepton tried to keep to the backstreets, the narrower passages that neither sun nor tourists could penetrate. The tourists were predominantly European and Japanese. The Americans were staying closer to home this summer. He went into a café for a cold drink, but found the heat indoors unbearable, so came away thirsty. The man who had been a dozen paces behind him walking in was still a dozen paces behind him when he walked out. Hepton smiled.

Where was he heading? In all honesty, he did not know. He stepped into a few shops, browsed, then came out again empty-handed. He crossed the expanse of Green Park with the man still behind him, and in Piccadilly he visited two large stores, taking lifts up, stairs down and back-door exits where possible.

He didn't know where he was headed, but he knew where he was avoiding going: the offices of the *London Herald*. Could he face Jilly? What would she say? Would she help him? He tried to rehearse various lines as he walked the streets. They all sounded false. They all *were* false. What was more important, however, was that he should shake this tail before he tried to contact her. Otherwise he would be drawing her into the nasty little web, and that was the last thing he wanted to do.

Lunchtime approached, and he felt hungry again. Breakfast at Heathrow seemed an eternity ago. He touched the roll of banknotes in his pocket and decided to treat himself to something at Fortnum's. But the queue for the Fountain restaurant was disheartening, so he left again. Besides, his clothes were looking decidedly shabby and slept in: definitely not the stuff of a Fortnum's luncheon.

One of the floorwalkers had kept a beady eye on him all the way around the ground floor.

He had been expecting a tail, of course. Now that Villiers had found him, he would want to keep tabs on him. But who *was* Villiers? He appeared to be some not-very-minor official at the Foreign Office. What was all or any of this to him? Hepton didn't know. But he did know one thing. Like a dog offered a bone, it was time for him to shake his tail.

At Piccadilly Circus there was a large record shop – new since his last visit to London and exactly what he was looking for. He entered the noise and the confusion of aisles. At the main door he had spotted a uniformed security guard, and had passed the alarm system with its warning to potential shoplifters. The place was well protected. He walked up and down the aisles, squeezing past this and that browser. He paused by a display of compact discs and saw, from the corner of his eye, the tail browsing a few aisles further along. He smiled and picked up a disc enclosed in a protective clear plastic sheath. On the back of the packaging was a price label and a barcode. Through the barcode ran a strip of silver. Pleased, he examined the disc again. *Barbed Wire Kisses* by The Jesus and Mary Chain. Yes, this would do.

He walked casually back along the aisle, towards where the tail was now enthusiastically reading the sleeve notes to an offering by The Dead Milkmen. As he was about to pass the man, he paused and put a hand on his shoulder. The tail flinched, but kept his eyes on the record. Hepton kept his hand where it was and brought his face close to the man's ear.

'I'm starving,' he said. 'I think I'm going to go to lunch now. Okay?' Then he moved quickly away towards the main doors. The man hesitated, then put the record back into its rack and followed.

Hepton was already on the pavement and hailing a taxi. Damn: the tail would have to hurry. He'd have to find a taxi too, in order to follow Hepton's taxi. As he was about to push open the heavy glass door, a sudden high-pitched whine came from behind him. The security guard was upon him immediately, hands on his shoulders, turning him around. The tail protested, but the guard's hands were patting his jacket, and one of them slipped into the left pocket, bringing out a compact disc.

The tail glared through the glass at Hepton, who was bending to get into his taxi. Hepton waved at him and grinned. Then the door slammed shut and the taxi moved off into the line of traffic.

'Where to, guv?' the driver asked.

'First, a clothes shop,' ordered Hepton. 'Nothing too flashy. And somewhere between here and the Isle of Dogs.'

He reckoned he would need a shirt, jacket and casual trousers. He reasoned that he would be less conspicuous dressed smartly, and also that he needed a change of clothes in any event, otherwise his description could be circulated too easily. It was tempting to relax a little, to forget that somewhere out there Harry was waiting, ready to kill him if she must. He would use his credit card to buy the clothes: even if Villiers had access to his credit card record, it would take a little time for the transaction to come to light. Villiers knew he was in London. The least Hepton could do was make it difficult for the man to circulate a description of him. That necessitated a change of clothes. A change of hair colouring would be an idea, too. And, while he was at it, why not a change of height and weight and sex?

Despite the terrors of the past twenty-four hours – or perhaps because of them – Hepton threw back his head and laughed. The cab driver glanced into his rear-view mirror.

'Glad somebody's happy,' he said. 'Journalist, are you?'

'What makes you say that?'

'We get a lot of journalists come into town at twelve o'clock for a drink, then have to get a taxi back half an hour later so they can start work again. Mad, those journalists are. You know the ones I mean, down at that new place in the Isle, where the *Herald*'s printed.'

'Oh yes, the *Herald,*' said Hepton casually. 'That's where I'm headed to, as it happens.'

'Thought you were,' the driver called, chuckling. 'I've got a nose for that sort of thing, you see. A real nose. But first off, let's see about getting you that clobber, eh?'

Part III

The result is a complex network of intelligence-gathering and communications installations throughout Britain ... There are two main reasons why there are so many such installations in Britain. First, geography. Britain may be a peripheral country on the north-west fringe of Europe, but to a military planner, things look different. Britain sits astride the shortest route from the US to Europe. American policy is 'forward defence' to prevent war on US soil. This involves monitoring Soviet activities as far forward as possible ... Second, there is the 'special relationship'. While some of the installations are purely British, most are either part of the US military system or linked directly to it.

Ian Mather, *Observer Magazine*, 19 April 1987

18

The Isle of Dogs was everything Hepton had been expecting. It was, in fact, a building site, a hotchpotch of half-completed monoliths and half-demolished houses. The headquarters of the *Herald*, however, if not what he had hoped to find (he had fond memories of *The Front Page* and *Citizen Kane*) was certainly what he had thought he might find. The metal and glass cube that was home to the newspaper was protected by a high security fence. A barrier lay across the road at the entrance to the site, and two security men watched from their little prefabricated building there, while video cameras scanned the perimeter.

'Checkpoint Charlie, they call it,' said Hepton's taxi driver, accepting the fifteen pounds' fare and a small tip. 'Cheers then.' And with that he wheeled the taxi around and away.

Hepton stared again at the construction before him, trying to find some hint of a soul. There was none. He walked towards the barrier. One of the security guards donned a cap and came to meet him.

'Can I help you, sir?'

'I'm here to see one of the journalists, a Miss Jilly Watson.'

'Watson, did you say?' The guard was already turning back towards his office. 'Follow me, sir. Expecting you, is she?'

'No, not really. I'm a friend of hers.'

'I see, sir.'

The other guard lazily watched several screens, each one showing a corner of the compound. There was a mug of dark brown tea in front of him, proclaiming its owner to be the *World's Best Dad*. Another bank of screens showed the interior of the large building behind them, where the workers moved like ants. The first guard looked through a sheaf of A4 printed paper on his desk.

'Watson, J. Extension three-five-five,' he said to himself. He punched several numbers into his telephone receiver, and, looking up, saw that Hepton was watching the screens. 'Good, aren't they?'

'Yes,' Hepton responded. It seemed everyone was a spy these days. And everyone had a camera trained on them.

The guard's call had been connected. 'Hello, it's the gate here. Got someone to see Miss Watson.' He listened to a voice speaking at the other end, then put his hand over the mouthpiece. 'What's the name, sir?'

This was the moment Hepton had dreaded. 'Martin Hepton,' he said.

'Martin Hepton,' the guard repeated into the mouthpiece. There was a pause while he listened again, then he motioned with the telephone towards Hepton. 'Wants a word, Mr Hepton,' he said.

Hepton took the receiver cautiously. 'Hello?' he said.

'Martin? Is that you?' Jilly Watson's voice sounded vibrant.

'Yes,' he said.

'What are you doing here?' But it wasn't a sniping question; rather, it was filled with honest and welcome surprise. Hepton lightened: she was *pleased* that he had come.

'I wanted to see you,' he said.

'Great! But they won't let you in here. You need passes and all that kind of stuff. We're not allowed visitors; a bit like a prison.' She laughed. 'If nobody gets in, nobody can steal our scoops, that's what they reckon. What time is it?' She checked her watch. 'One thirty already! Christ, I haven't eaten yet, have you?'

'No.'

'Well, that's settled then. You can take me to lunch. There isn't much around here, but there's a wine bar not too far. Do you have a car?'

'No, I came by taxi.'

'Well, wait at the gate and I'll bring my car round. Okay?'

'Fine.'

'Martin . . .?'

'Yes?'

'It's good to hear your voice.'

Click. The connection went dead.

'Coming down, is she, sir?' asked the first guard. Hepton nodded. 'Nobody's allowed in, you see,' the guard went on. 'Security.'

'Bloody daft if you ask me,' rejoined the second guard, cupping his hands around his mug. The first guard now took off his cap and sat down.

'Ours not to reason why,' he said.

Hepton nodded agreement, but he wasn't about to complete the couplet.

The guard operated the barrier from inside the gatehouse, while Hepton slid into the reassuringly familiar seat of Jilly's red MG sports car. She leaned across to peck him on the cheek, then waved towards the gatehouse and revved the car out onto the main road.

'You look great!' Hepton shouted above the wind and the sound of the engine.

'So do you,' Jilly replied. 'You never used to dress like that.'

Hepton examined his newly purchased clothes. 'I'm on holiday.'

'In London?'

'Yes.'

'And you thought you'd surprise me. How lovely.' The smile left her face. 'I did mean to get in touch, Martin. I didn't want to lose you as a friend. But . . .'

'Forget it.' He tried to steel himself; this wasn't the time to become emotional. 'So how's the job?'

'Oh, fine.' But her voice had taken on a false edge.

'Really?' he prompted.

'Well, no . . . not really. In fact, it's awful. I seem to get all the shitty jobs to do, all the really boring things. I think the editor likes the idea of me, he just doesn't like *me*. If that makes any sense.'

Hepton nodded. 'It makes sense.' He could no longer contain his next question, his first real question. 'Have you heard anything from Mike Dreyfuss?'

'No, nothing, I sent some flowers to the hospital in Sacramento, but I don't know if they arrived. Did you know they'd taken him to Sacramento? They tried to keep it a secret, but our sister paper in the States found out.' She sighed. 'Poor Mickey.'

'Yes. I'm trying to get in touch with him.'

'With Mickey? But why?'

So he told her.

They sat at a corner table in the wine bar. The waitress had cleared away their plates and brought them coffee. There was an inch of wine left in the bottom of the bottle, and Hepton poured it into Jilly's glass. She had sat quietly and attentively all through lunch, while he had continued his story. Now and then she would ask a question, in order to clarify some point, but other than that she was silent. Hepton remembered the day she had ordered him to teach her about satellites. She had been the same then.

Occasionally she jotted a few notes into a clean page of her Filofax, and when Hepton had finished talking, she drew a thick line beneath what she had written so far, then numbered the individual points.

'Well?' he asked. 'Do you think I'm going mad, or is something happening out there?'

She gave her answer some thought. 'I don't think you're mad, no. But at the moment you don't really know what's going on, you don't have any proof that anything's going on, and you'll have a hard job convincing anyone that anything's going on. Despite which, I believe you. But then I'm a reporter, we'll believe anything.' She saw that Hepton was looking dispirited and squeezed his hand. 'You're safe now, Martin. You've got me to look after you.' He smiled at this, but knew she could see he was tired; more than that, he was drained. He needed rest and sleep and to forget about the past few days for a little while.

'Come on,' she said. 'I'll put lunch on expenses, then give the office a ring.'

'Why?'

'To tell them I'm not coming in this afternoon. I'm going to be working on something, and you're going to be resting.'

'I am?'

'My flat's not far from here. You can stay there while I go into town.'

'What are you going to do?' Hepton did feel drowsy, but then he'd had the larger share of the wine. He could feel the effort in each word he spoke aloud.

'I'm going to see what I can find out about this George Villiers character, among other things.'

'Jilly . . .'

'What?'

'You're sure it's okay for me to go to your place? I mean . . .'

'It's all right, Martin. There's no other man around just at the moment. Christ, I wish I had time for one.' She paused, then tapped the Filofax. 'I want to take a look at this. God knows, it'll make a nice change for me to do some sleuthing again. Who can say, there may even be a story in it.'

Hepton was asleep on his feet by the time they reached Jilly's apartment block by the river. He had been expecting, if anything, an old converted warehouse, but in fact the block was of recent design.

'Mock warehouse,' Jilly explained.

There was a security system at the main entrance, and each flat had its own little video screen so that callers could be identified before being let in. That might come in handy, Hepton thought to himself.

The flat itself wasn't huge, though Jilly stated that by London standards it was more spacious than most. The living area was open-plan, with a bedroom and bathroom off it. There was a narrow veranda – not for the nervous – outside the French doors that took up the far wall. And yes, there were views of the Thames, though fairly unsavoury ones. The river itself was a mottled grey colour, and across the water there were gasometers, a stretch of wasteland and not much else.

'You can see for miles,' Jilly said. 'Make yourself at home. I'll try not to be too long, though parking can be hell itself in town.'

'Where exactly are you going?'

She tapped the side of her nose. 'Journalists never reveal their sources, especially before they've visited them. It's bad luck.' She bent down to give him a peck on the cheek, then closed the door behind her and was gone.

Hepton was surprised. He really didn't feel anything more than friendship towards her now. When she'd been far away and inaccessible, he had longed for her, but now that they were together again, there wasn't the same spark. Perhaps Jilly had been right to come to London. Their affair would have fizzled out in any case, wouldn't it? Better to make a clean break. He lay along the sofa and closed his eyes, not intending to sleep. He just wanted to rest . . .

He awoke to the sound of a purring telephone. He hadn't been asleep long, and felt light-headed, disoriented. He reached for the receiver and picked it up.

'Hello?' he said.

There was a silence on the other end, a crackling of wires, and perhaps, in the background, someone's fluttering breath.

'Hello?' he said again. Still nothing. Then a short laugh.

'You've been a very bad boy, Martin.'

Hepton felt his fingers tighten around the receiver.

'Hello, Harry,' he said. The light-headedness left him. He was wide awake now. 'How was Leeds?'

There was that laugh again, laughter lacking humour but filled instead with cruelty. 'Leeds was a clever idea, Martin. I couldn't think why you'd be going there. Then I realised you'd found my little device.'

'How did you track me down?' Not that he was really interested, but he needed time to think.

'I spoke to your employer. He told me how depressed you'd been when your girlfriend moved to London. I thought it was worth a try.'

Hepton's mind was working now. There was no point mentioning to her that he knew about Villiers. It would be a cheap point to score, like throwing an ace onto a low card. No, he'd keep his ace for the moment. But he needed to knock her off balance. She was sounding a little too confident, and this, married to her thoughts of revenge – he could hear how bitter she was about Leeds – made her doubly dangerous.

'You should have killed me back at the nursing home,' he said. 'Don't think you're going to get a second chance.'

'What are you going to do? Run for it?'

'No, I'm going to wait right here.' For Paul, he was thinking. 'And when I see you, I'm going to kill you.'

The laughter this time had a hysterical edge to it. Good: his words were having their effect.

'That's fine, Martin,' she said at last. 'I'll see you soon then. I'm calling from just outside your building.'

And with that the telephone went dead. Hepton paused, put the receiver down and got to work.

19

Three short knocks followed by one long.

'Come in, Parfit.'

Parfit entered Johnnie Gilchrist's office. Gilchrist was pouring himself a drink.

'Want one?' he asked.

'Why not?' said Parfit. 'I'll have a small brandy, thanks.'

Gilchrist poured half an inch of Martell into a crystal glass and handed it to Parfit.

'Cheers,' he said. They chinked glasses.

Gilchrist took a mouthful of his own whisky, then smiled, shaking his head.

'I have to hand it to you, Parfit. Getting hold of a private jet like that. I won't ask what favour the owner owed you.' He paused, inviting Parfit to tell him anyway, but Parfit merely savoured his drink. 'How is the patient?'

'He's fine,' said Parfit. 'I don't think he was overly pleased about being brought in from the airport in a crate, but he'll get over it.'

Gilchrist smiled again, then sat down, gesturing for Parfit to do the same.

'How was the City of Trees?'

Parfit looked quizzical.

'That's what they call Sacramento,' Gilchrist explained, pleased that Parfit hadn't known. 'Home of the Pony Express.'

'More relevant, it's also the home of McClellan Air Force Base, which is where they landed Dreyfuss once they'd decided he shouldn't stick around Edwards. To answer your question, the City of Trees was . . . interesting.'

'So your gambit paid off?'

'What gambit, Johnnie?'

Gilchrist rubbed a finger around the rim of his glass. 'Leaving your man there so damned long on his own. You wanted to see what they'd try to get out of him, didn't you?'

'That's your interpretation. I was hoping for . . . a reaction.'

'I take it you got one?'

'Oh yes. You know a man called Frank Stewart?'

'*The* Frank Stewart? National Security Agency?'

'Yes, that's the one.'

'What about him?'

'He was there.'

'Good God. I wonder why?'

'I got the feeling it wasn't so much to do with Dreyfuss as it was to do with General Ben Esterhazy.'

'So Esterhazy was there too?'

'Yes, you were right about that. What's more, he was looking fairly rattled.'

'Oh? Any particular reason?'

'Several, I shouldn't wonder.' Parfit finished his drink and took the empty glass back to the drinks cabinet. He left it there and walked to the window, from where he watched the remnants of another demo as they chanted something incoherent, their fingers pointing towards where he was standing. He gave them a wave, which seemed to anger them further. 'Esterhazy's up to no good, Johnnie. I can't say yet quite what, but I'm getting closer.' He returned to his seat.

'Don't tell me about it, Parfit. It would only make me an accessory. Just tell me what you need.'

'Two things. Two names, to be precise. One is Cameron Devereux. He was a member of the ground control crew on *Argos*. I'd like to talk to him, face to face if possible.'

'And the other?'

'Is someone called Martin Hepton. He works on one of our own tracking stations back in England, somewhere in Lincolnshire.'

Gilchrist considered this. 'Must be Binbrook then. What of it?'

'Dreyfuss knows him vaguely, and wants to ask him about something.'

'Martin Hepton, you say?'

'Yes, why?'

'I had a message from George Villiers in London. He phoned

while I was asleep.' Gilchrist picked up some sheets of paper from the tray on the corner of his desk, finding the one he needed. 'Yes, here it is. It seems Hepton paid Villiers a visit, wanted to know how to reach Major Dreyfuss.'

Parfit sat back in his chair. 'Now that *is* interesting.'

'More than mere coincidence, you think?'

'So Hepton's in London?'

'It would seem so. Right, I'll get on to this Devereux character. Shouldn't take long.'

Parfit was already standing, ready to leave. 'Thanks, Johnnie.'

'Parfit?'

'Yes?'

'How big is this thing? Should I be starting to make noises in the direction of our masters?'

'I'd leave it for now,' said Parfit confidently. 'It might all blow over.'

Not that he believed it would. He just didn't want more people than absolutely necessary knowing he was on to something. It was all down to trust in the end, and Parfit didn't trust anyone. Not even Johnnie Gilchrist, not entirely.

20

Dreyfuss had been given a room containing a foldaway bed and not much else.

'Not so different from the crate,' he had commented on arrival. Not that he had minded the crate too much. He didn't want anyone knowing he was in Washington with the climate the way it was right now.

Parfit explained that most of the embassy staff were sleeping on the premises these days, so beds and furnishings were scarce. However, he did return a couple of hours later with a portable television, a radio and some books.

'If anyone asks where they came from,' he said, 'say they were here when you arrived.'

Dreyfuss nodded at this. He didn't want to know where these items had come from, and he didn't care where they had come from; he was just glad that *he* had them now, and not someone else. His room, such as it was, must have been a storeroom. At least he could think of no other use for a space measuring twelve feet by ten and tucked away in the furthest, highest corner of the building. There wasn't even a window, but there was a small skylight, desperately in need of a clean.

'I'd have been better off back at Sacramento General,' he commented.

'I really do doubt that,' said Parfit.

There was a knock at the door, and it was pushed open by a feisty individual wearing half-moon glasses. He was breathing hard, obviously unused to climbing the stairs to this attic level.

'Ah, Parfit,' he said.

Parfit introduced the two men.

'Major Michael Dreyfuss, this is Johnnie Gilchrist, a colleague of mine.'

'How do you do?' said Gilchrist, shaking Dreyfuss' hand. Then he noticed the portable TV. 'Nice-looking model. I've one just like it in my own room.'

Dreyfuss tried to avoid Parfit's eyes.

'So,' Parfit said, 'what brings you so far out of your lair, Johnnie?'

'I'll tell you. I've been trying to make contact with this man Devereux.' Dreyfuss and Parfit both looked interested, and there was nothing Gilchrist liked more than an attentive audience. 'Devil of a job I had, too.' He turned to Dreyfuss. 'These days, Major, the international situation being what it is, a diplomat's life is not easy. Not that it ever was.' He looked around the room. 'Don't believe I've been this far north in the building before. But I do recall some story – before my time – of some of the secretaries squeezing out of that skylight to sunbathe nude on the roof. One of them's supposed to have gotten herself stuck, and—'

'What about Devereux, Johnnie?' interrupted Parfit.

Gilchrist hated to have his stories ruined. His eyes blazed away at Parfit for several seconds, then he said simply: 'He's gone.'

'Gone? You mean disappeared?'

'Not in so many words. Apparently he was a bit shell-shocked when the shuttle crashed. So now he's on extended leave.'

'Do we know where?'

'You won't believe it, Parfit, but it seems he's gone to London.'

'London?'

Now Parfit and Dreyfuss exchanged glances.

'I'm not sure,' Parfit said, 'whether that's to our advantage or not. What do you think, Johnnie?'

'Well, we can have him traced and picked up easily enough.'

'Yes, but can he give us the information we need by telephone? I was rather hoping to speak to him in person. Any explanation he can give might be a bit technical, mightn't it?'

'Why don't we get someone who knows about satellites to talk to him for us?' Dreyfuss asked.

'Someone like Martin Hepton,' said Parfit.

'Hepton?' Dreyfuss sounded uncertain.

'He'd be perfect. For one thing, he knows about satellites, and for another, he's in London.' Parfit turned to Gilchrist. 'Get your man Villiers to find out where Hepton's staying. We need to speak to him.'

'I've just had a word with Villiers, actually,' said Gilchrist. 'He said Hepton had mentioned the name of a friend in London. Jill Watson. Villiers didn't reckon Hepton was headed there, but there's always a chance . . .'

Parfit noticed the numb look on Dreyfuss' face. 'What's wrong, Major?'

'I don't want Jilly getting mixed up in this,' Dreyfuss hissed. 'Anything but that. Keep her out of it, Parfit.' He grabbed at Parfit's wrist and held it tight. 'Keep her out of it!'

21

Hepton went to the door and studied the tiny surveillance screen. It showed the main door of the block, and, at the touch of a button, the interior hallway as well. There was nobody about. It was five o'clock. People would still be at work. More importantly, there was no sign of Harry.

He went back to his exploration of the flat. He found a chef's knife in the kitchen drawer and slipped it into his pocket. In another drawer he found a large box of matches. He shook it to convince himself of its contents, then slipped it into his pocket too. From the living room's waste-paper bin he took a copy of the previous day's *Herald*, then, so armed, returned to the front door of the flat and opened it.

He looked left and right along the corridor. All clear. Then he stared up towards where the smoke detector sat, a neat little unit flush-mounted into the ceiling. He had noticed it upon arriving. He always noticed ceilings.

That, Martin, he said to himself, is what comes of an adolescence spent staring upwards.

The rolled-up newspaper took a little encouragement, the first three matches failing to catch. He tore a few strips down the sides, then tried again. These strips caught and ignited the rest of the paper. The ceiling was high, and he stood on tiptoe beneath the smoke alarm, holding the newspaper as close to it as he could.

It took forever. His arm ached, and he wondered what he would say if someone happened to emerge from one of the other five apartments along the corridor. But no one did. The paper started to smoulder, the smoke rose, and finally the detector began to whine, setting off alarm bells all around the building.

Elated, Hepton darted back into the flat, stubbed out the flaming newspaper in the sink and poured some water on it. He went back to the video screen at the front door and saw that people were already emerging from their apartments, milling in the main hallway downstairs. He went out onto the veranda and waited. There was a stiff breeze and he breathed hard, staying calm. The Thames was smelling like a sick old pet, but he didn't mind that. He leaned out over the balcony and peered down onto the veranda of the flat beneath, then pulled himself back. There was no need to be rash. He could take the stairs to ground level, the same as the other inhabitants. He already had the evidence of his own eyes and his continuing life to the fact that Harry did not like a crowd. She enjoyed doing her slaying in private.

Suddenly he heard what he had been waiting for: approaching sirens. He rushed back inside and out into the corridor. A couple of people, looking as though they had been disturbed in the act of coitus, were standing by the lift, their clothes disarranged. The man was frantically pressing at the button beside the doors.

'I shouldn't think you'll get much joy,' Hepton informed him. 'These things shut off when there's an alarm. It's much safer to use the stairs.'

'Is there a fire?' the man asked.

'Yes, upstairs,' said Hepton. 'We'd better hurry.'

The three of them set off downstairs together. At the third landing, they joined a slightly larger group.

'*Is* there a fire?' someone asked.

'Yes,' the man with Hepton said, mimicking him. 'It's upstairs.'

Between the third and second landings, Hepton, to the rear of the small party, saw that someone was pushing their way back up through the descending group. There was always someone, someone who'd forgotten a treasured memento or the pet cat. He was about to remonstrate when he realised it was Harry. She was pushing hard now, her anger showing. And in her eyes he saw a kind of madness. There could be no doubting: she was out to kill him, witnesses or no.

Then she glanced upwards and, separated from him by only a handful of bodies now, saw Hepton. Her eyebrows rose in victory, and she dug a hand into the pocket of the checked jacket she was wearing. But the hand stuck there as somebody tried to squeeze past her downstairs.

'You should go back, love,' someone warned her. 'Save yourself. Never mind what's up there.'

Hepton turned on his heel and started up the carpeted steps two at a time, pushing hard as though his knees were mechanical pistons. The banisters were new. Dark polished wood with brass supports. His arms pulled hard on them, heaving his body upwards. He didn't pause at the third floor – he needed territory he could recognise. Instead he left the stairs at the fourth floor and ran back to Jilly's flat. Once inside, he closed the door quietly, then locked it. He realised that his right hand was gripping the kitchen knife. The video screen showed him the main lobby on the ground floor. People were beginning to move outside, some of them explaining to a fireman where the blaze was situated. Hepton could no longer hear the sirens and supposed they had been turned off. Well, he couldn't give them a fire . . . but fire was useful in other ways.

He walked quickly to the kitchen and filled the largest pot he could find with water from the hot tap. Then he manoeuvred it onto a ring of the gas cooker and turned the flame on full blast. It was Dark Ages stuff, but potentially effective. He pondered the contents of the food cupboard. The only pepper, though, seemed to be in the form of peppercorns. Useless. He cursed Jilly's yuppie lifestyle. Where were the tools? The saws, electric drills? The screwdrivers and spanners? What use was the broken edge of an empty champagne bottle against a killer toting a gun?

Then it struck him: Harry knew that Hepton had come to Jilly's flat. Therefore she would know Jilly's name . . .

And Jilly's name was engraved on the front door's silver nameplate!

Cautiously, Hepton took a few paces towards the door. He could hear no sounds. Maybe Harry had taken a wrong turn. He pressed his ear to the door. Still no sound. Then the world exploded.

The solid wood of the door splintered just a few inches to his right, beside where the battery of indoor locks was placed. There was a roaring in his ears, the result of the explosion. Another gunshot splintered more wood and severed the first lock's mechanism.

Hepton walked backwards into the kitchen. The pot was bubbling on the hob, and he lifted it with both hands grasped around the handle, walking back into the hallway just as a third shot severed the final locks and Harry's foot kicked the door open. She saw Hepton directly in front of her and raised the pistol, but then saw what he was holding . . .

Some of the water sloshed out onto Hepton's hands and wrists, scalding him, but he felt no pain as he held the pot out to one side like a tennis player preparing a double-handed return. He swung it forward, then jerked it back again. Harry was already half turning away from the water, and it caught her sideways on, spraying her clothes and her hair, splashing across one cheek, one ear, one tightly shut eye. She gasped, and Hepton threw the pot down, starting towards her. But her survival instinct was as strong as his, and blindly she brought the gun up and started firing. Firing wildly, but even a wild bullet was lethal.

Hepton dodged back into the flat, slammed the door shut again and ran. His eyes were focused on the open French doors. Then he was out on the veranda, and there was only one route possible. He swung one leg over the edge of the balcony, then the other. Crouched, gripping the steel rail, he let his feet slide off into space. He gained momentum, swinging his legs, the edge of the veranda hard against his stomach, then took one last swing outwards, started in again and released his hands. Like a high jumper, he felt his backbone graze the rail of the balcony below. Then his feet touched its solid floor and he pulled himself upright. Only to stare at the French doors, identical to Jilly's in every way except one.

They were firmly locked. He cursed. Somewhere above him, Harry had stopped shooting and was screaming instead.

'I'm going to kill you, Hepton! Going to shoot you to hell, you bastard!'

He looked left and right and saw with relief that the next apartment along had its windows open to the elements. There was no time to waste. He climbed nimbly onto the rail and leapt across the four-foot gap, landing safely and darting inside just as Harry arrived at the veranda diagonally above and, her sight restored, but still hurting, fired two shots into the balcony floor behind him.

He ran through the living room and pulled open the door into the hallway, taking the stairs down three at a time until he arrived in the lobby.

'Look, there he is now,' the man who had been standing at the lift said to a fire officer. He was pointing at Hepton.

'Excuse me, sir, I believe you know—' the fireman started, but Hepton simply pushed him aside and walked quickly from the building.

There were two fire engines parked outside, their blue lights flashing but the firemen themselves looking relaxed: just another false alarm. A bright red MG turned the far corner and began speeding towards the block. It was Jilly. He waited until she had almost pulled up next to the fire engines, then leapt forward from the crowd. She saw him and stopped the car, rising from her seat.

'Martin! What's happened?'

'I'll tell you later.' He heaved himself into the passenger seat. 'Just get us out of here.'

She hesitated, wanting to know what was going on.

'Let's go!' he shouted, and his voice frightened her. She started the car off, did a three-point turn and, watched by the huddle of neighbours, drove back the way she had come. Hepton tried scanning the rear of the car, both sides and the front all at the same time.

'Martin?'

'What?'

'What the hell are you up to?'

'Just keep driving. I'm looking for a black Sierra.'

'You mean that woman Harry?'

'Yes. She came to the flat. She's just tried to kill me.'

'Christ.' Jilly's face lost a little of its colour. 'Did she start the fire?'

'What?' He looked at her, then grinned. 'Oh, no, I did that. Don't worry, all I did was set the smoke alarm off.'

'So you could make a getaway?' Jilly seemed impressed. 'That's brilliant, Martin.'

'It might not have been if you hadn't shown up.' He noticed that his hands were stinging, and examined them. White blisters were appearing where the water had scalded him. Jilly grimaced.

'Those look sore.'

'They're nothing,' said Hepton, meaning it. He hoped Harry was in agony.

'So where to now?' asked Jilly.

'A hotel, I suppose.' He was still checking for a tail. 'I can't believe there isn't someone on to us. Drive into town, Jilly. That way maybe we can throw them off.' Looking out of the side window, he saw a red Vauxhall Cavalier driving very fast in the direction from which they were coming. Detectives, he guessed. On their way to a fire that never was. With any luck, they'd pick up Harry. But he doubted it.

'Well I must say, Martin,' said Jilly, attempting levity, 'this isn't the way I usually end my working day. Normally it's a gin and tonic at the wine bar.'

Hepton turned to her again. His look was contrite. 'I'm sorry you had to get mixed up in this, Jilly.'

'I'm not.' She was smiling. 'Besides, I haven't told you yet what I found out about your civil servant.'

'You mean Villiers?'

'Who else? Martin, you're not going to believe it.'

'Try me.'

'Well, your description of him was spot on. You know you said you thought he had some kind of military background? He was in the Royal Marines until not too long ago. A major, to boot. Pretty high up. There was a fight on Brown Mountain – at least I think that's what it was called. Anyway, somewhere on South Georgia. Villiers led his men into what turned out to be a trap. A lot of them were killed. It was hushed up here, of course. Bad for morale.' Jilly was warming to her story, and as she continued, she pushed a little harder on the accelerator. 'Villiers seems to have snapped. He'd seen plenty of action. Oman in the fifties, Belfast in the sixties and seventies. But something happened to him in the Falklands. After he saw his men die, he just couldn't stop killing the enemy, and when the enemy were dead, he turned on his own men. Kill crazy, they call it. Apparently it happens sometimes.'

'Christ,' said Hepton quietly.

'He was a good soldier, too.' Jilly slammed her foot on the brake as a red light loomed. She idled the car and turned towards Hepton. 'They had psychiatrists on him from the minute he landed back home. He seemed normal enough by then, but nobody was taking any chances. Bad for public relations, having a killer in your midst.'

'So they pensioned him off?'

'One of the disabled. They even gave him a medal, I forget which. It's in my notes.'

The car started off again, turning left at the lights.

'And the government hired him?'

'Well, yes, in a way. The Foreign Office gave him a job. His actual title is pretty vague, but he knows his stuff: countries, political climate, that sort of thing. God only knows why it had to be him you saw when you visited the FO.'

'Because,' said Hepton, 'he'd been expecting me.' His voice was level. 'He'd figured out, you see, that I was curious and that my curiosity would probably lead to Mike Dreyfuss.'

'But how could he know?'

'He's a cunning little bastard. Cunning enough to string us along, because he doesn't know we know about him. *That's* our big card. Meantime, he'll probably want to know just *how* much *I* know.'

'What about this Harry, though? She just wants you dead, period. Isn't she working for Villiers then?'

'I'm not sure.' Hepton thought it over. 'No, I'm sure she *is* working for him. Or, at least, they are both working for the same ultimate employer.' Harry's words were coming back to him: *my employers, who are, ultimately, your employers*. But what did it mean? 'In any case,' he said, 'I think Harry's become . . . what was that phrase you used? Kill crazy? Yes, that's what she is. Kill crazy.' He examined the cars moving past them. Then he turned to Jilly again. 'How did you find all this out anyway?' He was both impressed and curious to know.

'A guy I met at a party,' Jilly explained. 'One of the old guard of Fleet Street hacks. He's been around a bit, reported from Afghanistan, Belfast, Beirut, that sort of thing. It's a passion with him, the military. He's written a couple of books. He was able to tell me some of it off the top of his head. The rest he got by making a few phone calls. That's what you call a network. Every good journalist needs one.'

Hepton's mind was still trained on Villiers. 'Yes,' he said vacantly. A network . . . 'Anything else?'

'Isn't it enough?' Jilly sounded slighted. She was checking in her rear-view mirror.

'Yes, yes, I suppose so. Thanks for . . .' She was still staring in the mirror. 'What is it?' He turned and caught a glance, three cars back, of a dark-coloured Sierra. 'Shit,' he hissed, gripping the seat with his hands.

'Is that her car?' Jilly asked, her voice level.

'I think so.' Hepton looked back again. The dark car was in the process of overtaking one of the vehicles between them. He let out a sigh of relief. 'No, it's okay. It's not a Sierra. It's a bloody Cavalier.'

Jilly's shoulders relaxed too. She was nearing another set of lights. 'I think there's a shortcut here, unless they've blocked it off.' She signalled left and squeezed the MG into an alleyway. The high buildings either side seemed purpose-built to hem them in. There was a screech of tyres behind them. The Cavalier was following, speeding up. Hepton remembered the night Harry had tried to run him down in an alley almost as narrow as this, and every bit as deserted. Then he recalled that he had seen the red Cavalier before: hurrying towards Jilly's flat as they were making their getaway.

'They're chasing us!' he called.

Jilly responded to the Cavalier, pushing the MG down a gear and hitting the accelerator. They were running now, careering past parked cars, braking hard to take an almost impossibly tight turning into a two-way street. Hepton held on, teeth clamped together. Jilly was a good driver, but not good enough. They weren't going to shake the Cavalier. It was mere yards behind them now, and he peered through its black-tinted windscreen. Two men. Definitely men, though he couldn't have said more than that. Not Harry, then.

The extended blaring of a car horn brought his head round to the view to the front of the MG. It took him a moment to realise that the horn was their own, and that the heel of Jilly's left hand was hard against it. She had turned the headlights on full-beam, too. The traffic was becoming clogged. She scraped past a bus, paintwork peeling like confetti, but ahead the lights were at red, and the traffic was at a standstill in both directions.

'Hang on!' Jilly yelled, throwing the MG to the right, braking hard as she did so and spinning a full one hundred and eighty degrees. On the other side of the road now, the Cavalier roared past them, braking hard itself. There was a squeal as the driver threw his wheel round, bumping onto some central bollards. These stopped him, and he reversed, the traffic cursing angrily all around him. Jilly glanced back to see that the Cavalier had lost a lot of ground, and let out a whoop.

'Where did you learn a stunt like that?' Hepton gasped. His heart felt like a bird in a cage too small for it, fluttering against the bars. The breath came from him in short bursts.

'I didn't,' Jilly answered, clearly enjoying every moment of this. 'Put it down to instinct.'

'Fine. But every traffic cop in the area's going to have our description and registration in about five seconds flat.'

'Five seconds? Don't talk daft.'

'Haven't you heard of car phones?' Hepton yelled. 'Half those BMWs you just nearly totalled will be on them right now.'

'What are you saying, Martin? That we ditch the car and *walk*?'

'Just get us away from here,' he said, looking back again. 'And fast.'

Jilly looked in her mirror and saw that the Cavalier was not about to give up the chase. In fact, it was gaining at a steady rate.

'Bastards!' she yelled. The lights ahead were turning red. She held the horn down again and pulled the car into the middle of the road, passing the waiting line of traffic. There was a no-right-turn sign, so she threw the car to the right just as the other traffic was responding to the green light. Hepton looked out of his side window and saw a motorbike messenger heading straight for him. On Jilly's side, a white van was already braking, but too late. The front of the van hit Jilly's door, sending the sports car scudding sideways, where it collided with the bike. The driver was thrown clear, rolling like a pro. Another day in the city. Jilly tried to keep the MG moving, but her front driver-side wheel had buckled. The car protested, growling meanly.

'Last stop,' she said, face pale. The Cavalier was manoeuvring slowly, gingerly past the stalled traffic. Drivers were opening their doors to take a look at the mad bastards who had caused the accident.

'You ought to be fucking well locked up!' the van driver screeched. The bike courier, however, was casually examining some scuffs to his leathers, uninjured himself. Jilly got out of the car. So did Hepton. The Cavalier stopped beside them. Hepton's hand went into his pocket and found the knife he had taken from the kitchen.

'We could run for it,' Jilly said, but her legs were shaking wildly.

The doors of the Cavalier opened and the two men got out. Hepton recognised one of them. It was Sanders, the man from the Foreign Office. Sanders turned to his partner.

'You better stay here, Clive.' He surveyed the chaos. 'Try to clear this up with the police when they arrive.' Then he nodded in Hepton's direction. 'I'll take these two back with me in the car.'

The other man nodded slowly, not looking at all happy with his allotted task, but unable or unwilling to protest.

'Where are we going?' Hepton asked as he and Jilly walked to the car. His grip on the knife relaxed.

'I'm getting you out of this,' Sanders said, indicating the scene around them. He was shaking too, obviously not used to car chases and crashes. 'I would have thought that was reason enough for you to be grateful.'

'It is,' said Jilly. Even her lips had gone white with shock.

'How did you find us?' Hepton asked.

Sanders shrugged. 'I used a bit of initiative. Besides, what other leads did I have? All I knew about you, Mr Hepton, was that you had a friend in London called Jilly Watson who worked on the *Herald*. It wasn't too difficult to find out where Miss Watson lived. Then when I saw you racing away from the scene like that . . .'

'Someone tried to kill me back there,' commented Hepton, seeking a reaction. Sanders raised an eyebrow, nothing more. Hepton decided to try another tack. 'I lost your first tail, though, didn't I?'

'First tail?' Sanders seemed genuinely puzzled. Hepton beamed. He'd been right: Villiers was using the department for his own ends, without everyone knowing about it. Sanders, for one, didn't seem to be aware of the tail. He would bear that in mind.

'I'd still like to know where we're going,' he persisted.

'There's an old friend who wants to speak to you,' Sanders answered, his irritation showing.

'Who? Villiers?'

'Mr Villiers, yes. Indirectly. But someone else.'

'Who?' Jilly asked, wondering herself now; the mention of Villiers bringing with it a renewed sense of menace.

'A Major Michael Dreyfuss,' said Sanders, sliding into the driver's seat. 'Now come on . . .'

22

George Villiers was frowning when they arrived at his office. One hand rested on the telephone in a manner suggesting his frown had something to do with a recent call. He looked up as Hepton and Jilly entered. Sanders stayed outside, closing the door on them. The evening light was a deepening orange, casting long shadows in the room and creating a nimbus around Villiers' head.

'You really have caused us a great deal of trouble,' he stated. 'God knows whether we can keep it out of tomorrow's papers.'

'Blame your henchmen,' said Jilly, sitting down without being asked. She had regained her composure during the drive to Whitehall. Indeed, having realised that she was about to get away with breaking every traffic regulation in the book, she was on something of a high. She crossed her legs and folded her arms. 'They were like maniacs,' she explained, studying Villiers. 'Martin's life is in danger, and then they came racing after us. What were we supposed to do?'

Villiers' face showed no emotion. He turned to Hepton, who was about to sit down.

'*Is* your life in danger, Mr Hepton?'

'Oh yes,' Hepton said quietly.

Villiers appeared to ponder this, then picked up his telephone and waited.

'A pot of tea,' he ordered when the line was picked up. Then he replaced the receiver.

'What's this about Mickey?' Jilly asked.

'Mickey?'

'Major Dreyfuss,' Hepton explained.

'Ah.' Villiers paused. 'Sanders told you then.'

'He wouldn't say anything other than that.' Jilly was up on her feet again. She was nervy still; that much was more than obvious. Hepton hoped she could keep in control. It was a kind of madness to have come here, and yet it felt like the right course of action. The questions still needed answering, and who better than Villiers to do it?

'Right.' Villiers leaned forward, resting his arms on the desk. 'Well, it's true enough. After Mr Hepton called here, I was able to contact our embassy in Washington. Major Dreyfuss is there at the moment, though that must remain strictly between us. Ah . . .'

Sanders pushed open the door and brought in a tray, the cups chinking together as he moved.

'I hope you're a better tea-maker than you are a driver,' Jilly commented, the hint of a sneer on her face.

Sanders paused, but chose to ignore her. He left the tray on the desk in front of Villiers, then exited again. There was something else on the tray beside tea. It was a sheet of paper. Villiers slid it towards himself, glanced at it, then turned it so that the writing was facing away from him. His right hand went to his inside pocket and came out with a fountain pen, the top of which he removed to reveal a gold nib.

'Miss Watson?'

'Yes?' Jilly stopped pacing and came to the desk. 'What's this?'

'Routine, I'm afraid. I know Mr Hepton has already signed, as was required of him when he started work. If you would just . . .'

Jilly picked up the form and studied it. It was simple and to the point. It was the catch-all.

'The Official Secrets Act?' she said, smiling. 'Well, why not?' She snatched the pen from him and scratched her name on the paper, then handed back both paper and pen. Villiers looked satisfied, and slid the sheet into the top drawer of his desk. 'I don't mind signing something I'm quite willing to break,' Jilly said with finality. Villiers' satisfaction took the slightest of jolts. Jilly had picked up the teapot. 'Shall I be mother?'

Villiers accepted his cup with what grace he could muster. He was still playing the senior civil servant.

'So what's this about Dreyfuss?' asked Hepton, growing impatient.

'Ah yes, Major Dreyfuss. Well, he'd like a word with you.'

'With me?' Jilly said, hopefully.

'Alas, no, with Mr Hepton.'

'Me?' Hepton could not hide his surprise. 'Whatever for? He hardly knows me.'

'Yes, but he knows you by reputation, apparently. The embassy will be calling in another five minutes or so.'

'But what does he want?'

'I really can't say.' Villiers sat back, lips tightly closed, as though prepared to sit out the time before the phone call in silence.

'Tell us about the Falklands,' Jilly said nonchalantly.

Villiers twitched and leaned back in his chair, as though he had just been given a mild but unpleasant electric shock.

No, thought Hepton. This wasn't the time to give away secrets. He saw why Jilly had done it. She was a journalist, a journalist who knew something about the man before her. Her professional instinct was to go for the jugular, startle him into some kind of revelation, get him worried . . . but this wasn't a newspaper story. This was entirely more serious.

'Jilly,' he warned, 'not now.'

'Why not?' she snarled. 'Why not now?'

'Because I say so.' His voice was cold and hard, but his eyes were ablaze. She read his thoughts and seemed to understand them. Villiers had a bemused smile on his face.

'I'm sorry,' he said to Jilly, 'what was it you were about to say?'

Her cheeks were red. 'Nothing,' she said.

Villiers turned to Hepton. 'You know I served in the Royal Marines then?' Hepton stayed silent. 'You both seem to know a lot about me, Mr Hepton. Now why should that be? Why should a lowly civil servant interest you so much? Hmm?'

But now it was Hepton's lips that stayed tight shut. Villiers rose from his chair and turned to stare out of his window. Hepton glanced at Jilly, whose face looked pained. She mouthed, 'I'm sorry,' at him. He merely winked in reassurance. Villiers turned back to face them.

'I'm not sure speaking with Major Dreyfuss would be such a wise move,' he stated. 'I'd like you both to leave now.'

Hepton hadn't been expecting this. But he saw that it made sense. He had been brought here to speak to Dreyfuss so that Villiers could ascertain how much he knew about *Zephyr*. But now Villiers had discovered that Hepton knew about *him*, making the telephone call hazardous. Indeed, Hepton now saw, it was imperative to Villiers that Hepton and Jilly leave, since their call to Dreyfuss would doubtless include their suspicions of Villiers himself . . .

'We're staying,' he said. Jilly looked at him, uncomprehending.

'Not if I want you to leave,' Villiers said quietly.

'Nevertheless, we're staying.'

Villiers stared at him, then smiled, coming back towards the desk. 'You're a clever man, Mr Hepton. But you're also incredibly stupid.'

He reached out a hand to pick up the receiver of the internal telephone, but just at that moment the other telephone started ringing. Hepton leapt from his seat, grabbing Villiers by the shoulders and propelling him away from the desk, pinning him against the wall. Villiers was strong, and he struggled.

'Jilly,' Hepton hissed between gritted teeth. 'Answer the bloody phone!'

She did so. 'Hello?'

Villiers had stopped struggling. Hepton relaxed a little, then remembered the man's Marine training. A heel crushed down onto the toes of his left foot, and he gasped. Then two hands chopped into his ribs. Villiers crooked his index fingers and pressed hard against them with his thumbs. He jabbed the second knuckle of each rigid forefinger into Hepton's neck. Hepton's grip on him fell away. But when Villiers made to push him aside, Hepton clutched at him again, and the two men fell sprawling to the floor.

Jilly was shouting into the receiver. 'It's Villiers! He's trying to kill Martin! It's George Villiers!' She wasn't calling for help; she was just letting the facts be known.

Villiers, hearing her words, let out a growl. His hands went to Hepton's throat again. Hepton drew back a fist and punched him deep in his stomach. Villiers had been Royal Marines, yes, but not for some years, years spent behind a desk. His gut was soft, and the blow winded him, giving Hepton time to climb back to his feet. He swung a foot at Villiers' head, but Villiers' reactions were still fast. He dodged the swing and grabbed Hepton's leg, tugging him off balance and down onto the floor again, clambering atop him.

The older, heavier man's weight was enough to pin Hepton down. A hand scrabbled at the desktop and came away again clutching a paperknife. Too late, Hepton remembered the kitchen knife in his own pocket. He caught Villiers' wrist, but Villiers had found new strength. The knife pushed downwards against Hepton's resistance. Villiers was smiling now, a look of tranquillity on his face. Close combat was his true calling; killing was his destiny . . .

The office door opened and Sanders looked in. His mouth fell open at the sight of his superior kneeling on top of Hepton with a knife poised above his throat.

'Christ almighty!' he gasped.

He loped towards the two men, and as Hepton watched, he seemed to turn his body sideways, raising one leg. The leg flexed, shot out, and a well-shod foot slapped into Villiers' jaw, cracking his head to one side and throwing him off Hepton. Hepton scrambled to his knees, but Villiers was already on his feet. He seemed to take in the whole situation – Hepton, Sanders, Jilly still talking on the telephone – at a single glance, and started for the door.

'Sir . . .' Sanders laid a restraining hand on his shoulder, but Villiers pushed him aside and ran out.

'Get after him,' Hepton ordered.

'What?'

'You saw him. He was going to cut my fucking head off. Get after him!'

Sanders hesitated, then crossed to the other telephone, dialled two digits and spoke.

'Security,' he said. 'Sanders here. I want George Villiers apprehended. Yes, that's right. No, it's not a joke. He's trying to leave the building. I want him stopped.' He slammed the receiver down again and looked to Hepton, who nodded at him in thanks.

'Martin?' Jilly was saying. She was holding the receiver out towards him. 'Martin, they want to speak with you . . .'

The problem with the secure line, a line unlikely to be tapped into by prying ears, was that it made voices sound as though they were trapped somewhere between an anechoic chamber and a sardine tin. There was a flat, dull lifelessness to the sound, with occasional bursts of jangling metallic tone.

Was it any wonder then that Dreyfuss did not sound like the man Hepton had met one day for lunch with Jilly? But Hepton was intrigued by the secure line, too. Did it use a satellite link? And if so, how secure could it ever be? He took several deep breaths as he took the receiver from Jilly. She was shaking, and he placed a hand on her shoulder to let her know he was all right.

'Is that you, Martin?'

'Yes.'

'Mike Dreyfuss here. What the hell's going on?'

'A man just tried to kill me. Lots of people seem to be trying to kill me of late. This one was a civil servant.'

'Is Jilly okay?'

'She's fine.' Hepton glanced across towards where Jilly, her arms folded in front of her, leaned against the wall. She nodded and smiled, confirming his opinion.

'What?' Dreyfuss seemed to be conferring with someone at his end of the line. 'Hold on, Martin,' he said. Then his voice was replaced by another.

'Mr Hepton?'

'Yes.'

'My name's Parfit. We haven't spoken before.'

'Parfit?' Hepton repeated, his eyes on Sanders.

The young man, who had been pacing the room as though still unable to believe the scene he had just witnessed, drew himself upright at the sound of the name. His eyes turned to Hepton.

'I work at the embassy here in Washington,' Parfit was saying. 'What's all this about George Villiers?'

'He wants me dead.'

'But why, in God's name?'

'That's a good question, Mr Parfit. It has something to do with the reason I've been trying to get in touch with Major Dreyfuss.' There was a knock at the door. A uniformed guard opened it and had a short whispered conversation with Sanders.

'Oh?' Parfit sounded intrigued. 'And what reason is that, Mr Hepton?'

The guard had gone. Sanders looked towards Hepton and shook his head: there was no sign of Villiers. Hepton couldn't help wondering how hard the guards had tried. He also wasn't entirely sure that he could trust Sanders himself. Yet here he was, having the conversation he wanted with the people he needed to speak with. He took another breath, his heartbeat slowing a little, the roaring in his ears more of a gentle breeze now.

'The day the shuttle crashed—' he began. But Parfit interrupted.

'Wait one moment, would you, Mr Hepton? I'm going to put you on our conference facility, so that Major Dreyfuss can participate.'

Hepton waited impatiently.

'Okay, go ahead now.'

He began again. 'The day the shuttle crashed, about the time *Argos* was launching a satellite or whatever it was doing up there, *our* satellite went haywire. A friend of mine had an idea what had happened, but he ended up dead. Before he died, he gave me one word. That word was *Argos.*'

There was silence at the other end. Hepton glanced towards Sanders, who was listening intently.

'Martin?' It was Dreyfuss' voice. 'What do *you* think happened?'

'I'm not sure. But people are getting killed because of it.'

'All right then,' said Dreyfuss. 'Listen, I've got part of a sequence. I wonder if you know what it means. The whole sequence was much longer, but all I have are the first few letters and numbers.' He paused. 'Ze/446.'

Hepton smiled. He could have completed the sequence for them if they wanted.

'That's an easy one,' he said. 'It's *Zephyr*, of course. It's part of *Zephyr*'s identification code.' His smile vanished. 'How did you get hold of it?'

'One of the crew on the shuttle had it on his screen. It kept flashing up.'

Hepton's blood went a few degrees colder. 'Then you were trying to lock onto *Zephyr*.' It was a statement.

'That's just what I was thinking.'

Parfit's voice came on the line. 'Tell me about *Zephyr*, Mr Hepton.'

'What do you want to know?'

'What exactly does it do?'

'It's an all-purpose satellite, as versatile as we want it to be.'

'What was it doing the day it went haywire?'

'Not a lot. We'd been running some regular checks on it.'

'Well, what might it be doing now? Any specific jobs it was supposed to carry out?'

'A few. The big one, I suppose, is monitoring the troop pull-outs.'

'The pull-outs?'

'Nobody's supposed to know. But we've been keeping an eye on the US bases in Britain.'

'But why?'

'To make sure it all runs smoothly. There are some protest groups, including one pretty big one called USA Stay. They said they intended to stage some kind of resistance. You know, linking hands around a camp, or putting a padlock and chain on the gate. Symbolic stuff mainly. But the brass wanted to know what they were up to.'

'The brass?'

'Yes, the military. They've been keeping an eye open. A couple of high-rankers were on site when *Zephyr* malfunctioned.'

Hepton was trying not to be melodramatic. He wanted to state facts rather than his own suppositions, just to see what Dreyfuss and Parfit might make of it. This was the first time he had told any-one the story – Jilly excepted – and it felt good. Almost like the confessional.

'Then,' he continued, 'a friend of mine who works beside me thought he had something on his computer, some data showing interference with *Zephyr*. Next thing I know he's been rushed to hospital, and soon after that he's supposedly hanged himself in a closet. Then a woman called Harry tried to shoot me, run me over, and shoot me again.'

'Harry?' Parfit sounded almost excited.

'Yes. Do you know her?'

'I think so. We had a run-in with her four or five years ago. I thought she'd retired.'

'She tried to kill me.'

'Surprised you're still alive then. Killing is her job. But how in hell is she mixed up in this?'

Hepton stared fixedly at Sanders. 'My friend, the one who died. He told me to watch for someone called Villiers. I think Villiers and Harry are working together.'

'But working on *what*?' asked Parfit. 'That's the question. What does this satellite . . .'

'*Zephyr*,' said Hepton.

'Yes, *Zephyr*. What does it *do* exactly when it's hovering over its target?'

'It takes photographs and sends them back to control.'

'Control being where?'

'Binbrook.'

'Are these still photographs or videos?'

'Stills, mostly. The data is beamed down to us, and the pictures develop on a machine almost instantaneously.'

'Ingenious,' Parfit said, as though he meant it. 'A little like a fax then?'

Hepton smiled again. 'A little, yes.'

'But clear?'

'Clear enough. In focus, if that's what you mean.'

'Ingenious,' Parfit said again. Then: 'Sorry, hold on a second, will you?' There were muffled sounds at the Washington end, the sounds of a conversation. Hepton thought he heard the name 'Johnnie' mentioned at one point. Then Parfit's voice came back, loud and more or less clear. 'Sorry about that. Right, so are we any further forward, do you think?'

'Well, we know that *Argos* locked onto *Zephyr,*' said Hepton. 'Probably using the satellite it was launching. What we don't know is why. I had the idea it was all some kind of secret test, trying out some capability of the satellite that the powers-that-be wanted to keep hidden from even the ground controllers.'

Parfit seemed to consider this. 'Hmm,' he said at last. Hepton wasn't sure whether it was an interested 'hmm' or a sceptical 'hmm'; the scrambler was still robbing the voices of any emotion. Then Parfit cleared his throat, and Hepton thought he could hear Dreyfuss whispering something, a name . . .

'As Major Dreyfuss has just reminded me,' Parfit said, 'there is a man who might help us. His name is Cameron Devereux. He's the other reason we called. Devereux was Major Dreyfuss' contact at mission control. What you need to realise is that *Argos* was meant to crash, and with no survivors.'

'A suicide mission?'

'I doubt whether the crew knew that, though they must have known why they were up there in the first place. One of them tried to strangle Major Dreyfuss.'

'Strangle Dreyfuss?' Hepton saw the effect of his words on the room. Sanders, who was starting to sit, now stood up again, and Jilly looked aghast.

'This man said something about needing to bury a coffin. Does that mean anything to you?'

'No, nothing. So what about this Devereux?'

'He might well know something about the sabotage. And if so, he *may* also know what the mission was.'

'So talk to him.'

'Yes, but he's gone on vacation to London.'

Hepton rested against the edge of the table. 'Has he now? And you'd like me to talk to him?'

'Well, you might understand him better than we amateurs could.'

'Okay, Mr Parfit. Where is he staying?'

'A hotel on Park Lane, I believe. The Achilles. Our intelligence sources have just come up with it. He booked in yesterday.'

'I'll go there this evening.'

'Good man. Take care, won't you? If Harry's supposed to have—'

'Yes, I know.'

'Who's there in the room with you? I mean, besides Miss Watson. I've already spoken with her. Or rather, I've already had her screaming at me that you were being murdered before her eyes.'

Hepton's smile returned. Yes, ten minutes ago, Villiers had held a knife to his throat. Yet now he could smile about it, could brush it aside and get on with whatever action was necessary. He felt changed inside, in some profound way. He felt stronger.

'Sanders is here.'

'Sanders?' Parfit recognised the name. 'He's a good man. Take him with you when you go to see Devereux. Any sign of Villiers?'

'I think he's escaped.'

'Hmm. Well, he can't get far. Put Sanders on, would you?'

'Sure.' Hepton held the receiver out. 'Parfit wants a word,' he said.

Sanders looked at the telephone as though it might be about to bite him. Hepton didn't know who or what Parfit was, but he knew he was important enough for the mere mention of his name to scare Sanders half to death. He jabbed the receiver towards the young man, who licked his lips and stepped forward to take it from him. Gingerly, the way someone might handle a snake for the very first time.

'Hello?' Sanders said.

Hepton went over to Jilly and quietly filled her in on the details of his conversation with both Dreyfuss and Parfit. She listened sporadically, still shocked from the earlier struggle.

'I should have clouted him,' she said, replaying the moment over and over again in her head. 'I should have helped you, Martin. But instead I just stood there, yelling into the bloody telephone. Asking someone in *America* to help. Isn't that crazy?' And she gave a tiny, nervous laugh.

He hugged her, and felt her arms pull him inwards, and the feel of her brought back such memories . . .

'Er . . .?' The voice was Sanders'. 'Miss Watson?' She relaxed her hold on Hepton. 'Major Dreyfuss would like a word.'

Hepton couldn't help but feel a twinge of jealousy at Jilly's reaction. She let go of him, a schoolgirl grin appearing on her face, and almost skipped to the telephone.

'Mickey? Hello there. How are you? Did you get my flowers? You did! I tried telephoning the hospital but I could never get through.'

Sanders seemed embarrassed as he approached Hepton, his eyes everywhere but on Hepton's own. His voice when he spoke was muted.

'Look, about Mr Villiers . . .'

'Villiers is a maniac,' hissed Hepton. 'You people have known that all along, but he was useful to you so you conveniently ignored the fact. What's more, he's working with another bloody maniac called Harry.'

'But I don't understand. What has he done?'

Hepton considered this. There was no way of knowing, not without apprehending Villiers himself, or perhaps talking to the American, Devereux. He shrugged.

'What was Parfit saying?'

'You're to be given twenty-four-hour protection. Meantime, we'll put out a full-scale search for Mr Villiers. Well, not exactly *we*, since it'll have to be handled by the other lot.'

'The other lot?'

'You'd probably call them MI5.'

'What about Parfit?'

'He's MI6.' Sanders was perking up now. 'That's who I work for.'

'And presumably who Villiers works for too?'

Sanders stared at him. 'Yes, well . . .'

Hepton heard Jilly laugh, and glanced across to where she was sitting, perched on the edge of the desk, looking relaxed and with the telephone cord playfully twisted around one finger. Funny how people could change from moment to moment . . . She was ending her conversation. She dropped the receiver back into its cradle and hugged herself, looking radiant.

'He sounds fine,' she said.

'Yes,' Hepton agreed.

'I just wish . . .' But she didn't finish the sentence. Hepton was looking sad, and right now she felt like cheering up the whole world. She came to him and hugged him to her. Then pulled away to examine his face. 'We're going to be all right too, aren't we, Martin?'

'Of course we are,' he said, sounding more confident than he felt. He reached into his pocket and brought out the kitchen knife. 'As long as we've got this,' he said. Jilly recognised it.

'That's from my kitchen!' she cried. Then she laughed and hugged him again. 'What were you going to do with it? It's as blunt as my editor's sense of humour.'

'I don't know,' Hepton said. He was still studying the knife, trying to answer her question. 'I think I was going to kill Villiers with it.'

'Ugh!' said Jilly, giving a little shiver. 'What happened to him anyway?'

'He can't be found in the building,' Sanders explained, his voice taking on a tone of apology. 'We're still looking.'

'But how hard?' asked Hepton. 'How hard are you looking? Who else is in on this thing besides Villiers and Harry? It seems to stretch halfway around the world as it is!'

Sanders' voice became a monotone. 'You can trust me,' he said. 'Now if you'll excuse me, I'll be back in a few minutes. Would you like anything? More tea? Something stronger?'

'I could murder a gin,' said Jilly.

Hepton realised that his own throat was dry. He nodded.

'Two G and Ts then,' said Sanders, opening the door. 'I'll see what I can do.'

True to his word, two dusty glasses were delivered by a bemused security man a few minutes later. Hepton sank his in two gulps, then sucked on the tiny slice of lemon. Jilly savoured hers, reclining in Villiers' chair, her feet on the desk.

'Cheers,' she said.

'And don't we deserve it,' observed Hepton.

The door opened again and Sanders re-entered, looking pleased with himself.

'Right,' he said. 'It's about that knife of yours.'

'The Sabatier?' Jilly's face was quizzical.

'That's right,' said Sanders. He was unbuttoning his jacket. 'Anyway, you won't be needing it now.' He tugged the left side of his jacket open. Strapped beneath his shoulder was a brown leather holster, from the top of which peeped the butt of a small, fat handgun. '*This*,' he said, 'is what we need. Especially when dealing with Harry. Now, shall we go?'

23

On the way to the Park Lane Achilles Hotel, Sanders told them about Harry.

'It was four or five years ago. I'd just joined the department . . .'

What department? Hepton was tempted to ask.

'I remember meeting Mr Parfit for the first time. He struck the fear of God into me.'

Sanders seemed excited. Hepton decided that the secret agent hadn't seen much action in his musty set of offices. He didn't appear to be over-experienced either, driving a little too fast, potentially attracting attention. And now that he had been assigned to protect Hepton and Jilly, he was much less reticent, much more talkative, much more like a human being.

Hepton wondered why it was, then, that he liked him less this way.

'Mr Parfit had spent months on the case. There was going to be an assassination attempt.' He turned to them. 'I won't say on whom. But the identity of the assassin was what we couldn't uncover. We were looking for a regular, you see, a Carlos the Jackal or whatever. But it turned out to be a woman, a young and good-looking one at that.'

Hepton could feel Jilly bristling at this.

'The beautiful Harriet, in other words,' Sanders continued, unaware of Jilly's glowering face. 'She was the assassin.'

'So what happened?'

'Oh, Parfit tracked her down, or at least his team did. She did a runner and was never heard from again. Until now.'

'What about Villiers?' Hepton asked, his voice as neutral as an idling engine. Not that the Cavalier's engine *was* idling. Sanders pulled past some evening traffic and cut into the stream again just ahead of a purring Jaguar.

'I've worked with Mr Villiers for two years. When I started with him, I was told he was a bit . . . well, that he might be prone to . . . outbursts.'

'What did his job entail?'

'Nothing very much. He just waited. When advice was needed on one of his specialities, he'd be called for.'

'That must have been tedious.'

Sanders nodded. 'He hated it. Desk-bound after years of combat training. God knows, I'd hate it too in his position. They say he was a great soldier.'

'You mean good at killing people?' Jilly asked. Sanders reddened, but didn't answer.

'Did you ever suspect he might be involved in something?' Hepton asked him. 'Something you weren't allowed to know about?'

Sanders shook his head. 'Mr Parfit asked me a similar question on the telephone back there. I'll tell you what I told him: I didn't suspect anything. I'm still not sure that I do . . . I mean, it could all be some ghastly mistake, couldn't it?'

'No,' said Hepton flatly. 'No mistake.'

The car had reached the top of the Mall. Buckingham Palace lay directly in front of them. Hepton watched intently as a slow-moving line of army trucks approached from the other direction and drove past, heading in the direction of Trafalgar Square.

'There's a lot of troop movement at the moment,' said Sanders, attempting a change of subject. 'To do with the pull-out, I suppose. I'm against it myself. The pull-out, I mean. I think most people are.'

'Not me,' said Jilly. 'I'm glad they're going.'

Sanders stared at her in his rear-view mirror but kept his thoughts on her politics to himself.

'What about Harry?' asked Jilly. 'What else do you know about her?'

'We don't know much,' Sanders admitted. 'But there was plenty of speculation at the time. Fifteen years ago, a brigadier general's unruly daughter went missing in Germany. She left a note saying she was running away. She was fifteen, rebellious. A lot of anarchist literature was found in her bedroom.'

'And her name was Harriet?' Jilly suggested.

'No,' said Sanders. 'Her name wasn't Harriet. But her mother's name had been. Her mother was dead. The story went that the general used to get roaring drunk and hit his wife, made her life hell. She committed suicide when the daughter was eight or nine.'

'Well, well,' said Hepton, very quietly, filing this information away.

Hyde Park Corner came next, and then they were sweeping into Park Lane itself. Sanders entered the right-hand-turning lane and cut across the oncoming traffic, bringing the car to a stop outside a flat-fronted hotel of marble and smoked glass, which seemed very similar to the other hotels clustered around it. Three steps led to a line of six glass doors, behind which lay tantalising glances of a marble reception hall lit by sparkling chandeliers. In front of the steps stood a liveried doorman, and above him was a large canopy proclaiming the single word *Achilles*.

Sanders got out of the car and locked his door. When Hepton closed his own door, he watched the button on the inside of the window slide neatly into place of its own accord.

'A wonderful thing, central locking,' he mused.

Jilly was staring at the hotel's frontage. 'The things I'd do for a long, hot bath,' she said.

The doorman was coming towards them. 'You can't leave it there, sir,' he called, gesturing towards the Cavalier.

Sanders reached into his inside pocket and brought out a wallet, which he flipped open.

'A security matter,' he said. 'We shouldn't be too long.'

The doorman studied the ID carefully. 'Well,' he said at last, 'I suppose that'll be all right then. Want the manager, do you?'

'That's quite all right.' Sanders beamed back at him. 'We'll manage.' He moved past the doorman and up the steps.

'I thought he was supposed to be our bodyguard?' Jilly whispered as they followed, leaving the bemused doorman staring at their backs.

'He is.'

'Well he's not doing a very good job then, is he?'

'He's a bit too keen on playing the spy,' Hepton agreed. 'We can't afford to relax, Jilly. I think we're going to have to cover our own backs, rather than depending on Mr Sanders to do it for us.'

'Well, as long as we've got the kitchen knife, we should be safe,' said Jilly.

They entered the hotel lobby. The doorman was looking at the car now, checking colour, make and registration. Then he walked briskly up the steps and pushed open the doors. The car's occupants were at the reception desk, their backs turned to him. He went to a bank of public telephones along the wall nearest the door, picked up a receiver, inserted a ten-pence piece and dialled seven digits. He had to wait seconds only for a response.

'Achilles,' he said, identifying himself. 'I need to speak to Mr Vitalis.'

'Mr Devereux, please,' Sanders said to the woman behind the reception desk. She was wearing an identity badge and a well-worn smile.

'Room two-two-seven,' she said. 'Can I call him for you?'

'No thanks. That's floor two, room twenty-seven?' Sanders checked. The woman nodded, not about to waste a spoken answer. 'Thank you,' he said, turning from her. He stood for a moment, seeming to be deciding between the lift and the stairs. 'Stairs,' he said finally.

'You take the stairs,' Jilly objected. 'I'll take the lift. It's been a long day.'

Sanders stared at her. 'A lift is a trap, remember that. Once you're inside, there's no way out.' He started walking towards the pink-carpeted staircase. 'I'll see you up there,' he called.

Jilly looked to Hepton for a decision. Hepton shrugged his shoulders. Wearily they began to follow Sanders. He was right, though, that was the annoying part. He had obviously had some training in this sort of thing, while they were amateurs.

They climbed, counting the seventy-two steps to the second floor. The corridor was vacant, little noise coming from the rooms themselves. This was a hotel for the wealthy – businessmen as well as holidaymakers. And the wealthy had gone out to play in the London evening. Two things struck Hepton at the same time. The first was that Devereux might not be in; the second was that someone of his standing shouldn't be able to afford the Achilles. Hepton had seen the three-figure room charges displayed beside the desk.

They passed an ice machine, a drinks dispenser and an electrically operated shoeshine, then stopped outside a door.

Room 227. Sanders paused, listened, then knocked. There was silence. He knocked again. Nothing. He rested his hand on the door handle and checked that the corridor was still empty. As he was about to turn the handle, the door was opened from within. A man in shirt and trousers stood there, hair unkempt, the shirt rumpled, socks but no shoes on his feet. He had obviously been awakened from a nap, and was trying to stifle a yawn. When he saw that the three figures outside his door were not members of the hotel staff, he widened his eyes a little, trying to rouse himself.

'Yeah?' he said.

'Mr Devereux?' Sanders had fixed a sympathetic smile to his face.

'That's right.' His voice was American. There was an innocence to it that Hepton had noted before with American accents.

'Mr Devereux, my name's Sanders, I'm from the Foreign Office. We've come to talk to you about Major Michael Dreyfuss.'

'About Mike?' Devereux was wide awake now. A note of anxiety crept into his voice. 'What's wrong? Jesus, don't tell me he's up and died?'

'Oh no, he's quite fine. But he did telephone from America. He wanted us to talk with you.'

Devereux took in all three faces individually, wary still. Then he threw out an arm and pulled the door open to its fullest extent. 'You'd better come in,' he said. But looking into his room, at the sprawl and untidiness there, he seemed to change his mind. 'No, wait, on second thoughts, let me meet you in the bar in five minutes.'

Sanders seemed disapproving, but managed to keep the smile more or less intact. 'Right you are,' he said.

The door closed, leaving the three of them out in the corridor, much as they had been before.

'Sounds good to me,' Jilly said. 'One of you men can buy me a very large drink.' She was already heading back towards the stairs. Hepton began to follow, but saw that Sanders was staring at Devereux's door, his bottom lip clasped between upper and lower teeth.

'What's wrong?' he asked.

'How do we know he'll come to the bar?' Sanders whispered. 'I mean, he could do a runner.'

'He didn't look the running type,' Hepton offered, turning to follow Jilly.

Sanders watched him go, in an agony of sorts: should he stay and wait for Devereux, or follow his charges? A low growl left him, and he stalked back down the corridor after them.

It took Jilly less than a minute to finish her first gin. She examined the tall glass, still half full of unmelted ice.

'Better make it a double next time,' she said. She caught the waiter's attention and he walked smilingly towards her, knowing a potentially good customer when he saw one. Jilly ordered her double, but Hepton and Sanders shook their heads. Hepton was nursing a half-pint of lager, Sanders a tomato juice. They were seated at a corner table – at Sanders' insistence – from which they could watch the door to the hotel lobby and still have a view of the other occupants of the cocktail lounge. Not that there were many occupants to watch. The resident pianist was playing to a table of four well-dressed women, their clothes younger than their years. They applauded every tune, but quietly, politely, and he bowed his head each time, accepting gracefully, as he hoped to accept their drinks and their tips.

Two businessmen stood at the bar, slowly smoking cigars, sipping whiskies. They glanced around the room occasionally, looking first at the table of women and then over towards Jilly. They weren't hopeful; just looking.

'This is nice,' Jilly said without much attempt at sincerity.

Then Sanders, who had been the most subdued of the three, almost leapt from his seat, waving frantically towards the door, where Cam Devereux was standing. Devereux saw him and approached the table. Sanders sat down again, looking relieved and more animated again. Devereux squeezed into the booth beside Hepton. He had washed, changed his clothes and combed his hair. He had also had time to think, and was more wary than ever, as his first question showed.

'Who did you say you were?'

But the waiter was walking briskly in their direction, awaiting Devereux's order.

'Glenlivet, plenty of ice,' Devereux said, just as briskly. When the waiter had gone, he repeated his question. Sanders was about to respond, but Hepton beat him to it.

'I'm Martin Hepton. This is Jill Watson.'

'And you both work for the Foreign Office, too?'

'No,' said Jilly. 'We're friends of Mickey.'

'Mickey? You mean Mike Dreyfuss? How long have you known him?'

'Since school,' Jilly answered.

Devereux nodded slowly. 'I haven't known him more than six months,' he said. 'But he seemed like a great guy.'

'No need for the past tense,' Sanders said. 'He's still alive, remember.'

'Yeah.' Devereux's voice was like melting ice. His drink arrived and he gulped at it.

'This is a nice hotel,' Sanders noted aloud. 'It must be costing you a fortune.'

Devereux smiled and looked straight at Sanders as if to say: I know what your game is. 'I'm not paying for it,' he admitted. 'My employers are picking up the tab. Necessary R and R.'

Sanders was relentless. '*Is* it necessary?'

'Hell, yes,' Devereux said loudly. 'You ever see guys you'd gotten to know torched in the blink of an eye? Guys you respected suddenly dead, and all the time they're dying you think maybe you can do something to help, but you can't? Jesus!' His face was red now, and his voice had grown deeper. There was a silence at the table while they waited for him to calm down.

'Another drink?' asked Hepton, whose own glass was empty.

'Look,' Devereux said, 'let's just cut the shit, okay? What do you want?'

Hepton didn't know quite where to start, but both Jilly and Sanders had turned to him, expecting him to speak. 'Major Dreyfuss telephoned us,' he began. 'He was wondering what you know about the crash.'

'What's it to you anyway?'

'Our lives are in danger,' Jilly said quickly, 'and we want to know why. We're scared.'

Devereux seemed confused. '*Your* lives?'

'And that of Mike Dreyfuss,' Hepton continued. 'You see, I work at the control base for the *Zephyr* satellite, and somehow that satellite is tied up with the *Argos* shuttle. It looks as though the shuttle was trying to tap into *Zephyr*. We don't know why. Maybe *Zephyr* was doing something – something secret and something somebody wanted to know about.'

'Send a satellite to trap a satellite, huh?'

Hepton smiled. 'Maybe. But then the shuttle crashed, making the whole thing look like a suicide mission.'

'Not suicide,' Devereux said sharply, examining his empty glass. 'Murder. Sabotage, if you like.' He took a deep breath. 'Hell, I don't know why I'm telling you this . . . or maybe I do.'

He paused again, as if thinking things through. Then he began to speak.

'The day of the launch,' he said, 'some new guy turned up in the control room. He had a console tucked away in a far corner. A console they'd brought in the previous week. Well, he told me his name, but not much else. I can't even remember now what he said his name was. He knew what he was doing, though; I mean, he knew how to operate the computer, but he wasn't like one of us. I took a look at his screen that day, and he was in touch with the onboard computer. It was as if he knew something we didn't.'

'Such as?' asked Hepton.

'Such as that the whole onboard computer program had been fixed before the shuttle went up, and all it needed was the touch of the right buttons in the right order to bring a doomsday code into operation.'

'A doomsday code?' The question was Jilly's.

'Self-destruct,' Hepton explained. '*Zephyr* has one too, in case it falls into the wrong hands.'

Sanders was enthralled. 'So this man caused the shuttle to malfunction?'

Devereux was staring into his glass still. He'd played these scenes out a hundred times before in his head. 'You should have seen his monitor. It was like a Christmas tree, all these lights . . .'

There was a pause. Hepton broke it. 'Did you tell anyone about this?' He was thinking how closely Devereux's story followed his own, or even Paul Vincent's.

'Yes,' Devereux said. 'That was when they *strongly* suggested that I take a holiday.'

Hepton nodded. 'So what's it all about, Cam?'

'Hell, I don't know. I don't *want* to know.' Devereux looked up from his glass at last. 'No, that's a lie. I *do* want to know. I can tell you this: that wasn't a comms satellite *Argos* was launching. It was something else, something secret. Something for the military. There were a couple of the chiefs on site to watch the launch . . .'

Hepton remembered the brass who had watched over his own side of things. It couldn't be a coincidence.

'. . . and I figured the satellite must be some kind of intelligence-gatherer. Maybe a communications intercept.'

'Did the rest of the crew know?'

'The ground staff knew, or at least we guessed.'

'But what about the shuttle crew?'

'Well, Mike Dreyfuss didn't know. But as for the rest of them . . .' Devereux shrugged his shoulders. 'What does it matter, they're dead now.' He turned suddenly and held his glass aloft, yelling towards the waiter, 'Another one of these!' Then he looked back at Hepton. 'Have I told you anything you didn't know?'

'Oh yes,' Hepton answered thoughtfully. 'Quite a lot.' There was one thing, one innocuous thing Devereux had said, that kept echoing in his head. *A communications intercept*. Something didn't ring true, but he couldn't think just what.

24

As Sanders drove them to the safe house in St John's Wood, Jilly dozed drunkenly in the back seat, her head resting in Hepton's lap. Hepton himself felt wide awake and stone-cold sober. He saw Devereux's face again as they took their leave of him at the Achilles Hotel. The American's eyes had looked dull and unfocused, a man tired of living; or at least of living with lies. A man haunted by his own fears.

From time to time, Hepton glanced back to see if any cars were following them, and each time he did so, Sanders would offer a confident 'I'd have spotted them by now.' Which didn't make Hepton feel any easier. The late-evening traffic was dense, and as they stopped at lights alongside a black cab, Hepton studied the foreign-looking male passenger, who, catching his eye, bowed his head slightly as though in acknowledgement before the lights turned green and both vehicles moved off.

'Why St John's Wood?' he asked Sanders.

'Because that's where the nearest Security Service safe house is.'

'But you're not MI5, are you?' Hepton didn't know much about spies, but he did know that MI5 – the Security Service – handled intelligence work at home, while MI6 – the Secret Intelligence Service – covered foreign operations.

'Yes,' Sanders agreed, 'but unfortunately the Security Service has to be in on this too. After all, we're *in* Britain. This is their territory. But since the United States is involved also . . .'

'It's a joint operation, then?'

'I believe there have been a couple of meetings today to clarify the situation. Not that we enjoy working together, you understand. It's a matter of trust.' Sanders glanced round at Hepton. 'You're lucky, actually. Their safe houses are a bit nicer than ours.' He smiled.

They passed Lord's Cricket Ground and continued up Wellington Road. Hepton had vague memories of a student party he had attended twenty years ago at a flat somewhere near Grove End Road. The hostess' parents had bought the place for her. The night of the party, her friends had done their level best to wreck it. So much for peace and love.

Sanders turned left off Wellington Road and drove slowly down a narrower street of detached and semi-detached houses, some of them compact, others rising to three and four storeys. He stopped beside one of the smaller detached houses and flashed his lights once. A man appeared from nowhere and opened the garage attached to the side of the house. Sanders negotiated the car into the space and switched off the engine. Behind them, the garage doors were being pulled shut again, though the man operating them remained outside.

'Home sweet home,' Sanders said. 'You lucky swine can get some rest now. I've still to write my report and meet with my bosses.'

The garage lights came on, and Hepton eased Jilly out of the back of the car. Sanders had opened another door, connecting with the house itself. Together they helped Jilly through it, along a carpeted hall and into a small, well-furnished living room, where she collapsed onto the sofa. Sanders pushed his hair back into place and straightened his tie.

'Journalists,' he said, staring at Jilly. 'Right, I'd better be off. There are two bedrooms upstairs. Kitchen on the other side of the hall. Toilet next to the door to the garage, and bathroom upstairs. I think one of the bedrooms even has an en suite.'

'All mod cons,' said Hepton. 'Is there a telephone?'

'Yes, but I shouldn't try using it. It just routes you straight through to a watcher team.'

'Watcher?'

'Surveillance.'

Hepton glanced around the room. 'Bugged?' he asked.

Sanders shrugged his shoulders. 'Oh,' he said, remembering something. 'And if you need anything, either pick up the phone or tap on the kitchen window. There are a couple of security men front and back. Otherwise, sleep tight.' He made to leave.

'See you in the morning,' said Hepton.

A few minutes later, he heard the car start up and reverse out of the garage. He went to the living room window to peer out. A tiny front garden separated the house from the pavement and the street beyond. Sanders' Cavalier backed noisily into the road and started off, gathering speed. Hepton could see no sign of the security man, who presumably was closing the garage doors again. In the lamplight on the other side of the road, an overdressed woman stopped to let the tiny dog she was walking do its business in the gutter. She looked middle-aged, her face heavily made up. Hepton stared hard through the window at her, trying to find Harry's features beneath the make-up. But he couldn't. And the woman didn't even glance across the street. She just watched her dog, cooing at it, and then walked on again, her heels noisy in the silence of the night.

Hepton turned towards Jilly. Her eyes were open and she looked around in bemused fashion, studying this new environment.

'Where are we?' she asked, her voice slurred.

'Come on,' he said, feeling himself relax for what seemed the first time in days, 'I'll show you to your room.'

Hepton's sleep was dreamless, and he awoke early, refreshed. He ran a bath and lay in it until the water turned from hot to tepid. There was a portable radio on the windowsill, and he switched it on, letting the morning's news programme wash over him like so much water. There were traffic reports, relaying stories of five- and six-mile tailbacks on some of the roads into London. The world, it seemed, kept on going as though it were just another day, and in London that meant millions of people setting off to work.

The thought was too much. He sank beneath the water, then surfaced again. Drying himself, he switched off the radio so he could concentrate. There was an idea in his head, an idea about what was going on. But what could he do with it? That was the problem: apart from Jilly, there was no one he could trust, not completely. So he mulled over his idea and tried to fit together the remaining pieces of the puzzle.

In the kitchen, he found all he needed to make breakfast. There was bacon in the fridge, and eggs, butter and milk. A fresh loaf of bread sat on the breakfast bar, along with a new carton of orange juice, a jar of coffee and a pack of tea bags. There were pots of honey and marmalade in the cupboard, and a bowl of sugar, too. Everything had the look of having been put there only the day before.

He set to work, and even found a tray to put everything on before climbing the stairs. Outside Jilly's room he paused, wondering whether it was necessary to knock. It wasn't. The door opened suddenly from inside, and there stood Jilly, already dressed and looking fit and well. There were no signs of the night before, other than dark patches beneath her eyes.

'Good morning,' she said, opening the door wide to let him in. 'Is that for me?'

She sat on the edge of the bed and accepted the tray, draining the glass of orange juice before starting on the food.

'Aren't you having any?' she asked, chewing on a triangle of toast.

'Not hungry,' Hepton said. He sat on the padded stool beside the dressing table. Then he noticed that her hair, though drying, was wet. 'How long have you been awake?' he asked.

'Not long,' she answered. 'I heard you in the bathroom, so I got up and took a shower.'

Yes, he had forgotten she was in the room with the en suite. 'So how are you feeling?'

'My head's a bit groggy. I suppose I drank too much. But then we didn't have anything to eat last night, did we?'

'No, we didn't,' said Hepton, recalling that this was true. Neither of them had professed much of an appetite after the events of the afternoon.

Suddenly he heard a noise on the staircase, feet moving upstairs. He turned his head towards the open doorway just as Sanders appeared there. If anything, the young man was more smartly dressed than ever. He wore a stiff-looking pinstripe suit, with polished black shoes, white shirt and plum-coloured silk tie. Hepton wondered if perhaps he had been promoted overnight.

'Ah, good,' Sanders said. 'You've eaten.' This was plainly not true: Jilly had not yet touched the plate of bacon and egg. 'Sorry to rush you,' he continued, 'but there's a meeting in forty minutes at HQ. They'd like you to be there.'

'Who would?' Jilly asked through a mouthful of toast.

'Wait and see,' said Sanders, obviously flustered. 'Now come on, will you, please. The traffic's diabolical out there.'

They headed back towards the West End, Sanders driving with even less grace than usual. Hepton asked about George Villiers.

'We've scoured the FO building. No trace of him. There are guards outside his flat, but he hasn't been back there either. He does own a house somewhere in Scotland, but I think it unlikely he'd go there, although we're keeping an eye on it. No, he's vanished. But don't worry. If he pops his head up from the trenches, we'll have him.' He grinned at them.

Jilly gripped the back of the passenger seat and pulled herself forward. Sanders flinched instinctively.

'This is serious, you imbecile,' she said.

Then she sat back again, bathing in Sanders' silence. Hepton patted her knee affectionately and she winked at him. It had been a performance, but that wasn't to say she hadn't meant it.

As they neared Park Lane, Hepton decided that their destination must be the Achilles Hotel again, but they continued past it, then snaked left into Curzon Street. The Cavalier pulled abruptly into the side of the road and stopped. Someone opened the rear door from outside.

'Go with him,' Sanders ordered, sounding not a little petulant. Hepton and Jilly got out of the car, and the man who had been holding open the door now closed it. He was much the same age as Sanders, and dressed only a little less well.

'If you'll follow me,' he said as Sanders drove off. Then he took them up to and through the imposing doors of the Security Service's main headquarters.

There were six of them seated around an oval table of antique design but modern construction. When they had made themselves comfortable, the man at the head of the table called out, 'Thank you,' and the door was closed from the outside by one of two security men. Jilly and Hepton sat together, their section of the table blank and highly polished. In front of the others – three men and one woman (who had smiled conspiratorially towards Jilly, but not at Hepton) – were brown files and differing quantities of paper: typed reports, minutes, even a photograph or two. The man at the head of the table ran a hand over his face, as though checking the closeness of his morning shave.

'It's good of you to come,' he began. 'My name is Sir Laurence Strong.' He was in his seventies, but his physique still matched his name, and he had a head of thick silvered hair. Nor did he appear to require spectacles, though in these days of contact lenses it was impossible to tell for sure. He introduced himself as 'Sir' not out of any wish to impress, but because it was a fact. 'This,' he continued, gesturing towards the woman, 'is my personal assistant, Louisa Marchant.' She smiled again, including Hepton in her compass this time. She was younger than Sir Laurence, in her early sixties perhaps. Smaller and plumper, too, with steel-rimmed glasses behind which her sharp blue eyes glistened. Sir Laurence now nodded in the direction of a man of similar age to himself. 'Allow me to introduce—' It was as far as he got.

'Blast you, Laurence, I can make my own introductions.' The man turned to Hepton and Jilly. His face was stern, as though he were late for something else of more importance. What Sanders had said was true: the two intelligence services did not get on, even at their upper echelons. 'Blake Farquharson,' the man said. Then, with a glance towards Sir Laurence, 'Not yet knighted. This is *my* assistant, Tony Poulson.' His finger was stabbing towards the man next to him, who nodded agreement. Farquharson and Poulson were like young-and-old versions of the same person: same thinning hair, same thick black-rimmed glasses, same grimly set faces and worry lines.

'Fine,' said Jilly. 'We know who you are now, but not *what* you are.'

'Of course.' This from Sir Laurence again, seeming more urbane with every moment. 'I'm director general of what you probably know as MI5.'

'Ditto MI6,' snapped Farquharson.

Jilly nodded satisfaction, trying to look less impressed than she actually felt. She knew journalists who would give their non-writing arm for the chance to sit in the same room as the heads of both intelligence services.

'So,' said Hepton, 'what can we do for you?'

'Well, for a start,' said Sir Laurence, 'bearing in mind that Miss Watson is a journalist, though with no disrespect to that estimable profession' – there were smirks at this – 'we would remind you both that you have signed the Official Secrets Act. Now, that being understood, really what we'd like is your version of events thus far.'

Jilly nodded towards the file in front of him. 'Isn't it all in there?'

He laid a proprietorial hand on the cover of the file. 'Oh yes,' he said. 'But these are . . . facts. What we'd like now are opinions, thoughts.'

'Thoughts?' She leaned forward in her chair. 'I've been doing plenty of thinking this past day, and I'll tell you what I think.' Hepton had to admire her. Coming to London had made her more assertive, not afraid to voice her opinions or to ask for other people's. She held up one finger. 'I think you don't want the American troops to pull out of Britain.' Another finger. 'I think the military is planning a coup, and I think you're going to let them do it.' A third. 'I think they're being aided by the Americans, and I think both countries are going to turn themselves into fortresses.' She paused, but no one seemed ready to refute her allegations, so she continued. 'What I'd *like* to know is how much the government knows.' The three fingers became one, pointed straight at Sir Laurence. 'How much do *you* know? The prime minister *is* still head of the Security Service, isn't that right?'

Sir Laurence took this outburst quite calmly – they all took it calmly. He cleared his throat. 'Yes,' he said, 'that much is true, Miss Watson. The PM is titular head of the Security Service. However, as for your other . . . thoughts, I'm afraid they are rather off-beam. I'll admit, though, that we had been thinking along similar lines ourselves. We've had inklings, for example, that something is simmering, and that the chefs are the chiefs of staff of our own armed forces. That much is true. A coup seemed a feasible explanation. However, it was difficult to go to the PM with what were merely inklings—'

'Especially now,' interrupted Farquharson, his voice more reasonable than before, and obviously not wishing Strong to be allowed to tell too much of the story by himself. 'What with NATO bickering, and this blasted pull-out and all. You see, the military bigwigs have been whingeing, and they've also been currying favour within Parliament, seeking out supporters, that sort of thing. In the current climate, the government wants to remain on friendly terms with the military, so anything we might say would in all likelihood be taken as paranoia or even jealousy. Though,' he added as an afterthought, 'both *those* notions are preposterous.'

Having had his say, he sat back and folded his arms. Sir Laurence continued. 'What Blake is saying is that we couldn't find many friendly ears to listen to us. Yet we *knew* something was going to happen.'

'So,' asked Hepton, 'just what *is* happening?' Jilly's notion of a coup had crossed his mind too, but he had rejected it for something a little more frightening.

There was silence in the room as eyes sought out other eyes, looking for answers. Sir Laurence spoke first.

'We aren't sure. We planted agents in some of the more important military offices – new clerical help, that sort of thing. Risky, and so far we've been able to shed no new light.'

'And meanwhile,' interrupted Farquharson, 'I've got agents abroad trying to find out what they can.'

'Including Parfit,' stated Hepton. Farquharson glowered at him.

'Yes,' he said, 'including Parfit. He's one of our best men. I hope you'll be able to meet him.'

'What does that mean?' asked Jilly, frowning incomprehension.

'It means,' said Farquharson, 'that he's on his way here. And bringing Major Dreyfuss with him. Things are getting too uncertain in the States, and we want the major out of there. Now, tell us about your meeting with Cameron Devereux . . .'

Part IV

Theoretically, the smallest size that can be detected by spy satellites is just a few inches. Not quite enough to read the headlines on a newspaper but enough to tell what kind of newspaper you are reading. There is not a square inch of the globe that cannot be photographed or monitored in this way. Somewhere, deep in a vault in the Pentagon and its Soviet equivalent, there is a photograph which if magnified will reveal your house and the make of car you are driving away from it. Oh, and be careful what you say on your car telephone.

Guardian, 13 March 1987

25

They left the embassy compound in a van that claimed to belong to *DC Hygiene*. Dreyfuss, dressed in overalls and uneasy in the passenger seat, asked Parfit – also in overalls and driving – what the company did.

'They deliver roller towels for the toilets, that sort of thing. Gum?'

He noticed that Parfit was offering him a stick of chewing gum.

'No thanks,' he said.

'Take one,' Parfit ordered. 'Delivery men around here all seem to chew gum.'

Dreyfuss took the stick, unwrapped it and folded it into his mouth. Parfit did the same, then popped the tube back into his overall pocket. He was checking in his wing mirrors. There was a car following them, but that was okay – it was from the embassy, and would stay with them for the next few miles until they could be sure no one else was on their tail. Until then, they were due to drive around – not too fast, not too slow, just driving – as though between destinations. When Parfit was satisfied, they would head out to the airport, where another car filled with his men would be waiting, watching to see that they made it to the terminal building without incident. He had arranged for two more men to be posted inside the terminal building itself, but after that, once they had headed into the departure lounge, they were on their own.

'You seem to have plenty of men at your disposal,' Dreyfuss had said when told the plan.

'I'm using just about every member of staff the embassy has,' Parfit had replied, smiling. 'When Johnnie finds out, he'll be livid.

The embassy's going to be deserted apart from himself and a few typists. I reckon our need might be greater than his.'

Dreyfuss tried not to think about it, but found himself thinking of nothing else. His mouth was dry, and the gum wasn't helping. He wanted to return to Britain, of course he did. But somehow the more plans Parfit concocted to make sure they would do so safely, the more worried Dreyfuss became, for if these precautions were necessary, surely the danger must be necessarily as great? Yet Parfit carried no gun, no weapon of any kind. *A weak man needs a weapon*, he had once told Dreyfuss. In that case, Dreyfuss thought now, I must be weak as a deathbed grandmother. For the thought of a very large gun was all that seemed to soothe him just at the moment.

'Relax,' Parfit said; it sounded like another command. 'We're only delivery men, just driving around doing our job. We don't need to look so tense or grip the seat like that.'

Dreyfuss looked down and saw that his hands were indeed clenching either side of his seat, the knuckles white. He loosened them and folded his arms instead.

'You still look tense,' Parfit said.

'That's because I *am* tense, for Christ's sake. If I try to let my arms hang down, I just know I'll end up waving them wildly and screaming to be let out of here.'

Parfit laughed. Dreyfuss wasn't sure he had heard him laugh before, and found the sound strangely reassuring.

They drove in silence for a while, until they were crossing the Potomac River.

'We may as well take a look at the Pentagon while we're here,' said Parfit. 'After all, you *did* want to see a bit of the United States, didn't you? It said so on your application form for the *Argos* mission.'

Dreyfuss turned to him. 'You're enjoying all this,' he hissed.

'I enjoy my work, yes,' Parfit admitted. 'Sometimes I do, anyway. Haven't you ever been part of a team who had a rival team? At football, maybe, or cricket?'

'I was never very interested in sports.'

'Well,' said Parfit, unperturbed, 'try to imagine it. Here's us, and we're up against the military – people like Esterhazy.'

'You seem to forget that *I'm* military,' Dreyfuss said.

Parfit glanced towards him. 'Well, try to set that aside for a moment. So it's an us-and-them situation, and I want *us* to win the game.'

'But it isn't a game.'

'Yet in many ways it is *exactly* that. And if you forget that it's a game, you start playing the wrong way. So far, the opposition has been in a strong position, because we don't know what they're up to. But now they've started making mistakes – letting you live was only the first. People are getting suspicious, people like your friend Hepton. And to cover their mistakes, they – whoever they ultimately are – are starting to take bigger and bigger chances, which only force them further and further into the open. So yes, I *am* enjoying myself, because at last I think we've got a chance of beating them. What about you?'

'I'm delirious,' said Dreyfuss blandly, causing Parfit to laugh again, louder this time.

After another half-hour or so, Parfit decided that they should stop at a roadside café.

'I thought we were supposed to keep driving?' said Dreyfuss.

'We're still early,' replied Parfit. 'And I'd rather we spent the spare time away from the airport. Nobody's following us, so why not stop for a coffee?'

'Okay, if you say so,' Dreyfuss said.

They pulled into a parking area beside a large café proclaiming *ALL DAY ALL NIGHT BREAKFAST/BURGER*. It wasn't until Dreyfuss was studying the large, plastic-coated menu, seated beside Parfit in one of the booths by the window, that he realised this capitalised mouthful was in fact the name of the establishment.

A waitress approached, looking as well used as the dishcloth with which she wiped their table.

'What can I get you?' she asked tiredly.

'Just coffee, please,' said Parfit. Dreyfuss nodded. 'Two coffees,' Parfit corrected.

'Cream?'

Parfit nodded, and the waitress tore off a sheet from her pad, left it on their table and walked back towards the counter.

'Americans used to say "cream" and mean it,' Parfit said conversationally. 'Nowadays they almost always mean "creamer", and that's a polite way of saying "whitener", which in turn means monosodium glutamate. A long way from cream.' Dreyfuss didn't appear to be listening. 'You can't believe words any more,' Parfit continued.

Dreyfuss turned his head to look at him, then narrowed his eyes. 'What the hell are you talking about, Parfit?'

Parfit considered. 'Nothing,' he said, shrugging his shoulders.

'What exactly are we doing here?'

'I told you, killing time.'

'And I don't believe you.'

The door to the café was opening, bringing in another customer. Parfit leaned close to Dreyfuss' ear.

'Don't say anything about our leaving,' he whispered.

The man walked over towards Dreyfuss and Parfit's booth, then slid into the seat opposite them. It was Frank Stewart.

'Hello,' he said.

'Mr Stewart,' Parfit said by way of greeting.

'What's he doing here?' Dreyfuss' voice had become strained.

'Parfit thought we should meet,' said Stewart. He was admiring their uniforms. 'Nice disguise.'

'It's the only way to travel,' said Parfit.

'So what can I do for you?' said Stewart. The waitress was coming near. 'Coffee and a half-pound cheeseburger, medium rare,' he called. She nodded and started back to her counter, yelling the order through to the kitchen. Stewart shrugged. 'I'm starving,' he said.

'Yes,' said Parfit, 'I thought a little chat might be of benefit to both of us. Esterhazy's walking a very thin line.'

'Oh?'

'If you're able to keep a close watch on him, without his knowing, then you might be doing yourself a great service.'

'Keep talking,' said Stewart. He picked up a sachet of sugar, tore it open and emptied it into his mouth.

'There's not much more I can add,' said Parfit. 'I'll need a telephone number where I can contact you twenty-four hours a day.'

'You're doing this unsanctioned,' Stewart observed. 'That's a dangerous game for us both.' His eyes were interested but full of caution. He hadn't survived this long without covering every bet on the table.

'What makes you think—'

'Because,' Stewart interrupted, 'you stipulated this meeting be strictly off the books. That smacks to me of a solo outing, and I've never been keen on one-man shows.'

'This isn't exactly a one-man show,' Parfit said. 'But you're right. So far, there are more suspects than people I can rely on.'

'But you're willing to take a chance on relying on me? Why?'

'Because you want to nail Ben Esterhazy,' stated Parfit. The waitress was approaching with their order. The three mugs chinked together as she carried them.

'I can't argue with that,' Stewart said, chuckling. He stared at the burger as it was placed in front of him. 'No, sir,' he said, picking it up, 'I can't argue with that.'

Dreyfuss lifted his mug to his lips. He wasn't sure he liked the way Parfit seemed to be breaking the rules. He was certain that this meeting had been set up without the knowledge of anyone in the embassy. Sure, too, as Parfit's whispering had warned, that Stewart didn't know they were about to leave the country. Parfit was trying to have it all ways. He seemed confident that such was not only possible but entirely feasible. Yet Dreyfuss still wasn't sure of his motives or his ultimate goal.

He wasn't sure about anything any more.

They stayed long enough to finish their coffee, then left before Stewart, shaking his hand.

'Be careful out there,' he said, grease from the burger glistening on his lips.

Dreyfuss smiled but said nothing. He said nothing, in fact, the rest of the way to the airport. What was there he could say and be sure of getting a truthful answer to? Absolutely nothing.

The airport car park seemed, to Dreyfuss' eyes, to be full. An attendant told them as much, but Parfit insisted on driving around.

'Somebody's bound to be coming out,' he said. The attendant shrugged his shoulders and left them to it. Parfit knew exactly where he was going, however. He drove purposefully towards where two cars were parked side by side, their drivers reading newspapers. He blew four times on the van's horn, three short, one long, and the driver of one of the cars threw his paper onto the passenger seat, started his engine and drove off. With a certain amount of elegance, Parfit eased the van into the now vacant bay. He turned to Dreyfuss again. 'Easy when you know how,' he said. 'Right, you first.'

Dreyfuss had been told what to do. He got out, walking around to the rear of the van, where he opened the doors and pulled himself in, closing them after him. In the back of the van were two parcels, one marked 'P' and one 'D'. He opened the second package, revealing a two-piece suit, shirt, tie, socks and shoes. All in sober colours, and all in his size. He unzipped his overalls and began to change. Once he was dressed, he left the van again and got into the passenger seat of the second car, whose driver acknowledged his presence with a grunt and a 'You took your time,' before continuing with his reading.

Now Parfit went to the back of the van, reappearing less than two minutes later dressed in similar garb to Dreyfuss and looking more comfortable now that he had shed his workman's clothes. The driver saw him, folded his newspaper and got out of the car, moving to the van and climbing into the driver's side. Parfit meantime slid behind the steering wheel of the car. He watched as the driver moved off in the van, then looked left and right. Appearing satisfied, he touched Dreyfuss on the shoulder. Dreyfuss felt the touch like an electric spark, and flinched.

'Stay calm,' Parfit advised, 'for the next hour or so at least. Right, we're going in now.' He checked his watch. 'We'll go straight to Departures. Okay?'

Dreyfuss nodded and opened his door again. The car had a central-locking mechanism, and he watched as Parfit locked the driver's door and all four door locks engaged with a silent movement. Then Parfit opened the boot and brought out two small suitcases and two attaché cases. He handed one of each to Dreyfuss.

'Just some clothes, a few magazines, the usual stuff a businessman would take on a trip. Remember, we're only going to London for a couple of days. We're based in Washington—'

'At an international law firm. I remember.'

Parfit nodded. He seemed preoccupied now: perhaps he was growing just a little bit nervous himself. 'Oh,' he said, remembering something. He dug a hand into his jacket and brought out two passports, one of which he handed to Dreyfuss. 'There you go, Stephen.'

Dreyfuss opened the passport. It was a brilliant fake; in fact, it was more: it was for real. A real passport, bearing a real name: Stephen Jackson. Occupation: solicitor. Stamped with American visas, and with evidence of holidays spent in Greece, Canada, Tunisia. Next of kin: a father, Bernard Jackson, who lived in Dundee.

'There aren't too many Bernards in Dundee,' Dreyfuss commented. Parfit seemed to take this criticism seriously.

'Good point,' he said. 'I'll have a word with the chaps who make these up.'

The photograph was of Dreyfuss: of course it was. They'd had it taken only yesterday, at the embassy. But a make-up artist had erased a few lines from his face, and given more hair to his forehead. The result was that the man in the picture looked a few years younger; as young as he would have been when the passport was supposedly validated.

'I'll hang on to our tickets,' said Parfit. 'Okay?'

'Fine,' said Dreyfuss, slipping the passport into his jacket pocket. There was something else in there. He brought out a wallet. Opening it, he found money in dollars and sterling, a UK driving licence and three credit cards. 'Christ,' he whispered, amazed.

Parfit tapped the cards.

'Don't run up too much of a bill. We always ask for the money back sometime.' Then, having locked the boot, he was off. Dreyfuss picked up the attaché case and suitcase and hurried after him.

26

Dreyfuss was impressed by the performance. Parfit had assumed the brisk but awkward walk of the busy businessman, and even his face seemed to have grown new worry lines, his eyes proclaiming a head filled with spreadsheets and data analysis. There was no doubt about it: at the law firm, Parfit was the one who looked after the accounts. More, he made sure everybody paid.

Dreyfuss was no actor, however. He watched the other travellers intently, seeking out the potential assassin or arresting officer. There were video cameras trained on every angle of the building's interior. Somewhere in the security room, someone would be watching him. He prayed they wouldn't recognise him. His photograph had been in all the newspapers, hadn't it? They were sure to spot him.

They had joined the queue at their chosen airline's London check-in desk. The people in front of them looked innocent enough: businessmen mostly, one elderly couple, two young men travelling together. The young men had short hair and wore checked shirts and denims. They didn't have much luggage, either. But it was the haircuts that worried Dreyfuss. They looked like regulation down-to-the-wood cuts, the kind only an armed forces barber could perfect. Dreyfuss knew; he'd been there.

When the crew cuts got to the front of the queue, he tried to listen in on their conversation with the smiling clerk. It all seemed normal. Small talk. They wanted smoking seats, and there seemed to be a problem about this. At last, their seat numbers having been allocated, they headed off in the direction of the departures lounge, watched by Dreyfuss.

'Stephen?'

It took a moment for him to realise that Parfit was speaking – speaking to *him*. He was Stephen Jackson. But who was Parfit again? James Pardoe? Farlow? Yes, Farlow: James Farlow.

'What is it, James?' he said. He was perspiring now, and could hear his heart thumping through his inner ear. Parfit smiled at him, his eyes warning him not to panic.

'You need to put your suitcase in here.' He pointed to a gap in the desk where a set of rollers waited to send their suitcases hurtling down towards the baggage loading area. Dreyfuss nodded embarrassedly and handed over his case. 'There aren't any window seats left,' Parfit said. 'Is that okay?'

'I don't mind where I sit,' Dreyfuss blurted. The clerk was staring at him now. Dreyfuss attempted a grin, which seemed to frighten her further.

'Fear of flying,' Parfit explained to her, accepting the two boarding cards. 'He'll be fine once we're up.'

They walked towards the departures lounge, Dreyfuss on legs made of drinking straws filled with putty, Parfit looking a little less confident than before.

'Hang on in there,' he hissed.

'I'm trying,' Dreyfuss said. He was breathing deeply, trying to calm himself. Not much longer, he was thinking. Then I'll be home. Home and dry. 'What about the agents you said would be here to cover us? I haven't seen them.'

'They wouldn't be doing their job if you could recognise them. Don't worry, they were back there near the desk.'

'But we're on our own now, aren't we?' Dreyfuss whispered noisily.

'We can manage.'

Their tickets and boarding cards were checked again, and their briefcases put onto a conveyer belt that transported them through an X-ray machine. A man in a suit, a large plastic ID badge clipped to his breast pocket, gestured for them to walk through the metal-detecting gateway, after which he ran a hand-held, more sensitive detector over them. Then his assistant – an only-too-willing assistant, Dreyfuss thought – slid his hands down each man's suit, under the jacket collar and lapels, down the back, smoothly over the trousers and up along the inside legs.

'Thank you, sir,' he said to Dreyfuss with the hint of a smile. Dreyfuss did not smile back.

'I don't know about you,' Parfit said as they picked up their cases and walked on, 'but I need a drink.'

'Count me in,' said Dreyfuss. He was feeling calmer now. The worst was over, wasn't it? Then it struck him: the last time he had flown had been on a private jet, and the time before that . . . on *Argos*. His legs lost their rigidity again.

'Do you want anything in duty-free?' asked Parfit, pointing towards the glossy spending mall. Dreyfuss shook his head. 'I can never resist the malt,' Parfit said. 'Coming?'

'I think I'll just give my face a splash of water first,' Dreyfuss said, nodding towards where a door proclaimed itself the gents' toilets.

'Fine, I'll come with you.'

'People will begin to talk,' said Dreyfuss.

Parfit looked surprised. 'You just made a joke!' he said. 'That's more like it. Now come on, and stop looking so damned worried all the time.'

Only one cubicle was in use when they entered the toilets. Parfit gestured towards it and winked, reminding Dreyfuss not to break their cover. Dreyfuss nodded and, while Parfit went to the urinals, stood in front of the gleaming row of washbasins, examining his features in the splashed mirror. He looked fairly dreadful, like some old cancer patient: face pasty grey, eyes dark, cheeks hollow, and sweat cloying his hair. Another man came in and hurried into a cubicle, slamming the door shut after him. Dreyfuss heard him unbuckling his belt.

He ran some cold water and rested his hands in it for a few moments before starting to wash his face. He felt better almost immediately. Parfit was standing behind him, zipping himself.

'Ready?'

'Just give me a minute,' Dreyfuss said. 'I'll catch you up in duty-free.'

'Well . . .' Parfit looked dubious, but a glance at his watch told him they didn't have very long before they would be boarding. He could visualise that bottle of Glenlivet sitting waiting for him . . .

The door of the first cubicle, the one that had been occupied when they came in, snapped open. A teenager came out, his face flushed, and made for the exit, his eyes to the floor.

'Wonder what he's been up to,' said Parfit with a wink. He checked his watch again. 'Don't be long,' he pleaded.

'Two minutes,' Dreyfuss said, watching in the mirror as Parfit left. Alone, he relaxed a little more. He let the water out. As it gurgled down the plughole, a man in his forties pushed open the door and entered the toilets, nodding towards Dreyfuss as he made for the urinals.

'Helluva day,' he commented, but Dreyfuss wasn't sure whether the man was talking to him or to himself. He ran more water. The man came to the basin next to him, gave his hands a quick rinse and rubbed them vigorously beneath the fan dryer. Then he left, the dryer still whirring away noisily. Dreyfuss splashed his face again, rubbing at his eyes this time, pressing fingers to sockets. He spat some water back into the basin and re-examined himself in the mirror. A toilet was flushing, and the cubicle door behind him opened. A squat man wearing spectacles and a shirt too small at the neck came waddling out. Dreyfuss smiled into the mirror, and the man seemed to smile back, but kept on coming . . .

Dreyfuss saw the cheese wire. It was twisted around the man's pudgy little hands, wads of cloth stopping it cutting into the pulpy skin. It took no more than a second for the man to hoist it over Dreyfuss' bowed head and pull tight. But in that second, Dreyfuss managed to prise his fingers between the wire and his unprotected throat, so that when the wire tightened, it cut into finger joints rather than neck. But it hurt like hell, and kept on digging, rending the tissue, sending blood trickling down Dreyfuss' right hand. He watched in horror in the mirror as his eyes began to bulge, his tongue to twitch. The man was pulling him backwards, putting him off balance. With his free hand, Dreyfuss lashed out, finding first the man's glasses, then his eyes, gouging at them. The man cried out, but the noise was all but masked by the greater noise of the cubicle finishing its flush and the dryer finishing its cycle.

When both stopped, there was an eerie silence, punctuated only by the choking sounds from Dreyfuss, the squeaking noise his shoes made as he sought purchase on the floor, and the shrill breath of the small man who was slowly but steadily murdering him. Dreyfuss' whole head felt aflame, his eyes watering, ear canals singing like the sea. His chest felt tight as a drum skin. The thought of dying in this antiseptic place was appalling.

A picture flashed in his mind: Hes Adams' fingers around his throat. The picture gave him strength, and he lashed out again, but with his left foot this time, sending it backwards with a donkey kick into the small man's knee. The man gasped in pain but did not release his grip on the wire. Dreyfuss tried again, his eyes blurrily fixed to the mirror, hypnotised by the blood that was now dripping from his hand onto his shirt. His lips were drawn back from his teeth, the grin of a monkey. Monkeys grinned when they were terrified. This time the kick landed high on the man's soft thigh, causing no reaction. Dreyfuss tried to cry out but couldn't. He was losing strength, his whole body tingling with electricity. Movement was becoming difficult. Inside his head, someone opened the door of the furnace. He was on fire, and hell-bound. But he'd take the little bastard with him. He threw himself backwards, slamming the killer against the hard partition edge between two cubicles. Then he reached a hand around again. The hand was becoming numb, and it scrabbled over the man's clothes like a tiny blind animal, finding the crotch. He used the last of his strength to squeeze. The killer howled.

Then, from the corner of his eye, he saw the door swing open and Parfit enter. From then it was as if everything was happening in slow motion. Parfit approached the man from the side and gripped him by his furthest shoulder, pinning him against his own body sideways on. Then he brought his arm back in a straight line and sent it thudding towards the man, heel of palm connecting with ear. The man's head whipped to one side and there was a horrifying snap, as though a dog had bitten into a bone. The hold on Dreyfuss tightened further still, then relaxed.

He realised that Parfit was holding the small man – now a dead man – upright while he attempted to ease the cord away from Dreyfuss' throat. He did his best to help, then, suddenly released, staggered to the basin, gripping its edge with his left hand while he stared at his crippled and bloodied right hand. He ran more water and held the fingers beneath the cold spray. As he stared in the mirror at his purple face, the colour of a newborn baby, he felt his stomach wrench, sending a spume of vomit into the basin.

Parfit had eased the corpse to the floor. He was staring at it as though it were something unbelievable, something out of his ken. But the way he had dealt with the man proved to Dreyfuss that it very much was *not* out of his ken. It was what he did, when necessary, as part of his job description.

'Are you okay?' Parfit came to the basin and examined Dreyfuss' neck, then his bleeding hand. 'Run more cold water. Keep it under the tap.' He went over to the corpse again. 'We need to get rid of this bastard before somebody wants to use the facilities.'

There was only one sensible hiding place. He heaved the body upright in one swift movement and walked with it into the furthest cubicle, where he dumped it unceremoniously onto the pan. Closing the cubicle door, he examined the lock. It was a simple thing, made simple so that no one could stay locked in. He brought a coin from his pocket and inserted it into the screw thread next to the 'engaged' indicator. Holding the door closed, and turning the coin in the thread, he moved the indicator from green to red: the cubicle was locked.

He allowed himself a moment's pause, then turned back to examine the rest of the interior. There were drops of blood on the floor, but they couldn't be helped. What worried him more was Dreyfuss' injured hand, and the fresh bloodstains on his shirt. He checked his watch, wondering if they could last out the time until boarding. If the body was found before then . . . or if Dreyfuss' wound was too deep . . .

'I'll be all right,' Dreyfuss said, then gagged. His throat was like fire. Hadn't he been through this before and survived?

'You've got more bloody lives than a cat,' Parfit acknowledged, smiling. Then, seriously: 'But this was my fault, and I'm sorry.'

'Don't be,' whispered Dreyfuss – the least painful way of talking. 'I'm beginning to enjoy strangulation.'

'How's the hand?'

He lifted it from beneath the water. The cuts on each joint were clean and deep. He tried flexing the fingers. Blood began to pour again.

'Fine,' he whispered. 'What do we do now?'

'What do you want to do?'

Dreyfuss thought it over. What choice was there? 'Get on the plane,' he said.

'Then that's what we'll do. But first I have to make a phone call, and this time you're coming with me.'

'What made you come back?' asked Dreyfuss.

'They'd run out of Glenlivet,' said Parfit, attempting levity. 'Now let's see that hand.' He inspected the damage. 'It's bad,' he said, 'but I don't suppose I need to tell you that, since it's so bloody obvious.'

'And bloodily obvious.'

'Another joke,' Parfit said appreciatively. 'You're tougher than I thought, Major.'

'The name's Stephen,' said Dreyfuss, 'and don't you forget it.'

They wrapped wads of toilet paper around each finger, then Parfit's handkerchief around the whole hand.

'We'll get some sticking plasters at the sky shop,' he said. 'The hand will keep bleeding, but you probably won't die before we land.

If we get ice with our drinks, we'll make up a pack with the cubes and you can press that against it. Okay?'

'Never better,' said Dreyfuss, his voice laryngitic. 'Who are we going to telephone?'

'There's only one person I can think of right now. Frank Stewart.'

The telephone was one of a row of four. Parfit brought a paper napkin from his pocket. The napkin was from the café, and on it Stewart had scrawled a telephone number.

'He's going to be a bit surprised to get a call so quickly,' said Dreyfuss.

'He's going to be absolutely furious,' Parfit said, having pressed home the digits, awaiting a response at the other end.

Dreyfuss was intrigued. But he was also full of pain, and couldn't separate the two. They'd used a packet of cotton wool and a whole box of plasters on his hand, but he could feel the blood soaking through already. They'd also bought aspirin, and he'd swallowed half a dozen. He needed a drink.

'Stewart? It's Parfit. Listen, I need some help. No questions, just help. I'll explain later. What?' Parfit listened. 'No, we're at the airport. Yes, flying out.' He held the receiver away from his ear as Stewart's stream of invective flew out. Then, as briskly as it had started, it ended. Parfit returned the receiver to his ear. 'I couldn't tell you, Stewart. It would have meant too many other people knowing about it. Anyway, the point is, we've encountered a slight problem. That problem has been dealt with in the short term, but some cleaning-up needs to be done.' He listened again. 'In the gents' toilets,' he said at last. 'International departures. Last cubicle along.' There was another pause. 'How long will it take?' He nodded and smiled. 'That's great, Stewart. What? No, he's fine. I will. Goodbye.'

He slipped the receiver back into its cradle. 'Stewart sends his love,' he said to Dreyfuss.

'But can we really trust him?' Dreyfuss asked, his throat raw like sunburn.

'From the way he was questioning you in that hospital in Sacramento, it was quite obvious he hadn't a clue what was going on.' Parfit had started walking, and Dreyfuss walked with him, his whole arm throbbing. They were nearing the long, gleaming bar of the departures lounge. Parfit kept talking as they walked. 'We're up against generals, not spooks,' he said. The barman was ready to serve them. 'Scotch on its own,' Parfit ordered. 'But bring over the ice bucket, will you?' He turned to Dreyfuss. 'What'll you have?'

'Whisky,' croaked Dreyfuss. 'A double.'

The barman nodded and moved off to fix their drinks.

'Keep talking,' said Dreyfuss. 'It might take my mind off the bleeding.'

Parfit needed no further prompting. 'There's not much more to tell. Stewart will watch Esterhazy like the proverbial hawk.' He smiled again. 'It's a bit like the old days, special relationship and all that.' The smile faded. 'Of course, we can't trust the NSA *too* far, maybe not very far at all, but Stewart . . . well, I've got a feeling about Frank Stewart.'

The drinks had arrived, and with them the ice bucket. Dreyfuss reached his left hand into the chill centre of the white plastic basin and pulled out a cluster of cubes, which he dropped into his right-hand jacket pocket, packing them around his fingers and his palm. The barman was watching him but had seen worse behaviour in Departures.

'Cheers,' said Parfit, glancing towards the toilets. 'Here's to absent friends.'

'Cheers,' said Dreyfuss, before downing his drink in two hungry gulps.

Three musical notes preceded an address over the tannoy, announcing that their flight was boarding. Parfit patted Dreyfuss' back.

'Come on,' he said. 'In-flight drinks are gratis, I believe. The first one's on me.'

Dreyfuss grimaced. 'Plenty of ice with mine,' he said, feeling the damp in his pocket and not knowing whether it was evidence of melting ice or of his warm blood soaking through the compress.

'Plenty of ice it is,' said Parfit.

27

Hepton had the idea that everyone knew more than they were telling. Fair enough, he thought: probably *he* knew more than he was telling, too. And it was with this in mind that he asked Jilly if she knew of any restaurants where the public telephone was out of sight of the dining area, and preferably close to the toilets. They were sitting in the Curzon Street building, drinking tea and waiting for Sanders to come and pick them up. The spy chiefs had thanked them for attending the meeting, and had hoped there would be no need to meet again.

'I'll second that,' Jilly had said.

'I suppose I can think of a few,' she said now. 'Why do you want to know?'

'I want to make a telephone call, but I don't want Sanders knowing about it. For one thing, I don't trust him. For another, I don't want him to know who I'm telephoning. Everyone who gets involved in this thing seems to be in danger.'

'Who *are* you going to telephone?'

'Nick Christopher.'

'Your friend at the base?'

'Yes. Don't ask why, not yet. Are any of these restaurants close to here?'

'One's fairly close.' She was rising to the challenge. 'It's Italian. There's a wall phone downstairs, just next to the kitchen and the toilets. All the tables are upstairs. Would that do?'

'Perfect. All I'd need you to do is keep Sanders occupied while I'm downstairs.'

She smiled archly. 'If I know Sanders, that shouldn't be difficult.'

There was a knock on the door of the room, and Sanders' head appeared. 'Sorry I'm late,' he said. 'Another job.'

'Well, you *should* be sorry,' Jilly said, sounding peeved. She rose from her chair. 'Just for that, Sanders, lunch is on you.'

He shrugged his shoulders. 'Anything to oblige.'

'Good,' said Jilly, taking his arm. 'There's this little Italian place off Regent Street . . .'

Hepton, marvelling, followed.

Jilly had judged things perfectly. Sanders was keen to get on in his career, and slightly in awe of his superiors. He also felt a little aggrieved at having been left out of the top-level meeting, and his attention was total as, seated at a corner table in the restaurant, Jilly began to tell him all about it. He wanted to know every detail, and she was only too willing to tell. Soon, with a few tantalising lies thrown in to make the mixture even more intriguing, she had him hooked, a child to her fairy tale. They had just finished the first course. Hepton had ordered a veal dish to follow, though he hated veal on principle.

'That dish is very special, sir,' the waiter had informed him, pointing it out on the menu. 'You see, it says there it takes thirty minutes to cook.'

It did indeed warn of this, which was why Hepton had chosen it. He didn't want to be on the telephone downstairs and have his food waiting for him upstairs, causing Sanders to realise that he was away from the table. He had to be sure of a gap between the first course and the main. So he had nodded, and Jilly had caught his reasoning.

'That sounds good,' she had said. 'I think I'll change my mind and have the veal instead of the chicken.' The waiter had nodded, scribbling on his pad. Then Sanders had joined in.

'Make that three veals,' he'd said, and they had all smiled.

'Excuse me a minute,' Hepton said now, lifting his napkin from his lap and dropping it onto the table. Sanders nodded, but hardly paid any attention. Jilly had started another story about the meeting. Hepton rose to his feet and walked towards the back of the restaurant. An arrowed sign told him that the toilets were downstairs, and he descended the staircase slowly, his heart thumping furiously.

The wall phone was not in use. It was a modern chrome effort, with a blue receiver. It accepted most coins, and Hepton searched in his pocket. He came out with one pound and seventy pence. He checked his watch. It had just crept past one o'clock. Good: the rate wouldn't be at its most expensive. He probably had enough. He picked up the receiver, dropped in the money and saw it register on the liquid crystal display, and dialled.

'Hello?' said a voice on the other end.

'Yes,' said Hepton, 'I'd like to speak to Nicholas Christopher, please. He works in control.'

'I'll see if I can find him. Who's calling?'

'It's his brother, Victor.'

'Hold on.' The phone went quiet.

Hepton bit his bottom lip, then changed his mind and bit his top lip instead. Someone was coming down the stairs. A fat man in shirt and tie: one of the diners from upstairs. He pushed open the door to the gents' and, once inside, started whistling the background music from the restaurant's hi-fi. Hepton turned his attention back to the amount of money he had left. The LCD was ticking down, but there was still plenty of time.

He hoped Nick Christopher would recognise the code. One night, they had gone off base to a local pub, where the landlord had informed them that there was a disco in the village hall. After a few beers, they had visited the disco, and Christopher had dragged them onto the dance floor to introduce themselves to two young women.

'I'm Nick,' he'd shouted over the music, 'and this is Vic. Nick and Vic.'

In private, that nickname – Vic – had stuck to Hepton for a few weeks, producing a smile every time as it reminded them of that night and that disco.

The receiver suddenly came to life.

'Brother Victor,' said Nick Christopher knowingly. 'I thought you were on holiday?'

'I am. Can you talk?'

'Yes.'

'I mean, is there anyone with you?'

'Well, I'm at my console.'

'So there *are* people around you?'

'Not many, but yes. Look, give me your number and I'll call you back.'

'Okay, but hurry.' Hepton recited the telephone number and put down the receiver. A good portion of his money, unused, came clanking out, and he scooped it back into his pocket. The phone started to ring. 'Yes?' he said.

'Okay, I can talk now.' Christopher's voice was not as hale and hearty as it had been in the control room.

'What's happening, Nick?'

'I don't know, Vic. It's been pretty weird here since I last saw you. Fagin asked me if I had any idea where you were. He said he needed to contact you about something. And now . . . we're moving out.'

'What?' Hepton's face creased in puzzlement.

'Moving out. The place is being closed down temporarily. Something to do with fitting a new system. I don't know, something like that anyway. So everybody's getting two weeks' R and R.'

'But what about *Zephyr*?'

'She'll be stationary. There's going to be a skeleton staff to keep an eye on things. Fagin and a few others.'

'What others?' It was beginning to fall into place now.

'I don't know. But none of us. So, anyway, why did you call?'

Hepton had almost forgotten himself. 'Oh,' he said, reminded. 'I've got a big favour to ask.'

'Name it.'

'I want you to send me a video tape of Buchan airbase. As recent as you can manage, so long as it's after the *Zephyr* malfunction.'

'You've got to be joking!'

'I'm deadly serious.'

'What the hell for? I could end up in jail for a stunt like that.'

'Look, Nick, remember what I told you about Fagin and Paul and everything?'

'Yes, I remember. But Paul's dead now, isn't he? They said you were the one who found him.'

'I was. It wasn't suicide, Nick. It just looked that way. If we're going to find his killers, I need that tape. And if you could also send one of Buchan before *Zephyr* went haywire, that would help too. This is an emergency, Nick. I mean, life and death.'

'Well, maybe, but . . . Christ, I can't just—'

'You're shutting down, right?'

'Yes.'

'So it should be easy.' Hepton thought fast. 'Stuff's being moved about, boxed up, what have you. Say a couple of video tapes go missing, it's bound to happen.'

'Okay, so I put them in my pocket – then what? Down to the local post office?'

Hepton hadn't thought about that. He didn't want to involve Sanders – or anyone else he didn't feel able to trust. But if he wanted the tapes tonight . . . And he *did* want the tapes tonight.

'Nick, do you still go to the Bull?' The Bull was the public house closest to the base. It was a brisk evening walk, and a pleasant one in the summer months.

'Not for a while.'

'Could you drop in tonight? Just for a pint?'

'And take the tapes with me?'

'That's the idea.'

'I'm not sure I can get them that soon.' Christopher paused. 'Will you be at the Bull?'

'I'll try.'

'The thing is, there's a lot of logging to be done before we shut down. I'm not sure Fagin will spare me enough time. We were working till ten last night. I was so tired afterwards, I just collapsed into bed.'

'Look, Nick, try your best, will you?'

He seemed to give this serious thought. Hepton was under no illusions: Nick was a nice enough guy, but he was no hero. Look after number one, that had always been his creed. There was an all-too-audible sigh on the line. Then he spoke.

'Okay, Martin,' he said. 'If you want cloak and dagger, you can have it. I'll be in the Bull at seven.'

'Thanks, Nick.'

'You owe me one.'

'I won't forget. See you tonight.'

Hepton put down the receiver and turned towards the stairs. Sanders was standing there, three steps up, arms folded. He had obviously heard some of the conversation.

'Where are we going?' he asked.

There was no point lying. 'Binbrook, Lincolnshire. To the *Zephyr* base. I have to meet someone there.'

'Can I ask why?'

Hepton moved past him and started upstairs, Sanders following.

'No,' he said. 'But it could mean a whole lot of brownie points for you.'

'I still need to know why we're going to Lincolnshire.'

Hepton stopped and turned to him. 'Is there a video recorder in the safe house?'

'Yes.'

'Good, because we're going to be watching some videos later on, after we come back.'

Sanders nodded. 'Why didn't you just tell me?'

Hepton fixed his eyes on those of the younger man. 'Because you worked for Villiers,' he said. 'And because for all I know, you still do.'

Sanders shrugged. 'You're entitled to your opinion,' he said. 'But like it or not, I'm coming with you tonight. What about Jilly?'

'I'd rather she didn't go with us. No real reason.'

'You think it could be dangerous?'

Hepton managed a wry smile. 'These days,' he said, 'who can tell?'

Of course, Jilly was furious. She didn't want to be left out, and the fact that Hepton wasn't telling her much about the trip only served to kindle her curiosity further.

'Damn you, Martin Hepton! You were always too secretive, that was what I hated about you!'

Her words bounced around inside his head all during the drive. In the end, she had calmed a little, thrown herself into a chair and picked up a newspaper, using it as a shield against him. No matter how pleasant the house in Marlborough Place was – and it *was* pleasant – it was still a prison, a place of detention. There were two guards to look after Jilly, but they didn't only stop people entering the house; they stopped them leaving as well. And if Jilly was nothing else, she was a free spirit. Hepton could vouch for that.

Always too secretive. Damn you.

Yes, he'd been secretive. He had told her about his work, but not *all* about it. There always had to be something held back, something left unsaid. And he had never talked much about himself anyway, preferring to hear Jilly talk about her own life. It was so much more lively and vibrant, so much more interesting. So much more . . . open.

'I'd still like to know,' Sanders yelled. He was driving fast, with the car radio tuned in to the closing overs of a cricket match and the windows open to let some early-evening breeze into the stifling interior. The sun was coming lower in the sky. Soon, Hepton was thinking, soon it'll start getting dark earlier . . . Except that in some places it already was getting dark earlier.

'What?' he said.

'I'd still like to know,' Sanders called, 'what's on these videos.'

'Me too,' Hepton murmured. 'Me too.'

*

They were later arriving at the Bull than Hepton had intended: traffic jams all the way out of London, and major roadworks on the road north. Even Sanders' most manic driving had been unable to make up all the time they'd lost. So it was nearly eight when they pulled into the pub's gravel car park. There were a dozen or so other cars there. Hepton gave each one a searching inspection as Sanders passed them and stopped at the furthest point into the car park, then executed a three-point turn and drove slowly past the double line of vehicles once again. Hepton looked at him and saw that Sanders was inspecting the cars as meticulously as he himself had done. Satisfied that they were all empty, he pulled up close to the car park's entrance, ready for a quick getaway.

'Here goes,' he said. 'I'm dying for a pint.'

They walked into the bar by its car park entrance. There were couples at three tables, and a group of possibly underage teenagers huddled around another. A game of darts was taking place, and three men propped up the bar, as though the activity gave their life all meaning. The barman smiled at Hepton and Sanders as they approached.

'Evening, gentlemen. What's your poison?'

'Two pints of Courage bitter,' Sanders said. He turned to Hepton. 'That okay with you?'

Hepton nodded dispiritedly. There was no sign of Nick Christopher in the spacious bar, and it was well past his designated time. Either he'd been and gone, or he wasn't coming. Had Fagin got to him? And if so, what would happen next? Everyone in this bar could be implicated, could be working for Villiers and Harry. He tried not to stare, but it wasn't easy.

Sanders was managing to look casual about the whole business. Just two men out for a drink. He raised the straight glass to his lips, gulping at the first couple of mouthfuls.

'Not a bad pint,' he said.

One of the three men nearby seemed to hear him, and turned his head.

'You from London?'

Sanders smiled pleasantly. 'Not originally. But I live there now.'

'Thought you did,' said the man, turning back to his friends. 'Beer's like piss down there,' he informed them. 'And the water, you can't drink the water. Been through seven pairs of kidneys before it gets to you, been pissed out seven times before you drink it.'

His friends wrinkled their faces and chuckled. Sanders reddened. He was trying to keep up the facade, but Hepton could see he was having trouble. His eyes had acquired a fiery tinge to them, and his free hand rubbed at his armpit, just where the holstered gun nestled.

'Cheers,' Hepton said, trying to distract him, lifting his own glass to his lips.

Sanders twitched his head towards a table and carried his glass over to it. Hepton followed closely, placing his beer on one of the mats on the highly polished tabletop. The men at the bar were sharing a joke. He couldn't help thinking they were discussing him, and he too reddened slightly at the cheeks.

'Where's your friend, then?' Sanders asked, his voice sharp, kept low only through the greatest restraint.

'I don't know,' Hepton said. 'Maybe he couldn't make it.'

Sanders shook his head. 'So what do we do now?'

'Go back to London?' Hepton offered.

Sanders stared hard at him. 'Where are these video tapes?' he asked. 'We'll just have to go fetch them.'

It was Hepton's turn to shake his head. 'That isn't possible.'

'Why not?'

'It would mean going into the lion's den.'

'Better that than sitting in this particular den.' Sanders threw a baleful glance towards the bar.

'I could try phoning him again, let him know we're here.'

Sanders considered this. 'Might be an idea,' he said.

Hepton stood up. 'Back in a second.' He took a look around but could see no sign of a telephone. He went to the bar. The barman had the same fixed smile on his face.

'Yes, sir?'

'Do you have a telephone?'

The barman shook his head theatrically. 'Not as such, no. We don't have a public telephone, but there's one behind the bar.' He reached down and lifted an aged Bakelite handset onto the counter. 'Provided it's a local call, that is.'

'Oh yes,' Hepton assured him. 'It's local. We were supposed to be meeting a friend here, but we got held up. He's probably been and gone.'

'Would that be Mr Christopher?'

Hepton stared in surprise at the man, who was fussing beneath the bar again. 'Yes,' he said.

'Ah,' said the barman, as if this explained everything. 'Mr Christopher said there'd just be the one of you. Victor, he said it would be.'

'Yes, that's me.'

'Only,' the barman continued, 'he said he couldn't stop, since things are so busy back at that spy place of his where he works. So he asked me to give you this.'

Hepton stared at the plain white plastic carrier bag. The two black video cases were visible inside.

'Dirty films,' said one of the locals. 'That's what we thought, isn't it, Gerry?'

The barman's smile broadened, and the three locals gave throaty laughs. Hepton joined them, elated.

'No,' he said. 'Not dirty films. Just tapes of a friend's wedding.'

'Including the honeymoon?' rasped the first man, causing more laughter.

Hepton had brought a ten-pound note from his pocket.

'I think this calls for a round,' he said. 'Whatever these gentlemen are having, and one for yourself.'

The barman nodded, lifting the telephone back off the bar-top, and the three locals made appreciative noises, none of which sounded like 'thank you'.

'Nothing for yourself, sir?' one of them asked Hepton as the pint glasses were being refilled.

Hepton shook his head. 'We really should be going,' he said.

They watched as he went back to his table and spoke a few words to the Londoner. Then both men left the bar without so much as a wave of the hand or a nod of the head, carrying the bag with them.

'Forgot all about his change,' the barman noted drily.

'In that case,' said the oldest of the locals, 'keep the beer coming, Gerry.'

At one of the tables by the window, where a middle-aged couple were sitting, the wife suddenly produced a portable telephone from her handbag. The man took the phone and pressed a lot of digits, then waited. Eventually he said a few words, not much more than a sentence, and in a quiet voice. Then he gave the contraption back to his wife, who replaced it in her handbag. They finished their drinks and left the pub, the woman bowing her head slightly towards the bar as she left.

'Cheerio then,' the barman called in response.

'There's a lot of queer folk about,' said one local. The others nodded agreement and went back to their drinks. The rest of the night was to come as something of an anticlimax.

28

Hepton considered that he had seen Sanders' driving at its absolute worst. The journey back to London, however, served to impress upon him that this was an age without absolutes. Sanders seemed seized by demons, and determined to get back to the relative safety of the city as soon as he could. The men at the Bull had angered him, that was for sure. He was used to being undermined by his superiors, but not by people he would consider his inferiors by a fairly large margin. The needle on the dashboard flickered wildly around the seventy mark on the narrower roads, and Hepton felt sick in his stomach, the beer inside him sloshing wildly. On wider roads, they hit one hundred and ten miles per hour. It was, thank God, the only thing they hit.

Hepton, however, said nothing. He too was keen to get back to the safe house. Keen to watch the video tapes and see what he might discover. It was dark when they arrived, the sky spotted with yet darker clouds. The air was growing chill, so that they had to close the car windows and put on the heater for a little while. The night became greenish-yellow as the London street lights began to shine.

'Here we are,' Sanders said as they entered St John's Wood and turned into Marlborough Place. There had been little conversation on the drive back. It struck Hepton that the two of them had nothing in common, and that if they had not been thrown together like this, they would never have chosen one another as companions.

'Hold on,' Sanders said in warning as the car approached the house. His eyes had narrowed to slits, his face close to the windscreen.

'What is it?' Hepton was looking, too, but could see nothing out of place. Sanders drove past the house without stopping. 'What is it?' Hepton repeated in a low hiss.

'Too many lights on.'

'What?'

'All the lights inside the house are on. So is the light outside the front door, and the one to the side of the garage. It even looks as though there might be lights on in the garden.'

'So?' Hepton didn't want to think about what Sanders might be implying.

'So, something's wrong.' He pulled the car in to the kerb and stopped, shutting off the engine and killing the lights.

'What are we going to do? Just wait here? Jilly's in there! We can't—'

But Sanders was staring at the number plate of the car parked in front of them. The car itself was a Vauxhall Cavalier like his. He seemed not to have heard Hepton's outburst.

'Funny,' he said. 'That's Thommo's car.'

'Thommo? Who's Thommo?'

'The other lot. MI5. He's one of their . . . well, men.' He stared at Hepton, his face draining of colour. 'We better go in, but slowly. Keep with me.'

They opened the car doors and closed them – as Sanders instructed – quietly. Sanders was already pulling his gun from its holster as they approached the house. Hepton was frantic now. What had happened? There was no one to meet them at the front door, no guard. Sanders pushed open the door. There were voices coming from within, though muted. Everyone was being very quiet indeed. Then someone came into the hall, saw them, and turned his head back into the living room.

'Sir,' he called. 'Visitors.'

Another man, balding but not yet middle-aged, his moustache thickly black, popped his head into the hall, stared at Hepton and Sanders, then lifted his eyes towards the ceiling and gave a great groan of relief.

'Sanders, you bastard. Thank God. I thought they'd got you.'

Sanders was slipping his pistol back beneath his arm. He had become very businesslike, his voice like something lifted from cold storage.

'Fill me in,' he said.

The man looked from Sanders to Hepton, then back to Sanders. Sanders turned towards Hepton, who knew what he was going to say and cut in first.

'I'm not leaving. I've got a right to hear it too.' He looked at the man. 'Is Jilly all right?'

'She's not here,' the man said levelly. 'They've taken her with them, I suppose.'

'What about Bentley and Castle?' asked Sanders.

'Dead,' said the man. 'A neat job, clean. One knifed in the back, the other done with a garrotte.'

Neat, clean. Hepton was thinking of only one person: Harry. Sanders seemed to have read his mind, and nodded towards him before turning again to the man.

'All right, Thommo. I need details.'

'When you weren't here, I had to contact your department.'

'I appreciate that. Has anyone arrived?'

'Not yet. We only got here ourselves quarter of an hour ago.'

'Did you get anything on tape?'

'That's how we knew. No voices, though, apart from the woman's.'

'Jilly,' Hepton said. His voice was close to cracking.

'So if your surveillance team heard it all,' Sanders said, his tone accusatory, 'how come everyone had gone before you got here?'

'Surveillance is just that, Sanders. They called us, we came. All told, it took us about five minutes. But by then . . .' He shrugged his shoulders.

'This is a mess,' Sanders said, rubbing his temples.

'Jilly,' Hepton repeated. Sanders put an arm around him.

'Go sit down,' he ordered, 'I'll fix something to drink.'

Hepton began to move towards the living room.

'Not in there,' the man said. 'That's where we took the bodies.'

Sanders nodded. 'Go upstairs, Martin. I'll bring a drink up to you.'

Hepton felt beaten, utterly beaten, for the first time in what seemed an age. Harry had won, Villiers had won, they'd all won. And he had lost. He nodded his head and began to climb the stairs. Sanders and the other man – Thommo – were speaking together in hushed tones before he had reached the first-floor landing. He caught a few phrases.

'Clean-up party . . . how did they know? . . . tapes . . . phone call . . .'

Tapes! Hepton looked down and saw that he was clutching the carrier bag to his body. He ran his fingers over it. He still had the tapes. He walked across the landing, but instead of going into his own room, he entered what had been Jilly's. She had been reading:

there was a paperback lying open, face down, on the bed. It was one of the titles from the living room shelves, a modern romance. On her bedside cabinet sat a cup half full of tea. Hepton touched it; there was still a hint of warmth to it.

He had no doubts at all about who had taken Jilly. He even thought he knew why: as a warning to him, a personal warning not to go any further. They had to be desperate. They must know that it was not only Hepton's battle now; that others were involved. Yes, they *had* to know that. And yet they still wanted to scare him off. Why? Because of what he thought he knew, that portion of the secret he had not yet revealed to anyone? Whatever the answer, it was clear that they still saw him as a threat.

That thought gave him heart.

What was more, the sooner he solved the final riddles, the sooner he might be reunited with Jilly. But he had to be careful. Her life was in *their* hands now, in Harry's hands. He had to be very careful indeed. And sitting here wasn't going to do anybody any good. He needed a TV monitor and a video recorder. Ideally, he needed two monitors and two recorders – good recorders at that, with a freeze-frame facility that actually froze the frame, and didn't make it twitch or smear. A hard image, that was what he needed.

He realised that he wasn't going to go to pieces; that the worst was over. He felt calm and controlled. God knows why, but he did.

There was a knock at the door, and it opened. 'Oh, there you are.' Sanders entered, carrying a bottle of whisky under his arm and a crystal glass in each hand. Hepton shook his head.

'That's not what I need,' he said. 'What I really need is a TV lab. Your surveillance personnel probably have one. Get me there, then I'll show you what's on these.' He slapped the tapes.

Sanders studied him, to ascertain whether he might be suffering from shock or something similar. All he saw was determination and a mind ready for work.

'I'll call in,' he said. 'I think I know just the place.'

'One question,' said Hepton. 'How did they know about *this* place?'

Sanders shook his head. 'I wish to God I knew.'

29

It was after midnight, but the man they had summoned back from his bed and his wife to this cold building in the middle of a bleak industrial estate near Notting Hill seemed not to mind.

'No, really,' he said. 'This is what makes it all worthwhile.'

'I hope you're right,' said Hepton. The man had introduced himself as Graeme Izzard. Thommo had assured them that he was the best 'pictures' man in the business.

'I work mainly for Special Branch,' Izzard told Hepton. 'Serious Crime, that sort of thing. You know, someone walks into a building society and shoots dead a teller. They capture the whole thing on camera, but the image is too blurred to be recognisable. I clean it up until it's sharp from arsehole to breakfast time. Which reminds me . . .' He looked at his watch, then turned to Sanders. 'There's an all-night caff, just up the road and turn right. You can't miss it. There'll be about a dozen cabs outside. It's where the drivers go for their break. Get us, let's think, something hot, a sausage sandwich, something like that. Plus some cold sandwiches for later, corned beef or salami. And tell Alfie, the man behind the counter, that Izzard says he's to give you a flask of tea. Got that?'

Sanders looked devastated. He had been demoted to tea boy by a man if anything a year or two younger than himself, with straggly shoulder-length hair and a T-shirt advertising a heavy-metal band. This was the third blow of the evening.

Hepton's first impression of Izzard had been similarly coloured by his youth – he looked no more than twenty-six or twenty-seven – and his clothing. He had a London accent, too, harshly grained, the sort of voice heard at market stalls and football matches. But there was no doubt that he had a certain swagger that told you not to muck him about or underestimate him.

He offered Sanders a five-pound note from a wad pulled from his jeans pocket, but Sanders shook his head and stumbled away, still shell-shocked. Izzard watched the door close behind him.

'Stuck-up sod,' he said. 'I hate bloody SIS. Mind you, the other lot are no better. Give me Scotland Yard every time. Their heads aren't in the clouds. A bit more down-to-earth, you know?'

Hepton nodded, unable to think of any reply. Izzard had brought them into a large warehouse of modern corrugated construction. There were crates neatly stacked against one of the high walls, but this was no ordinary warehouse. Much of the floor space was taken up by another, smaller building of more solid, prefabricated construction. Izzard went to the door of this smaller building and unlocked it. An alarm sounded, and he switched on the lights before finding another key on his heavy chain and turning it in the alarm box, cancelling the ringing. He looked satisfied. They were in a small antechamber. On another door was a numerical keypad and a tiny keyhole. Izzard pushed five digits and turned a slender key in the lock, and the door clicked open.

Inside this room, there was an air-conditioned chill. Izzard swung an arm around proudly. 'The lab,' he said.

Hepton, used to technical labs, nodded, impressed. There was hardware aplenty: computers, monitors, video cameras, recorders, a huge studio-style machine for editing and splicing film, projectors, and workbenches covered in all manner of electrical instruments, bits of chopped film, broken-open cassette cases. The place was a mess, evidence that a lot of work was done here.

'All this Russian-doll stuff, a box within a box within a box, it's really to cut down vibration from outside more than anything,' Izzard explained. He bounced on the floor in his Dr Martens shoes. 'Decoupled from the rest of the building,' he said proudly. 'That was my design, actually.'

'This is incredible,' said Hepton. He had been attracted to the computers, and stood over one now. He frowned. 'I don't recognise—'

'That's my design, too,' said Izzard, running a finger over the keyboard. 'We do our own software and, in this case, hardware. It's just a number-cruncher, really. Do you know about computers?'

'I work in a tracking station,' said Hepton.

Izzard looked impressed and pleased. His face became more

boyish than ever. 'You track satellites?' Hepton nodded. 'I love all that stuff. Signals intelligence, comms intelligence.'

'That's what's on these tapes,' said Hepton, brandishing the bag. Izzard looked like a child offered sweets.

'Yes?' he said, reaching out a hand. 'Well then, let's put them on the machine and take a look.' His tone became more serious. 'What is it that you want exactly?'

'I want to examine the pictures,' Hepton said, following Izzard to one of the benches. 'Side by side if possible.'

'Very possible.'

'And then maybe concentrate on a few shots.'

'I can put them side by side on the same screen.' Izzard turned to him. 'If you like.' Hepton smiled and nodded.

Izzard brought the tapes out of the bag. There was a note inside one of the boxes. *You owe me a beer, Vic!* He handed it to Hepton, then turned his attention to the tapes themselves.

'Hmm,' he said. 'High-resolution tape, and plenty of it.' Even Hepton could see that there was a good deal of tape on each spool: perhaps as much as a couple of hours' worth. Yes, he owed Nick Christopher a beer.

He noticed that he had rested his hand on a small modem. He tapped it.

'Ever done any hacking?' he asked.

Izzard's face lit up again. 'Yes, years ago. I used to love it. What about you?'

'I've done a little.'

'I got into a couple of big companies' systems,' Izzard said, warming to his tale. 'Left messages there for the staff. Stuff like: "Do you know what your wife's up to right this second?" Childish, but still a lot of fun.'

Hepton smiled. 'Wasn't it difficult working out the code words?'

'Hellish difficult, yes.' Izzard had put down the tapes. 'Typing in everything from aardvark to zygote.'

He went to a large steel cupboard and opened it. There were bits and pieces of equipment arranged along the shelves inside. He found what he was looking for and brought it out, closing the door again. It was a small black box, the size of one of Nick Christopher's crossword dictionaries. Built into its top surface was what looked like an old-fashioned LED pocket calculator.

'It was difficult,' Izzard said proudly, 'until I made this.' He handed Hepton the box. Hepton examined it, but without success. The several home-made switches and push-buttons were unmarked.

'I give up,' he said. 'What is it?'

'It's another number-cruncher of sorts,' Izzard explained, pleased that Hepton hadn't known. 'Some of the companies use long numerical codes, and those were the worst to crack. All I needed to do was plug this box into my modem and it did all the work for me.'

'Ingenious,' said Hepton, examining the box more carefully.

'No,' said Izzard, 'what's *really* ingenious is that I cooked up a chip that put the other computer on hold while *my* computer was pumping the code numbers into it.'

Hepton saw the implications at once. 'So you didn't need to sign off and try again every time you got the code wrong?'

Izzard nodded his head vigorously, then gave a childish, high-pitched laugh.

'Brilliant,' said Hepton. 'I hope you took out a patent on it.'

'No,' said Izzard, calming a little. 'But I sold the idea to the military for fifteen thousand pounds.' He lifted the black box out of Hepton's hand and returned it to its cupboard. 'God knows what they wanted it for,' he said with finality.

As he closed the cupboard, a buzzer sounded. 'That'll be our spy,' said Izzard, 'wishing to come into the cold.' He pressed a button on the wall, and the door clicked open again, admitting Sanders.

'Cheery lot, those cab drivers,' Sanders said grumpily. He was carrying a cardboard box. Hepton could smell the waft of fried sausage coming from within it, and realised he was hungry.

Izzard seemed to know what he was thinking. 'Never work on an empty tum,' he said, making for the box.

As the work continued, becoming ever more painstaking, Sanders fell asleep perched on a stool, his head and arms resting on a bench top. Izzard, however, seemed to grow more awake as the night progressed, while Hepton, though not feeling tired, began to feel disoriented, even hallucinatory for a few strange minutes.

Having examined the two tapes, they ran them side by side, and then started freeze-framing particular shots, shots of similar buildings taken from similar angles. On the top left corner of each was an hour-and-minute counter, and they used this to align the two tapes temporally, checking differences in light and in the quality of the shadows cast by the evening sun. Izzard never seemed satisfied, and would run a section again, sharpening the focus, enlarging a shot onscreen: this enlarging process was again of his own design and the unit he operated his own construction.

'I haven't perfected it yet,' he admitted, though the results were, to Hepton's eyes, impressive enough.

At four o'clock, Izzard suggested they pause for breakfast. Sanders was snoring, so they left him to his sleep and went outside. Birds were chirping hesitantly in the distance, and a few early cars and lorries were on the road. After the cool of the lab, the morning seemed already oppressively warm. Izzard walked with hands in pockets.

'I think I can see it,' he said.

'What?' Hepton asked, still coming out of his brief hallucinatory stage.

'What it is you've been looking for. I can see it now.' Izzard turned to him. 'They're not the same place, are they?'

Hepton smiled. 'No,' he said. 'They're not.' He was pleased that Izzard could see it, too. If he could see it, then everybody could see it. It wasn't just in Hepton's mind. 'I should have realised right back at the beginning,' he explained. 'One day I was watching Buchan and it got dark at a certain time. Then *Zephyr* was got at, and suddenly it was starting to get dark earlier at Buchan.'

'Except that it wasn't Buchan,' Izzard noted.

'That's right,' said Hepton. 'That's what this is all about. Someone doesn't want us to see what's *really* going on at Buchan. So instead they've rigged a lookalike.'

'A mock-up.'

'Yes. But a very good mock-up. A bit too good.'

'How do you mean?'

'I think it must be a real airbase, but not one of the other ones the USAF has been using. We've been watching all of those at one time or other. It must be RAF.'

'Excuse my ignorance, but if all you do all day is watch these pictures, wouldn't someone *notice* that it wasn't Buchan?'

'Not really,' said Hepton. 'For one thing, our remit wasn't to watch the bases so much as watch their perimeters for protesters.'

'Weird,' said Izzard. 'Not so long ago, they were protesting about the Americans *being* here. Now they're protesting about them *going*.'

'Besides,' Hepton continued, 'we mostly examine still photos, and still aerial photos look much the same. We would be checking for things that were *different*, not things that looked the same. We're only technicians, remember. We're not spies.'

Izzard nodded, deep in thought but enjoying himself.

'This base, the one they're using, it's south of Buchan?'

'Yes, someplace where it gets dark earlier than it does in Scotland at this time of year; somewhere down here.'

'There are plenty to choose from.'

'Not very many would fit the bill. It should be easy to find which one it is.'

'This begs two rather large questions: why, and how?'

They had reached the café. There were no taxis outside now. Shifts had either ended or not yet begun. The glare of strip lighting made Hepton squint as they pushed through the door. A small, sweating man was standing behind the counter, wiping it down with a rag. He looked up as they entered.

'This is a late one for you, Graeme,' he said to Izzard.

'I wouldn't mind, Alfie, but the overtime rate is diabolical. Give us two of your special breakfasts, will you?'

'Coming up. Where's my flask?'

Izzard opened his arms in apology. 'Sorry, Alfie. I forgot. It's back at the lab.'

'Well, never mind. Do you want any tea?'

'Coffee for me, black and sweet. What about you, Martin?'

'Black, no sugar, please,' said Hepton.

The man nodded and started to work.

'How and why,' said Hepton. 'Yes, you're right. But we're very close to answering both. I can feel it. I can almost answer the "how" right now, though it's only guesswork.'

'Go ahead.' They had seated themselves on padded benches either side of a Formica-topped table. Hepton rested his elbows on the table, hands supporting his head as he thought things through.

'Well,' he said. 'A shuttle, the *Argos*—'

'The one that crashed?'

'Yes, the one that crashed. It was up there launching a communications satellite. Except the satellite wasn't just your normal COMINT satellite, it was an intercept.'

'An intercept?'

'Yes. Its purpose was to lock on to *Zephyr*. While it was locking on, *Zephyr*'s transmissions went haywire. But nobody minded that, because as long as the transmissions returned eventually, everyone would put it down to a glitch, nothing more. Some top brass from the military were on site when it all happened, just to check that the operation went smoothly. It did, more or less. Except I noticed how pleased they were looking, and one other person, a friend of mine, caught a hint of the interference. They murdered him and wiped his disk.'

Izzard whistled softly. Hepton paused, then continued.

'So what do we have? We have *Zephyr* apparently back to normal, except that it isn't, not quite. Because whenever we lock on to one particular spot – Buchan – the other satellite breaks in and transmits its own pictures to *Zephyr* before they're transmitted to the ground station.'

Izzard was shaking his head. 'This is too big for me,' he said. 'I'm used to bank robbers and spies, not conspiracies in space.'

'Conspiracy is right. The Americans and the British are in on it for a start. But the governments don't seem to know, only the generals.'

The door opened and a well-dressed man came into the café. Hepton glanced up at him, but was too intent on his story to pay him much attention. The man slid into the booth next to theirs, so that his back was to Izzard's back. Alfie was still in the kitchen, his frying pan sizzling.

'Only the generals,' Izzard repeated. 'So whatever's happening, what can we do about it?'

'I really don't know. We could persuade Whitehall that something's going on, but the suits in Curzon Street didn't seem to think it would produce much joy. What we need is proof, absolute proof.'

'Well, you've got that, haven't you? I mean, the tapes?'

'But what do they prove? Not *what's* happening, only that something *is*.'

'So go to Buchan. Take a look for yourself.'

'Yes,' said Hepton. 'Yes, maybe you're right.'

The newcomer swivelled on his bench so that he was facing their booth. Hepton glared at him, realising that he had heard every word. The man looked pale, tired. Not a killer, not just at the moment.

'Mr Izzard generally *is* right,' he said.

Izzard's head cracked round at the sound of the voice. Then his face broke into a grin.

'Why don't you join us?' he said. The man got up and did so. Izzard was still grinning. 'Once,' he said to Hepton, 'I went to lunch and came back to the lab, and I'd been in there ten minutes before I realised this sneaky sod was in there too. Just sitting, out of my line of vision, and absolutely still. A professional voyeur, that's what you are.'

The man took the remark as a compliment. He was holding out a hand to Hepton, who was wondering now where he had heard his voice before.

'Parfit,' the man said by way of introduction. 'We've spoken on the telephone. You must be Martin Hepton. They told me you'd come to see Izzard. And since Graeme spends more time in this establishment than in his lab, I thought I'd try here first.'

Hepton shook the proffered hand, a look of disbelief on his face.

'Parfit?' he said. 'Christ, when did you get back?'

'A couple of hours ago.'

'Is Dreyfuss with you?'

'Well, the safe house didn't appear to be safe any longer, so I've booked us into a hotel. He's resting there.'

'Does he know . . .?'

'About Miss Watson?' Parfit's face darkened. 'No. We were in a bit of a skirmish at the American end. Major Dreyfuss was injured. He lost some blood.' He saw the shocked look on Hepton's face. 'He's fine, really. I had a doctor patch him up. Believe it or not, there was one on the plane. There we were halfway over the Atlantic, and this poor chap was stitching a couple of the major's fingers. Quite exciting really. I didn't judge him fit enough, however, to take the news of Miss Watson's abduction. In fact, I *was* wondering . . .?'

'If I'd tell him?'

'Something like that. No real hurry. I'd like to be filled in first on what's so exciting about these mysterious tapes.'

Hepton looked to Izzard, who spoke. 'No problem there,' he said. 'We'll show you.' Alfie was approaching with two large plates. Izzard smacked his lips. 'Just as soon as we've had breakfast, eh?'

When he had seen what they had, Parfit was in no doubt about what had to be done.

'I'll send some men to Buchan, see what they can come up with. Not a lot, I shouldn't think. Security's bound to be tight. We'll also check on the other airbases south of there, see if we can find out which one they're using as a mock-up.'

He made the phone calls from the lab. Izzard sat on a high stool, pinching the bridge of his nose between his fingers and yawning: the night had finally caught up with him. Sanders was wide awake, however, and looking ready to impress Parfit, if such were possible. He'd still been sleeping when they'd arrived back at the lab, but had been shocked into wakefulness by the sound of his superior's voice, only then to feel acute embarrassment at having allowed Hepton and Izzard out of doors without his knowing about it.

Hepton had passed his own nadir and felt numb but not sleepy. He listened to the efficient phone calls with an appraising ear. Parfit didn't waste a single word, and his instructions were as foolproof as seemed possible. When he had finished, he replaced the receiver and turned to the room.

'Well, that's as much as we can do from here. Thanks, Graeme. Can we offer you a lift?'

But Izzard shook his head, in the middle of a protracted yawn, and gestured with an arm. 'I'm only five minutes' walk away,' he said.

Parfit nodded and turned his attention to Hepton. 'I think you'd better come back to the hotel with me,' he said. 'I can't think of anywhere safer to keep you, and you can see Major Dreyfuss.'

'That'll be fun,' Hepton said in an unemotional voice. Then: 'Where's the hotel anyway?'

'Only the best,' said Parfit. 'What better cover is there than an expensive West End hotel?'

'But not on Park Lane?' Hepton asked, growing uneasy.

Parfit caught his tone. 'Just off it,' he said. 'Why?'

'Because Cam Devereux's in the Achilles.'

'Ah.' Parfit nodded his understanding. 'Don't worry, we're in the Bellevue. Two streets back from the Achilles. Not so expensive either.' He turned to Sanders, who all but stood to attention. 'You can go home, too, Sanders. Get some rest. But I'll want your report on my desk by ten o'clock.'

'Yes, sir.'

Hepton knew Sanders would get precious little sleep: he'd work through the morning to perfect his report and buff it to a conspicuous sheen. He was a company man all right. Hepton shook hands with Izzard.

'Thanks for your help,' he said.

'Any time,' said Izzard, easing himself off the stool. 'But try to make it daylight hours, okay?'

'Okay,' said Hepton, with the glimmer of a smile. Then, to Parfit: 'Let's go see Mike Dreyfuss.'

'Wait a second,' said Hepton, checking from the car window. 'This isn't the way to Park Lane.'

'A slight detour,' Parfit said. 'It won't take long.'

They were in a maze of elegant town houses, somewhere in the midst of unimaginable wealth, otherwise known as Belgravia. The car pulled in to the kerb. The streets were silent; there was little to remind Hepton that he was living in the dangerous tail-end of the twentieth century. But there were subtle hints: alarm boxes above most of the tightly shut doors, a latticework of metal bars across a basement window. Little Fort Knoxes all in a row . . .

'Here we are,' said Parfit.

'Where?'

They were standing at the bottom of a short flight of stairs leading to a doorway. To the side of the door were a dozen nameplates, evidence that the house had been divided up into apartments. Hepton turned at the sound of a car door opening. The vehicle had been there when they'd arrived, but he'd spotted no signs of life. Now two men emerged. One stayed by the car while the other came to the steps, climbed them, and turned keys in the door, opening it. Coming back down the steps, he handed the keys to Parfit.

'Thank you,' said Parfit. The man returned to the car. Both men got in. Hepton realised that they were keeping guard.

'What is this place?' he asked.

'This is George Villiers' home,' Parfit explained. 'Come on, let's take a look.'

The reception hall was huge and elegant. There was some mail on a marble table. Parfit browsed through it, finding nothing of interest. They took the near-silent elevator to the third floor, where Parfit opened one of two doors on the landing. The nameplate had been removed.

'Why are we here?' asked Hepton. He breathed in the stagnant air of the long hallway. Parfit walked noiselessly towards the far door and pushed it open. A lounge, leading on to further rooms: dining room, a small study, and past this the bedroom. The apartment seemed to be a series of conjoined rooms, shaped in a 'U' around the hallway. Hepton repeated his question, but Parfit appeared intent on his surroundings, as though planning to make an offer on the vacant property.

'He didn't own this, you know,' he mused. 'I thought he did, but he didn't. It was supposed to be an inheritance. That was the story.'

'Who does own it then?'

Parfit smiled at Hepton, his eyes hooded and intelligent as a crow's. But instead of answering, he walked on from one room to another. Hepton caught him up as he was beginning to speak again.

'I never liked him. I was against his recruitment from the start.'

'Why didn't you stop him then?'

Parfit's smile this time was bitter. 'It wasn't up to me,' he said. 'I really had no say in things.' His eyes sought Hepton's. 'All I do is clear up the mess. Treatment rather than prevention, you see.' Hepton could feel the man's irritation. It filled the room and threatened to burst from it. 'My superiors recruited him, not me. Blake Farquharson recruited him. Well, he had his reasons, I suppose.' The emotion was melting away again, or rather was being shovelled back into some hidden cellar. But still there.

Why, Hepton wondered, was he being shown this side of Parfit, a man he barely knew?

Parfit walked on, through the study and into the bedroom. The bed was narrow, the room small and airless. There were no ornaments, nothing to brighten it or make it more than just a place for resting.

Resting and waiting. Hepton could imagine Villiers lying here at night, nothing distracting him from his thoughts, and his thoughts filled with death, glory, deceit.

There was a piece of card on the bed's one pillow. Hepton lifted it and turned it over: *SORRY YOU COULDN'T MAKE IT TO THE BURIAL.* The message was printed. Parfit read it, then took the card from Hepton and slipped it into his pocket.

Hepton started opening drawers, flicking through books in the study. He didn't doubt that some team specialised in such things had been through the apartment before him. But perhaps he knew what he was looking for better than they did. There were few clues, however. He switched on Villiers' word processor, only to find that what disks there were had been wiped clean, or had been empty to begin with.

Coffin . . . burial. The words rang in his head, growing loud, dissonant. He was wasting his time here. Why had they come?

They were leaving the apartment when it dawned on him. He remembered the book well. It had been one of the first he had ever read . . . well, the first without pictures in it. A bear was terrorising an isolated village. The backwoodsman hunted it. He tracked it to its lair, but found the lair empty. The man was fascinated by the cave, examined every inch of it. Then found the bear and killed it. Yes, Hepton remembered. He remembered, too, the way Harry had come to his flat in Louth and waited for him there.

The hunter gains strength and insight from the lair of his victim. Parfit was a hunter. And he had brought Hepton here because he wanted him to be a hunter too.

Satisfied, both men headed to Park Lane.

30

If Dreyfuss took the news of Jilly's abduction better than they had expected, it could probably be put down to a mixture of painkilling drugs and jet lag. His right hand was heavily bandaged up to and past the wrist, and he lay on the hotel bed with his good arm falling across his face, shielding his eyes from the light.

He mumbled something.

'What's that, Mike?' Parfit asked. Dreyfuss took his arm away from his eyes and angled his head up so as to look right into Parfit's face.

'I said,' he spat, 'we've got to kill them. It's the only way. They're killing us; we've got to kill them.' Then he flung his arm across his eyes again and let his head fall back onto the bed.

Parfit stared at Hepton worriedly. Dreyfuss was exhausted, doped and shocked. It was a lethal cocktail. Hepton understood and gave a reassuring nod.

But in his heart, he agreed with Dreyfuss. The scent of Villiers was still in his nose.

Dreyfuss turned onto his side, letting his damaged hand fall onto the bedcovers, where it lay. He was drifting back to sleep again, looking much older than Hepton remembered him: older, sad and angry at the same time. Well, if half of what Parfit had related on the drive over here was true, Dreyfuss had been to hell and back. Hepton had the feeling that he too might have to visit hell before this was all over. A little part of him was looking forward to it.

'Get some sleep, Mike,' Parfit said. 'We'll see you later.'

Hepton was to share with Parfit.

'My room's got twin beds anyway,' Parfit explained, 'and it saves paying for another single. God knows, my expenses on this are big enough already. The accounting department is going to want my head on a block.'

'How do you explain away a four-star hotel?' Hepton asked.

Parfit shrugged. 'Well, there don't seem to be any safe houses any more, and the first place they'd think of looking after that is seedy anonymous hotels. This place isn't exactly seedy.'

'But anonymous?'

'Well, let's just say it's discreet.'

'One thing worries me,' Hepton said, watching Parfit opening the door to their room. 'How is it they keep being able to find us?'

'Search me,' said Parfit, pushing the door wide. The room was large, and Hepton didn't mind sharing. It was seven o'clock, and outside, the morning's traffic jams were building up nicely. Work was beginning for the day, and Parfit suggested they rest till noon.

'Suits me,' said Hepton. 'But listen, did I tell you about the clever little transmitter Harry planted on me?'

'No,' said Parfit, sounding uninterested.

'Maybe they're using something similar to keep tabs on us.' Hepton was becoming excited.

'Maybe,' Parfit said, his voice dull with drowsiness.

Hepton saw that he was making no impression on the man, absolutely none. He went to the door and peered out into the empty hallway.

'No guards?' he asked.

'No,' said Parfit, slipping off his shoes. 'No guards. Now that they've got Miss Watson, I shouldn't think you're in much danger. They'll try using her as a lever first. Sleep tight.' In trousers, bare feet and shirt open at the neck, he fell onto the furthest bed and turned his face away.

Hepton sat on the edge of his own bed. He lay back, resting his hands behind his head. His mind still surged with energy. The heavy curtains were only half closed, giving enough light to see by. He examined the ceiling, its ornate mouldings. He tried to empty his mind of thoughts, but they swam around like fish in a tank, this way and that, passing each other, almost touching, then darting away. He closed his eyes, but that just made his whole head swim. What was he doing? They had Jilly: how was he supposed to sleep?

He thought of Cam Devereux, only two streets away. Those scared, haunted eyes, the hollow voice. The man had been hiding something. But what? Hepton replayed the scene: the hotel bar, the pianist playing to a table of women, Devereux's hard American inflections as he told his story. Of how the stranger had come to the *Argos* control room, set himself up at a console and . . .

Why do that? Why put him at a console in the main control room, with the full knowledge of the controllers? Drawing attention to the very man who was to be *Argos*'s executioner. It didn't make sense. Surely if he'd needed to be on base at all, they would have placed him somewhere away from curious eyes, in a room of his own, with his own terminal.

Yes!

Hepton swivelled his legs off the bed and stood up. Parfit was breathing heavily, already deep in slumber. Hepton went to the door and eased it open, slipping out into the corridor. He closed the door again, making sure not to dislodge the *Do Not Disturb* sign swinging from the brass knob. Then he walked silently, purposefully along the corridor and down the stairs into the main lobby. The Bellevue was no smaller than the Achilles, but made a show of being inherently more intimate. The reception clerk recognised him and made an obsequious bow from behind his desk. Hepton gave a casual wave and went to the revolving door, entering it and pushing softly. The door tumbled round until it discharged him onto the pavement and into the smells of the city: exhaust fumes and damp trees.

The same doorman as before was standing in front of the Achilles, and opened the door for Hepton as he climbed the steps. 'Good morning, sir,' he said.

'Good morning,' Hepton returned, entering the hotel.

He walked purposefully to the stairs before remembering that Devereux was on the second floor. So he crossed to the lifts instead. One was already waiting, and he stepped in. What was Devereux's room number again? He had forgotten, but remembered the room itself, along towards the end of the corridor, past the ice dispenser and the shoeshine machine. The lift cranked its way upwards, jolted to a stop and opened. Hepton stepped into the dimly lit corridor and turned right. Past the ice machine . . . the drinks dispenser . . . the polisher . . .

Yes, this was it: 227. A couple came out of the room opposite, talking about the breakfast they were about to eat. They glanced back at Hepton, who stood hesitating outside Devereux's door, then went on their way.

Hepton was about to knock on the door when he saw that it wasn't properly closed. There was the slightest of gaps, but he couldn't see into the room. Suddenly a sickening sensation hit him in the pit of his stomach. He leaned back into the corridor, brought up his foot and kicked open the door with the heel of his shoe. The room was dark, a crack of daylight coming through the closed drapes. And there was a funny sweet smell, like the gas he'd been given once as a child in the dentist's chair. He found the light switch and flipped it. Devereux was in bed, naked. Another figure, fully dressed, was crouched over him, holding a hypodermic syringe into his upper arm. The face had jerked upwards to look at Hepton.

One side of it was scarred by long white water blisters, edged with redness.

It was Harry.

'Oh Christ . . .' Hepton whispered, the hair prickling on his neck.

Harry's lips twisted into a delinquent smirk as she looked down at the prone body and saw that the syringe was empty. She retracted it, then seemed to examine Devereux's blank face before turning her attention to Hepton. But by then it was too late. Hepton had grabbed the door handle and pulled the door tightly shut. He locked both hands around the handle. He had her now. He had trapped Harry! He looked up and down the corridor, but it was empty. Still, soon someone would appear from a room, ready for breakfast, and he would order them to telephone Parfit. The main thing was—

'Hello, Martin.' The voice was faint, lacking any trace of emotion or feeling. Hepton resisted the temptation to place his ear against the door, the better to hear her words. He remembered Jilly's flat, the bullets splintering past him through the wood panelling. 'Long time no see,' Harry continued. 'I've just been tidying up a little.'

His voice was firm. 'Where's Jilly?'

'You should be dead by now. You know that, don't you? You've turned into a real challenge, Martin. I enjoy a challenge. I'll enjoy killing you.'

'I asked where Jilly was.'

'Does it matter? We've got her. If you want her alive, quit now.'

'Quit what?'

Her laughter was as cruel a sound as Hepton had heard. 'Just quit,' she said. 'You know what I mean.'

He looked around him again. There was still no one in the hallway. His arms were aching from holding the door closed, yet Harry had not yet attempted to open it.

'You didn't have to do that,' he said.

'Do what?'

'Murder Devereux.'

'Orders,' she said. 'That's all.'

'Orders from Villiers?'

'Ah, you know about Villiers. Yes, I'd forgotten that. Stupid man. He should have been more careful. But no, not Villiers. These orders came from overseas. Someone's been keeping tabs on Mr Devereux, someone besides your friends and you.'

'Oh? Who?'

'It doesn't matter. But the Americans have been getting nervous, so they asked—'

'All that matters is that the coffin gets buried,' said Hepton.

His words had their effect. There was silence from behind the door.

'Too many people know now, Harry,' he went on. 'Too many for even you to be able to shut them all up. You can't bury it.'

She laughed again. 'I don't see anyone stopping us. I see a lot of mice chasing their own tails and squeaking, only no one's paying attention to them because no one *wants* to pay attention to them. Because what *we're* doing is for the best.'

'Who's we, though? You and Villiers? The chiefs of staff? Who?'

'Bigger than that, Martin. Much, much bigger. Coffin.'

'But what does that mean?'

'It's an acronym, of course. You know how the armed forces and the bureaucrats love acronyms.'

An acronym: the letters standing for other words. 'What's it an acronym for? I never was much use at crosswords.' He realised that she'd hooked him. He was interested, despite himself. But her voice had become faint, as though she were moving away from the door, forcing him to bring his head closer.

'I'm going to kill you, Martin,' she said, 'the way I should have done right at the start in your flat. Don't think I didn't consider it. I could have put it down to a burglary. But it seemed messy at the time. It still isn't a necessity, not now we have your friend Miss Watson. But I'm going to do it anyway.' Her voice was very faint now. Hepton kept his head and body clear of the door, expecting a shot. None came. Then he heard the sound of exhausted breathing from along the corridor.

A thickset man had just reached the landing from the stairs. He was pausing at the top, trying to regain his breath. He stared along the corridor and saw Hepton.

'What do you think you are doing there?' he called. Then he started moving forward, quickly for his size. 'This is Mr Devereux's room.'

'I know,' Hepton said. The man moved towards the doorway, but Hepton gripped his arm with one hand and pulled him back, keeping the other tight on the door handle. 'There's a murderer in there,' he said.

The man's eyes widened; not in shock, Hepton realised, but in mild surprise only.

'A murderer?' The accent was difficult to place. Mediterranean? Eastern European?

'That's why I'm holding the door shut. She's still in there.'

'A she? And her victim?'

'He's in there too. Will you go for help, please?' Hepton was becoming exasperated. Who bothered to ask questions when a killer was around? But the man made no sign of moving. He seemed deep in thought. Then, his eyes on Hepton, he reached into his trouser pocket and produced a tiny gun, so dainty that it might have been a trick cigarette lighter. It might have been, but Hepton thought otherwise.

'Help has arrived,' the man said. He took two paces back from the door and pointed his gun at it. Hepton knew instinctively what was expected of him now. He released his grip on the handle, stepped back and gave the wood a mighty kick. The door flew open and the man crouched lower, still levelling the gun . . . But apart from Devereux's corpse, the room appeared empty. More than that, it *felt* empty. Hepton studied the scene. He couldn't imagine Harry hiding under the bed or in the wardrobe. The windows were double-glazed, impossible to open, so there was no escape route there. Which left only the bathroom. He looked at his new-found accomplice, who nodded in understanding. Together they walked to the bathroom door, the man pausing only quickly, expertly to check for any sign of a pulse in Devereux's wrist. There was none.

The bathroom door was slightly ajar, and Hepton glanced into the white-tiled room. A thick splash-proof curtain had been drawn across the shower. He pushed open the door and pointed to the curtain. The man aimed his pistol again, and Hepton yanked the curtain aside. The cubicle was empty. Hepton exhaled noisily and raised his eyes to the ceiling, where they stayed.

'Look,' he said. The man looked up too, and saw that the ceiling was a false one, with one small section pushed aside to reveal a dark gap.

'You think she has escaped?' the man asked in a whisper.

Hepton considered. No, the ceiling would not support a body's weight, and besides, where could it lead? Nowhere. He dashed back into the room and looked around. The wardrobe door was open now. Inside, the suits and shirts had been pushed along on their railing to allow a body to squeeze into the space. He placed his head in the wardrobe. He could smell soap: Harry's soap. He ran to the door and looked down the corridor, but there was no sign of her.

'Give me your gun,' he ordered. The man seemed startled. 'Give it to me.' He snatched the weapon from the man's hand and ran out of the room. He headed down the corridor towards the main staircase, and took the steps two at a time. There were guests in the reception area, buying newspapers, talking to the desk clerk, about to walk off breakfast. They stared at Hepton as he made for the glass doors, pushed through them and stood on the top step. The traffic below was snarled, becoming angry. The day was hazy. Still no Harry.

A moment or two later, he heard some foreign words behind him and turned to see the man barking something at the hotel's doorman. Then he walked towards Hepton, smiling, his hand held out palm upwards.

'My gun, please.' Hepton handed the pistol back, and the man slipped it into his pocket.

'That was Russian you were speaking,' Hepton said. The man ignored him.

'We had better be going,' he said.

'But a man's dead,' Hepton protested.

'Good reason for us not to be here, my friend.'

'Who are you?' Hepton asked.

'Come on.' The man gripped his arm. 'We'll take a ride.' He propelled Hepton towards a waiting black cab. Hepton hesitated, but climbed into the back of the taxi, followed by the man, who told the driver to head towards Holborn. Then he turned to Hepton. 'I'm sorry for Mr Devereux,' he said. 'But there's nothing more to be done. My name is Vitalis, and yours is . . .?'

'Martin Hepton.'

Vitalis nodded, giving no indication that he recognised the name. 'Were you a friend of Mr Devereux?'

'In a way. And you?'

'Yes. I suppose you could call me a friend.'

'A friend who carries a gun.'

Vitalis smiled, but said nothing.

'A friend who carries a gun because he fears danger,' Hepton continued. 'Because he *knows* Devereux's life is threatened.'

Vitalis shrugged.

'Who are you?' Hepton persisted.

Vitalis didn't respond. 'The time for questions is past,' he said. 'Now is a time for action.'

Hepton found himself agreeing with this.

'The assassin,' Vitalis said, 'you said it was a she.'

'A woman,' Hepton said. Vitalis nodded. 'You were his . . .' Hepton sought the correct word and found it. 'His controller. You were Devereux's controller, weren't you?'

'What makes you say that?' Vitalis' tone was amused.

Hepton nodded to himself. 'Cam told me,' he said, 'about some mysterious man at the *Argos* base. But the only way he could have known about such a person was if he had gone investigating, opening closed doors, that sort of thing. Because the mystery man would have been in a room of his own, with his own computer and everything. But why would Cam be spying? The answer's simple, isn't it?' He fixed Vitalis with his gaze. 'He *was* a spy, he was spying for *you*.'

'Bravo, Mr Hepton,' said Vitalis. 'Yes, well done.'

'And he had come to London to defect?' It was an educated guess.

'He thought his useful time was over. It happens.'

Another question was on Hepton's lips, but he swallowed it back. If Devereux were about to defect, why would the Russians keep him on so long a leash, and leave him unprotected to boot? *His useful time was over.* His useful time was over, and so he was expendable . . . Hepton stared at the driver's back. Was he too a spy? When would the killing stop?

'Where are we going?' he asked.

'Don't be alarmed. We're dropping me off near my place of work, and then the driver will take you back to your hotel.' Vitalis' eyes twinkled. 'I presume you are staying in a hotel?'

Hepton made no answer. Vitalis just nodded and smiled. He seemed amused by everything.

'I think I know you now,' he said. 'I think I know Martin Hepton. And I want to help you.'

'Why?'

Vitalis held out his hands. 'Because I am a generous man. So Devereux told you about the man he saw at the *Argos* base, the man in the storeroom that had been fitted with a computer console and a telephone?'

'Didn't I just say as much?' Hepton said, hoping to tease a little more out of this man. The traffic had cleared, and they were nearing Holborn. There wasn't much time. There were storerooms at Binbrook, too . . .

'And he told you about the telephone?'

'What about it?'

Vitalis paused to consider whether to tell or not. Hepton could feel his fists tightening. He wanted to hit this man very hard, to force something from him other than this casual chatter. To wipe the smile off his face. He looked at the driver again. The driver was looking back at him in the rear-view mirror. His eyes were hard like marbles.

'The telephone,' Vitalis began. 'Devereux was intrigued by the telephone.'

'A modem?'

'No.' He shook his head. 'It had no dial as such. You couldn't call out, you see; all anyone could do was pick up the receiver. Devereux picked up the receiver and waited.'

'And?'

'And he was connected to somewhere here in England, Mr Hepton. To some kind of listening base. To a man who called himself Fagin.'

Fagin. The line led straight to Binbrook. Hepton tried to look composed but shifted in his seat. Vitalis seemed to know the exact effect his words were having. He glanced out of the window.

'This will do,' he called to the driver, who pulled the cab in to the kerb. 'Now, my friend Mr Hepton, can I offer you breakfast?'

Hepton shook his head. 'I don't eat with strangers.'

Vitalis shook his head. 'I am not a stranger. Well, perhaps I am. But we have a common enemy, it would seem. We have our ideas as to what is going on here. But that is not so important. All my people want to do is to observe, for the sake of our own safety.' His eyes were arch. 'Do *you* know what happened, Mr Hepton?'

'No,' Hepton said, shaking his head again.

'That is a lie,' Vitalis noted objectively. 'But I will let it pass. You will have your own reasons for saying nothing. As I say, we wish only to observe and to protect our interests. Now that Mr Devereux has been terminated, I profess I am more worried than I was. It proves . . . well, something at least.' He shrugged. 'It is your affair, Mr Hepton. By which I mean it is the West's affair. Do you know a Mr Parfit?'

Hepton considered another lie, but paused so long that a lie would have been obvious.

'Yes,' he said at last.

Vitalis seemed satisfied. 'Please give him a message from me. Tell him to remember Warszawa in '87. Goodbye, Mr Hepton.'

He stepped nimbly from the cab, gave some money to the driver and was gone, walking up High Holborn with the brisk step of a man on his way to work. Hepton thought about following, but the driver was awaiting his orders. Still, he was damned if he'd let him know where he was staying.

'Green Park,' he said. He would walk from there.

31

It took Parfit a couple of minutes to come fully awake, and while he washed in the bathroom, he made Hepton relate his story twice more. He seemed unmoved by Devereux's murder and the near-assassination of Hepton himself, but was interested in Vitalis. He was also interested in the acronym.

'I wonder if our code-crackers can come up with anything for COFFIN?' he mused, then shook his head. 'Tell me about Vitalis again.'

'Do you know him?' Hepton asked, admitting to himself that he wasn't going to get any sympathy for his own traumas.

'I should say so. We're old adversaries. He's not so active these days, of course. His cover is a bookshop somewhere near Holborn.'

'He's a Russian spy, though,' Hepton protested.

'Yes?' Parfit didn't seem to see his point.

'And you know where he is. Why hasn't he been arrested? Deported?'

Parfit laughed. 'Because then they'd just send home some of ours. Besides, it's nice having him here. It means we can slip him the odd piece. Let him decide whether or not it's true.'

Hepton shook his head. 'The more I know, the less sense it makes. What did he mean about Warsaw in '87?'

'Oh, we were having a bit of trouble out there. The Polish secret police were cracking down a bit too heavily on our diplomats, being a bit obvious in their operations, that sort of stuff. We could have done something about it ourselves, but we passed on a message to Moscow and let the Kremlin deal with it. They slapped a few wrists, and things calmed down again.'

'So what does it mean?'

'It means we're being allowed to deal with this mess ourselves, without outside interference.'

'You think he knows what this is all about?'

'Oh, he'll have more than an inkling.' Parfit had dried his face and was now combing his hair. He looked at himself in the mirror and swept a stray strand back behind his ear. 'More than an inkling,' he repeated. 'After all, as you said yourself, Devereux was his man.' He turned to Hepton. 'Let's get Major Dreyfuss and head for my office. If they wanted rid of Devereux, you can bet a shilling they want rid of Dreyfuss too.'

'But why did they want rid of him?'

'You mean Devereux? Probably because they realised what his game was, that's all.'

Hepton stood for a moment, wondering how Parfit could take it all so rationally, so calmly. Then, aware that he was alone now, he made a dash for the door and followed the cool secret serviceman to Dreyfuss' room.

Dreyfuss was quiet during the short drive towards Westminster Bridge. Hepton sat with him in the back, while Parfit sat with the driver in the front. Parfit had a briefcase on his lap; in it was a cellnet-style telephone, with which he made a steady stream of calls. The driver paid no attention to these, busying himself with the heavy, slow-moving traffic instead. His style of driving was the antithesis of Sanders': careful, methodical, courteous. All the same, the traffic being what it was – and London drivers being what they were – he had to fall into the shunting rhythm of the cars around him, slamming the brakes on, pulling away fast, then slamming them on again. Each jolt seemed to make Dreyfuss wince. Hepton saw that he was holding his right arm with his good left hand, trying to steady it against unwanted motion.

'You should have that in a sling,' he observed. But Dreyfuss did not reply. Parfit, hearing Hepton and glancing in the rear-view mirror, saw the sheen of sweat on Dreyfuss' forehead, indicative of continuing pain.

'Take some more tablets,' he ordered.

'I'm fed up with being doped,' Dreyfuss said through bared teeth. 'I'd rather have pain and all my faculties intact than being in that bloody stupor all the time.'

'Suit yourself.' Parfit made another call.

Dreyfuss turned to Hepton.

'First Jilly. Now Cam. We're letting these people get away with murder.' He nodded his head towards the passenger seat. '*He's* not going to do anything about it. Not if it involves scandal. He's paid to cover things up, not let them get into the open.' Dreyfuss' voice was becoming conspicuously loud, but Parfit made a show of not listening. 'If we're going to do anything, Martin, it's got to be you and me.' His eyes, the pupils tiny pinpoints, were boring into Hepton's. 'You and me.'

'Yes,' Parfit commented, 'you've done so well on your own, haven't you?'

Dreyfuss made a face at him behind his back, then winked at Hepton. 'You and me,' he mouthed noiselessly, before sitting back and watching from his window.

Hepton watched from his window too, but he wasn't really seeing anything. He was thinking over what Dreyfuss had said; that, and a lot more besides . . .

32

Blake Farquharson was waiting for them in Parfit's office. Hepton had expected that their destination would be Whitehall and the Foreign Office. But in fact they had travelled south, past the Houses of Parliament, over Westminster Bridge and into Westminster Bridge Road. Their destination was a large office block, where passes once more had to be issued before they headed up in the lift towards Parfit's floor.

Parfit's office, too, was modern, belying his old-world appearance. The desk was cream-coloured and constructed of metal and plastic and chipboard. The chairs were made from tubular steel, their fabric a gaudy lime-green design. There was a large cabinet against one wall, protected by a steel rod and a tumbler lock. Beside it stood a smaller filing cabinet, again protected from prying eyes. The windows were covered by prodigious quantities of net curtain – to stop glass from a potential bomb blast spraying the room, as Parfit later explained. There were calendars and year-planners on two walls, and a coffee table upon which sat a teapot and three mugs, whose interiors were growing cultures not dissimilar in colour to that of the chair fabric.

And in one chair sat Blake Farquharson, though he stood when they entered.

'Hello, Parfit.'

'Good morning, Blake.' The two men shook hands warmly, like old friends after a separation. 'You've already met Martin Hepton. This . . .' Parfit gestured towards Dreyfuss, but Farquharson interrupted.

'. . . Must be Major Dreyfuss,' he said, holding out his hand.

Dreyfuss stared at it, but kept his own by his side. Then Farquharson noticed the bandage and brought his outstretched hand up to his mouth, using it to shield an embarrassed cough.

'We had a spot of bother,' Parfit explained. He had gone to his desk and was sifting through the mass of paperwork awaiting him. He read the top sheets thoroughly, while the rest of the room kept an awkward silence. Dreyfuss had grabbed one of the chairs and was trying to make himself comfortable. Hepton preferred to stand, and went to the window. Parfit put down the sheets. 'Sanders' report,' he stated.

'Yes,' said Farquharson, 'I read it while I was waiting. I'm not sure about Sanders. He's keen, but . . .'

'That's his problem,' Hepton muttered.

'What's that?' Farquharson barked.

Hepton turned to him. 'Your Sanders,' he said. 'He's all enthusiasm, no brains. I'll give you an example.'

'Please do,' Farquharson said slyly.

'Okay, when we went to talk to Cam Devereux – who died this morning, by the way, not that you'll lose much sleep over *that* small fact – the doorman at the Achilles told us we couldn't park where we'd parked. Sanders flashed some kind of ID, which the doorman studied.'

'Yes? Is that all?'

'No,' said Hepton. 'I went back to the hotel this morning. I tried to catch a killer, and a Soviet agent helped me.'

Farquharson's eyes opened wide, and he looked to Parfit for confirmation.

'Vitalis,' Parfit said in a neutral voice. Farquharson nodded.

'And this Vitalis,' Hepton continued, getting to his point, 'stopped on the way out of the hotel to have a few words with the doorman; a few words in Russian.'

'Is that so?' Farquharson looked to Parfit again. 'That's a useful piece of information.'

But Parfit shook his head. 'We've known about the doorman for a while.'

'Well, Sanders obviously didn't know about him,' Hepton said, his voice increasing by a decibel or two. 'Besides which, I've been thinking over what Mike was saying in the car.' At the sound of his name, Dreyfuss became attentive. 'He was saying,' Hepton continued, 'that you seem to know a lot but aren't prepared to do anything about it. It strikes me that he hit the nail firmly on the head. You know about Vitalis but don't do anything about him; you know about the doorman at the Achilles but don't do anything about *him*. And now you know almost everything there is to know about this COFFIN business: it's to do with satellites, and Buchan airbase, and Major Villiers, and Harry, and General Esterhazy, and most probably my boss Fagin. But' – he began to space his words for effect – 'you're not doing one damned thing about it.' He paused, and noticed how loud his voice had become. Dreyfuss was smiling encouragement at him and applauded silently as he finished.

Farquharson didn't like being shouted at. His cheekbones were veined with blood, his voice tremulous. 'Well then, let me tell you a few things, Mr Hepton,' he said. 'We need proof, solid hard factual proof. Because RAF stations and tracking stations and their like are out of our jurisdiction. In fact, there's precious little that *isn't* out of our jurisdiction. The intelligence services have no formal powers. We have to work with Special Branch, and they're not convinced so far by what we've told them. We can't get Number Ten to listen to us, because frankly the PM has been got at by military advisors and MoD officials. Our agents in the field have found nothing, so there's precious little we can do at this moment. Except wait.'

'What?' Hepton was yelling now. Yelling out all his fear and frustration, all the last few days of madness and murder. 'Wait for them to pick us off? Look, whatever this COFFIN is, it's been buried. How do we find something once it's buried? We don't. The longer we sit here, the more chance they've got of getting away with whatever it is they're getting away with while we sit here!'

'Bravo!' Dreyfuss called. He was smiling grimly.

'Who told you the coffin was buried?' Parfit asked in a purposely quiet voice.

'What?' Hepton asked.

'Who told you?'

'Harry did. Well, sort of. She certainly didn't deny it.'

'And you believed her?'

'Why would she lie? She was going to kill me.'

'But she didn't.' Hepton began to see Parfit's point. 'Now answer me another question: why is the *Zephyr* ground station being temporarily decommissioned?'

Hepton pondered this. He gave up and shrugged his shoulders.

'I'll tell you,' said Parfit. 'Or rather, I'll tell you *my* interpretation. The coffin *isn't* buried yet – not quite. But they know we're getting close. They'll put a ring of steel around Buchan, but they can't stop *Zephyr* spying on them from space. That's why they went to an extraordinary amount of effort to nobble it. But because we're closing in, they want to make doubly sure, so they're sending the sky-watchers home until the burial's complete. That means there's still time for an exhumation.'

'Fine,' said Dreyfuss coolly. 'So what do we do?'

Parfit turned to Farquharson, his eyes asking the same question.

'We wait.' Farquharson saw that Hepton was about to protest and hurried on. 'We wait until we see what information comes back from Buchan. If there's enough to present to the PM, then I'll arrange a meeting.'

'And if there isn't?' There seemed no ready answer to Hepton's question. He repeated it.

Farquharson looked to Parfit, but Parfit's face was a blank.

'We've got video tapes,' Hepton continued. 'Don't *they* count as evidence?'

'They indicate that something's going on,' said Parfit quietly, 'not what that something is.'

'You mean they're not enough?'

'What do you think?'

Hepton considered. The tapes suddenly seemed very small in comparison to the scale of the conspiracy.

Dreyfuss was shaking his head. 'You're going to let them get away with it,' he said bluntly.

Farquharson slapped the desk. 'Get away with what exactly? We don't know what's happening, do we?'

But Dreyfuss only smiled, as if to say: *I've got a damn good idea.*

33

The first report arrived just after they'd eaten a lunch of sandwiches and tea. The tea came in disposable beakers, which was a relief to Hepton, who had feared the offer of one of the mouldy mugs. He was finishing his last cheese sandwich when the telephone rang. Parfit, himself still chewing, picked up the receiver.

'Yes?' he said. He listened, his eyes fixed to the wall in front of him. 'Is that everything?' he said finally. 'Thank you.' He replaced the receiver in its cradle and swallowed some tea.

'Well?' asked Farquharson.

'That was our man in Buchan. He's been past the base. Heavily guarded, and not very subtly. He stopped to ask why, and was told that there had been anonymous threats concerning the pull-out. He says there *is* a pull-out taking place, but there's also a lot of work going on. He thought perhaps they were busy dismantling something.'

'Dismantling something?' Farquharson repeated. 'What sort of thing?'

Parfit shrugged his shoulders. 'He couldn't be sure that it was dismantling.'

'So it could be building work then?' said Hepton.

'Building work?' Farquharson sounded sceptical. 'But that would be noticeable, wouldn't it?'

'Not if it was underground,' said Hepton. 'As in "burial".'

'That's the impression I get,' Parfit agreed. 'They've got to be building something underground.'

'Such as?'

He shrugged again. 'If we knew what COFFIN stood for, we might get an answer.'

'So,' Dreyfuss said, pointing at Farquharson, '*are* you going to go see the PM?'

Farquharson was flustered. 'What with?' he exclaimed.

Dreyfuss got to his feet. 'With everything you've got. It all adds up to quite something, after all, doesn't it? Drag the PM up to Buchan if you have to, but do *something*!'

Farquharson looked to Parfit, but saw in him no ally ready to leap to his defence. He examined his trouser legs thoughtfully and picked a thread from one. 'Very well,' he said. 'I'll do what I can. May I use your phone?'

'Be my guest,' said Parfit.

Farquharson picked up the receiver and punched out a few numbers. 'Hello,' he said, 'it's Blake Farquharson here. Any chance of a word with the chief? Yes, I'm afraid it *is* urgent. Urgent as in very.'

Hepton and Dreyfuss were given leave to visit the canteen, situated in the building's basement.

'I'll get someone to show you where it is,' said Parfit.

'We'll find it,' Dreyfuss snarled. But he calmed almost immediately and apologised. 'I'd just like Martin and me to have a little time to ourselves, to talk about, well, Jilly. Is that okay?'

Parfit looked cowed. 'I'm sorry,' he said, 'if it seems we're not doing enough to locate and free her. I admit it's needle-in-a-haystack stuff, but we *are* trying. Try to relax a little. I'll join you shortly.'

'No rush.'

Whether irony was intended or not, Parfit caught some in Dreyfuss' words. No rush indeed. Farquharson had gone off to Downing Street. The prime minister had agreed to give him a ten-minute interview, starting at quarter past four, which barely gave him time to gather together the relevant details and assimilate them. Still, actually gathering the details was a job for Farquharson's PA, Tony Poulson. Poulson would be panicking right about now, and the thought pleased Parfit greatly. What Farquharson saw in the man was quite beyond him. He had even instigated his own highly furtive investigation of Poulson's past and private life, but with precious little success: the man was as clean as a nun's conscience. But then how clean was that?

He sat behind his desk, wondering if he should have insisted on accompanying Farquharson to Number Ten. He stared at his door, thinking of Dreyfuss and Hepton. Pity the canteen wasn't bugged, but no member of staff would have stood for it . . .

Parfit was a patient man, but also a man who enjoyed the occasional slice of action. He had, for instance, thoroughly enjoyed breaking the man's neck at the airport in DC. He hoped one day to enjoy killing Harry. But it had to be sanctioned. Given that sanction, he was ready to fall on Villiers, Harry and the rest with the most extreme prejudice he could muster. A nod from the PM, that was all he craved right now. His men were ready to act. He'd arranged for Special Branch to turn a temporary blind eye. And he had the necessary tools of his profession to hand. A nod was all he needed. But he doubted he'd get it. All the same . . .

He went to the door and locked it, then crossed to the large cabinet, worked the combination and drew the steel rod out from its resting place. Pulling the cabinet open, he revealed his small but lethal arsenal. Pride of place went to his two preferred handguns, a Walther PPK and a Browning nine-millimetre pistol, the latter's magazine already engaged, thirteen rounds ready for the firing: unlucky for some. He tested its weight. Both guns had been stripped, oiled, checked and rechecked since last use. He put them back and examined the other firearm, a Heckler & Koch MP5 sub-machine gun. Several years before, Parfit had accepted a challenge from an SAS captain to spend some time with the regiment's Counter Revolutionary Warfare Unit as they played out a close-quarters scenario in what had become known as the Killing House. This was a closed environment in which they had to imagine three terrorists were holding a hostage. The captain's summary of Parfit's performance had been frank: 'That was fucking awful. You killed each and every one of them, the hostage included.' But then that had been Parfit's intention, since his job usually entailed tidiness of the most rigorous kind.

Still, he had liked the feel of the MP5s used by the unit, and had acquired one, its serial number removed. Now he touched its barrel, thinking of Harry. Did he hate her so much because he saw so much of himself in her? It was a question he would rather not answer. He lifted the MP5 fluidly to his shoulder and took imaginary aim at the office door.

'Hello, Harry,' he whispered.

There were no windows in the canteen, and the air conditioning was working flat out just trying to dissipate the smells of cooking, of hot fat and baked beans. Sad murals the colour of mud played over the walls, while afterthoughts such as room dividers and pot plants merely added to the institutional feel of the whole. Hepton and Dreyfuss were the only inhabitants. They had been given cold stares and lukewarm tea by one of the canteen staff.

'Too late for food,' she'd snapped.

'Thank God for that,' Dreyfuss had added in an undertone as she poured tea from a huge tin pot. The tea was the same colour as the wall decoration, which gave Hepton an idea as to the mural's genesis.

They sat at the only table not to have been wiped and stacked with four upended chairs. The table came from the same family, it seemed, as Parfit's desk upstairs: cream plastic and chipboard. This was a sad country, Hepton thought, a stupid country. But it still didn't deserve to be handed over to Villiers and Harry.

'It's not a coup,' Dreyfuss stated. 'A coup would be simpler, more out in the open.'

'Maybe the Yanks want to annex us?'

Dreyfuss shook his head. 'They did that a long time ago. It's just that nobody noticed. No . . . I don't know.' He threw up his hands. 'And neither do that lot upstairs. There's only one way to find out.'

'How?' Hepton was sure they were working along similar lines of thought. Dreyfuss' answer confirmed it.

'Your little tracking station.'

Hepton nodded. It made sense, didn't it? The only way Villiers and his crew could keep an eye on the Buchan operation was to use Binbrook. He thought about what the Russian Vitalis had told him. That Cam Devereux had found another room in the *Argos* base. There could be another room at Binbrook, too, a whole series of rooms, fitted with computers and screens showing what *Zephyr* was *really* seeing. Now that he considered it, he realised that there *were* portions of Binbrook that were off-limits to personnel. Locked doors: someone had called them storage areas, someone else had said they were disused and awaiting redecoration. Those locked doors might well be hiding a small, dedicated tracking station. A box within a box, like Izzard's. And if such were the case, there would probably be someone there to watch: someone like Fagin, of course, but perhaps also Villiers himself. And where Villiers was, Jilly might be . . .

'What are you suggesting?' he asked.

'I'm suggesting . . .' Dreyfuss brought his head closer to Hepton's. His eyes burned with something other than drugged or drugless pain, 'that we do something other than sitting around here on our arses. There isn't much time. I'm not saying that we go barging in there, but is everyone on the base in on this COFFIN thing? I think the answer is a definite no, or they wouldn't be moving them out. Okay, so there's the chance that you' – his finger made a circle in the air – 'could move freely inside the base. As far as they're aware, you've been on holiday. So just tell them you've come back early.'

'What about you?'

'Me?' Dreyfuss considered this. 'Do you know how they got me from Washington airport to the embassy? In a crate. After that, a car boot will come as something of a luxury.'

'A car boot?'

He nodded slowly. 'Of course,' he said, 'there is a snag. First, we need a car. We could hire one, I suppose. I've got all sorts of false documents and credit cards on me.'

'What about Parfit? Are you suggesting we do this without him?'

'That's exactly what I'm suggesting.'

'But why?'

'Because I don't trust him. I don't trust anyone in this whole thing who hasn't been hurt. You've been hurt, I've been hurt, and right now someone could be hurting Jilly. You've seen how Farquharson operates. He's scared of COFFIN. He's not going to do anything.'

'We don't know that.' But Hepton's voice betrayed his feelings. The time for action had come. He knew his way around the Binbrook base, and Dreyfuss was right: alone, he might stand a good chance of gaining entry. Once inside, he could . . .

'I could tap into their intercept,' he said.

'What?'

It was becoming quite lucid now. Somehow he'd known all along that this moment would come. The moment when he could put his skill to the test. A moment of challenge.

'I could tap into their intercept,' he repeated. Dreyfuss listened hungrily. 'I'm sure I could. I could screw up their entire system.'

'But won't there be alarms? Protection circuits? That sort of thing?'

Hepton nodded. 'Oh yes,' he said. 'There'll be codes. Entry codes. We'd have to crack them.'

'That could take for ever.'

This time he shook his head. 'I've got a friend,' he said, 'and he's got a little box . . .'

Dreyfuss thought things through. Gain entry to the camp, gain entry to the control room, break into the spoiler satellite . . . Hepton could work on that, while he, Dreyfuss, could look for Jilly. And for Villiers. A lot of ghosts were crying out for revenge. So were a few of the living.

'Right,' he said. 'If you think it's worth a try, I say we leave now, this second. Before Parfit and his boss have a chance to hold us back. I get the feeling somebody's been holding us back all the way along. Like bloody fish on a line. Allow us a bit of play, then reel us back in. Seeing what we know, how far we'll swim. Hoping we'll tire, so that we're easy to land . . .'

But Hepton wasn't listening. He was watching a young man who had entered the canteen and was studying one of the snack-vending machines at the far end of the room. He waved a hand, but it wasn't necessary. He had already been recognised. The man, smiling, approached their table.

'Hello again,' he said. 'I didn't think I'd be seeing you so soon.'

Hepton motioned towards the man and turned to Dreyfuss. 'Let me,' he said, 'introduce you to Mr Sanders. Sanders, this is Major Mike Dreyfuss.'

'How do you do?' The two men nodded. Dreyfuss was looking to Hepton for guidance.

'Sanders here,' Hepton explained, 'is a marvellous driver. He has a very fine Vauxhall Cavalier.'

Now Dreyfuss saw what he was getting at. His smile when he turned back towards Sanders was rapacious.

'Is that right?' he said. 'A Cavalier?'

'Yes,' said Sanders, pleased at their interest but unsure just *why* they were interested. 'It's parked in the garage downstairs.'

34

Later, Sanders was able to reflect that that was the moment, really, when he lost his job. Because he didn't see what they were getting at. Because he told them about the modified engine, modified for speed. Because when Major Dreyfuss asked to see the car, he didn't check with Mr Parfit. Because he accompanied them past the security guard and down to the parking bays. Because he turned his back on them to open the door of the Cavalier . . .

And then woke up with a sore head and the drip of oil on his face. Staring up at the underside of a car and realising he had been knocked unconscious and hidden beneath the vehicle in the bay next to his. His bay, which was by then conspicuously empty.

The walk he took back upstairs – walking because it was slower than taking the lift, and he wished to defer the inevitable – was funereal. Yet necessary. There was no way he could hide what had happened. He had to tell Mr Parfit.

He was breathless when he reached Parfit's floor, and realised with some surprise that he had just walked up eight flights of stairs. He remembered none of it.

He knocked on Parfit's door.

'Yes?'

He turned the handle and entered. Parfit was seated behind his desk, his hand poised on the telephone as though expecting a call.

'Ah, Sanders,' he said. 'Come in. If it's about your report, I really haven't had a proper chance to read it yet, but I'm sure it's . . .'

He stopped short. There was oil in Sanders' hair, and the boy looked deathly pale, looked, indeed, beaten about a bit. Then it dawned.

'Oh my God,' he said. 'Where are they?'

'They've taken the car, sir. The Cavalier.'

'Get me another car!' Parfit had already picked up the receiver and was dialling. 'Hello?' he said. 'Let me speak to Detective Inspector Frazer.' He put his hand over the mouthpiece and spoke to Sanders. 'We've got to find them before they leave London.' He removed his hand. 'Hello, Craig? Parfit here. Yes, long time no see. I want a favour. A very important one. Can you get your lads to keep their eyes peeled for a red Vauxhall Cavalier.' He asked Sanders for the registration, and then repeated it down the line. 'Thanks, Craig. Goodbye.' He stared hard at Sanders. 'I thought I told you to get us a car!'

'Yes, sir.' Sanders dashed out of the room, holding his neck where the fist had chopped down on it.

When the door was closed, Parfit took a deep breath and stared at his cabinet. It was time. He was about to rise from his chair when the telephone rang. He picked it up without thinking.

'Parfit?' said the voice. 'Blake here.'

'Blake.' Parfit's heartiness was bluff, and nothing but.

'I've had my say, but the PM reckons it's too amorphous – actual words, "too bloody vague". We're to gather a bit more intelligence before we can act.'

'It may be too late by then.' Parfit was thinking: it may be too late right *now*. The cabinet beckoned.

'Nevertheless, those are the orders from on high.'

'Since when did that stop us, Blake?'

'I don't know what you mean,' Farquharson said, his tone full of meaning. It was time to tell him.

'Dreyfuss and Hepton have left us, headed who knows where.'

The silence on the line was as piercing as any scream. There was a cough of static before Farquharson's too-calm voice said, 'What will they try to do?'

'That's what I'm wondering myself, Blake. I'd say they're capable of trying anything, and I do mean anything.'

'Oh my God.'

'So, PM or no PM, it looks as though there is no alternative. No point in my hanging around here either, so I'm going out into the field.' Parfit paused. 'With your permission.'

Blake Farquharson knew what 'going out into the field' meant in Parfit's terms. He thought quickly but hard. But then, as Parfit had said, there was no alternative.

'Of course,' he said. 'You must do what you think fit.'

'Thank you, Blake.'

'But promise me one thing.'

'Yes?'

'Keep it as low-key as possible.'

'Trust me, Blake.'

'What if you don't find them?'

'Oh, I think I'll find them. I've got a sneaking suspicion I know exactly where they'll be headed.'

He put the receiver down. Then picked it up immediately.

'Get me Downing Street, please.' He waited for the connection to be made. 'Hello? Ah, hello. This is Tony Poulson, assistant to Blake Farquharson. I believe Blake had a meeting with the PM scheduled for this afternoon. I was just wondering—'

'Haven't you been told?' The voice on the other end of the line was curt to the point of rudeness. 'Your boss took ill.'

'Took ill?'

'Had to call off. After the bloody lengths we went to to find ten minutes for him in the PM's schedule. No one is amused, Mr Poulson. Good day.' And the line went dead.

Parfit's smile was part vindication, part acceptance of the betrayal. Farquharson had never intended keeping his appointment. It was a delaying tactic, as had been so much of the game thus far. Parfit had run a check on the lease on Villiers' apartment. The route to ownership had been circuitous, cleverly so, keeping one name as far away from prying eyes as possible. The name had been Farquharson's. He owned the flat, as he owned its former occupant.

Well, nothing could be done about that now. He could leave Farquharson for the moment. For now, he had better things to do. He didn't doubt that Hepton and Dreyfuss would be making for Binbrook, and that if they actually got there, they would inflict at least some damage, perhaps even enough damage. He phoned Frazer again.

'Craig?' he said. 'Cancel that request, will you? If your lads see the car, let me know about it. But don't apprehend.'

The larger the web had grown, the smaller its circumference had become, almost in defiance of the physical laws. Not that laws meant much any more. Parfit put down the receiver and went to the cabinet. There was, as always, no real alternative.

35

Graeme Izzard didn't seem surprised to see Hepton, and greeted him like an old friend. Hepton had ordered Dreyfuss to stop the red Cavalier beside the taxis outside Alfie's café. Inside, Izzard was tucking into the all-day breakfast.

'Morning,' he said by way of greeting.

'It's late afternoon, in case you hadn't noticed,' Dreyfuss commented. Hepton and Izzard shared a conspiratorial smile: for Izzard, it was the start of the day.

'What can I do for you?' Izzard asked, his mind more on the tussle he was having with a particularly tough slice of middle bacon.

'It's about your little device,' Hepton began, 'the one you showed me last night.'

'Which one? I seem to remember I showed you hundreds.'

'Yes, but you kept this one in a cupboard. A relic of your hacking days . . .'

Thirty minutes later, Dreyfuss and Hepton left the industrial estate, Hepton driving and Dreyfuss clutching a small black box topped with an old calculator fascia. An unmarked police car was idling near the entrance to the estate. Five minutes later, the call went through to Parfit.

It was past six o'clock when Hepton drove up to the security barrier of the tracking station. A change of shifts was taking place. A young, unsmiling man – a stranger to Hepton – was being replaced by Bert, who had been at the station as long as anyone. Hepton sounded his horn, but Bert, not recognising the car, came out of the hut to check. Seeing who it was, he broke into a gap-toothed grin.

'Mr Hepton sir. I thought you'd gone off on holiday.'

'I was called back. Something about the place shutting down for a while. I've got to collect my things.'

'Ah, yes, shutting down. As from tomorrow, so they tell me. Mind you, *I'll* still be here. You always need security.' Hepton nodded agreement. Bert was giving the car's paintwork a cursory examination. 'I see you've been buying yourself a new car, Mr Hepton.'

'No, it's on loan. I had a little mishap with the Renault.'

'I'm sorry to hear that.' Bert was walking around to the back of the car. Hepton watched him in the wing mirror.

'Anything the matter?' he called.

'Should there be, Mr Hepton?'

'No,' he said, laughing. *Just don't look in the boot.*

'Yes, sir, a very nice car this. Hired, did you say?'

'No, it's a friend's.'

'I suppose I should log it in,' Bert said. He had finished his tour and was returning to the driver's-side window. 'All cars are supposed to be logged, aren't they?'

Hepton shrugged. 'I suppose so,' he said casually.

'Then again,' Bert reasoned, 'if you're only coming in to pick up some stuff . . .'

'That's all.'

'And you've just borrowed this car . . . well, I suppose it hardly matters, does it?'

'Whatever you think, Bert. So long as it won't get you into trouble.'

'Well then, I'll just go and raise the barrier.'

'Thanks, Bert.' Hepton thought of something. 'Oh, Bert?'

'Yes, Mr Hepton?'

'That security man, the one who just clocked off. He's new, isn't he?'

'Started yesterday. His name's Ken. Quiet bloke, keeps himself to himself. But he seems to like the job.'

'Right.' Hepton seemed satisfied with this, so Bert walked away from the car and towards his office, where a moment later he pushed the button that raised the barrier, allowing Hepton into the compound. Hepton gave a wave as he drove in, making for the other side of the administration building. There were plenty of parking spaces in front of the block, but he wanted to be far away from prying eyes. Thankfully, a few cars had parked at the rear, in a sort of courtyard enclosed by a picket fence, a hedge and an emergency generator, itself surrounded by high iron railings. Hepton did not drive to the furthest corner: there were no other vehicles there to provide cover. Instead, he made for the busiest point, where two cars had parked a bay apart, with another car a little distance in front of them. He manoeuvred the Cavalier into the narrow space between the two cars and turned off the engine. Yes, the new security man on the gate liked his job . . . They were moving their own men into the base. Slowly but surely, COFFIN was taking over.

He opened the driver's-side door as far as it would go without denting the car next to him and squeezed out, then closed the door again but did not lock it. He wasn't planning on staying long, and their leave-taking might have to be rapid. Unlocking a door took time, time they might not have.

He looked around. The place was quiet. There was a security camera trained on the back of the admin block and on the path that led towards the control building, but no camera, he knew for a fact, covered this rear car park. He unlocked the boot.

Dreyfuss blinked into the light and quickly, silently, pulled himself out of his foetal position. While Hepton relocked the boot, Dreyfuss did some limbering exercises. The boot had been a tight squeeze, and he was thankful he'd only needed to be in it for the last mile of the drive. He shook his arms loose of any stiffness and straightened his clothes.

'I thought your pal at the gate was going to ask to see inside,' he said.

'To be honest,' answered Hepton, 'so did I. But I already had a story ready about the boot being jammed shut.'

'Very likely,' Dreyfuss said. He was taking deep breaths.

'Okay,' Hepton said. He pointed towards the meandering line of paving slabs, cracked and showing tufts of wild grass. 'That's the path we take. There's a camera trained on it beginning and end, so look relaxed. Pretend I've just arrived on base and bumped into you.'

'Fine,' Dreyfuss replied.

They set off, Dreyfuss with his hands in his pockets and seeming to listen intently to what Hepton was saying, not that Hepton was saying very much other than reminding him of the layout of the tracking station's interior. At the end of the path stood a hefty-looking steel door, and on the wall next to it a numerical keypad, topped by yet another video camera. Hepton tried to look nonchalant as he pressed home the combination 52339, then waited. There was a ca-chunk as the several locks on the door disengaged. He gave it a push, and they entered a sort of antechamber. Against one wall stood what looked like a clocking-in system, but instead of identifier cards, Dreyfuss saw that each slot held a plastic-coated name badge, and beside each name a photograph. Hepton reached for his own badge and tagged it to his trouser pocket. Dreyfuss took the first badge he saw and did likewise. He had been informed: *Some guys clip them to their shirts, others to their trousers. If we tag them to our trouser pockets, there's less chance of someone noticing that you're not the face on the ID.*

He had also been warned about the wall opposite this one, which was made of glass. Behind it, in a small room filled with video screens, sat another security guard. Hepton waved to the guard, who smiled and waved back, then pushed on through the interior door, Dreyfuss following mutely. Now they were in a long corridor, and walking briskly. Dreyfuss felt a kind of complete terror overtake him. They were getting deeper and deeper into this, almost too deep to facilitate any hope of escape. Hepton misread his companion's fear.

'Don't worry,' he said. 'I reckon that with the shutdown, and the change of staff, nobody's going to think a new face suspicious. In fact, we couldn't have picked a better day, all things considered. The only thing that bothers me is that there *are* so many new faces, all of them probably connected to COFFIN. That guard back there, for instance. I've never seen him before in my life.'

Dreyfuss nodded his head. 'So what if he checks up on us?' He was trying to walk at the same pace as Hepton, but it was difficult not to fall a step or two behind and let him take the lead. After all, Dreyfuss had little idea where they were going. But he had to *look* as though he knew. He stared at the floor, matching his footsteps with those of his guide, and so concentrating grew less frightened and less nervous.

After a moment, he realised that Hepton hadn't answered his question. The silence was answer enough in itself. Any check, and they'd be doomed. Suddenly a voice sounded behind them, and both men froze.

'Hey! Martin! Hold on!' They turned slowly towards the voice. A man was approaching them, grinning. 'Martin, what are you doing back?'

'Hello, Nick.' This was what they hadn't wanted, but could hardly hope to avoid: close contact with someone who knew Hepton well.

'Did you get the tapes?' Nick Christopher asked.

'Yes, thanks,' answered Hepton.

Dreyfuss' good hand rested momentarily on Hepton's arm. 'I'll see you later,' he said, smiling towards Nick Christopher before moving off down the corridor. Christopher stared after him.

'Who was that?'

'Some new guy,' said Hepton.

'I get the feeling I've seen him somewhere before.'

'Oh?' Hepton was staring at Dreyfuss' back too, wondering where he was headed. Their plan, hatched on the way here, now seemed woefully inadequate and as full of holes as a disassembled circuit board. But then even on the way here it had seemed so. He turned to Christopher. 'Going to the control room?'

'Yes.'

'Me too. Come on.' They started down another corridor, away from Dreyfuss.

'But what are you doing back here? What was all that with the tapes?'

'I'll tell you later. Is Fagin about?'

'Somewhere, yes. Why?'

'I just need my console for an hour or so, and I'd rather he didn't know about it.'

'What are you going to do?'

'Nick.' Hepton came to a stop, gripping Christopher's shoulder. 'Remember Paul Vincent?'

'Of course.'

'He was murdered. If I can get on my computer for an hour, I think I can catch his killers. But I need your help.'

Christopher stared at him as though Hepton were mad. But Hepton's look was that of a sane man, a scared man, a man doing what he had to.

'What do you want me to do?'

'I want you to protect me. Try not to let anybody interfere with the computer.'

'No problem. But can't you tell me why?'

'Remember when you were younger, when you played with computers for fun rather than for work?' Christopher nodded. 'Did you ever do any hacking?'

Now Christopher smiled. 'Sure, everybody tried it at some time or other.'

Hepton nodded. 'That's what I'm going to attempt now. I'm going to try the scariest piece of hacking you'll ever see.'

Nick Christopher's face lit up. 'All right!' he said. 'Let's go.'

They were nearing their destination. Hepton needed to know what lay ahead. 'Have the new controllers arrived?' he asked.

'The skeleton staff? Yeah, most of them. And a few of the old gang have already left.'

Hepton nodded. 'And you don't know where Fagin is?'

'No idea.'

The storerooms that weren't really storerooms, he thought. It was perfect: as long as he was there, keeping an eye on his satellite, he was free to go to work. He pushed open a final set of doors.

The large central control room was chaotic. Some people were tidying their desks, some were monitoring *Zephyr*. There was a holiday mood in the air, jokes and laughter. Furniture was being moved, consoles dismantled or serviced. A few of the new faces looked at Hepton curiously as he moved past them. He tried to smile and nod affably. Well, he was already in the lion's cage; he might as well stick his head in a gaping mouth . . .

He passed Paul Vincent's desk. It was being dismantled. The computer had already been taken away. He touched the desktop with one finger, then walked to his own console, pulled the chair out and sat down. There was a fine layer of dust on the screen, and he wiped it with the palm of his hand before switching on. A few of the original crew, the genuine crew, saw him and called over. He waved back.

'Just in to tidy up a bit,' he explained. Any one of them could be in on it, could be part of the COFFIN conspiracy. He had to move quickly. But then he knew all the moves, didn't he? He'd been working them out for what seemed like days. He made the link with *Zephyr*'s onboard computer and checked its co-ordinates. It was just about right. Very soon now, within the next hour, it would be over Buchan. That gave him a little time to crack the access code. He already had two passwords he reckoned to be likely candidates – COFFIN and ARGOS. Then he'd let the computer work on the numerical sequence, if one existed, going through random combinations until it found the right one.

He pulled from his pocket Izzard's black box. If he remembered the instructions correctly, it would help save time. And time above all was precious. At any moment, he might be discovered. The new faces around him might twist suddenly with hate, guns pulled from pockets. Fagin might appear, or Villiers, or Harry. He didn't know how long he had. He only prayed it was time enough.

36

Dreyfuss walked slowly along this corridor and that. Two men walked past him carrying large holdalls. They smiled, assuming him to be one of the replacement crew perhaps. He smiled back and kept walking. A door was open, allowing him a view of an empty office. The desk had been cleared, but there was a clipboard lying on top of it. He darted into the room and darted out again, carrying the clipboard now. He held it against his chest, keeping his injured hand in his pocket. The hand had stopped giving him pain. Now, it just throbbed. Nobody seemed to be paying him much notice. He hoped Hepton was all right. Dreyfuss' part in the plan was more nebulous. He had to find Jilly, supposing they were keeping her here. It was an outside chance, though, wasn't it? Still, Hepton had told him about the disused stores. It was as good a place as any to look.

'Mr Fulton?' There was a man walking towards him. 'Mr Fulton?' he repeated. He was trying to examine Dreyfuss' name tag.

Dreyfuss looked down at it and saw that *Peter Fulton* was indeed typed there, with an indecipherable signature scrawled beneath. The small photograph was of a man younger than Dreyfuss, the hair fairer, and wearing glasses.

'Not a very good likeness,' the man noted.

Dreyfuss smiled, trying to look younger than his years. 'It was taken a while ago,' he said. He pointed to his eyes. 'And the contact lenses make a difference.'

The man thought for a moment, then nodded. 'Quite so,' he said. He gestured along the corridor with his arm. 'The guard on the main door told me you'd arrived. Shall we go?'

'Of course.' Go where? Dreyfuss was thinking. And who the hell was he supposed to be anyway? It would be just his luck if this Peter Fulton were crucial to the running of the station. They'd be asking him questions he couldn't possibly hope to answer.

'Everybody's ready,' the man said. Dreyfuss groaned silently. 'When did you arrive?'

'Oh, not long ago.'

The man nodded, seeming satisfied. He looked as though he had other things on his mind, which was fine by Dreyfuss. They walked through one set of doors, then another. At least they were progressing into uncharted territory. Dreyfuss checked each door they passed with his eyes, not sure what clues he might be given to Jilly's whereabouts: a scream perhaps, or a muffled cry? Guards outside the door?

They came to a security door. There were numbers on its handle, and the man pressed three of these before turning the handle itself. In this new corridor, things were quieter, cooler. There was a slow hum of air conditioning, the low sounds of distant voices. They came to a final door, and the man opened it, gesturing for Dreyfuss to precede him into the room. A very attractive young woman sat on a chair, watching a bank of TV screens, switching between surveillance of one part of the base and another. One side of her face was heavily made up.

The door closed solidly behind Dreyfuss, and when he turned, the man was pointing a Beretta pistol directly at his chest.

'The guard was right,' he told the woman, who had risen to her feet. 'Someone did take Peter Fulton's pass, unaware that Fulton flew off on holiday yesterday.' Dreyfuss' heart sank. 'I recognised him as soon as I saw him,' the man continued. 'Major Michael Dreyfuss, isn't it?'

'At your service,' Dreyfuss said softly. 'And you are . . .?'

'Didn't I say?' The man had come round to stand beside the woman. He bowed his head slightly, but the pistol never wavered. 'I'm George Villiers; you may have heard of me. And this is Harry.'

On hearing Dreyfuss' identity, a keen look had come into Harry's eyes. She examined him as though he were some rare species, some rare and *endangered* species.

'Where's Jilly?' Dreyfuss asked, his voice as brittle as a thread of ice.

Villiers ignored him. 'Harry,' he said, 'Major Dreyfuss came into the station with another man. I went and took a look at the main door just to be sure, and I was right – guess whose pass is missing all of a sudden?'

'Whose?' Her voice was soft and feminine.

'Martin Hepton's.'

The laugh was cavernous beyond her slender frame. She went to the desk and lifted an attaché case onto its surface. The locks clicked, and she pulled the case open. Inside was the most lethal-looking handgun Dreyfuss had ever seen. It resembled a heavily modified target pistol, with a long shining silver barrel. There was a sight in another compartment of the case's moulded interior, and she fixed this along the pistol. Then she closed the case again and brought a plastic carrier bag out from the bottom drawer of the desk, placing it over her left hand, which was now grasped around the carved butt of the gun. It didn't quite look as though she were merely carrying an empty bag, but the gun was sufficiently disguised. She touched the fingers of one hand to the scald marks on her face. Finally, wordlessly, and on silent feet, she walked to the door, opened it and left, closing it behind her.

Dreyfuss looked at Villiers, who appeared impressed by the performance. 'Where's Jilly?' he repeated.

'She's safe. For the moment. Why don't we sit down? I'm sure there are questions you want to ask. We have a little time until Harry returns. Fire away.'

Dreyfuss sat on the chair Harry had been using. Villiers, however, remained standing, leaning against the far wall next to another door.

'Okay,' said Dreyfuss. 'What's COFFIN?'

'An easy one to start with. Very well, let's take COFFIN's lid off.' Villiers smiled at his own joke, but Dreyfuss remained unmoved. Villiers' face lost its humour. 'COFFIN, Major Dreyfuss, stands for Combined Forces International Network. It has an interesting history. I myself was unaware of it until quite recently. By then, COFFIN had decided it needed a few agents in the field, people who couldn't be traced back to it. People, in other words, outwith the armed forces. Eventually they came to me, and were able to introduce me to Harry. Really, she's the more . . .' he seemed to search for the right word, '*professional* of the two of us. But I'm afraid we're very lowly figures, comparatively speaking.

'COFFIN came about by accident,' he continued. 'You see, generals don't always agree with their governments, and they command more respect from their men than do politicians. Well, a lot of generals – from the United States, the other NATO countries, even a few of the non-aligned states – got together and found that they had a good deal in common. More in common, in fact, than they did with their own countries' leaders. So they started to swap information, intelligence, that sort of thing, all very informally, very *sub rosa*. That seemed to work to everyone's advantage, so they started trading all kinds of things.'

'What kinds of things?'

'Oh, tactics, armaments, maybe even a few men for certain special missions. Of course, no one ever questioned orders, and so no one ever knew that the generals were doing more and more off their own bat, without anyone else knowing about it outside the forces themselves.'

Dreyfuss whistled, trying to sound impressed. Damn it, he *was* impressed, 'But how could you hope to keep something like that secret?'

'Easily enough,' said Villiers, warming to his subject. 'For one thing, who did they have to hide it from? A few men from the MoD and the more investigative of our journalistic profession. But the thing was so big – *is* so big – that virtually no one can see it! That's its beauty.'

'Then why the need for a burial?'

'Look around you, Major Dreyfuss.' George Villiers paced the floor like an actor of old. This was his big soliloquy, and he knew it, but to Dreyfuss he was all amateur dramatics. Amateur dramatics or no, he still held the Beretta. And while he held the gun, Dreyfuss could do little but listen.

'American defence strategy is forward-thinking,' Villiers was saying, 'forward meaning Europe, so as to prevent war on American soil. The American generals weren't happy about the enforced pull-out. It's all down to trust, and they weren't about to trust a civilian Britain not under the US umbrella. Anything might happen. We all might become bloody Europeans, and it's a short step from there to Euro-communism. They decided it wasn't *right*. So it was decided that a base was needed, an underground base, away from prying eyes. RAF Buchan was chosen as the intended site. It has a surveillance system, a few dozen staff and even a couple of silos.'

'Silos?'

'Nuclear silos, Major. Built when Britain was expecting to play host to American missiles.'

Dreyfuss' throat was suddenly very dry. 'Are there missiles, too?'

Villiers nodded eagerly. 'Yes,' he said. 'Isn't that amazing?'

'It's impossible.'

'Oh no, I assure you that it is *fact*. The missiles were already here. Instead of dismantling them, our cousins merely moved them around, stripping off a bit here and a bit there, then rebuilding new missiles from pieces of the old. Simplicity itself. After all, they already had more missiles here than anyone knew about.'

'But why do you need silos?'

'For the first strike.'

'What?' Dreyfuss' head spun.

'Buchan is merely the UK base. There are others dotted all over Europe. They are the centres of attack for a series of forthcoming coups, apparently by the armed forces of each country, but in reality by COFFIN. Soon after that, we launch the missiles.'

'But why, for God's sake?'

Villiers laughed. 'I took you for an intelligent man, Major. Think about it. Can you see Eastern Europe accepting such a series of coups so close to their borders and – if you'll excuse the pun – their satellites? No, they'll be forced to attack. But they'll be too late. *We'll* have hit them first!'

'This is mad.'

'No, it is completely sane, Major.'

'You're saying nobody's *noticed* any of this?'

'Buchan is isolated, as are the other chosen bases. The fact that the troops were pulling out gave the perfect cover for some excavation and building work. There was already a small underground chamber there, to protect the systems against nuclear attack. We disguised a building programme as a dismantling programme. The Scots are a wonderful nation, Major. They keep themselves to themselves, and so long as no one's interfering with them, they're happy to turn a blind eye to most things.'

Dreyfuss nodded. 'But,' he said, 'you couldn't hope to hide the construction work from the skies?'

'Exactly. Which is where *Zephyr* came in. I must say, the generals proposed a simple but ingenious idea. Tap into the surveillance satellite, and you can transmit anything you like. So that's what they did.'

'But I was on the shuttle that launched the pirate satellite.' It was a comment, nothing more. Dreyfuss was still looking for a chance to wrest the gun away from this insane man.

'Indeed you were,' Villiers said, smiling again. 'There was little that could be done about that. The mission had been planned for ages. The US pull-out was supposed to be amicable. To have suddenly announced that a Briton was no longer to go up in the shuttle would have been more than a mite suspicious.'

'More suspicious than blowing the shuttle up?' Dreyfuss felt queasy now, thinking of how heartlessly the crew of *Argos* had been dispatched.

'Yes.' Villiers seemed surprised by the question. 'I mean, shuttles do crash, don't they? Anyway, the generals made *Zephyr* work for them, rather than against them, which is a brilliant strategy. Of course, having decided that a Briton must go up, COFFIN had to be sure that the least capable member of the shortlist was chosen.' He was really enjoying himself now. He waved the gun across Dreyfuss' body, then up and down from head to toes. 'So there was the least risk of your seeing anything suspicious and reporting those suspicions back to Earth before the crash-landing. It all worked well enough, except that you survived the landing. At first, everyone thought you had amnesia, and decided to allow you a lease of life. And by the time General Esterhazy realised what a threat you really were, it was too late. You'd gone. And now here you are.'

'Yes, here I am.' Dreyfuss shook his head. 'I still don't understand, though. The ground crew, the technicians who worked on the *Argos* satellite, they must have *known* its purpose.'

'Why should they?' Villiers opened his arms for a second: not long enough for Dreyfuss to consider charging him, but enough to give him hope of a later opportunity. 'They built to a military design. They didn't need to know what that design's intention ultimately was, and' – Villiers stressed his final words – 'they just followed orders, the way they'd been taught.' He stared at the screens for a moment, then pointed to one. 'Look,' he said, 'there's your friend Hepton now. He's in the control room.'

Dreyfuss looked. Hepton was seated at his console, unaware of the camera trained on his sector of the room.

'Won't be long now till Harry finds him,' Villiers said. His face took on a glaze of sincerity. 'But what you really must try to understand,' he continued, 'is that COFFIN is operating for the greater good. It's *defence* we're talking about.'

'It's more like murder we're talking about,' Dreyfuss growled.

Villiers' gun hand twitched. 'The greater good,' he repeated, robotically. Dreyfuss remembered then what Parfit had said about Villiers: a cold-blooded killer with a history of instability. He tried to calm himself. The last thing he wanted to do right this second was die.

'Well, if that's what you believe,' he said evenly.

'We *do*, Major Dreyfuss. Believe me, we do.' Villiers paused, seeming to drink in his own sense of power. 'Any more questions?' he asked. Dreyfuss shook his head. 'Then if you'll follow me, or rather, *precede* me through here . . .' He lifted his left arm to unbolt another door.

Dreyfuss stood, taking a final look at the surveillance screen. He had no way of letting Hepton know Harry was on her way. 'Where are we going?' he asked.

'I thought you wanted to find Miss Watson?' said Villiers. 'Besides, you haven't seen half of what we're doing here. Not nearly half.'

Then he pulled open the door to another world.

37

It had all gone smoothly at first. Hepton had done a spot of hacking in his time, and the process still intrigued and enthralled him. Once, he had found himself hacking into a company's computer at the same time as another hacker. They had exchanged greetings before the other hacker identified himself as a member of the Chaos Club in West Germany; he was hacking from the Ruhr Valley into a computer system in Milton Keynes. Contact with the Chaos Club had taught Hepton much about hacking, and for a time he'd been hooked. But after a while, personnel records and medical files ceased to hold their one-time interest, and he'd given the sport up.

Like cycling, however, you never forgot the 'how'. Having accessed the *Zephyr* onboard computer, he found that COFFIN 762 was the code to unlock the interface between the two satellites, or rather between their two computers. The code was simple enough: COFFIN hadn't been expecting anyone to attempt an access, or to have the knowledge so to do. Otherwise they would not have been so unimaginative with the password, and they would surely have used a less simplistic numerical combination. Izzard's black box had done its job, finding the number sequence in a space of minutes.

Nick Christopher was watching over Hepton's shoulder, interested and excited but trying to look unimpressed so as not to draw undue attention to the console.

But meantime, Hepton was stuck. He'd got this far, but progressing any further seemed an impossibility, for there was a further code to be gleaned, and he had run out of ideas.

What is your name?

COFFIN

Thank you, COFFIN. Please wait.

What is your identifier number?

762

Identifier number accepted. Welcome to interphase control at 19:45 hours. You have fifteen minutes online remaining before engagement of protection circuitry. Do you wish to access:

1. Classification?

2. Interlock?

3. Transmission?

4. Quit?

Hepton wasn't sure, but had taken a chance on Interlock, pressing the number 2 on his keyboard.

Interlock control required. State access password.

And that was where he had so far drawn the blank. He was in, but he wasn't in. He could speak to the damned computer, but it wouldn't do what he wanted until he'd found the password. COFFIN had already been used, so it wouldn't be anything similar. He had an idea.

ZEPHYR

Incorrect password. Please try again.

He sat there staring at the screen. If not ZEPHYR, then what?

'Try *Argos*,' Nick Christopher suggested. Hepton typed in the letters.

Incorrect password. Please try again.

Hepton snarled, then typed in *FUCK YOU* and pressed the keyboard's return button.

Fuck you too, 762, came the onscreen reply.

'I hate computers with an inbuilt sense of humour,' Christopher commented. Then he touched Hepton's shoulder. Hepton looked up and saw that a security guard had entered the room. The guard stopped and held a murmured conversation with one of the new controllers. Hepton didn't like this one bit. He reached around the side of the computer screen and turned the brightness and contrast knobs as low as they would go, blacking out the screen. Then he turned to Christopher. The guard was looking in their direction now.

'Does that guard know you?' Hepton whispered.

'I've seen him around,' Nick said, trying hard not to sound nervous.

'Yes, but has he seen *you* around?'

'We've nodded to one another in the corridor.'

'Does he know your name?'

Nick shrugged. 'I don't think so. We're not *that* close.'

Hepton's hand went to his trousers and unclipped the ID badge, slipping it into the pocket. 'Do you have a name badge?' he whispered. As well as the official ID, some of the staff owned larger, rectangular badges made from stiffened card and boasting name only. These had been given out at the beginning of the *Zephyr* project, a stopgap until the proper IDs had been made. But Nick had held onto his, finding its inverted mistake – *CHRISTOPHER NICHOLAS* – amusing. He reached into his shirt pocket now, brought out the badge and laid it in the palm of Hepton's hand. Pretending to fuss with his keyboard, Hepton attached the badge prominently to his own shirt.

A moment later, the guard confronted them.

'Yes?' Hepton asked imperiously. The guard stared at the name tag, then at Nick, whose face he recognised. He seemed confused, shook his head.

'Nothing, sorry,' he said, moving away again. Hepton watched from the corner of his eye as the guard said a few reassuring words to the controller, then left the room. He sighed and turned the screen back on. He was still no further forward. He stared upwards, seeking inspiration, and found himself gazing into the single black lens of a video camera, angled into the room from one corner.

'Shit!' he said. 'I forgot about that.'

'About what?'

'That camera.' Its red light was on, too. There was no doubt about it: it was beaming his picture back to security. Perhaps he had even less time than he had thought. He stared around the room. Two controllers were laughing over a photo in the newspaper . . .

Newspaper!

'Nick,' he said, 'do you still do those crosswords?'

'Yes, why?' Nick Christopher sounded scared: he had an inkling now that this was all very serious after all.

'Got a thesaurus?'

'Sure. Stay there.' As if Hepton were going to leave! A moment later, he returned with a large paperback book.

'Look up zephyr for me,' Hepton ordered.

Christopher started flipping through pages. 'Why zephyr?' he asked.

'Because I don't suppose Argos will be in there, and we've already used coffin.'

'Okay.' Christopher had found zephyr in the index, and now sought the correct section. 'Three-five-two,' he said to himself. 'Right, here we are.' He held open the book, his hands tense, as though he might at any moment tear the pages in half.

'Start at the top,' commanded Hepton.

'"Breeze",' Christopher read.

Hepton typed the word in: incorrect.

'"Breath of air".'

Hepton was dubious, but typed it anyway: incorrect.

'Next,' he said.

'"Waft", "whiff", "puff", "gust" . . .'

Hepton entered all four individually: incorrect.

'Damn this thing!' he cursed.

One of the older operatives came up to the console.

'Hi, Martin,' he said. 'What happened to the holiday?'

'Just clearing things up, Gary,' Hepton said, his grin as tight as a rictus.

Gary took a look at the screen.

'It's a game,' said Christopher grimly. Gary sensed that he wasn't wanted.

'That's nice,' he said, moving away. Hepton watched him go.

'Next,' he said.

Christopher had lost his place. There was a pause while he found it.

'Next!' Hepton hissed.

'Jesus, Martin, I'm doing my best. Hold on, here we are. "Capful of wind".'

Hepton stared at him, saw he was serious and shook his head. Then tapped the letters in anyway. Incorrect.

'"Light breeze", "fresh breeze", "stiff breeze",' Christopher concluded, closing the book with a thump.

'That's it?' Hepton asked.

'That's it.'

'Okay.' Hepton thought hard, seeking another way.

'What about a dictionary?' Christopher suggested.

Hepton nodded vigorously, then, while the large red book was being fetched, rubbed at his aching temples. Time was rushing by. Soon he would run out of his online allocation, and the satellite's computer would warn its guardians that someone was attempting to tamper with it. They would try to shut him down right then . . . that was supposing security didn't get to him first.

'Here you go.'

Hepton took the book. There was a mark on the cover where Nick's palm had left some sweat.

'What are you looking for?' Christopher asked.

'Straws to clutch at,' muttered Hepton. He turned to the back and found zephyr. '"The west wind",' he read aloud, '"gentle breeze, the god of the west wind".' He closed the dictionary and handed it back, then turned to his keyboard. The west wind. Well, what the hell. He started to type.

WEST WIND. Then the return key.

There was a pause, and he held his breath, then:

Incorrect password. Please try again.

Nick Christopher cursed quietly, but Hepton was staring at the screen. There had been a pause, a very slight pause, before the computer had responded. As though it were checking . . . As though it weren't sure. He typed again, his fingers solid on each plastic key.

WESTWIND. This time with no space. Then the return.

There was another pause, if anything longer than the first, then the screen kicked into life.

Welcome to interlock option on interphase. Do you wish to:

1. Change interlock coding?

2. Enter interlock program?

3. Check interlock co-ordinates?

4. Oversee interlock?

5. Disengage interlock?

Nick Christopher sucked in air and leaned lower towards the screen. 'You've done it!' he gasped.

Hepton almost leapt out of his chair, but gripped its arms with his hands instead. Yes, he was in! He was right there in the nerve centre of the American satellite! He wondered if someone somewhere in a tracking station in the US was watching a screen and beginning to worry. He hoped so. Because he was going to give them a show.

Christopher slapped his back. 'You clever sod,' he whispered, his voice trembling. 'You've actually done it.'

'Now watch this,' said Hepton. But Nick's attention had switched to something else. He was looking over towards the far door, his antennae twitching.

'She's new,' he said. 'Must be part of the skeleton crew. A bit tasty for a skeleton, though. No, wait a second, I've seen her before . . .'

Hepton, curious, looked up for a moment from his screen and saw Harry standing just inside the far door, holding it open as her eyes swept the room. She seemed to be carrying a plastic bag.

He froze momentarily, watching her. 'She's the one who's been trying to kill me,' he stated, his voice cool. Then he concentrated on the screen again. Any second now she would see him. And she would kill him. But he had so little time left anyway, so little time to crack the whole COFFIN thing wide open. And what a foul stench he'd release. So rotten and pungent that no one could ignore it any longer. It didn't matter if he died right here and now, just so long as he wrecked their plans.

'Hello, Martin.'

She was in front of him, standing on the other side of the console, her head and shoulders visible above the monitor, the rest of her body hidden from his view. He didn't glance up from the screen. Instead, with quiet pressure from his left index finger, he pressed the number 2.

ENTER INTERLOCK PROGRAM

A message flashed onto the screen: *WARNING! INTERPHASE USER TIME NOW UP. INFORMING CONTROL OF THIS TRANSACTION. PRESS RETURN TO CONTINUE. YOU ARE NOW BEING MONITORED BY CONTROL.*

Monitored by control: that meant someone would now be watching his every move, ready to negate it if they could. (Harry in front of him! Don't think about her!) He had to finish this quickly, but without allowing them to work out just what he was up to. (Harry standing right there, a rustling of plastic. The carrier bag.) It wouldn't be easy.

'Hello, Martin,' she said again. 'Bring your hands where I can see them.' And this time he did look up. He couldn't help himself. He gazed towards her dark glassy eyes. And found himself staring down the barrel of a gun, so close that he could swear he could see the bullet resting at the end of the long, long chamber.

Then the gun seemed to speak. 'Goodbye, Martin.'

38

'What the hell is this?'

Villiers had ushered Dreyfuss into a series of rooms, separated by glass wall dividers. The rooms were packed with electronics Dreyfuss didn't – couldn't – recognise. It wasn't like in the old movies he'd seen, banks of flashing lights and huge rolls of tape rotating on their mainframe computer spools. It wasn't even like *Argos* mission control. It was cool and peaceful, and the machines made a low, soothing sound, while six dot matrix printers disgorged their data and a row of six television monitors showed a mixture of satellite pictures and computer graphics. DAT machines recorded without apparent end the digital transmissions from . . . well, wherever. Telemetry? Satellite waves? Computer language? Dreyfuss thought all three were possible. COFFIN seemed to have limitless access and limitless funds. But then COFFIN was potentially the largest army the world had ever seen.

And in a corner of this most impressive of the rooms sat Jilly.

Surrounded by state-of-the-art hardware, her captors had chosen a good old-fashioned method of securing her: rope bands looping around her body and the chair-back, and around her wrists; an adhesive gag for her mouth. Except that on closer inspection, Dreyfuss saw that the bands were made of thin plastic strips, secured by metal clips. Unbreakable, and painful to fight and chafe against. He ran to the chair and placed his hands on her shoulders. Her eyes were wild with surprise at seeing him, and she tried to speak, mouthing her frustration against the restraining pad.

'Are you okay?' he asked awkwardly, no other more sensible words coming to mind. She nodded briskly.

A man in a white coat was standing over one of the recording machines, checking line levels. He seemed relieved to see Villiers.

'Thank God!' he snapped. 'I'm a scientist, you know, not a bloody gaoler.'

Villiers ignored the outburst. 'This is Major Dreyfuss,' he said. 'And Major Dreyfuss, this' – pointing his gun hand at the man – 'is Henry Fagin, head of this . . . establishment.'

'A bloody pawn more like,' Fagin muttered, loud enough to be heard. He was still bent over his machines, moving from one to the next like a commander inspecting his troops.

'What *is* this place?' Dreyfuss said, looking around him. One hand still rested on Jilly's shoulder, kneading the skin gently, calming her.

The reply came from Fagin. 'It's a listening post. Off-limits to *Zephyr* personnel. They don't even know it's here. Officially, it's an offshoot of Menwith Hill.'

'Menwith Hill?'

'Yes. That's an NSA operation, American personnel. The job is SIGINT, signals intelligence, picking up all sorts of information while it's in transit.' He gave a sly glance in Dreyfuss' direction. 'Nothing's safe any more, not if it's being transmitted. It still gets from A to B, of course.'

'But on the way it's listened to?'

Fagin slapped one of the machines proudly. 'And copied. You name it: telephone conversations, rocket telemetry. Here, take a listen.' He flipped a switch and a stream of noise started issuing from the speakers set into the walls. 'Know what that is?' he asked, his face opening into a smirk. 'Computers talking to one another. Satellite computers.' He pointed earthwards. 'The ground asks *Zephyr* for close-ups of RAF Buchan.' His finger jerked skywards. '*Zephyr* transmits this request to the other satellite, which then sends it live shots of a base in Wales, made to look like Buchan.' He pointed downwards again. '*Zephyr* then sends these pictures to the ground. It's quite easy if you think about it.'

'You're forgetting, Fagin,' interrupted Villiers, 'Major Dreyfuss doesn't *need* to think about it. He was there when the satellite was launched.'

'And when the crew were murdered,' said Dreyfuss coldly. Villiers just shrugged.

'A US branch decision. What could we do?'

'I'll tell you what you *did* do, though,' said Dreyfuss, remembering Hepton's story. 'You killed a man called Paul Vincent, you tried to murder Martin Hepton, you murdered Cam Devereux, and God knows, that may only be the tip of the dagger.'

Villiers shrugged again but seemed, if anything, pleased by Dreyfuss' catalogue. He glanced at one of four clocks on the wall, each one set for a different time zone.

'Harry should have disposed of Mr Hepton by now.'

On hearing this, Jilly screamed behind her gag, her face purple with effort. Villiers was delighted by this effect and lifted his head to laugh. But a choking sound from Fagin cut him off.

'What is it?' he asked.

Fagin was studying one of the computer screens. He pressed a few buttons, then studied the screen again. 'There's a fifteen-minute access alarm on the interface,' he explained quietly. 'And it's just gone off.' He turned to Villiers, his eyes twinkling with humour. 'Somebody's trying to out-sting our own little sting.'

'Can you stop it?' Villiers sounded wary.

'Oh yes. Every time the intruder makes a move, I'll just order the computer to make another. A bit like chess. Strange, though. He's in, but he's not doing anything.'

As Villiers peered at the computer screen, Dreyfuss knew he had to make his own move. But Villiers wasn't his target: Fagin was. Fagin could wreck everything. He *had* to take him out. He threw himself forward and grabbed the scientist, pulling him to himself as a shield, then backed away. Villiers was already aiming his gun, undecided whether to risk the shot.

Fagin saw his hesitation. 'For God's sake,' he pleaded.

Villiers stared at him, then at Dreyfuss. Finally he brought his gun arm down, but then angled it away from Dreyfuss and his prisoner and began raising it again. Directly at Jilly's head.

'I think,' he said stonily, 'this is what's called an impasse. Except that you, Major, can do nothing with your hostage except hide behind him. While I, on the other hand, won't hesitate to shoot mine.'

And to prove it, he turned his head away from Dreyfuss towards Jilly, taking aim and beginning to squeeze the trigger.

'No!' Dreyfuss pushed Fagin aside and started forward again. But he was too far away from Villiers, far too far away. The gun moved in an easy sweep until it was pointed directly at him. The explosion in such a confined space was deafening, but the impact in Dreyfuss' chest was silent. He felt himself propelled backwards with great force, until, with a new and sickening sound of shattering glass, he slammed into and through one of the dividing walls.

Shards sparkled in his hair as he lay on the floor, a red stain spreading rapidly across his shirt. Villiers examined him through the sizeable hole in the glass wall, seemingly content, then turned back into the room. Fagin looked ghostly white, smoothing strands of hair back across his gleaming pate. And Jilly Watson . . . well, she was staring at Dreyfuss' still body with wide, tear-brimming eyes and horror carved into her cheekbones. Seeing this, Villiers smiled at her with a face that seemed to be transfigured before her very eyes, becoming quite mad and more dangerous, even, than ever.

But now Villiers' attention was drawn to Fagin. 'Don't just stand there!' he roared. 'Get to work! Let's see who stops Martin Hepton first: you with your computer, or Harry with her gun.'

There was chaos in the control room. Some of the men had risen from their consoles to stare wide-eyed at Harry, and more especially, at the gun she was pointing in Hepton's face. A few onlookers, caught between one desk and another, had frozen where they stood, while others had slipped out of the room. Harry didn't appear to see any of this. She had eyes only for Hepton. He was still seated at his computer but had taken his hands off the keyboard and placed them either side of it. His left hand rested on the desktop, his right hand on Nick Christopher's heavy dictionary.

'I can't believe,' Harry was saying, 'you thought you could just walk in here.'

'Why not?' said Hepton. 'You did, after all.'

She didn't seem particularly angry or vengeful or confident or nervous. She seemed . . . relaxed. A job was a job, and this was just another one. Hepton took pleasure in the scars across her face, the result of his boiling water.

'Now look,' Nick Christopher said from somewhere behind Hepton's shoulder. 'You can't just come in here waving a bloody gun—'

'Don't waste your breath, Nick,' said Hepton. His fingers had closed around the book under his right hand.

'That's right,' Harry said. 'Don't waste your breath.'

Hepton swallowed hard. He had one last card. 'I was sorry to learn about your mother,' he said.

Harry's eyes widened, then narrowed to slits. 'What?'

'Your mother,' Hepton repeated casually. 'I was sorry to learn that she committed suicide. Something to do with your father, wasn't it?'

'Shut up.'

'He was in the army, wasn't he? I find that odd, you see.' He paused.

'You find *what* odd?'

'That you should end up working for the military, working for everything your father stood for. Yet he was so brutal to your mother, to Harriet.'

'Shut up!'

'That was why you left home, wasn't it? Did the old drunkard like to give you a beating too, eh?'

It was enough. Harry's teeth were bared in absolute, mindless hate. She swung back the pistol and whipped it across Hepton's face. As it connected, he brought up his left hand and gripped Harry's pistol hand, *her* left hand, angling the gun away from him, while his right hand, now clutching the dictionary, swiped at her head, connecting heavily. The gun went off, its deadly charge hammering home into a computer screen, which sparked once before starting to smoke.

Hepton rose from his chair and placed one foot on the seat, using it as a springboard to launch himself over the desk, the computer, the monitor screen, landing heavily on Harry. His left hand still clutched her gun arm, while his right flexed and sent a clenched fist hard into her face. The contact was satisfying. She gasped, writhing beneath his weight. He could feel blood trickling down his cheek from where the pistol barrel had hit him. Then Harry's knee connected with his groin, and he felt searing pain. He retched, but held fast to her arm, and punched her again, in the mouth this time. But she was wrenching free of him, kicking out, and scrabbling with her free hand towards his face, his hair, his eyes . . .

Her nails were like tools as they raked down his already bloodied cheek, digging into flesh. He cried out and pulled away from her hand. She used the moment to kick again with her full weight, sending him flying into a desk. People were pouring from the room, not about to lend a hand. Even Nick Christopher seemed rooted to the spot, his eyes on the pistol. The pistol she was raising again, aiming. Blood dripped from Hepton's face onto the stone floor. His skin felt on fire. He prepared himself for a final assault, while four feet away Harry stood, blood flowing from nose and mouth, her trigger finger squeezing . . .

'Bastard,' she screeched. 'No more!'

'Harry!'

She froze at the sound of the voice. Her gun still trained on Hepton, her eyes peered towards the far door, where another gun was trained on *her*.

'Parfit!' she spat, arcing the pistol towards the door. But too late: Parfit's bullet hit home with a wet sound like an overripe peach hitting a wall. An inky pink spray covered Hepton as Harry fell back, her head crashing against a computer screen, cracking it, then her body sliding floorwards in a clumsy, ungainly mess. And there she lay, the gun still in her hand, but like nothing so much as a toy now, a rag doll with too little stuffing. Inelegant, and not at all tidy.

There were shouts, panic, pandemonium. Parfit didn't care, didn't bother identifying himself. He walked over to Hepton.

'Have you finished?' he asked. His eyes strayed momentarily to the corpse.

'What?' Hepton was still in shock, still reeling from a great feeling of being *alive*.

'Whatever it is that you're doing here.'

'Oh.' He was jolted back to the present. 'No,' he said, 'not quite.'

'Then get on with it.' Parfit looked around. 'Where's Dreyfuss?'

'He's gone off to look for Jilly.'

'Right.' Parfit handed him a clean handkerchief. 'Here, mop some of that blood off your face.' As he stalked off, Nick Christopher slumped weeping into a swivel chair, covering sticky red face with sticky red hands. Hepton looked towards Parfit's retreating figure.

'What took you so long?' he called with a grin, before walking back around the row of consoles to his own screen, where, numbly but fixedly, he began to go to work. 'Nick,' he said, 'I need your help.'

Nick Christopher rubbed at his eyes. His voice was hollow. 'What do you want me to do?'

Hepton pointed to the computer console next to his own. 'Get that thing up and running. Do you remember that TV satellite we hacked into a couple of months back, so we could get the porn channel?'

'Yes.' Christopher looked uncomprehending.

'Good, get me back into it, will you?'

Fagin stared at the screen. Villiers was growing ever more agitated beside him.

'What's happening?' he snarled.

'Nothing's happening,' said Fagin. 'Absolutely nothing.'

'Then Harry must have found him!' Villiers said.

'I don't think so,' Fagin answered. 'Look.'

He was pointing towards the screen. Numerical sequences were appearing, rows and rows of numbers.

'What are those?'

'I don't know,' said Fagin simply. 'Perhaps he's trying to confuse us.'

'What do you mean?'

'I mean,' Fagin explained, 'maybe he's using these to throw us off the scent of what he's *really* doing.'

'You mean you don't know? I thought you were supposed to be an expert?'

'In some things, yes. But when it comes to hacking, I think Martin Hepton might just have the edge.' Fagin's smile had a hint of pride about it. Villiers grabbed him and shook him.

'So shut it down,' he yelled. 'Close the whole thing down.'

Fagin did not resist. Instead he waited until Villiers had stopped shaking him. 'I can't do that,' he said. 'All we can do is wait for him to make his move – his *real* move.' Then he sat down in front of the screen, a grandmaster awaiting his opponent's opening gambit.

The room was empty now, with the exception of two live bodies and one very cold one. Hepton was in a chair on castors. Once Nick had tapped into the television satellite, he used this chair to wheel himself quickly between the two computer terminals – his own, locked into the *Argos* satellite and, consequently, into *Zephyr*; and the TV satellite. He worked fast and expertly, so that even Nick Christopher had trouble deciding what he was doing. Hepton was happy to explain.

'I'm going to marry these two bastards,' he said. 'I'm going to take over the TV satellite and lock it into *Zephyr*, then disconnect *Zephyr* from *Argos*. Resulting in . . .'

Nick Christopher saw it all now, and broke into a wide, devilish grin. 'You can't do that,' he said. 'Do you know—'

'Of course I know. I know what it'll do. What's more,' smiling too, he turned to glance at his friend, 'I really think I can do it.'

'What's happening now?' Villiers was frantic. What had happened to Harry? Why hadn't she disposed of Hepton?

Fagin rubbed his temples. He was too old for this, too old for

Hepton's tricks. 'He's doing *something*,' he said. 'But I don't quite know what . . .' His fingers worked slowly, methodically, on the keyboard, trying to cancel whatever Hepton was doing. Then it dawned on him. His voice became a whisper. 'He's using two terminals.'

'What?'

'He's using two terminals at the same time.'

'So open a second terminal! Now!' Villiers pushed Fagin against the console. Fagin reached to a second computer and started coding in. 'Perhaps there's still time,' Villiers said.

'Yes, perhaps,' agreed Fagin.

Jilly, however, saw what they could not. One of the monitor screens had burst into life. And instead of the aerial views she had become used to, she was watching a nature programme. The scene looked very much like Africa. Parched earth, creatures gathering around a drying pool of water. Then a voice.

'Quickly, the animals learn that old enmities must be put aside, for now at least. Water is necessary for their survival, so they gather around, forgetting that they are enemies, knowing only that life is their priority. Hunters and hunted sip side by side . . .'

Villiers and Fagin turned slowly, disbelievingly, towards the TV monitor. For that was, unmistakably, where the sound was coming from. Stuck to the top of it was a large piece of Dymo tape, on which was printed *ZEPHYR: LIVE PICTURES*.

Fagin began to laugh. 'I see what he's done now!' he roared hysterically. 'I see!'

'What?' screeched Villiers. 'What?'

'Look,' said Fagin, pointing to the screen. The wildlife programme had vanished, to be replaced by sharply focused pictures of Buchan, the camera homing in on the building work, the underground silos, the tips of the missiles themselves. Villiers opened his mouth in horror.

There was a deferential cough at the open door.

'Good evening, Villiers,' said Parfit, his gun extremely steady in his hand.

39

The screens began to jump around 8.15. Hepton's intention was always to wreck the interface, not merely snip the connection. The estimated viewing figures of seven and a half million, however, came as a bonus. For in linking up the satellites, he had projected the shots of what was really happening in Buchan to a Europe-wide audience. While two video tapes, one master, one backup, ran, capturing the moment for posterity, satellite receiver dishes across most of Europe started to pick up a new station. Early-evening quiz shows, old movies and wildlife programmes crackled and faded and were replaced by pictures of nobody quite knew what. Some pirate station, people assumed, and many of them settled back, waiting to see if there would be any pornography on display, as the tabloid newspapers had been warning and promising. But all they got until nightfall was pictures of a building site. At least, they mostly assumed it was a building site. Except that one repeated shot showed what looked to be a large and ugly missile, resting nose up in its near-finished silo . . .

The plug had been well and truly pulled on COFFIN.

Villiers and Fagin were easily subdued, and Jilly was released. But Dreyfuss was in a bad way. Parfit felt an uncomfortable moment of sentiment: one second the pleasure of terminating Harry; the next the grief of seeing the blood-soaked shirt and feeling the fading pulse. How many lives could a man have? Dreyfuss had used up a fair quota already, but Parfit was grimly determined that he deserved yet another. He staunched the wound as best he could and waited for the ambulance.

Jilly buried her face in Hepton's shoulder and let the tears come. They were tears of frustration rather than relief. Hepton, his work finished, didn't know what his own tears were. But he let them fall all the same.

40

General Colin Mathieson-Briggs was sitting in his office when the men from Special Branch arrived. He knew why they had come, and had prepared himself for the moment, his tie knotted tightly so that his head remained erect.

General Jack Holliday was not, however, to be found in his office. Like Mathieson-Briggs, he had been on site at Binbrook the day they had infiltrated *Zephyr*. He had timed the whole process. From initial interference to complete locking-on had taken just under four minutes. Not long enough for anyone to notice any mischief, surely? There had been risks, of course, but they were not so great as the risk of leaving Britain defenceless and dependent on unreliable European allies for future safety . . .

His wife found him dead in the woods near their country estate. Holliday had gone shooting with his dog, a young Weimaraner. She discovered him slumped against a tree, his head taken clean off, the dog anxiously licking and cajoling the corpse's hands and neck, its whiskers shiny crimson.

In France, Germany, Spain, Greece, Turkey, Finland, arrests were happening. And in the United States, too. Parfit had called Frank Stewart and given him the go-ahead to move in on General Ben Esterhazy and others, including, at the Pentagon, General William Colt. But without any apparent fuss or urgency: it had been decreed that the whole COFFIN affair was to be kept hidden from the world at large. In London, an anxious Home Secretary signed more D-notices in the space of an evening than in the rest of his term of office put together. It was all for the best.

Though Parfit had the devil of a job convincing Hepton, Dreyfuss and Jilly Watson of this. They were gathered around Dreyfuss' bed, a good old-fashioned English hospital bed in a good old-fashioned (albeit private) English hospital. Dreyfuss was recovering slowly, but convincingly, though it seemed to him he'd been through all this one time too many.

'So what did we accomplish?' he asked.

Parfit shrugged. 'What we set out to achieve,' he answered.

'So it just gets hushed up?' yelled Jilly.

Parfit knew of her fiery reputation and was at pains not to test it too far.

'The guilty will be punished,' he said.

'But not publicly!'

'Does it matter?'

'Yes, I think it does.' She was out of her chair now, stalking towards the window.

'I *could* remind you . . .' Parfit began.

'. . . That we've signed the Official Secrets Act,' Jilly finished for him. 'I know.' She sighed. 'But it's so bloody unfair, after what we've been through.'

'Jilly.' The voice of reason was Dreyfuss'. 'As Parfit says, does it matter? We've won.'

Jilly's arm snapped out towards Parfit. '*They've* won,' she said. '*He's* won. Not us, Mickey. Not any of us.' Her eyes went to Hepton, silent still in his chair, thoughtful, looking tired and numbed. 'Martin?' she coaxed.

He seemed to come awake. 'What?'

'What do *you* think?'

'I think satellite TV'll never be the same again.' Then he laughed, the others joining in. 'And I think I need a holiday.'

'That shouldn't present a problem,' said Parfit, checking his watch. 'I'm sorry, I've really got to go now. I have an appointment in London.'

'Getting your back slapped?' Jilly couldn't resist asking.

'Not quite,' he said. 'Can I offer anyone a lift?'

'Yes please,' said Hepton. He looked over towards Jilly, who paused, but finally shook her head.

'I think I'll stick around here for a little while,' she said. She gave a hint of a smile in Dreyfuss' direction, and he returned it.

'Fine,' said Hepton, meaning it. Parfit glanced at him.

'Shall we go?'

'Yes,' said Hepton, 'let's go.'

As the car – yet another black Ford Sierra – sped towards London, Parfit revealed the nature of his appointment.

'I'm seeing our friend Vitalis,' he said. 'Having dinner with him, actually, just to let him know what happened. He did the same for me after the Polish thing.'

'Will you tell him everything?' Hepton asked, staring at the passing scenery.

Parfit thought this over. 'Probably not,' he said. 'Almost certainly not. It doesn't matter, so long as he's told a little of it and doesn't have to find out for himself.'

'The special relationship,' Hepton said quietly to himself, musing. Then he asked the question that had been bothering him for days. 'How come COFFIN always knew where to find us?'

The question seemed to surprise Parfit. He raised his eyebrows and puckered his mouth. Then he shook his head with slow deliberation.

'It could have just been Villiers, I suppose,' he said casually.

'Or it could have been someone in *your* organisation. It could even have been you, Parfit, couldn't it?'

Parfit's eyes were on the road ahead.

'It could have been you,' Hepton repeated, enjoying this deliberate train of thought, 'because you wanted to get Harry. And because you wanted Harry, you were only too willing to set us up as bait. Catchable bait.'

Now Parfit barked out a laugh, though with a slight, noticeable edge to the sound.

'It's an intriguing thought,' he said. He was on the point of adding something, but he had already given away enough confidences. It would reflect badly on the Service if people found out that Blake Farquharson was in COFFIN up to his mottled neck. There had to be a quiet demise for Farquharson. An accident, perhaps, or heart failure. These things could be arranged. Parfit was, after all, an expert in damage limitation. He couldn't tell Hepton and he couldn't tell Vitalis. He couldn't even tell Frank Stewart, who was so looking forward to being there when Ben Esterhazy was arrested. No, it had to be the Department's secret . . . for the moment. The Department's secret that Blake Farquharson, head of the Secret Intelligence Service, had been a traitor at the highest level; a traitor not to his country so much as, in Parfit's mind, to his calling. He hadn't visited the PM that day; he had called from a public telephone kiosk and made his apologies. And he had been ever ready to slip information to

George Villiers – his protégé of sorts – and to Harry; as much information as was necessary. God might know why he'd done it; Parfit didn't.

He squinted ahead into the sunshine. The sky was blue, peppered with tiny high-level clouds. If the sky was blue, how come space was black? He could always ask Hepton. There was a lot he should ask Hepton, but this probably wasn't the time.

Blake Farquharson carried only one case as he left his home. A small case, the kind one might use on an overnight trip. Not that he was going on an overnight trip. He was fleeing for ever. He had some money in a confidential account, tucked away on a Caribbean island. They would find him eventually. But that didn't matter. All that mattered was that it shouldn't happen here, at home, in England.

The streets seemed quiet. He looked up and down for a taxi, and was elated to see one turn the corner in his direction. Its orange light was on, too, proclaiming it for hire. He waved an arm, and the taxi signalled, pulled into the kerb and stopped.

'Heathrow,' Farquharson ordered, getting in.

'Of course,' said the driver, his voice oddly inflected.

The taxi started off, and Farquharson stared at the driver. He looked familiar. In the rear-view mirror, the man's dark eyes wrinkled with pleasure.

'Yes,' he said, 'you do know me, Mr Farquharson. At least, I think you do. My name is Vitalis. You are about to leave the country. Probably for some warm climate. But might I suggest a slightly cooler one? Somewhere your old friends won't find you? At any rate, let us talk.'

Farquharson stared out of the window. The taxi was not travelling fast. He wrapped his fingers around the door handle and tried it, but it was locked. Vitalis was still smiling at him. Farquharson rested his back against the seat and closed his eyes. Slowly they filled with tears.

About the Author

Ian Rankin is the multi-million copy worldwide bestseller of over thirty novels and creator of John Rebus. His books have been translated into thirty-six languages and have been adapted for radio, the stage and the screen. Rankin is the recipient of four Crime Writers' Association Dagger Awards, including the Diamond Dagger, the UK's most prestigious award for crime fiction. In the United States, he has won the celebrated Edgar Award and been shortlisted for the Anthony Award. In Europe, he has won Denmark's Palle Rosenkrantz Prize, the French Grand Prix du Roman Noir and the German Deutscher Krimipreis. He is the recipient of honorary degrees from universities across the UK, is a Fellow of The Royal Society of Edinburgh and a Fellow of The Royal Society of Literature, and has received an OBE for his services to literature.